1

THE GRAVEBORN SERIES
BOOK ONE

THE STRANGE HOUR

R.G. WESLEY

First edition 2024

Library of Congress Control Number 2024914492

ISBN 979-8-9911343-2-3

CONTENTS

AUTHOR'S NOTE

This book contains adult themes, and depicts explicit sexual content and graphic violence.

PART I

"But if I'm not the same, the next question is, 'Who in the world am I?' Ah, *that's* the great puzzle!"

— LEWIS CARROLL, *ALICE IN WONDERLAND*

1

I dreamed of misty forests and a candle-lit cottage nestled in the bend of a whispering river that was wide and deep with secrets. Of damp logs covered in toadstools, mossy boulders and weathered gravestones, all wrapped up in the green smell of growing things. Of peace, and quiet, and profound solitude.

Maybe if I could ignore the trilling of the phone on my desk, I could be in that dream place, instead of the offices of Whitlock and Williams, attorneys-at-law. I sent a death glare at the phone, but it ignored me and kept ringing. Perhaps if I threw it across the room? I laid a hand on the receiver, my fingers itching, but picked it up instead.

"This is Clark Williams' desk, Seph speaking."

I *mhm-ed* and *yes-sirred* while the man on the other end of the phone yelled about how his wife—soon to be ex—would never see a goddamn dime of his money. I doodled mindlessly on my notepad, sketching the daydream the call interrupted. One of the perks of having an excellent memory meant that I didn't need to take notes. But it also meant that I was often bored out of my mind, and that the lengthy tirades of our divorce clients rang in my head long after the workday ended.

This particular diatribe was coming to an end, and I promised to have Clark Williams—the blue-blooded asshole I worked for—call him. Not likely.

A knock on my cubicle wall had me turning after I hung up the phone. I dimly wondered if all cubicles were inherently soul-sucking, or if mine was special. The white-flecked plastic panels mocked me with their blankness, reminding me that I didn't have any family photos to cover them with, nor plants or art or even useless knick-knacks that signaled I'd been somewhere or done something.

"Seph? Did you hear me?" Bri leaned against my cubicle. I should have known she was there, what with the smell of fresh herbs that always followed her. Her black hair framed a heart-shaped face, and light makeup complimented her smooth, tanned skin. Bri was my only friend at work—well, my only friend, period—and visited me as often as she could get away from her desk. She, at least, was able to move around the office, whereas I was chained to the thrice-damned phone.

"Sorry." I gave her an apologetic shrug. "I was just...plotting a new assassination attempt for Clark." It was only a fantasy that served as an outlet for our frustration, but still...more enjoyable than I would have thought.

Bri rolled her amber eyes and dropped into a cross-legged position on the floor of my cubicle. "I've been brainstorming something innovative we could do to him with a pair of tweezers. Anyway, I was saying that Whitlock is loaning me to him," she said, using air quotes around *loaning*, "while he's on vacation."

"Gross." I wrinkled my nose.

"How long do you think it will take Clark to even notice I'm here?"

"He doesn't pay attention to us lesser mortals. I've been at this office for...." I grimaced. "Four years, and he can't even get my name right."

"Everyone knows your name is Stephanie. Or, was it Melanie?" Bri said, trying to hide a smile. She could never quite pull off my dry humor.

"My name is Penelope this week. Or perhaps, the bootlicker."

Bri scoffed and tucked hair behind her ear. "Bootlicker, my ass. When are you quitting?"

I rolled my eyes. "You *know* it's my greatest desire to be screamed at by rich, greedy assholes. I am living the dream. Plus, what would you do without me?" It wasn't, but even if I did figure out what else I wanted to do, I needed to pay my bills. I might hate this job with the intensity of a thousand suns, but at least it was a predictable sort of hell.

"I'll be fine. Whenever I get sick enough of it, I'll leave and end up wherever the wind blows me. You, on the other hand, are wasting that big brain of yours. You could do anything, Seph. Be anything."

I sighed, tired of this conversation. Every couple months, Bri urged me to quit so that I could *find myself* and *live my potential*. But I wasn't sure how to find my potential, even if it walked up and slapped me in the face.

"What I want is to be left alone." I arched my brow in a way that I hoped conveyed annoyance. Bri, who was used to my standoffishness, ignored it.

We'd become friends by way of being the quietest people in the office, and had sort of drifted together like two jellyfish in the ocean that happened to cross paths. Our mutual love of shit talking really cemented the friendship.

"Wrong," she said, pointing a finger at me. I batted it away, but grinned. "You need people. You can't just pretend that no one else exists and go hide in a cemetery. It's impossible to live on books and silence alone."

"But I can. And I do." Bri didn't hide her aversion to my macabre interests, but I wasn't bothered.

"I will never understand why it doesn't weird you out," she said.

Because the dead can't torment you like the living can. Instead, I said, "They're peaceful. You should try it sometime."

"No thanks," she replied, wrinkling her pert nose. Bri's idea of a perfect day was more along the lines of trying some insane spa treatment, like being scrubbed raw with walnut shells, then slathering goo on our faces while meditating. I shuddered involuntarily. But the rules of friendship dictated that I do those things sometimes, so I suffered in silence. Because Bri truly was the best friend I'd ever had in my twenty-six years in this world.

"Want to come over and watch *Buffy* tonight? I'll get popcorn," I cajoled.

Bri was about to reply when her eyes widened and her mouth snapped shut. She stood abruptly. "Mr. Williams, I was just—"

"Leaving?" he supplied. Clark Williams was a large man, with thick, straw-colored hair that I suspected wasn't natural, and large, square teeth, which were too horrible not to be. His jaw was thin and his lips were thick and wet, giving him a strong resemblance to a parrot fish.

Bri nodded, then slipped around him. Once she was behind Clark, she mimed texting. I gave an almost imperceptible nod, then turned my attention to my boss. His musky cologne was strong enough to choke a horse, forcing me to breathe out of my mouth.

It was true that Clark barely paid attention to me—but when he did, I always felt like an ant being fried under a magnifying glass.

"I need you to proofread and edit these. Have them ready by Thursday morning, eight sharp." Clark dropped a banker's box onto my desk with a loud thunk. I flinched, my eyes traveling upward from the box and finally landing on his face. He wore a smug grin on those fish lips.

Those files would take more than two days to finish, after all the other drudgery I had to do.

My fingers crept toward the flower-shaped birthmark on the inside of my wrist. I rubbed it, a tic I'd carried since childhood. "But, it's Tuesday. I'm not sure I can—"

"Thank you, Daphne. That's all." Clark's eyes floated over my head, like he'd already forgotten the conversation, or that I was even there. He filed out, taking his reek with him.

I wanted to chuck the box at him and tell him to do it himself. To demand to know why he got such pleasure out of abusing his position and crushing people who didn't have enough power to say no. I imagined storming out of the office, telling him exactly where he could shove those files.

But no. No. I took a deep breath, forcing back the fury that licked up my throat. I was a coward and complacent and cared more about living in my head than living in the real world.

After staying an hour later than usual, I hefted the ten pound box, then made the commute back home in my ancient Toyota.

Full, mature trees lined the streets, their brilliant fall color popping against late afternoon light. I rolled my windows down and breathed deeply, ridding my lungs of Clark's lingering stench. The air was crisp, carrying the scent of woodsmoke and leaf litter. Halloween was in a few days, and the temperature had been steadily dropping all week.

I pulled up to my apartment and slammed the car door with more force than necessary, thinking of how I would need to cancel on Bri tonight, when a dark shape on my neighbor's porch moved.

"Hello, dear." The voice creaked like an unoiled hinge, and was, unfortunately, very familiar.

I jumped a foot in the air, winging my keys into a nearby bush in the process. Closing my eyes, I prayed for patience before turning to face my neighbor. Mrs. Parham was semi-lovingly known behind her back as the Devil of Chesapeake Street.

Mrs. Parham looked like a typical sweater-knitting, cookie-baking, cheek-pinching grandma. Her iron gray hair was permed and coiffed, and she wore one of her many pastel colored twin sets—periwinkle today.

"Oh...hi," I mumbled, turning to retrieve my keys.

"I didn't see you leave for work this morning."

The sweet old lady uniform belied Mrs. Parham's ability to sniff out secrets faster than a CIA operative. She rocked on her wide front porch, even though the late afternoon was chilly. Apparently gossiping and spying on your neighbors was an all-weather sport.

Living next to her had unfortunately earned me the top spot in her inquisition. I imagined that she was largely disappointed, as my life was utterly boring. I had nothing to hide from anyone.

"I left earlier than usual," I lied. What I'd actually done was park my car on a side street and snuck out of my back door, but that was on a need-to-know basis. "Well, goodnight." I hurried inside without waiting for an answer.

My apartment was small and on the shabby side, but it was home. Almost everything was thrifted, but it was impossible to see scuffs through the unrelieved black I'd painted the furniture. Except for the couch, which Bri claimed she was going to bring to the county dump if I didn't take it off her hands. It was deep and wide, the color of oyster shells and soft as a cloud. I had the sneaking suspicion that Bri was loaded, but I never would have asked. We didn't really discuss our pasts.

Dropping my bag with a heavy thud, I stretched, rolling my shoulders before crossing the few steps from the kitchen to my tiny room. The decor matched the rest of the apartment, except that it was crammed with books. They lived on the floor, the windowsill, the space atop my dresser. I'd promised myself that I would keep it to one book-case only, but I had a negative amount of willpower and a habit of haunting bookstores.

Spotting my copy of *Alice in Wonderland* laying on the floor, its spine cracked wide open, I bent to pick it up. "How did you get down there?" I asked, stroking a hand over the cover.

The book was ancient and tattered, the pages well-thumbed and dog-eared. In truth, I found Alice mildly annoying. But the story had gotten me through some difficult times. It was an escape that dulled the perpetual ache of sadness in my chest, if only for a little while.

Hesitating, I extracted a worn photo, edges fraying, from where it was tucked behind the title page.

It showed a little girl sitting in a pretty blond woman's lap. The girl had a tangle of brown waves, and she wore a face-cracking grin, displaying a missing front tooth. The woman's smile was softer, but even so it was obvious they had the same wide set to their mouths.

There was nothing else of my mom in me, not in the shape of my eyes nor my pointed chin. My skin was tawny, while hers was milky white. My eyes, a brown that leaned toward green in the light, were yet another relic of the half of me I knew nothing about.

I didn't even know why I kept this photo. Maybe it was some evidence that there had been a time when I had curled up in her lap, woven my fingers through hers, sought comfort in her softness.

Whoever that little girl had been, however she'd felt back then—she was long gone.

Tucking the photo back inside the book, I shelved *Alice* and pulled a thick sweater over my head. The files could wait.

I headed out the back door of my apartment, where a quick shortcut through the woods led me to the graveyard.

Gravesville, North Carolina, was completely unremarkable apart from the fact that there were more dead people in the town than live ones. We had the most cemeteries per square mile in the continental United States. They ranged from large and immaculate to tiny plots of roadside graves. As my great-aunt Gracie would've said, you couldn't spit without hitting one.

The sun was setting over Gravesville Historic Cemetery, all those rubies and oranges and violets melding together to create the leavings of an artist's palette. The last rays of light pierced through the clouds to brush the tops of the trees and disorderly rows of headstones, gilding angels and weeping women. Although I'd seen this view many times, it always managed to wedge itself into a soft place in my chest.

The cords of tension threaded through my neck fell away, and I breathed deeply, finally letting go of my shitty afternoon. The cemetery's tranquility was already working its magic.

I followed the paved path deeper into the graveyard, through the willow grove and around a small pond with its defunct fountain. Then I veered deeper into the gravestones until I arrived at my habitual thinking spot. The mausoleum was the grandest in Gravesville Historic Cemetery, a resplendent gothic revival with arched windows and curved finials.

This was my favorite time of day, when the sun went down and the moon rose to hang in the velvet twilight. It felt like a time where anything was possible, where magic, real and imagined, could come out of the shadows. Where the world in my head and the world outside it were more similar than they were different.

Great-aunt Gracie called this time the strange hour. She was the one who had always been ready with tales of magic and moondust, witches and sorcerers, and princesses in high towers. She'd instilled her love of stories in me, feeding me a steady diet of classics and novels, mystery and new fiction, fantasy and romances. I'd gorged on them, tucking all of those words into my lonely places.

Because lonely I had been, for most of my life. As a child I'd been half wild with it, until I found the tiny graveyard in the woods behind my mom's house. Something about those worn headstones had called to me, bid me to lay on down and stay awhile. Promising comfort and turning silence into company.

A crow cawed, startling me. The black bird perched in a tree that had already shed its leaves, stark and beautiful in its nakedness.

It must have been calling to its mate, because a second crow landed beside it with an answering cry. The pair of them sat like twin shadows in the fading light. Or, were they crows? The birds were large and sleek, and somewhere in the recesses of my mind I remembered that ravens often traveled in pairs and were mistaken for crows. I shook my head. Ravens in the graveyard. How cliché.

Was I also a cliché? I had a roof over my head, I was employed, had food to eat and a friend who cared about me. But for some reason tonight, the mediocrity of my life chafed against some unfamiliar emotion that pressed against my ribcage, unyielding and sharp. It was strange, like a little kernel of....

Longing. Yearning. Desire.

I stood abruptly, my breath suddenly loud in my ears. It was time to go. Back home, to my work and the life that I had, not the one that I fantasized about. Daydreams were one thing, but real wanting had teeth sharp enough to wound.

My long strides ate up the ground as I headed back toward the path. The moon was full and bright, hanging in a navy sky that was turning blacker by the minute. Clouds scudded, blown by a light wind that made the dry autumn leaves rustle in the trees. The temperature had dropped, and I exhaled puffs of vapor. A chill ran down my spine that had nothing to do with the cold.

It had turned into the kind of night where vampires came out of crypts to stalk their prey, and werewolves howled at the moon.

"No," I reprimanded myself. "No werewolves, and definitely no vampires." One of the downsides of the overactive imagination I'd never grown out of was that I had the tendency to scare myself. Often. That, and the irritating habit of walking into lamp posts.

I picked up my pace, walking as quickly as I could without breaking into a run. Through the willow grove, where long tendrils of leaves brushed my arms like they were bending down to catch me. Wind whistled through holes in the knotted bark, creaking softly. My steps fell harder and faster.

After I passed the pond, the only obstacle remaining between me and home was the grove of oak trees that flanked the cemetery gates. The little patch of woods loomed like those in a dark fairytale, specifically the type where little children wander off and get lost, only to be found and eaten by a wicked witch. Butterflies winged in my stomach and tried to flutter up my throat. I couldn't stay here and wait until morning, could I? No, that would be even worse than going through the trees.

The moonlight cast shadows on the ground that ruined my depth perception, and I staggered, only to catch myself on a low hanging branch. During daytime the woods looked like another world, with their thick vines that twisted around headstones displaced by thick roots. I usually loved it, but tonight I couldn't wait to be clear of them.

After a long minute of lurching around in the dark, the break in the trees lay just ahead. I let out a soft sigh of relief.

But as I reached the treeline, a glowing pinprick illuminated the darkness. It flared red for a moment, then faded to orange. I realized that it was the end of a lit cigarette, and on the other end of the cigarette was a man.

2

───────

The man blew out a cloud of smoke that looked like an apparition on the wind. I froze, and would've screamed if my throat hadn't gone desert dry. Compromising, I let out a raspy, strangled breath. What were those moves from the self-defense course Bri signed us up for last year? Although, I wasn't sure how much self-defense would work against an undead being of the night.

He was pale, with a shock of chestnut hair that curled to his collar. The bright light from the full moon illuminated a pair of cunning eyes and a wicked smile. His clothes were all black, shrouding the rest of him in a cloud of darkness.

Taking another lazy drag, he flicked his cigarette to the ground, crushing it underneath a booted heel. Wait, did vampires smoke? I wracked my brain for everything I'd learned in my years of watching glittering teenagers prance across my television screen.

"Nice night," he said breezily. His voice was lightly accented—British, maybe, but my untrained ear couldn't distinguish it.

Ducking, I stepped left to walk around him. The stranger shifted so that he was directly in front of me again. Alarm bells began to ring in my head.

"Sure. Nice," I said, taking another step. I waited for the man to get out of my way, but he only pulled another cigarette out of his sleeve and held it to his lips. The tip glowed again, and the smell of smoke twined with something else, something lightly sweet.

"Can I...help you?" The hoarseness in my voice belied any confidence I tried to project. I pressed my thumb into my wrist, massaging my birthmark to try and reclaim some calm.

The man peered at me with shadowed eyes. "I don't know. Can you?" After a long pause, I realized he was actually waiting for me to answer him. But, I knew better than to stand in the dark with strange men.

Part of me wondered if he would chase me if I ran, like a fox scenting a rabbit. Then my stomach dropped when I remembered my cellphone was still in my work bag. *Damn.*

As if the stranger could smell my fear, he chuckled, low and throaty. "I'm not going to hurt you, for Asael's sake."

"I don't have any money. I don't have anything on me." I realized the mistake as soon as the words left my mouth. *Double damn.*

"I'm not going to rob you, either. Even I have my pride."

"Get out of my way, then." My eyes roved over his shoulder, ready to flee, but I would barely be able to see anything in the dark, let alone run.

"I'm not in your way," the man said, gesturing to the open spaces between the trees. Technically true, but his presence was imposing, larger than life.

Keeping my eyes on him, I hastened past, making it only a few feet before I crashed into a headstone. The hard granite bit into my knees and I lost my balance, teetering for a moment. Realizing too late that I was going to fall, I thrust my hands out in front of me and toppled over the headstone, landing in a jumbled pile.

At least I hadn't hit my head; that would've been just what I needed, to knock myself unconscious. I rolled and slowly sat up, favoring my left hand. A tingle of electricity rolled through me, like I'd just touched a hot wire.

"Shit," I hissed. My palm smarted, and even in the dark it was obvious there was a gash clear across its center. Blood, just a black smear in the moonlight, spotted the headstone and dripped down my arm in rivulets. I followed the trail of blood to the epitaph that marked the grave. *The body dies, and the soul wakes.*

Oh, damn it to *hell*.

A pale, elegant hand extended toward me, pulling me up on my uninjured side before I had a chance to protest. I hadn't even heard the man come over, which was one point in the vampire column. But, his touch was solid and warm, not at all how I imagined the undead would feel.

Without letting go of me, he reached for my other hand and gently turned it palm up to study the cut. "Ouch," the stranger said. "That looks painful."

"I'm fine." I pulled my hand out of his grasp and tugged my sleeve over it, hoping that pressure would stem the bleeding. The wound stung like fire and began to throb in time with my heartbeat.

"Are you sure? I can help you with that."

I looked up to see that his eyes were locked on my hand, tracing a line from the gash to where my blood was smeared on the ground.

"It's nothing." I shoved my hand in my pocket. "I'm not having a conversation with a stranger in a cemetery at night," I said, half turning away from the man. *That's exactly what you're doing now*, a small voice in my head reminded me. Adrenaline was making me brave, and despite myself, I felt a tingle of interest.

"Oh, but they're the best kind." He grinned rakishly, tilting his head as he studied me.

I shrank under his gaze, but didn't take my eyes off of him. "Do you make a habit of it?"

For some reason he found that hilarious, and his laughter split the night air like shattering glass. "Yes, in fact. I find graveyards to be… inspiring. They contain all sorts of surprises, wouldn't you agree?"

"I…I guess. But why—what are you doing here?"

The man exhaled tendrils of smoke from his nose, like a fire-breathing dragon. "A little of this, a little of that. It's my luck that I would find a lovely woman here, perhaps doing the same?" He raised a perfectly arched brow.

"I'm not doing anything." My jacket pocket was wet and sticky, soaked through with blood. I needed to get home and clean up. And, hell, those files weren't going to read themselves.

"I'm going now," I said. But I must have looked at the man for a second too long, searching his face for answers, because he spoke again.

"What's your name?" His voice lost the jocular, mocking tone, turning soft and serious.

Maybe that's why I told him.

"Seph," I answered.

"That's an unusual name, Seph."

I grimaced. "I wouldn't have chosen it."

"And what would you have chosen?"

"I don't know. Something normal." I had thought about this, at length. But even though I would have gladly become an Ann or an Elizabeth, I just couldn't picture it. It would be like wearing a shoe that was three sizes too small.

"Is there something irregular about your name?" the man asked, arching his brow again. He truly had skill.

"Yes. Well, no. Sort of."

"Now I'm intrigued."

So was I. The strange man was compelling, with a magnetic quality that made me want to spill all of my close-kept secrets.

"Persephone," I blurted. "My name is Persephone." Immediate regret filled me, and I clamped my lips shut to prevent any other personal information from spilling out.

The man smiled again, sharp as a blade. "Ah, so that explains it."

"Explains what?" I asked warily.

"Why you're walking in the land of the dead."

The prickling at the back of my skull was from the cold, wasn't it? Not a sense of recognition, of feeling some strange familiarity in the words he spoke. Before I could answer him, the stranger stiffened, cocking an ear.

"My apologies, but I should be going. Enjoy your evening," he said, inclining his head in a short bow. I was momentarily bewildered, although I'd been on the verge of leaving, too. Right?

As I stared at the man, who was now looking into the distance, I felt the sudden urge to turn around. Had I heard a noise, or seen a flicker of something in the corner of my eye? I glanced over my shoulder and walked toward the movement, but no; nothing was there, except for the gloom.

Shrugging it off, I turned to address the stranger again. Only headstones and moonlight stood in place of where he'd been.

What in the fresh hell was going *on*? I turned a circle, searching the darkness for him, but I was most definitely alone. I returned to where we had our strange conversation, looking for any evidence that he actually existed and wasn't a figment of my imagination.

There was no trace of the man, not even footprints or the cigarette butt he'd casually thrown on the ground. But no, there *was* something. A small playing card winked up at me, the white backing glowing pale in the darkness.

I reached for it, then paused. I had a sudden, inexplicable feeling that I shouldn't take it. I thought of other girls who had touched something they weren't supposed to, like Sleeping Beauty pricking her finger on a spindle, or Snow White taking a bite of that poisoned apple.

But I was no fairytale princess, just an ordinary person with a strange name.

I picked up the card, turning it over in my fingers, then released the breath I'd been holding. See, I hadn't turned into a pumpkin, had I?

What I'd taken for a playing card turned out to be something else. The image of a courtly, medieval man was painted on the card, pointing diagonally toward the top and bottom corners. Red roses climbed the edges of the yellow frame.

I flipped the card over. *Jupiter's Books and Stationery* was stamped in small, but ornate, calligraphy along its edge. I'd never heard of such a place in Gravesville, and I could say with unerring certainty that I knew every bookstore in town.

It warranted further exploration, but not when the cold was settling into me like a houseguest who had overstayed their welcome. I shoved the card into my unbloodied pocket, smothering the stir of unease that I was taking something that most definitely did not belong to me.

Somehow, walking the remaining distance home, I didn't feel frightened anymore. I'd already encountered the scary stranger in the dark, and it had been...diverting. Intriguing. Curious.

But, where had he come from, and how did he disappear so quickly? What had he really been doing wandering around in the cemetery? Okay, I had been too, but that was different.

As I slid my house key into the locked door, I recognized the nagging thought that was jiggling around in a corner of my brain.

The stranger knew my name, but I didn't know his.

I was late. Very, very late. Dreams about moonlit cemeteries and foreboding strangers had plagued me for the last few nights, and the poor sleep was finally catching up to me. I'd overslept all four of my alarms, and even now felt the dream clinging like a film on my skin.

My hands clenched the steering wheel of my car, and I let out a hiss. The gash on my palm bit like it had a sharp set of teeth, although part of the skin had already started closing. It had seemed so deep, had bled so much—although, maybe my imagination made it out to be worse than it actually was. Per usual.

But none of that mattered, because Clark was going to skin me alive anyway. I hazarded a glance at my car clock and felt my heart rate increase the closer it ticked to eight o'clock.

After hitting three red lights and stopping at every crosswalk, I pulled into the parking lot of work, tires squealing. Flinging myself from the car, I grabbed the banker's box and ran to the door, then sprinted up the first flight stairs. Through the open plan office, then—

"Excuse me."

I whipped toward the voice, my heart galloping from running. "What?" I barked at the man who had just risen from a highly modern and extremely uncomfortable waiting room chair.

Belatedly, I realized that wasn't the best way to address a client. Especially a client who looked as expensive as this one.

The man wore a perfectly tailored dark suit that hinted at serious musculature beneath, with a crisp white shirt unbuttoned at the throat. Broad shoulders filled out the jacket, and his long legs ended in shiny black shoes.

"I'm looking for David Whitlock," the man said. His voice put me in mind of the rich dark roast I'd spilled on my blouse this morning. I tried not to look down at the stain.

"He's not here," I answered, already turning. The wall clock read three minutes past eight.

"It's important," he said, walking toward me. A subtle, woody smell preceded him. It was pleasant, not at all like Clark's heavy musk.

"I can't make him appear," I said, unable to fight my rising annoyance. Client or not, he was in my way. "He's in Bali, or Fiji, or Tahiti. Something like that."

The man arched a dark eyebrow that had a small white scar running through the middle. How had a suit gotten something like that? Although, now that I'd gotten a good look at him, he didn't seem as comfortable in the fine clothing as I'd first thought. The man tugged a cuff and shifted on his feet, like maybe those shiny shoes pinched a little.

And his face.... Well, he didn't look like our usual clientele of rich guys trying to get out of their prenups. He appeared around my age, slightly rough around the edges, with a fine-boned nose. His hair, a dark shock against pale skin, curled slightly around his ears. It brought to mind swashbuckling pirates and buried treasure. All he needed was a gold hoop through his ear to complete the look.

The man reached inside his jacket and showed me a wallet with a badge and ID card tucked inside. *Alexander Eames, Captain, City of Gravesville PD*. Not a pirate, then.

"This is a police matter," he informed me, keeping his tone friendly.

What the hell had Whitlock done? I shifted the banker's box to my hip, eyes flicking toward the clock again. I couldn't very well ignore a cop, could I? "Do you want to leave him a message?" I offered.

"It would be more helpful if you could give me his personal number," Captain Eames countered.

I studied him again as he ran a hand over a jaw that held a day's worth of scruff. His eyes were a deep, olive green, with a corona of gold around the pupil. I was surprised to find that they were kind. Gentle, even.

"Hold on." I set the box on the ground, shaking out my tired arms before snatching a business card from Bri's desk. Scrawling Whitlock's cell number on the back, I handed it to the captain. "Here. It's around..." I did a quick calculation. "Midnight his time. I'm sure he wouldn't mind answering a call from Gravesville's finest."

The corner of Captain Eames's mouth quivered for a moment, like he wanted to smile. "I'll keep that in mind. Thank you, Miss..." he trailed off, looking at me expectantly.

"Hart," I answered. Even though I should have been sprinting from the room like my pants were on fire, I lingered for a moment. Yes, the captain was handsome in the extreme, but there was something else about him that made me want to stay, even if we didn't speak another word to each other. "But you can call me Seph."

"Seph," he echoed, saying my name slowly, as if he was tasting it. "In that case, you should call me Alex."

Alex. I rolled it over in my mind, feeling its smooth curves and hard edges. Now, that was a name that fit.

"It was nice meeting you," he said. "Perhaps I'll see you again." There was something else behind his eyes, like he had just asked me a silent question and was waiting for an answer. But he turned and walked toward the stairwell, his posture impeccably upright.

Reality slammed into me like a ton of bricks. "Shit, shit, shit," I muttered, hefting the box and scurrying down the hallway to Clark's office. I caught a glimpse of navy walls and mahogany bookcases through the open door, along with an empty desk.

Finally, I'd caught a break. Going straight in, I placed the box atop the squat desk then beat a hasty retreat.

Or I would have, had Clark not been standing in the doorway, blocking my way out.

3

————

"Oh, hi." All of the air in my lungs fled in a single breath. "I was just...."
I trailed off at his stare.

"I know what you were doing," Clark said, taking a step toward me.

I involuntarily backed up, bumping against his desk. Adrenaline threaded through my blood, making me lightheaded. *Just calm down. He can't do anything—it's broad daylight in the middle of the office.*

"I'm so sorry—"

"It's 8:10. I was scheduled for court at nine. I had to cancel," he said in a voice that could have shredded me to ribbons. "Your carelessness just cost this firm thousands of dollars."

"I overslept, but—there was a cop, and he...and I...." Clark didn't give a rat's ass about why I was late. No excuse would satisfy him. I walked toward the door, head down, but he didn't step aside.

Clark grabbed my elbow as I brushed past him. I recoiled, but he tightened his grip, digging in.

"Let go of me," I said, fighting to keep my voice even.

"This won't be tolerated again. I can replace you immediately and without consequence." Then he released me so quickly that I questioned for a second if he'd actually touched me. But my arm smarted, and disgust made my breakfast threaten to resurface.

How was it possible that I was so cold, but also on fire? Anger, embarrassment, and fear all twined together into a hot ember that slid from my throat into the pit of my stomach.

"The money you cost the firm today will be deducted from your pay," Clark said. "Now get out of my office."

But I couldn't make myself move; I was rooted to the spot, somehow feeling both like a statue and a wobbly bowl of jello. Part of me knew that I had bills to pay and that this was just part of the everyday bullshit of being a woman. But another part disagreed. It was the little ember burning inside my belly. When it spoke, I listened.

Fuck that. Show this privileged moron that he has no right to put his hands on you. Make him regret every time he's ever ignored you, belittled you, or made you feel trapped in this dead-end job.

"Out. Now," Clark commanded.

I was so close to walking away, so close—until he flicked his hand at me. That flick ignited the ember, turning it into a roaring bonfire in a millisecond. I heard rushing in my ears, and realized it was the blood surging through my body, my heart set to pounding.

The overhead lights in their expensive fixture flickered once, then popped. Clark looked up, alarmed, but my attention was fixed on him.

"No," I snapped, my voice hot enough to spit flames. "No, I will not *leave*. Not until you apologize. Oh, and my name is Seph, by the way, not fucking *Daphne*."

I paused to take a breath, and Clark tried to cut in, spluttering at me.

"How dare you—"

"No, how dare *you*," I hissed. His eyes widened in shock. "I may answer your phone and bring you coffee, but even I know that I can litigate your ass into next month for putting your hands on me. And actually, I don't need your fucking apology, because I *quit*. I'm instituting a new policy, which is that I don't work for pricks anymore. And, I mean this most disrespectfully; fuck *all* the way off."

Clark's mouth worked furiously open and shut. He resembled a fish more than ever, like he'd been abruptly yanked out of the water with a hook in his mouth, gasping stupidly for air. I turned on my heel and strode away, my ears ringing and my hands trembling.

We had an audience. My co-workers—former co-workers—had filtered in, morning coffees and briefcases still in hand. I passed wide eyes and open mouths, not bothering to stop at my cubicle on the way out. It wasn't like I had anything to take with me.

I fled down the stairwell. Overhead lights flickered and died in my wake. Clearly the building had some kind of electrical problem. "Shit-hole office," I muttered.

Chilly fall air cooled my flushed cheeks as I rushed back to my car. It had only taken twenty minutes for my life to change completely; to go from employed to unemployed, from complacent to...whatever that had been. God, what had come over me? No, I didn't want to think about it. I needed to keep moving, to keep my thoughts at bay for as long as possible.

I drove on autopilot, not noticing where I was until the simple iron gates of Crestbridge Cemetery came into view. Parking, I got out of the car then let my feet take me wherever they wanted. I barely felt like I was occupying my body at all; it was as if I had a bird's eye view of the graveyard, watching my long strides eat up the ground.

Crestbridge wasn't neatly planned out like Gravesville Historic Cemetery. Paths meandered like forks in a creek around irregular groupings of headstones that were set at odd angles by time and erosion. The reds and yellows of autumn leaves lay perched loosely on the trees, ready to fly off at any moment. I caught the rich scent of freshly turned earth. A distant part of my mind noted there must have been a burial recently.

I wandered until my legs felt like lead. Then I dropped down on a rickety bench where the path diverged, and the throbbing pulse of emotion began to fade. I closed my eyes, seeking that leading hot edge of anger, but it slipped from my grasp.

My phone buzzed in my bag but I ignored it. The sound was distant, but annoying enough that when it rang again, I picked it up without looking at the display.

"Hello?" I answered dully.

"Seph, are you okay?" Bri's voice was like a hug, soft and warm. "When I got in this morning, everyone was saying that you screamed at Clark and quit."

"Well...yeah. That's basically it."

"What did he do to you?"

My heart swelled with affection for Bri, even as I brushed angrily at a tear that spilled down my cheek. "I can't talk about it right now," I whispered. "But I think I had to do it."

"Of course you did. Whenever you're ready to talk, I can't wait to hear about how you bitched him out. You *did* bitch him out, right? Because that would have been a missed opportunity."

A smile forced its way over my frozen lips. "I did."

"You're a badass, and fuck him."

I groaned, kneading the headache that was building in my temple. "I don't know about that. I feel...numb. And angry."

Bri made a shushing sound. "You're going to be okay. Should I come over?"

"No, I don't want you to get in trouble by association. Everyone knows we're friends."

"I'm so quiet, hardly anyone even notices I'm there," Bri replied.

I choked out a laugh. "True."

"I don't have experience with rage quitting, but I think you should go home, pour yourself a large glass of wine, and binge *Bridgerton*."

Bri's advice, while usually sound, was not always something I agreed with. "It's nine in the morning."

"And?"

"I'll start with coffee."

Silence hung over the line for a moment. "Cut yourself a break, Seph. Just go home, and we'll cross whatever bridge comes next together."

Normally, I would have ducked Bri's sympathy. I didn't want or need anyone to feel sorry for me. But today, it felt nice to have someone who cared about me in my corner.

"Thanks, Bri."

"Always. You know, I'm kind of jealous of your freedom. Maybe I should quit, too. I don't think I can stand working in the same office as he-who-shan't-be-named anymore."

Freedom? the voice of reason in my head asked. *How about financial freedom? How are you going to pay for your apartment without a job? And who's going to support your book habit?* With a mental shove, I pushed down the little voice and all of the unpleasant things that were attached to it. Those worries would be for later. Much, much later.

"I appreciate the solidarity, but please don't quit on my account," I said.

"Party pooper," she mock-pouted. "Hey, should I come over tomorrow morning? We can debrief and stuff our faces with sugar and caffeine."

"That sounds excellent. Thanks, Doctor Bri. You made me feel better."

"Seph, you know I've got you. Now go home and relax, and I'll see you tomorrow."

I hung up, surprised that I felt lighter. I may have acted on impulse, but maybe it wouldn't be all bad.

The worn peaks of the Blue Ridge Mountains bumped against the horizon to the west out of the car window. Most of the leaves had already dropped at higher elevation, and the bare trees reminded me that winter would be here soon. I loved all of the seasons in Gravesville, because they felt like they belonged to me.

Gravesville wasn't only my home now, but was where I'd been born just over twenty-six years ago. After my dad left and my mom realized he wasn't coming back to his bride and infant daughter, she packed up our life and moved us to Virginia to be closer to relatives.

I'd returned to Gravesville thinking I might find a part of myself that had been left behind here, like a dropped earring or a missing sock. It was the part of me that felt a little out of step with the rest of the world, like I was going left while everyone else went right. But I hadn't found it, and over the past couple of years I'd stopped trying.

I wasn't a praying woman, but I'd sent one up hoping Mrs. Parham wouldn't be rocking on her porch when I returned home. That request had been denied, perhaps due to the aforementioned habit of only doing it when I wanted something.

Our homes were mirror images of each other, except that mine was split into an upper and lower apartment, while hers was a single family. She rocked on the worn blue rocking chair with a pile of yarn in her lap. Was it normal to be that fast at knitting? The needles clicked and flashed like a whirring piece of machinery.

"Hello, dear!" she said without looking up. "What are you doing home so early?"

Usually, I would grit my teeth, make some agreeable noises, and retreat inside. But I was too tired to hedge. "I went postal on my boss and quit my job."

Her needles faltered before resuming their rapid movements. "Well, I am sorry to hear that." She didn't sound sorry at all. In fact, it seemed like she was fighting with the corners of her mouth to keep a straight face.

"Yeah, well." I unlocked my door and was halfway through when she called me back.

"Persephone, wait a moment." Mrs. Parham set her needles on the rocking chair and came to the porch railing. I stilled, instantly regretting my moment of candor.

"Would you like to come in for a moment? Have a coffee, or... perhaps something stronger?"

"I...." Damn it. Refusing her could put a target on my back. But, did I really want to drink with my old lady neighbor? Mrs. Parham looked back at me with keen eyes, waiting.

Oh, why the hell not? It was already turning out to be the strangest day I'd ever had. This would be the cherry on top. "Sure."

"Wonderful. Come along."

It was mildly unsettling seeing the inside of my neighbor's house, because the living room looked exactly like mine. Gas fireplace, big bay window, and weird angled closet for the water heater.

Except for the absolute explosion of doilies. I blinked slowly. Lace was *everywhere*, covering surfaces as far as the eye could see—on table tops, the television stand, the arms and back of the couch. There were even some framed on the petal pink walls. Jesus, Mrs. Parham must not do anything but knit.

I found her in the sunny kitchen, standing on tiptoe as she reached into an upper cabinet. Her fingertips barely grazed the bottom of it.

"Here, let me help you." I walked over, arm already outstretched, but she turned to face me with a bottle of bourbon and two glasses in hand.

"That's quite all right, dear. I may be vertically challenged, but I have my workarounds."

"But...." I looked from the bottle to her tight-lipped smile. "Sorry, I thought—nevermind."

Mrs. Parham set the glasses on the counter, pouring a stiff measure of deep amber liquid into each before handing me one.

"When one door closes, another opens. To your new beginning, Persephone."

God, this was weird. But I clinked my glass to hers when she offered, then knocked back a healthy mouthful.

"Thanks, Mrs. Parham," I said, grimacing as the bourbon burned a path down my throat before settling warmly in my stomach.

"Oh, call me Evangeline, dear. No need to be formal."

We stood in heavy silence for a moment before I blurted the first thing that came to mind. "I like your knitting."

"I've had a lot of time on my hands since Uriel passed. My late husband," she clarified.

"Oh, I, uh—I didn't know."

"He's been gone for four years now. I moved to Gravesville right after he passed. Around the same time as you, actually. Too many memories, you know." The creases in my neighbor's face deepened. She looked...sad. No wonder she was so nosy. She must have been lonely.

My heart softened toward her. I settled for nodding my head with what I hoped was appropriate solemnity.

"Where did you move from?" The alcohol loosened my tongue, putting me at ease.

She waved a hand. "Canada. Tiny little town you never would've heard of."

"Ah." I gulped more bourbon.

"Enough about me. I hardly know anything about you, dear, even though we've lived next to each other all these years."

That was on purpose, but I couldn't tell her that. Mrs. Parham's bright hazel eyes studied me, and for a moment it felt like she could see into my thoughts. Glancing away, I said, "There's not much to know."

"Oh, I doubt that."

I turned my head sharply and our gazes met. Another prickle of familiarity, just like the one I'd felt in the graveyard the other night, tingled down my spine. I shivered involuntarily. No, it was just the bourbon clouding my head.

"Everything all right, dear?"

"Fine," I answered, setting the glass down abruptly. "I should go. Thanks for the drink."

Mrs. Parham followed me out, not commenting on my rudeness. "Goodbye, my dear," she said to my retreating back. "You be careful now, and take care of yourself."

The odd feeling lingered even after I was safely ensconced on my couch, letting the squashy cushions cocoon me in comfort. Why would Mrs. Parham warn me to be careful? I hardly led a risky life.

What about talking to that stranger in the graveyard? an irritating little voice in my head asked.

"Shut up," I mumbled, grabbing the remote and flicking on a mindless reality show.

Even someone who was as carefully non-participatory in life as I was experienced a little excitement from time to time. I would put it all behind me, although some part of me knew my life wouldn't go back to the way things had been. It couldn't. Because now I was the kind of person who had said something instead of staying invisible. Who had left a mark on her own life.

The combination of bourbon and droning voices made me drowsy, effectively shutting down any rebellious thoughts. I laid down, head pillowed on my arm, and let sleep take me.

4

———

Screams woke me, and it took me a second to realize that they were coming from me. I'd fallen asleep, had some kind of nightmare involving creatures with red eyes and sharp teeth.

Sweat plastered hair to the back of my neck, and my hands trembled. A wave of nausea roiled in my stomach, and I levered off the couch to dart to the bathroom. I just made it before I emptied the contents of my stomach—mostly bourbon—into the toilet. I flushed it down, then leaned back against the wall, pushing damp hair off my forehead.

I hadn't had nightmares like that since I was a child. Even though I tended toward daydreaming during my waking hours, my fantasies usually didn't follow me into sleep.

I rinsed my mouth clean in the sink, then padded into the kitchen to make a cup of tea. While I waited for the kettle to boil, I tried to collect the fragmented memories of the dream. There was a cemetery—not unusual for me, but...creatures had been waiting for me. Monsters that sliced at me with teeth and claws. Thinking about it made my heart jackhammer in my chest.

The kettle whistled, and I steeped the tea, swirling the bag around in the steaming water. "It was just a dream. An alcohol-induced nightmare. Get a grip, Seph."

Still, there had been pain. Real pain. Feeling foolish, I held my arms out in front of me, examining them. The only mark I had was the bandaged-covered gash on my palm. I peeled the bandage away to take a peek.

"What the hell?" A pinkish scar spanned my palm. I walked to the window, holding my hand up to the buttery afternoon light. This morning it had been a raw, angry scab. How was that possible?

Massaging the bridge of my nose, I tried to banish my thoughts. I'd take a walk to clear my head. And not to the cemetery.

I took a shower to scrub the rest of the nightmare away, then got dressed and walked into the city.

Gravesville's oldest part of town, dating back to the early 1800s, looked like something out of a fall movie special. Jack-o-lanterns and warty gourds dotted storefront stoops. Sidewalk signs promised a variety of pumpkin-inspired craft beers and treats, while skeletons sat on benches in jaunty poses.

With a jolt, I realized it was Halloween. Trick-or-treaters would soon be out collecting candy and getting up to mischief. I normally would have handed some out, but clearly not this year.

Skipping the buzzing bars and restaurants, I turned down a side street. Here, the cheesy decorations had been replaced with frosted glass windows that had more to do with privacy than ornamentation. The old brick buildings were run down, with chips in their once grand facades and spiderweb cracks in the window panes.

I was the only soul on this street, and the quiet rang around me conspicuously, only broken by the click of my boots against the sidewalk. It seemed impossible that the bustling stores I'd passed were only a street away. I walked mindlessly, zoning out until I came to a bright sign that hung above a basement doorway. It was hard to miss, given the pulsing, neon crystal ball.

Psychic Readings

Was that exactly what I needed, or a terrible idea? I imagined an old woman with heavily lined eyes, wearing a turban and foretelling my doom in heavily accented English. Perfect.

I wouldn't say there was anything inviting about the place, just looking at the outside. The door was a heavy and imposing steel that weighed about a million pounds. After dragging it open with all of my rather limited strength, I pushed past a curtain and found myself in a small, dark room.

The smell hit me first; citrusy, strong but not unpleasant. The room was painted a deep purple that bordered on black, and the wall directly across from the door had a mural of an open hand with lines and symbols drawn across it. Underneath the mural was a table with a few chairs crowded around, also upholstered in that same deep eggplant as the walls. Floor lamps covered with scarves were placed randomly around the room, giving off just enough light so that I didn't trip over my feet.

I almost missed the small woman sitting in an overstuffed armchair in the corner. She rose and walked over to where I stood just inside the door, teetering on the edge of turning right back around and leaving.

"Welcome," she said, her voice soft and tinged with the south. Definitely not Romanian, then, which wasn't the only incorrect assumption I'd made. Instead of being swathed in a long black dress and a turban, she was dressed in light, loose clothing, and wore her blond hair down around her shoulders. I guessed she was around my mom's age, although it was hard to tell in the dim light. "I'm Constance. How can I help you?"

"Um. Hello," I said, trying to figure out how to extricate myself now that I'd been noticed. I took another step toward the door, my back brushing against the curtain.

Constance smiled. "First time, honey?"

"Yeah. Um, yes, I mean."

"Well, you look about as nervous as a cat in a bathtub. Why don't you come on over here and sit down. Can I get you something? Tea, water?"

"I'm fine, thanks," I replied, as she herded me toward the table under the mural wall. I was trapped by the manners my mother insisted upon. "I actually think I need to go. I was walking around and lost track of time." Constance gave me a searching look that seemed too direct for her guileless, cornflower blue eyes.

"I'll be just a minute," she said, not giving me an option to refuse, and floated behind yet another purple curtain. The woman truly couldn't have been more at odds with the goth decor.

She returned quickly with a steaming mug that matched the citrus scent of the room, setting it in front of me. "You'll feel better if you drink that. Calms the nerves, lemon balm."

When I didn't immediately drink, she sent another direct look toward me. I sipped from the mug. It was actually good, the citrus taste melding with something sweet and slightly grassy. My pulse settled and something like ease slid down my throat. I looked up at Constance to find her wearing a knowing smile.

"What did I tell you? Now, what ails you, my dear?"

"I—Is it that obvious?"

"Only to someone who's looking," she said kindly.

That was all it took to have me spilling my guts about what happened at work, to share my anxiety and relief and fear that suddenly overflowed like a too full cup, leaking over the edges and dripping into a puddle on the floor.

What was wrong with me? I kept my thoughts and feelings locked up nice and tight, please and thank you. Because if I didn't, I wasn't sure I'd ever be able to get them back inside.

But there was something about this stranger, who made me tea and put her hand on my shoulder with a comforting squeeze, that made me want to tell her the story of my whole lackluster existence. She listened completely, never looking away or interrupting me until I finished.

"Well, that is quite a tale. And I have to say, good for you. That Clark seems as worthless as gum on a boot heel, and sounds like you're well shot of him. You're a brave young woman, Seph."

"Stupid, maybe. Or reckless," I amended.

"Stupid and reckless can still be brave. In fact, those are usually the primary ingredients. Sounds like you took a step in the right direction. Now, it makes sense why your wanderings brought you to me. Just sit tight and I'll give you a reading, if you'd like."

It was harmless, remember? When I walked in, I thought it would be a silly little distraction, something I could share with Bri tomorrow as *see, proof that I didn't hole up and ruminate about how I ruined my life.* But now? Now, I felt like this woman who was a study in contradictions might be able to see through me too clearly. I took a deep breath.

"Sure. Why not?"

"Excellent." From underneath the desk she pulled out a deck of cards and fanned them across the table, then performed a complex shuffling move.

"This is tarot. You may be familiar?" I shook my head. "That's fine. All you need to do is think of a question that you want to ask the cards. Something open-ended, usually. Do you have anything in mind?"

What question didn't I have? Should I ask what the job market was looking like? Or, if I was going to come into some unexpected money? Unlikely, but worth a shot.

Constance watched me agonize. "Don't think about it too hard, honey. Try asking not about what you need to know, but what you want to know. Your heart's desire, if you will."

No one had ever asked me about my heart's desire before. Hell, I'd never even asked myself that. What *did* I want? *You want to know what else is out there for you*, a little voice answered. It came from the vicinity of my sternum, and felt small but bright, like that first flickering spark that started a fire. *You want more than what's beyond the pages of your books and the walls of a graveyard.*

Constance handed me the cards. "Cut the deck, then set them here." She tapped the center of the space between us. I did as she said, holding tight to that spark as I handled the cards and placed them on the table.

She gave me one more searching look, then flipped ten cards off the deck, arranging them into a pattern as she went. Some of the cards faced me, and some were upside down. Constance was silent for several long minutes as she studied them. I also looked at the cards, hoping the illustrations would give me some insight into their meanings.

There was a woman and a lion, men sitting on thrones, and a skeleton in knight's armor. But that wasn't what made my heart skip several beats. There, right across from me, was the same card I'd found in the cemetery two nights ago, the one that was now sitting on my dresser. The medieval man with his arms pointing in opposite directions toward the sky and the ground, behind the little table with a scattering of objects laid upon it. Roses climbed the top and bottom edges, framing the scene.

"What's that?" I asked, pointing to the familiar card.

Constance flicked her gaze to me. "The Magician. He symbolizes willpower, creation, and manifestation. Here, in your spread, he is in the place of what is reflected in your subconscious, what truly drives you." Then, that studying look again, drilling into me like she was fixing a loose screw. "Traditionally the Magician represents magic, of course."

"Magic?" I supposed that made sense, what with my love of fantasy. "What about this one?" I gestured to the skeleton knight.

"That card is Death. It's in the place of the outcome of your question."

"Oh." My hands turned clammy, and I wiped them on my jeans.

"It doesn't mean actual death, at least not in this case. Death represents radical transformation, sacrifice, new beginnings." Constance looked down at the cards again. "It seems like your problem has to do with making a decision. You're at a crossroads in your life. Makes sense what with you leaving your job," she mused. "You're not feeling ready for all that life is throwing at you. There's deeply rooted insecurity here."

I laughed. "That's not news to me."

"You know, making fun of yourself is part of that." I stopped laughing. "You've got something good coming as part of your journey in the form of a new relationship. Could be your soul mate, or could be a deep, lifelong friendship. But you'll struggle, too. There's tyranny, obstacles, rebirth, betrayal, with a good bit of suffering thrown in. I'd say all in all, you're in for a hell of a time here. But it's going to be worth it. You're working toward who you really want to be, and finding your true self along the way. Looks like she's going to be pretty special. Magical, even."

I was still focused on tyranny, betrayal, and suffering. I rubbed at my birthmark like it was a lucky penny. Not exactly the news I wanted to hear about my path in life, but I reminded myself that this wasn't real. Just like the crystal collection Bri bought me for my last birthday, it was fun and pretty to look at, but was just as false as their sparkle.

"Well, sounds like I'll be busy, at least. Thanks for the reading. How much do I owe you?" I asked, digging around for my wallet.

"No charge."

I stopped digging. "I can't let you do that."

"Why not? This is my place, and I make the rules, my dear. Consider it a gift, and when you've finished your journey, come back and see me. That'll be payment enough."

She might be waiting a long time, if that was the case. But the least I could do was play along, especially because of her generosity. "I will. Thank you, Constance."

"You're most welcome. Take care, now." She clasped my uninjured hand, then seemingly on impulse drew me into a hug. Startled, I made to pull away, but she had already let go, rubbing her arms as though she'd been shocked.

"Are you okay?"

"Fine. Just fine." But her eyes told a different story.

She drew something from her pocket and offered it to me. An asymmetrical stone pendant dangled from a thin gold chain. The stone was silky and striped with reddish-brown and black streaks, almost like a tortoise shell.

"Why don't you take this as well? It's called Tiger's Eye. Just a little good luck charm," Constance said.

"Ah...sure." Did I really want that shitty necklace? No, but I did want to leave. Constance seemed like a kind woman, but I was starting to get an odd feeling from her. *This is what happens when you go to the woo-woo people, Seph.*

Constance dropped the necklace into my outstretched hand. "Goodbye, Persephone," she said to my retreating back.

I waited until I got to the street to let out the breath I'd been holding. I was positive I hadn't told Constance my name.

5

The street was still hushed when I emerged from the shop, like someone had thrown a blanket over it.

I held Constance's gift up to the light. The necklace looked like something from a souvenir store at the beach—cheap, and a little tacky. I shoved it in my coat pocket and strode back toward the center of town, annoyance rising with each step. The reading had been a silly waste of time. There was no reason to think what she'd predicted was actually true.

Reality crept back in. I was jobless and would probably be broke within a month. If I had to move back in with my mom and Scott....

I stopped in my tracks and groaned, burying my face in my hands. Please, not my stepfather. I'd do anything to avoid Scott's particular brand of feigned interest that managed to be both condescending and dismissive.

"You lost, girl?"

Flinching, I turned toward the voice. A man sat on the steps of a building under a sign with peeling letters that read *Eric's Electronics Repair*. His torso was thick but his limbs were stick-like, like he was a bug that crawled out of the bathtub drain.

"No." I looked around, shocked to find that I'd somehow been walking not toward the hubbub of main street, but away from it. How had that happened? I shoved my hands back in my pockets and turned around, my strides growing longer.

"What's your hurry?" the man called.

I glanced over my shoulder and saw that he was behind me, way too close for comfort. I hadn't even heard his footsteps. The hairs on the back of my neck stood on end, but I ignored him and kept going, hoping he would get the hint and crawl back under whatever rock he'd come from.

In case he didn't... I slid a hand into my bag as I had in the psychic shop, but this time I found my house keys. I put them in my pocket, then inserted the keys between each finger. My hands were vise-like, the cold metal biting into them.

"I said, where are you going, lily girl?"

His voice was right in my ear. I ran, but the man grabbed my sleeve and dragged me toward him. The scream I wanted to unleash froze in my throat. There was something wrong with his eyes. They were too dark, the irises bleeding out into the whites like an errant ink blot.

The man yanked up my left sleeve, exposing my wrist. I cried out as I tried to wrench away. He touched my birthmark with a pallid finger in which the nail beds were too long, and the ends too sharp. Bile rose in my throat and disgust crawled over my skin. I jerked away, a burst of fear rising so hot and bright that if he'd been able to see it he would've gone blind. He let go with a wheezing gasp, his eyes rolling like a panicked animal.

Almost as if another person was in charge of my body, I whipped my keys out of my pocket and jabbed the man in the throat. He dodged, but the sharp points scraped along his skin in shallow slices. Dark rivulets of blood poured from four identical wounds. He gurgled, releasing me to clasp his neck with both hands.

I ran toward the main street, but got no farther than a few steps before a figure sprinted from an alleyway, moving impossibly fast.

I recognized the lean build and dark hair. It was Captain Eames —Alex.

What the hell was *he* doing here?

Alex shoved the man against a building, but my assailant brought one of those pincer-like hands to his neck. They grappled, and I stood frozen, watching in horror.

Then, almost as suddenly as it began, it was over. Alex had the attacker on the ground, a knee in his back, wrists restrained.

Alex met my eyes. "Are you all right?" He ground his knee harder into the man's back when he tried to squirm. *Jesus H. Christ on a raft.* Was this really happening?

"I'm...." I looked down at my exposed wrist. A reddish tinge informed me I'd probably have a bruise from where the man had grabbed me, but that seemed to be the worst of it. "Fine," I finished.

The assailant gave a muffled grunt from where his face was buried in the pavement. Alex dug his phone out of his pocket, then pinned it to his ear with his shoulder. He took a pair of handcuffs out of his other pocket and secured them around the man's wrists.

He muttered something too low for me to make out, then lowered the phone. "Someone will be coming to pick him up, couple minutes tops."

Alex dragged the man over to a stair railing and adjusted the cuffs so that his hands straddled the metal rail. The man's inky eyes roved over us and he bared his teeth, rattling the cuffs. Blood streaked his neck, soaking his shirt collar. Was it my imagination, or were his teeth longer and sharper than they ought to be?

Alex took my elbow and steered me to a nearby bench, farther away but still within sight of his prisoner. He guided me down gently, taking a seat beside me.

"What the actual fuck," I whispered to the universe. What had I done to deserve this shit show of a day?

Alex's voice was level and calm. "Did he touch you?"

"Yes." My thumb found my birthmark and stroked it. Alex's eyes followed the line of my forearm to the small, pale mark that stood out against tawny skin. "But I'm fine."

"Even so. Mind if I have a look?"

"Hm? Oh...sure." Then, I took complete leave of my senses and blurted, "You look different." He was no longer wearing the fancy suit from this morning, but a pullover and jeans.

"It's hard to take down bad guys in a suit," he said, giving the ghost of a smile, one corner of his mouth lifting crookedly. My face heated as our eyes met, my heartbeat stumbling.

He looked at me—really looked, like he could see down into all of my dusty and cobwebbed corners, places that I hadn't dared touch for years. Or maybe ever. I dropped my gaze and my heart started again, fluttering rapidly as if to make up for its momentary lapse.

Alex took my hand, then paused. I nodded my permission for him to continue, my throat uncomfortably tight. He traced the red mark on my wrist, as delicate as a butterfly's wings grazing a flower. Everywhere he touched tingled like my muscles were waking up from a long nap, and even after he removed his fingers my nerve endings sang.

I hadn't noticed the silence that ensued, but he asked, apparently not for the first time, "And your name is Steph, right?"

"Seph," I answered, feeling muddled and slow.

"Seph," he repeated, and some buried part of me couldn't help but like the sound of my name on his lips. "Sorry. Is that short for something?"

I was sure that Alex was trying to keep me distracted from the moaning psychopath across the street. If only he knew the distraction I needed was from my overactive imagination and wild hormones.

"Yes," I replied, but didn't elaborate further.

A white, nondescript SUV beeped its horn then stopped in the middle of the street. Then a man jumped out, pulling off aviator sunglasses as he approached, and ruffling blond hair that was just a little too long to be tidy. His heavy-lidded, sea green gaze was assessing, but there was a spark of mischief behind the vigilance.

"Hiya, Cap," he said, his voice a thick southern drawl. "I assume that's the asshole in question?" The newcomer inclined his head toward the cuffed man.

"That would be correct. Seph, this is Sergeant Hollis Aldridge."

"Hi, Sergeant," I said. The sergeant's eyes crinkled in the corners, like he was holding back a laugh.

"Pleasure to meet you, ma'am." He thrust out his hand and took mine, drawing my knuckles toward him and bowing. I twitched my hand out of his as soon as I could without being rude. I'd never met a cop who'd been so...not like a cop. Instead of a police uniform, he wore a pair of well broken-in jeans and a long-sleeved shirt that showed off defined muscles.

"Sarge," Alex said in what could have passed for a warning tone.

"Right," he said, winking. "On it."

He strolled lazily over to the assailant, but there was only steel in his eyes as he dragged the man into his car. The sergeant shoved him into the backseat, and with a salute to me and Alex, drove away.

"Can I give you a lift home, Seph?" Alex said.

"Huh?" He was going to think I had a hearing loss at this point.

"A ride home. I can take your statement on the way."

Oh, of course. Would they be filing charges? Would I? "Right," I managed.

Alex led me to another unmarked SUV parked on the other side of the alleyway he'd come out of. A blue and red siren sat on the dashboard, and the front seat was separated from the back by a grated partition.

His sudden appearance at the passenger door startled me. How could someone so tall be so quiet? He gave an apologetic nod, then opened the door for me.

The car's interior was spotless and smelled fresh, like the woods. I gave Alex my address, and we set off down the darkening street.

We were quiet until we hit the main part of town, cruising by the shops and restaurants that looked inviting and warm. Why hadn't I just gone to one of them, or the bookstore, or anywhere except for where I'd ended up?

Little ghosts and witches and vampires skipped along the streets, going from shop to shop trick-or-treating. My blood ran cold at the thought of the person who attacked me roaming the same streets as these children.

"Can you tell me what happened?" Alex asked, keeping his eyes on the road as he navigated downtown traffic.

"That guy asked if I was lost. I was by the computer place, off Oak. I said no, I wasn't, and he started following me. I didn't realize it until he'd already caught up with me. He grabbed my arm, and then...." And then he'd released me as if he'd touched a hot stove. "Then I punched him in the neck with my keys." I blanched. I'd *drawn blood*, hurt someone. I'd never harmed another living being in my life.

"Sounds like it was self defense. Where were you headed?"

"Back toward main street."

"And where were you coming from when you saw him?"

I hesitated. It was embarrassing, but I didn't want to lie to the police. "There's a psychic shop...I think it was on Church Street. That's where I was. It's stupid." I glanced over at him. His profile was all angles and hard jaw. Yeesh. His eyes flicked toward me, and he gave that ghost smile again.

"Get anything good out of it?"

"Nothing, other than a two-cent necklace and some tea."

"Was there anything odd about the place? Anything that caused concern?"

"No, nothing. The woman who helped me was really nice, actually."

"You didn't see her use the phone at all while you were there? Send a text?"

"No. Well, I didn't have my eyes on her every second. She went into the back to make tea. Why?"

"Just routine questions," he said. I stole another glance, but his face gave nothing away, no tell or hint that it *was* anything out of the ordinary. Did he think that Constance had something to do with it? Innocent bystanders, even the woo-woo ones, didn't deserve to get dragged into this mess.

"I don't think she was involved," I said, as we pulled up to my apartment. "I'm good at reading people, and she didn't give me any bad feelings. Anyway...how did you get there so fast? I didn't notice anyone else on the street, and you came flying out of nowhere."

Alex turned toward me, leaving one hand on the wheel and the other on the center console. Suddenly, the car felt extremely small. I shifted toward the door, rapping my elbow on the handle. Pain tingled up my arm, and I bit down on my tongue to stop a groan.

"The whole force is out patrolling on Halloween. I heard you scream." His eyes tightened, and his lips compressed into a line.

"Oh." I hadn't noticed any cops out when I'd walked down main street. And...I didn't remember screaming. But it had all happened so fast, so maybe I couldn't trust my recollection. A spot behind my left eye throbbed as if in agreement. "Thanks for the ride."

"You're welcome. We pride ourselves on door-to-door service at the Gravesville PD." He opened the center console and pulled out a scrap paper and pen. It was a torn receipt from Big Buck's Military Surplus. "I'll give you my number. Call if you remember anything else. And I should get yours, too. So that I can follow up."

"You don't need to write it down. Just tell me." At his hesitation, I prompted him again. "I'll remember."

"If you're sure." Alex recited his phone number, and I committed it to memory. "That's an interesting talent. And a useful one."

"Most of the time. But—nevermind." I held out my hand for the receipt and pen that he still held. "Unless you can memorize mine?"

He shook his head. "No, I don't think so."

I jotted down my number, then handed him the receipt. I was careful to hold it near the end so that we didn't touch.

"You know...it's strange that I've never seen you before today, then suddenly you're everywhere I am." I stilled, shocked by the words coming out of my own mouth. What compelled me to say that? I'd talked more in the last few days than I had in the past three years. And it *was* just a coincidence. I reminded myself that when people actually left their homes, they saw other people. If I did it more often, it wouldn't be so surprising.

"This city isn't so small. I haven't seen you before. I'd have remembered," Alex said. His eyes were so clear that I saw my reflection in them. Wide eyes and a tangled mass of hair, lips parted slightly.

My pulse beat thickly. *Just get out of the car, Seph. Open the door, and walk away.* "You must have been here for a while. If you're a captain, I mean." My fingers flexed on the door handle. It was like the connection between my brain and my mouth had been severed.

"I've been here for a few years. Law enforcement...it runs in the family."

"Oh."

"Are you doing an internship at the law firm?" he asked.

I raised my eyebrows. I looked young, but I didn't think I'd still get mistaken for college-aged. "No. That's where I work." I closed my eyes reflexively. "Or...worked. I, uh, quit. Today."

Alex's thick, straight brows drew down. "I'm sorry."

I shrugged. "It's been a long time coming. I'm better off now, anyway." Maybe.

"I see. Did you grow up around here?"

"No."

Silence pressed on my ears. "I need to get back," Alex said. "Teenagers will be coming out soon."

"Right. Um, thanks again." I suddenly felt all of the events of the past few days pressing on my shoulders like an insurmountable weight. My body sagged, and I had the desperate, mad desire to bury my face into the curve of Alex's neck.

"Take care. And be careful," Alex said, taking my measure again. "I'm sure I'll be talking to you soon."

"Okay." I fished my keys out of my bag but stopped when I saw their ends coated in gummy red. Congealed blood. Shit. Buzzing started in my head, and my chest tightened. I closed my eyes and tried to concentrate on my breathing. Warm hands closed over mine.

"Just breathe. Here, like this." Alex guided my head between my knees, and I could have died of shame, except that it helped. The buzzing receded instantly and my heart rate slowed. I felt as relaxed as I had when I'd drunk Constance's tea.

"I'm okay," I said, sitting up. Lingering mortification burned in my cheeks, but Alex looked understanding—sympathetic, even.

"Here, let me have those." He took the keys that had fallen to the floor and wiped them off on his shirt.

"Oh, don't do that, you'll get blood on—your shirt," I finished. He handed the keys back to me, and they shone as though they were brand new. Even my ancient clover keychain glimmered bright green with new life, the years of grime removed. I turned them over in my hands, marveling. "How did you do that?"

"Do what?" he asked. He looked politely curious, nothing beyond a dutiful public servant that probably wanted the weird lady out of his car.

"Never mind," I muttered. "Thanks again."

"Hey," he said, as I was about to close the car door. "Put my number in your phone."

I gave him a brief nod of acknowledgement because I didn't trust myself to speak, then hurried to my front door. Before I turned the key in the lock I looked over my shoulder, but all was quiet in the light of the street lamps.

6

———————

Someone was trying to break down my door. I closed my book and tossed it onto the coffee table before throwing off my blanket. Extracting myself from the deep couch cushions was a challenge, but I managed it.

After arriving home the evening before, I had locked every window and drawn every curtain, then deadbolted the front door. While I'd managed to fall asleep, it was a restless night, and I woke every couple hours with my heart pounding. Eventually I'd turned to a book, trying to remind myself that everything was fine, and to banish the image of inky black eyes.

The pounding on the door continued. Judging by the faint glow of sunlight coming through the curtains, it was well past morning. I grabbed my phone off the kitchen island and saw five missed calls, all from Bri. Damn.

I hurriedly tugged on my robe, flannel monstrosity though it was, and padded down the hallway. Pulling back the curtain, I peeked out the front window. Bri stood there in a quintessential fall outfit, down to the plaid scarf and knee-high boots. I surveyed my overslept-chic and sighed.

"I'm opening the door. Don't punch me in the head!" I yelled. The pounding stopped.

Bri proffered a bakery box and coffee carafe. "I come bearing gifts."

I squinted against the bright midmorning sunshine. "You are my one true love." Then I took the box from Bri and sniffed. "Pecan roll?"

"Obviously," Bri said, flipping her silky hair over her shoulder. I threw the door open and ushered her inside.

She made herself at home, setting the coffee carafe on the island and pulling chipped mugs from the cabinet. The heavenly smell of yeast and cinnamon wafted to my nose, and I took the mug that Bri offered. Sweet baby Jesus, *coffee*. I relished the rush of caffeine through my veins, and my fatigue headache receded. "Oh, that's good."

"You are an addict," Bri said, pursing her lips.

"And you're enabling me." I inhaled long and deep, and Bri laughed.

"I know it's morning and all, but you look terrible," she said. Brutal, but fair. I didn't even want to know what state my hair was in.

"You will not believe the shit that's been happening to me." I slumped into a scratched counter stool, simultaneously taking a bite from the pecan roll. I moaned. "Can you imagine a world where these don't exist?"

Bri paused, then picked a croissant out of the box. "I wouldn't want to live there."

"Right? Anyway, things have been so weird."

"Spill it. Tell me all your secrets, Hart."

I told her everything, beginning with the man in the cemetery and ending with Alex dropping me off at my apartment. Well, almost all of it. She didn't need to know about my hormonal reaction to him.

"And, that's basically it," I said, picking out a muffin from the bakery box. I had already demolished my pecan roll by the time the story was through. "Wild, huh?"

When I was greeted with silence, I looked up from my pasty. "Bri?"

"Hm? I was listening," she said, although she was staring into the middle distance.

"Are you okay?"

"Sorry, I'm fine. Anyway, you poor thing. I'm so sorry." She hugged me, but I wiggled out of her grip.

"It's okay, Bri. I'm okay. Promise."

She held me at arm's length, scanning me as if assessing for battle trauma. "You are way too calm about this. And why didn't you call me last night? I would've come over in half a second. You shouldn't have been alone, you idiot."

"Hey, quit with the insults. I'm in a fragile state," I said. Bri eyed me licking crumbs off my finger.

"Fragile, my ass," Bri said. "You have this whole silent waif thing going on, but I see right through it."

My mouth dropped open. "Silent waif? How dare you!" I was joking, but part of what Bri said hit home. I was a waif, technically. Well, not an orphan, but the whole father abandoning me at birth thing qualified me for it.

"You're funny, and smart, and you can eviscerate someone with a single word. That's what I love most about you. And it terrifies me to think something could have happened to you, but I also know you can defend yourself. I mean, you put holes in the guy. So, no, you're not fragile."

Bri looked more serious than I'd ever seen her. Her forehead was dewy—almost glowing. "Okay, okay. I'm not fragile," I reassured her.

Then I pulled Bri in for a hug, because I figured this was one of those times I needed to follow the friendship rules. I leaned into her steadiness, and the tight knot in my chest loosened.

"There are scary things in the world, Seph," Bri said, the words breathy with her mouth close to my ear. "I want to be sure you can protect yourself from them."

"Bri, I'm fine. Like you said, I did protect myself. What's your deal?"

Bri stiffened, then pulled away, smiling softly. Her teeth were so white that they shone. That, in addition to her Disney princess looks, always made her look beautiful, put together, perfect.

"Hey, do you think you should get out of town for a while?" she asked.

"What are you talking about?" I said, confusion plain on my face. "Where would I go?"

"I have a lake house. Well, my family does. In the Smoky Mountains. It's empty right now because they're away. You should go there. Take some time."

My head spun. "So, you *are* secretly rich? Is that why you can work at Whitlock and Williams for peanuts and afford those shoes?"

I'd grown up among the rich, but was never one of them—and they never let me forget it. My mom cleaned their toilets, after all. Until she'd met my stepfather, and had become one of the country club wives she'd always been envious of.

Bri's cheeks pinked. "I don't spread it around. But I think it would be good for you to get away from here for a while. Don't you want a break from all of this? The mountains are gorgeous this time of year, and you can clear your head. Get some fresh air, go on some hikes. It'll be fun."

The vision of the misty forest and cottage I'd daydreamed about a few days ago—had it only been days?—filled my head. It *would* be nice to get out of town for a few days. I hadn't taken a vacation since...well, it didn't bear thinking about. There was no job for me to take time off from anymore, so it wasn't like I had to limit myself. Maybe Bri was right; it could be just what I needed.

"Maybe," I said, not wanting to dampen Bri's enthusiasm or get my own hopes up.

"Please, Seph. Think of it as a favor for me. I want you to feel safe."

I had to remember that Bri was kind, and generous. She was my friend. She'd always gone out of her way to make me feel included, and I, to the degree that I could, accepted it. "Okay, fine. I'll do it. But only because you begged me on your knees."

Her eyes cleared. "You're going to love it up there. Imagine taking a bath in the giant soaker tub," she spread her hands wide, "and having a glass of wine while looking at the most gorgeous view of the lake."

I was a sucker for a nice bathtub. "Sounds amazing." And like an escape from reality. I could do with taking a break from the shit show my life had suddenly become.

"I can have the house prepared in time for you to leave tomorrow."

"Tomorrow? Isn't that a little soon?"

"Is there anything stopping you from going?"

"Well...no. But I kind of feel like I'm being whisked away," I joked.

"You deserve to be whisked away. Tolerating Clark for four years means that you need every moment of recovery time possible. Leave tomorrow, stay for a couple weeks. Relax, think things over, then come back refreshed. I promise, you'll have a good time."

There wasn't really an argument against it. "That sounds perfect, actually."

Bri toasted me with her coffee cup. "To the start of your next chapter," she said. "Whatever you do, it's going to be great."

We clinked mugs. I hoped her prediction would come true.

I spent the rest of the day preparing for the trip, which consisted of giving my plants a good watering and trying to decide how many books were a reasonable amount for two weeks. Seven? Ten? I ended up throwing them all in my duffel bag, where they nestled comfortably against my oldest and tattiest sweatshirt.

It kept me busy, but I couldn't help peering out the windows periodically and rechecking the locks. The guy who attacked me was probably in jail right now. But I was still jumpy and on edge, probably not helped by all the caffeine I'd consumed.

Maybe a little bit of fear always stuck with you after something like that happened, knowing the world wasn't ever going to feel as safe as it did before. I had experienced something that I always thought happened to other people. Now it was like knowing that the shadows on the wall maybe weren't just shadows, but had turned out to be real life monsters.

As I ruminated, my thoughts turned to Alex and the string of events that predated our meeting. Meetings, rather. It all felt so bizarre, like I'd been dropped into the middle of someone else's story, not knowing the plot or any of the characters.

Shadows lengthened outside, the apartment growing dark while I packed. I'd been double-checking to make sure I hadn't forgotten anything when I found the necklace that Constance the psychic gifted me.

The necklace was on top of the tarot card I'd found in the cemetery, and I couldn't help but feel a sense of the uncanny when I saw them together. Two objects used in the magical arts, both found after strange situations.

I picked up the striped stone and studied it again. It was actually kind of pretty, not as cheap looking as I'd initially thought. Constance said it was a good luck charm. I decided to bring it. What the hell, I could use all the luck I could get.

I messaged my mom to let her know I'd be out of town. My excuse was that I had the opportunity to take an impromptu trip for the week with Bri. I knew she wouldn't like it if I told her I was going into the middle of the woods, alone, to run away from my responsibilities. Although, she of all people should understand that.

Logically, I knew it made sense to fall into a depression after the love of your life left a note saying that he was leaving for good, and not to go looking for him. But emotionally, I wasn't sure I could ever forgive the years that my mom had seemed as far away as a distant galaxy.

It required several messages back and forth, and an averted phone call, before my mom was mollified. She asked me the usual questions: how was I, how was Bri, was I dating anyone, why *wasn't* I dating anyone? I was such a nice girl, surely there had to be someone who could be convinced to like someone as...boring (okay, she didn't say it, but she might as well have) as me.

My mind conjured an image of the way Alex's eyes crinkled in the corners when he'd given that half-smile. My heart gave an unwelcome and totally unnecessary flutter.

Decidedly not thinking about him, I got into bed early. Too early, some would say, but I was utterly lacking in giving a damn. I cracked open a new book and dove eagerly into the heroine's world. After less than twenty pages I slid into sleep. Through my exhaustion, somehow I knew that I would see Alex in my dreams.

———

Adele's soulful voice blasted through my car's speakers as I sped down I-40. The gorgeous, sunny day couldn't have been more at odds with yesterday's gloom. Brilliant fall leaves sprinkled the road like confetti, providing little pops of color against the asphalt.

Perhaps it was because I was properly caffeinated for the first time in days, but things were looking up. A surprisingly good night's sleep with no nightmares hadn't hurt, either. I spared a moment of appreciation for Bri, glad that I accepted her invitation after all. I wasn't sure why I'd considered turning down the mountain air and promise of relaxation.

Highway turned into winding mountain roads, and I began the climb toward the lake house. The houses in the mountain's shadow were modest, growing larger and more stately the closer I got to the top. Imposing gates that flanked paved driveways appeared, along with discreetly mounted cameras. There must have been some serious money on this mountain.

My map's GPS signal went haywire when I was ten minutes away. I made three circles before I gave up on the signal, pulling up Bri's text about directions. She'd explained that they didn't have great cell service up at the lake, but that it 'added to the experience of being one with nature.' That's what the realtor must have advertised when they bought the house. It was a fancy way of saying, *if you get ax murdered up here, there's no one to call for help!*

Despite my doubts, Bri's directions were accurate, and I soon turned onto a long gravel driveway. The densely packed trees opened up and I was treated to a view of a grand house, all stone and wood and peaked roof. Was that a turret? My jaw dropped as I parked in front of the double-door garage.

Grand didn't really begin to describe the house; it was massive, more of a castle than the quaint home Bri had told me about. The facade was gray and brown stone, with wood beams running on the eaves and large picture windows. There wasn't just one turret, but two. They spiraled up into the sky, and instead of conical roofs they had crows nests. I bet the view went on for miles from up there.

Beautifully manicured gardens bordered the lawn, at odds with the wild thicket of woods that encroached them. I hauled my suitcase out of the car, then walked up to the imposing front doors. Standing over ten feet tall, they were monoliths of timber, glass, and steel. Very off-putting to ax murderers, I was sure.

Bri had given me a security code for the keypad, and I searched the facade, finally finding it hidden behind a carving of a flowering vine set right into the stone. I punched in the code, and the front doors clicked ajar and swung inward lightly, belying their weight.

If the outside of the house looked medieval, then it was in complete juxtaposition to the modern interior. I walked into a large foyer, where beautiful curved double staircases twined through each other. Everything was Scandinavian chic, with blond wood, glass, and clean white marble as far as the eye could see. The whole place was exceedingly bright, like the house floated amongst the clouds.

The lake that sparkled turquoise through floor-to-ceiling glass windows drew my eye. A long dock jutted out into the water about a hundred yards below, complete with a boathouse that was more square footage than my childhood home.

Bri wasn't just rich; she was *filthy* rich.

I dropped my bag by the ivory sectional couch flanking what could only be called an entertainment center, not just a TV, and headed toward the kitchen. The whole main level was an open floor plan, so all I had to do was pivot toward the mile of more white marble island that could seat a dozen. The same marble used for the counters continued up the wall into a backsplash that had a stunning waterfall-like effect. Everything in here was top of the line; from the looks of the stainless steel appliances, restaurant grade gas range, and wine fridge.

Overwhelmed by the opulence, I went down to the dock to let Bri know I'd arrived. Motion detector lights flared, following my movements on the stone path leading down to the lake. I only had one miniscule signal bar, but after a few seconds I heard a tinny ring, and my call connected.

"Hello?" Bri's voice sounded far away.

"You really undersold this place, you know."

Bri laughed. "I told you it was incredible."

"Please don't tell me this is funded by blood diamonds and ruin my time," I said.

"Hardly. It's family money. Does that help?"

"Marginally. It's gorgeous, and luxurious, and amazing. It just feels too good to be true that I have this place to myself for two weeks. Where are your parents when they're not here?" Another pause. "Bri, are you there?"

"Sorry, the connection is bad. I told you about the cell service, right?"

"You did. So?"

"They live out of the country."

"Really?" I asked. "Where?"

"In England."

"Why did I not know that?" A little voice reminded me that I didn't know that Bri had a lake house, either. I didn't know much about her past. But she didn't know much about mine.

Bri's voice started to break up on the other end of the line. "I think

I'm losing you," I said, pulling the phone away from my ear to check the service. Only one bar.

"Gotta— go—love—" A long beep signaled the call had dropped.

"Love you too," I murmured, then lowered the phone from my ear.

I spun a slow circle; there was a full bar in the boat house, a complement of all the water toys one could ever want, and a fire pit built into the dock. Shaking my head in disbelief, I began the hike back up to the house. It was time to begin the promised relaxation.

7

———

Daylight spilled into my bedroom, turning the darkness behind my eyelids to an orange glow. I rolled over, hugging the pillow closer to me, breathing in the scent of fresh lavender. Thank god it was morning.

Bad dreams plagued me most nights, leaving me eager for the rosy fingers of dawn to break the horizon. My fears always seemed more distant in the light of day. But still, there was a lingering sense of wrongness. Like the man who attacked me was lurking around the corners of bright and airy rooms, waiting to grab me again.

But nightmares or no, the past eleven days had been the most decadent of my life.

Yawning, I stumbled out of bed and into the bathroom. A palatial tub dominated the space that was decorated in shades of cream and green. I'd taken Bri's advice by enjoying the stunning view from the bath with a glass of wine. At dusk the lake transitioned from turquoise to violet, and the early evening light muted the burnished golds and brilliant reds of fall foliage, turning them into an impressionist painting.

I also spent hours upon hours reading, something I hadn't been able to do since high school. The primary bedroom suite included a cozy library area with a gas fireplace that had an expansive selection of everything from the classics, to cheesy romance novels, to contemporary fiction. It was my version of heaven.

The lake sparkling through picture windows greeted me like an old friend as I padded into the kitchen. I brewed coffee, then took my first cup into the sunroom—as had been my habit. Although, it was dangerous to form habits that couldn't last.

So far, I'd done a first class job of avoiding any thoughts of the future. Every time my mind started to drift in that direction, I backpedaled.

Except for one memory that kept circling, no matter how hard I tried to keep it at bay. It was a voice saying *I'll be in touch* that came from a pair of lips sculpted by a renaissance master, and eyes that you could wander into and never want to find your way out of.

Maybe I'd been taking too much advantage of the library's romance selection. But the truth was that I couldn't keep Alex out of my head. The lack of reception meant that even if he'd tried to call, I wouldn't know about it. I'd thought about reaching out, but I felt too...nervous, worried, guilty? Probably all of the above.

I pushed open the sliding doors and walked onto the deck, shivering in the fall air. Movement caught my eye as I looked out over the lake. It was from the closest neighbor's house, a woman running on a treadmill. The window framed her perfectly, like she was on a television screen. Maybe some exercise would be good for me. Maybe—

An ice cold hand wrapped around my wrist, grinding the bones together so that I gasped in pain. I whipped around and jerked my arm away, seeing a pale imprint of inkblot eyes. Breath gathered in my lungs, preparing for a scream to erupt.

But no one was there. Just the empty deck and the sound of blood rushing in my ears.

I could have sworn the pain was real. I held my arm up to the light, looking for any sign of redness. All I saw was my little flower birthmark, pulse thrumming like the beat of a hummingbird's wings in the hollow of my wrist.

Sagging against the deck railing, I released the breath I held. If my imagination was getting this out of control, maybe it was time to give up my hermetic seclusion.

I'd take one last hike, then pack up my things and rejoin the real world.

My car crunched over gravel at the entrance to the Norton Creek Trailhead on the north shore of Lake Fontana. The drive there had been beautiful, the forest colored in patches of red and gold, and the deep green of the pines. Sunbeams pierced through the rapidly shifting clouds, so that the sky was a patchwork of light and shadow.

Despite the sunshine, the dense canopy of these trees looked eerie up close. The forest's beauty was wild, less postcard perfect and more haunted woods. A light wind set branches swaying, and they rubbed against each other with a dry rustle as if they were reaching out to hold hands. *To hold secrets.*

No, Seph. No more stories.

I reached for Constance's necklace and thumbed the stone. That was real, not a fantasy of my own making. I'd brought the trinket with me—on impulse or intuition, I wasn't sure which. But now I was glad I had the little luck charm, even if it was all in my head.

The Smoky Mountains were chock full of cemeteries, and the Norton Creek Trail passed by several, which was why I'd chosen it. Mine was the only car in the lot at the trailhead, but I assumed there would be other hikers around, maybe even some who were thru-hiking the Appalachian Trail.

As I made my way down the rugged dirt path, I didn't see a single soul. There was plenty of rustling in the undergrowth; little forest animals preparing for winter, no doubt. A few deer picked their way daintily through the trees. The way the light shone through the canopy dappled their coats, turning them almost invisible in the shadows.

My thoughts wandered during the hike. It was restful, meditative, even, just to be. To allow myself to exist without the rest of the world watching and judging. The slight pressure I always felt in the company of others, even Bri, had evaporated.

After about two hours on the trail, I stepped off to rest and refuel on a fallen log. It was damp and covered with feathery green moss, but I didn't mind. The forest wasn't so eerie now that I was used to the quiet. The air smelled of damp earth and growing things. It made me feel vital and alive, like I was part of the forest ecosystem, too. Like I belonged somewhere.

It had all started with my name. Persephone Augusta Hart, gifted to me by my absent father. I wasn't sure why my mom even agreed to it—but she couldn't have imagined how hard it was to be stuck with the same name as the goddess queen of the underworld.

I'd shortened it to Seph as soon as I could, but the damage had already been done. So I'd hidden myself away, made myself small and invisible so that cruel words and damning judgments couldn't harm me.

While I'd been disappearing into myself, my mom had moved on and found a new home in my stepfather. In my loneliness I'd sharpened my tongue, so that when the other kids caught and cornered me, I left my own marks.

I took a deep breath, and cold air flooded into the knot of sadness that had been massed in my chest for so long that it was as much a part of me as my own skin. I wanted to curl into a ball, to sink into the soft carpet of moss and wrap my arms around my wounds to protect them.

I didn't know how long I sat there, the salt of my tears joining with the forest floor. All I knew was that when my face was dry, I felt better. Still raw, but maybe the weight was lighter and the ache was smaller than it had been.

After I found my way back to the trail, a harsh chirp sounded behind me. I glanced over my shoulder, then frowned. Had the smattering of small white flowers that surrounded the log been there a moment ago? I walked back and crouched in front of one, touching a velvety petal and tracing the round black stigma. Spring ephemerals, perhaps brought on by the trick of a warm day.

The weather was beginning to turn. An overcast sky covered the great boughs of the pines like a thick blanket. The wind picked up, clouds swirling fast, as dry leaves whispered in the treetops. The shiver that rolled down my spine was only partially to do with the cold, and I couldn't help wishing that I had some company now.

I was still determined to reach Norton Cemetery. As the cold claimed me, it became less of a want and more of a need to find it, like the graveyard was a magnet, pulling me in.

I trudged along until the dense thickets of magnolias thinned, and the winding path widened out into a large clearing. The cemetery spread before me.

There was an undeniable beauty about the place. Soft light from the overcast sky made the graves stand out in stark relief, and the contrast against the forest was striking. There were rows upon rows of headstones, some new, some so weathered that the inscriptions were no longer legible.

Walking along the rows, I relaxed again as I fell into a familiar rhythm. I played a game where I looked for the most interesting, unique names on gravestones. There were the classics, like William and Ann, but I also passed a Calliope and Fortunata.

Near a silvery birch tree at the edge of the cemetery was a crypt of mottled black granite. It stood alone on top of a small rise, like an easily defendable fortress. I shivered as I headed toward it; the air smelled like snow, all traces of the crisp fall day gone.

The crypt was set with an impregnable looking wooden door that had bulky iron hinges and a metallic pull ring in the center. I reached out but hesitated, my fingers hovering in the air inches away. Most likely it would be locked. It smelled like grave dirt and old bones, like every nightmare I'd ever had, the twisted fingers of terrible dreams reaching inside to—

"No." My voice broke the heavy silence that lay across the graveyard, startling a flock of black birds out of a tree. I'd never been afraid in a cemetery before. They were my refuge, the quiet places that welcomed me like an old friend. I wouldn't let what happened back in Gravesville ruin that for me.

I closed my fingers around the iron ring. Shocked, I let go and stared at the door. It was cold outside, but the metal felt like it had spent a day in a subzero freezer. Tugging my jacket down over my fingers, I pulled. The door opened silently.

The crypt was damp inside, and I wrinkled my nose at the strong musty basement odor. Strips of light pooled on the floor from narrow windows, providing dim illumination to the gloom. I counted twelve rectangular outlines where coffins were interred, and came closer to read their inscriptions. There were also a series of hollow niches carved into the walls, some empty and some holding ceramic urns. A shattered glass vase and long dead flowers were scattered on the floor beneath a ledge.

My breath crystallized into puffs that reminded me of the stranger's smoke from the cemetery. It was still too dark, so I used my phone's flashlight to read. *Josephine Baker McKnight, 1895-1975.* I wondered what kind of life she'd lived. Two of her children had died before her, so it must have been a hard one.

I turned away and the flashlight's beam swept across the crypt's stone floor, exposing a circular depression in its center. The circle had a mosaic style border, with carvings adorning the interior. There was some sort of inscription, but I was too far away to see clearly in the semi-darkness. Maybe it was a memorialization, or a quote. I liked to tuck away the good ones for future use.

I lowered to my knees and peered at the inscription. What I saw stopped my heart and froze me into place, my body as immovable as the flagstones beneath my feet. The world around me slowed until I felt like I was floating, rising high above the cemetery like a lost balloon.

The carving was of a fierce, avenging angel plunging a sword through a gothic skull. Underneath it read:

Here Lies
Persephone Augusta Hart
June 21, 1995 - November 13, 2021
Flectere Si Nequeo Superos Acheronta Movebo

I squeezed my eyes shut for one slow heartbeat, hoping my overactive imagination was playing tricks on me. Because there was no way that my birthday was carved into the unyielding stone. When I opened them and my name was still etched there, I stood and backed away, looking around and half hoping that someone would pop out and yell, "Gotcha!"

But it was just me and my own grave, the damp smell of the crypt turning into something foul and sinister. I spun and ran toward the doors, but they slammed shut when I was just feet away. I scrabbled for a handle that wasn't there.

Damnit, I hadn't realized that there was no way to open the crypt from the inside. Although I should have expected it, since it wasn't like the occupants would be leaving anytime soon. A hysterical bubble of laughter escaped my lips, echoing.

I'm going to die here, and no one will know where I am. The thought swirled around me, threatening to take me under in a tide of panic. My fingers clawed at the seam of the door, trying to find purchase.

Then, a noise sluiced through my fear like a river bursting its dam. A soft, screeching sound that had every single hair on my body standing on end rang through the crypt. I froze again, and terror rose from the pit of my stomach, curling its frosty fingers around my sternum. "Oh, *fuck*," I whispered, and turned around.

One of the rectangular plates that held the coffins began to saw slowly back and forth, inching open. A dark stain oozed out of the crevice then started to drip down the wall like melting wax. But no, it wasn't dripping; the shadow flowed across the stone, not touching it or leaving a mark as it slid toward me.

"This is not happening," I whispered to myself. "It's a dream. Wake up!" I slapped my face, and pain blossomed in my cheek, real and sharp.

The shadow was halfway across the floor, an unending dark wave that belied my terror with its fluidity. How could something so hypnotic be so dangerous? The smell was truly horrible now, a combination of rotten eggs and ashes. A garbled noise came from the shadow, like the scratching of a record.

I pressed my back against the door as though I could become a shadow myself to slip through and flee. The dark stain curled around my ankles, icy cold claws probing, seeking.

But...it didn't touch me. In fact, as the black mist sought to wrap around my waist, it drew back sharply. Almost like a flinch.

Then I was falling backward out of the crypt into a warm, solid wall, a pair of arms closing around my waist and dragging me away.

It was Alex, his eyes flashing and skin glowing with something more than just good genes.

At least if my final moments were one long hallucination, it would be a good one. I realized that I wouldn't mind at all if he was the last person I saw before I died.

Alex stepped around me into the crypt and spread his arms wide. A wind picked up, stirring the dead flowers on the ground and shoving the shadow further back. He growled words in an unfamiliar language, his voice echoing in my ears. Although I couldn't understand him, his tone made it clear that he wanted the thing to fuck off, and to do it immediately.

Pressure I hadn't realized was there lifted from the base of my skull. Then the shadow retreated into the crevice from which it came, like a tape being rewound. It simply disappeared without a trace, and the crypt returned to musty but benign normality.

Alex crossed to the rectangular drawer and slammed it shut. Stone rasped against stone, and I winced at the harsh sound. He murmured a few more words and swiped a hand over the lid, then turned to face me.

My first thought was that Alex was even more beautiful than I remembered. His dark hair was tousled, his frame tall and lithe. My second was that I finally had that nervous breakdown that had been threatening for the past twenty years. I opened my mouth to speak, but nothing came out other than a strangled squeak.

"Did it hurt you?" Alex asked, his steps measured and soundless. He hesitated for the briefest of moments before snaking an arm around my waist and ushering me into the graveyard.

The brightness of the overcast day compared to the crypt's gloom was startling but welcome. Gulping fresh air, I marveled at how I'd never noticed how delicious it was before. I stumbled and Alex pulled me upright, not releasing his hold by a millimeter.

"Do you have a car?" he asked, as if the world hadn't just completely upended itself.

"What?" I swayed again, clutching my birthmark to ground me. But no matter how I tried to will it away, sizzling black flickered at the edges of my vision, and an iron band constricted around my chest.

"Breathe," Alex commanded. "In through your nose and out through your mouth." That was familiar, but his voice was a million miles away.

"How are you here?" I said.

"I felt you. What did you think you were doing, coming up here alone?"

"I—I wanted to hike," I wheezed, then almost went cross-eyed as Alex spun us around to face the mausoleum. "What is it?"

"Company." He raised his free hand, and in his palm was a ball of licking blue flames. I blinked rapidly to clear the vision. But it hadn't changed, and with the fire in his hand and the fierce look in his eyes, he could have been a dark god.

"Oh, shit." My voice cracked, and I swayed.

"Don't faint," he warned, looking at something behind the mausoleum. "Can you stand?"

"I think." He released me and I leaned on a tombstone but managed to stay upright. The world stopped swimming, and my heart rate returned to a semblance of normal. The cemetery looked innocuous apart from the two of us, as out of place among the dead as the sun in the night sky.

"On second thought, we'd better go." His voice had gone tight.

"What?" I turned and stared at what had Alex's attention. Something large and scaly with long teeth and eyes like smoke. My knees threatened to buckle, and I slapped a hand onto the tombstone again.

"Hold on, let me find it—there. Come on!"

Between Alex's spread hands was a hole filled with undulating midnight silk, as though he'd split the fabric of the very air itself. It had a silvery sheen that captured the light, then diffused it across the surface like droplets of rain hitting a shallow pool.

"What," I breathed, "is that?" Chills ran up my spine, then turned into a whole body tremor. I clutched my waist, trying to hold myself together as everything around me, including *the freaking air*, unraveled.

Alex stepped back, letting his hands drop, and turned to face me. His eyes were like chips of dark green glass, his hard jaw clenched. "This is a gateway. And we're going through it."

The beast behind us gave an almighty roar, then Alex grabbed my hand and yanked us into the darkness.

8

Why had someone dumped an entire bucket of sand under my eyelids? They felt scratchy and raw, as did my throat. And holy mother of god, my *head*. It throbbed like the beat of a bass drum, pain ricocheting around my skull.

I burrowed deeper into the pillow, hoping more sleep would get rid of this horrible hangover. But I didn't remember drinking...and why did the sheets smell like cedar?

My eyes snapped open and I sat upright in bed. Images of the deathly shadow snaking across the floor of the icy crypt flashed through my abused brain, along with—

"Alex?"

I was alone. And this wasn't *my* room, not from back home nor the lakehouse. A floor lamp in the corner softly illuminated dark blue walls. There was a framed vintage poster of Shenandoah National Park on the wall opposite the bed, and a dresser tucked into the corner. It was neat as a pin, and as I got up I noted that the bed corners were tucked in with military precision.

Where the hell was I? The unfamiliar room added to my disorientation, and I grabbed for the cell phone that was in my pocket. Dead, of course.

"Well, shit," I muttered. As the what-ifs circled my brain, my eyes alighted on the window.

"If you're thinking of climbing out, I wouldn't. It's one o'clock in the morning."

I recognized that voice.

Alex was framed in the doorway, backlit so that his face was in shadow. He took a step into the room and the darkness cleared. I had a stray thought that he belonged in the light, with that golden starburst in his eyes that reminded me of the sun.

"Where are we?" My voice came out wobblier than I would've liked.

"My house. In Gravesville. Hollis brought your car back."

"Oh." It took a moment to sink in. Questions jostled for position. "How did he—why—how are we here? How did you find me? And...." *And what was that thing in the graveyard*, I wanted to ask, but I couldn't make my mouth form the words.

Alex came closer, but stopped when I shrank back. "You're safe now."

I rubbed my birthmark, looking around the room. It seemed real enough, but was it possible this had all been a dream? That at this very moment I was sound asleep in my bed at the lakehouse, never having woken up to begin with?

"I just...I don't understand." Tension crept up the back of my neck, settling in a tight mass around my shoulders. "What happened, exactly?"

"I don't think you would believe me if I told you," Alex said, his tone measured.

I shut my eyes, but that only intensified the pounding in my head. "Try me."

"Why don't you come downstairs?" Not waiting for an answer, he left the room. "Do you want something for your headache?" he called down the hall.

Hesitating only for a moment, I followed after him down a set of spiral stairs, skimming my hand along the polished banister. We walked through hallways the color of midnight and over jewel-toned rugs covering gleaming hardwoods. I counted at least four doors before we came to a sort of great room, then a kitchen.

The kitchen design reminded me of a forest in early morning light. Plants crowded butcher block countertops, and a huge picture window above the sink looked out onto mature trees strung with lights. Alex pulled a mug out of a silvery green, glass paned cabinet. He switched on an electric kettle and took loose tea from a wooden box on the counter.

"How do you know I have a headache?" I asked. My heart quivered in my chest like a skittish animal.

"It's all in the eyes." The kettle whistled, and Alex pushed the mug toward me. I wrapped my fingers around it, relishing the warmth. "Drink," he urged. "It'll help."

I did, and the pounding settled to a whisper. My throat felt better, too. "What's in this?"

"Sylvan's special blend. He's one of my...roommates. I have a few."

"Rent must be high," I muttered, sipping again. "Where are they?"

"Out. Look, we can sit, and try to figure this out."

Alex padded over to take a seat at a blond wood table. I noticed for the first time that he was barefoot. It felt strangely intimate seeing him like that, and I forced my eyes away.

"What do you remember?" he asked, sitting ramrod straight but making it look comfortable.

I traced a whorl on the table. "What I remember is impossible."

"Try me," he said, face betraying nothing.

"Well...there was a shadow." It seemed even sillier when I said it out loud, and warmth crept into my cheeks. "And you did something to make it go away. Then I remember you...you were holding fire, which is impossible, and then there was a...hole in the air."

The hollows in Alex's cheeks deepened. "That was all real, Seph."

"But how? That kind of stuff doesn't happen. I probably hit my head somewhere along the way." I probed my scalp, but there was no pain, not a bump or a bruise to explain the hallucination.

"That kind of stuff happens in my world. All the time."

Interest warred with reticence. "Your world?"

Alex reached out a hand, then stopped a hairsbreadth from my arm. "May I?" I nodded, and he drew my wrist toward him, touching a finger to the pale birthmark that stood out on my brown skin. An electric current zipped up my arm. "The sign of the lily," he said.

I pulled away, covering the birthmark with my other hand. "What, this? It's just a birthmark."

"I have one, too." Alex inclined his head toward me, and I didn't realize what he was doing until he pointed to a spot behind his right ear, pulling some of his dark hair aside.

It was the exact same birthmark. Not just similar, but its twin in everything but color—his was the inverse of mine, brown on white skin. Six long petals atop a slim stem, about an inch long.

"Coincidence," I said. It had to be. There was no other possible explanation that squared with reality.

"Is this a coincidence?" Sergeant Aldridge strolled into the kitchen, his cowboy boots clicking on the tiled floor. I tensed, not realizing that we weren't alone in the house.

Hollis held up his right hand, then flipped it so the back faced me. My lips started to go numb as I realized that riding just below his pinky knuckle was the same mark as mine and Alex's.

"Hollis," Alex warned, his jaw tightening.

"Seph already knows me. Don't ya, darlin'?" Hollis said.

I looked between Alex and the sergeant. "He's one of your roommates?"

"He is. And he was supposed to wait so you didn't get overwhelmed."

"I think it's a little late for that," I said.

Hollis laughed, bold and loud. "See? I told you so."

"Okay, so we all have matching birthmarks. How does that explain how you knew where I was?" I demanded.

Alex exchanged a brief look with Hollis. "I felt you."

"That doesn't make any sense. You can't just *feel* people." I stood. "I think I should go."

"Seph, please. It's not safe for you to leave right now."

"And it's not right for you to keep me here." I blurted what had been haunting the corner of my brain since I'd woken in Alex's bedroom. "You're not a cop, are you?"

"Not in the way you think. We're not that kind of enforcement," he answered.

I kneaded my forehead, the headache building again. "Can you stop being cryptic?"

"I'm trying—I'm not usually the one who tells people." Alex brought a hand up as if to scrub it through his hair, then rested it back on the table.

"But she has to know anyway, doesn't she?" a woman's voice said.

I turned to see the voice's owner leaning against the door jamb. She was beautiful, curvy and petite with waist-length black hair and features as even as a doll's.

Alex sighed audibly. "Davina, what are you doing here? You're supposed to be supervising patrol."

"Relieving Hollis at command. I thought you'd need the backup." She nodded at Hollis. "Go on, hotshot."

Hollis dipped his head and grinned at me. "I'll see you later, I'm sure."

Part of me relaxed knowing that there was a woman in the room, but my brain was spinning at the rotating cast of characters. "Who are *you*?"

"Davina. Alex's second in command. And you must be Seph."

My shoulders hovered somewhere around my ears, and I made a conscious effort to lower them. "Where are my car keys?" I said tersely.

Davina's brown eyes narrowed, perhaps at my tone, but I didn't give two shits what she thought. What *any* of them thought.

"You don't want to leave right now," she said.

I was on the verge of pounding my hands on the table like an irascible toddler. "Oh, because I'm in some sort of *danger*?"

"Alex is too gentle, so I'll just come out and say it. *We're* demon hunters." She pointed to her impressive chest. "*You're* attracting every demon and supernatural asshole within a fifty mile radius. Do the math. If you walk out that door, you're likely to get jumped by at least one or two on your way home. From what Alex has told us, it's already happened twice. Don't be stupid and make it a third time."

I opened and closed my mouth, but no words came out. Alex pushed up from the table, and suddenly I felt like the three of us were in the middle of a Wild West standoff.

"Supernatural?" The word felt clumsy in my mouth.

"Yes. Demons, witches, vampires, fairies, mermaids. The list goes on," Davina said.

Alex held a hand out like he wanted to stop the flow of words coming from her mouth. "While Davina might be lacking tact, she's right. That man who attacked you in downtown Gravesville wasn't a man. It was an atrax."

"A—a what?" I stammered.

"An atrax," Alex repeated. "A spider demon who entered this world through a graveyard, then somehow got past us and went after you."

It was the fourth time someone had said demon in as many minutes. "Right. Well, I don't need my keys. I'll walk."

I started toward the pocket door we'd come through to enter the kitchen, and Davina neatly sidestepped out of my way. But it slammed shut and the lock clicked when I was a foot away. I waited a beat, then turned to see Alex and Davina standing side by side.

"Nice trick. But holding someone against their will is a crime." The overhead lights flickered once.

Davina chuckled, low and smoky. "You think human laws apply to us? I'd like to see them try."

My eyes flitted around the kitchen, looking for something to pry open the door. The knife block was behind Alex, but Davina guessed my intent. She flicked a hand and they slid to the opposite end of the counter. "None for you," she cautioned, wagging a finger.

"Davina, enough," Alex said, cool and even. "Go to the command center and support the rest of the unit."

With one last flick of her hair, Davina sashayed out of the kitchen. The door opened for her, but snapped shut again once she'd gone through.

"Look, I don't know how you're doing these little tricks, but it's not funny." Fear clawed at my throat, and my voice wavered. "Please let me go."

"If you want to go, I'll make sure you get home safely. But if you could just hear me out one last time. I'm sworn to protect, and I would never hurt a human soul. That's a promise."

I so wanted to believe him, because if I did then maybe I wouldn't feel so terrified. "You have three minutes, then I'm jumping out the window."

"That's fair." A pause stretched between us before he began. "It happened a few days before Halloween. I was getting ready to patrol with the rest of my unit—my roommates—when I felt this...pull. It was like a...." He furrowed his brow. "Like an earthquake, with you at the epicenter. I followed the feeling, and found you. Then I learned your routine for the next couple of days, waiting for a chance to approach you."

"Wait—you were following me?" I hesitated. "You knew I was going to be at the office, alone?"

The corner of his mouth pulled down, exposing a dimple. "I had to confront you, to find out what you were. Then after the atrax attacked you, I saw your mark. When you left town, I knew you were at risk, so I followed you from a distance. I didn't know what else to do." There was regret under his mask of control, I was sure of it. "When initiates are found outside of the bloodlines, there are people who deal with it. And your age—it doesn't make any sense."

"Initiates of *what*? What does my age have to do with anything?" I ground out.

"Power manifests around nineteen or twenty. Sometimes twenty-one, but that's a stretch. You're what, twenty-five?"

I folded my arms. "Twenty-six."

Alex shook his head. "See, it's all wrong."

I didn't see. At all. "What power do you mean?"

"Arcana. Power, magic, energy—you can take your pick, it's all roughly the same."

The laugh rose from my gut. "You think I'm magic? Wait, you think that *you're* magic? Are you like, an amateur troop of magicians?"

He looked affronted. "No. How else would you explain what's happened to you?"

"Late onset psychosis," I suggested.

Although I knew everything Alex had told me, every moment I'd spent in this house so far was based on a lie, I couldn't prevent the curiosity. It had awakened something childlike in me, something that still held onto hope that maybe there was more to life than the disappointment that was always in my shadow. But hope was a dangerous thing, and it had no business here.

A sudden pulse of anger flared in me, like a viper rearing back to strike. The lights flickered again.

"I understand that you're scared. Helpless, even," he said. Was that a condescending smirk on his smug, handsome face?

I slammed my hands on the table with a bang. "I'm *not* helpless." A series of loud pops sounded as the light fixture exploded and glass rained down on us.

Faster than I could blink, Alex was at my side, yanking me from under the fixture that was now devoid of bulbs. Small pieces of glass glittered in his hair like water droplets. I felt warmth on my forearm, and saw a scarlet line snaking its way down to my wrist. Alex placed a hand over the cut. "Hey!" I cried, waiting for the sting to come.

It never did. He released me, and where there had been a thin streak of blood on my arm was a pale white line, like a pencil mark that had been erased. I gawked at it, then turned to Alex. "What did you just do to me?"

"I healed you." He gave me a considering look, then leaned over to pluck a piece of glass from my hair. "That didn't take long. How many times has it happened?"

The bastard had goaded me on purpose. "How many times has a light fixture exploded on me? That's the first, to my recollection."

"Don't be obtuse. How many times have you lost control like that?"

"You think that was *me*?"

"Come on, Seph. What other proof do you need?"

I touched the scar that had been an open wound moments before. "I honestly don't know." I wanted to go back home. Back to safety, back to where things didn't explode on my head and there were no monsters trying to kill me.

The kitchen door opened, beckoning. "Hold on just a minute. I'll follow you, make sure you get back safely," Alex said. He left the room, then poked his head around the door. "Please." He sounded sincere, at least. Or maybe I was just turning into a fool.

I waited for him in the foyer. Paintings hung on a gallery wall, their frames gilt and opulent. The whole place reeked of money.

He returned carrying a book bound in leather. The edges were soft and worn, as though it had been held by hundreds of hands. "Take this."

"What is it?" I reached for the book, interest flickering again. It was heavy, and I flipped it open to expose tissue thin pages.

"It explains our history, much better than I ever could."

What did it say about me that I trusted books more than people? That words on a page felt safer than the words coming out of his mouth.

I wasn't sure whether to feel grateful for Alex's offer to follow me home, or annoyed at the pair of headlights in my rearview mirror. They seemed like a lighthouse's beacon in the dark, promising safety. But I'd been taking care of myself for as long as I could remember. *You can't save yourself from things that go bump in the night*, a voice in my head whispered. On a harsh exhale, I slapped it down.

List the facts, I reminded myself. Alex, Hollis, and I—I didn't know about Davina—all had the exact same birthmark. Alex had shown up out of nowhere to save me from an attack, twice, then, if my memory was to be trusted—and it usually was—had pulled us through some kind of tear in reality to bring us back to Gravesville.

Well, when I put it that way...it did seem like the simplest explanation.

Alex walked me to the door when we arrived at my apartment, and I wondered if in another version of my life, we would have been coming home from a date instead of the bizarre night I'd had.

"So...what happens now?" I asked. I shuffled awkwardly, like some ungainly newborn colt.

"I'll assign someone to watch your house tonight. You get some sleep, then we'll figure out what to do tomorrow. Everything will be better in the light of day."

An empty promise, but I appreciated the sentiment. "Sure. Well... see you." I walked inside and gave him one last nod before I shut the door and flicked the lock. I had a fleeting thought that it might not hold against whatever was out there.

I sat on the couch, cocooning myself in a blanket. It was two o'clock in the morning, and I knew that I should go to sleep, but adrenaline sizzled in my bloodstream. Was my apartment safe anymore? It had always been my refuge, the place where I could be my full self without any prying eyes or judgements. But now it seemed like a trap more than anything, and I wondered just what exactly was lurking outside in the dark.

I stroked Constance's tiger's eye pendant that hung around my neck, the silky texture soothing as my mind raced in circles.

9

———

It would have been easy to convince myself that the last day was all a dream—if the leatherbound book hadn't been sitting on my coffee table like a grenade with its pin half pulled. But it was, meaning that however I'd ended up at Alex's house last night, that part had at least been real.

I'd gone back and forth a dozen times this morning, deciding whether or not I even wanted to open the book. Reading it would be validating what Alex had told me. That there was magic in the world, and that demons were coming for my blood.

And even worse, what if I actually wanted whatever I found inside? I paced, throwing heated glances at the book like it had wronged me somehow.

Maybe talking to Bri could ground me. It was a work day for everyone else, but I made a deal with myself then. If she answered I wouldn't open the book. And if she didn't...then I would.

I called her, and while the phone rang my heart knocked around under my ribs.

"Hello," Bri said.

"Hi, Bri—"

"You've reached Bri. You know what to do." There was a beep, then the voicemail recording started. I hung up the phone, then sat on the couch, laying back against the deep cushions.

I picked up the book and cracked its thick spine, the pages splaying open.

What I found written in dark ink on yellowed pages was an ancient tale of good and evil. It was about immortals who called themselves gods, the humans who worshiped them, and a fight for survival.

———

There was a pair of immortal twins, Malistir the Cunning and his sister Iznir the Fair, who resided in one of the worlds of the gods. They ruled their land as equals, while sitting upon thrones made of stardust and night wind.

But over millennia, Malistir grew discontented with his lot. He desired more. Why should he be confined to ruling one world, when there numbered as many worlds as drops of water in the oceans? Malistir would take them all, and rule as he saw fit, without interference from the other, weaker gods.

Malistir began to venture from his immortal realm, slyly spreading chaos and sickness, war and famine, disease and death. Eventually, he began to steal mortal souls and consume them for his own, storing the power he gained inside of a star that he plucked from the heavens.

Malistir laughed as the other gods, with their self-obsession and vanity, were blinded to what was happening under their very noses.

The corners of the worlds became darker places, and the shadows spread, until everywhere bore some mark of Malistir's evil. By the time the other immortals realized his plans and banded together, he had already sown resentment and sabotage amidst their ranks. Attempts to destroy Malistir were thwarted from the inside, and he continued to amass great power as kingdoms fell. The dark god picked up the broken pieces and molded them into places of madness.

However, there were some immortals who held out hope and continued to resist the spread of evil. Malistir's twin, Iznir, was one of their leaders. She hatched a desperate plan to fight her brother.

Iznir knew that the immortal gods alone would not be able to destroy the darkness that was already near invincible. So she left her immortal world and began to save souls, just as her brother reaped them.

Iznir and her band of fellow immortals selected the most capable mortals they could find—those who possessed not only physical strength, but valiant hearts, courage, and cunning—and gifted them with speed, strength, and magic—everything they needed to fight and subdue Malastir's forces. There were many more mortals than gods, after all. Where Malistir saw only weakness, Iznir saw potential.

These chosen were called Guardians, the protectors, because they were the gods-touched, the ones who were given power to eradicate the darkness that dominated the worlds. To differentiate the chosen from other mortals, Iznir and her followers marked them with her sign— the lily, the symbol of rebirth.

The war raged for a thousand years or more, in the skies and on the ground, in the seas and under the land, but in time the Guardians joined forces over all the worlds and defeated Malastir and his armies. The evil ones were destroyed or bound in prison worlds for eternity.

Even after the threat was defeated, the Guardians formed what became the Aureum, the demon hunters that watch the gateways between the worlds, and protect their lands from an evil that never rests.

———

I closed the book slowly, images of gods and humans wielding swords and lightning bolts filling my head. It was the type of fairytale I would have loved as a child.

Suddenly, my birthmark felt like a burning brand.

I picked up the phone again, texting the number I had memorized. Then I poured two fingers of bourbon and downed it in a gulp, wincing at the burn. I wouldn't have more, but I needed that liquid courage in order to have the conversation that was coming.

My doorbell rang half an hour later. Alex was on my front stoop, just like I'd asked him to be. After I let him inside, the already tiny front hall felt much more cramped. I was glad I'd decided to shower and wash my hair so that it fell in tidy waves around my shoulders.

"Who's your neighbor?" Alex asked by way of greeting. He wore a dark gray turtleneck that highlighted his broad shoulders. I pulled down the sleeves of my black hoodie and took the couch, claiming my space.

"Mrs. Parham—or, Evangeline. Was she on her porch?"

"Yeah. Knitting. Even though it's forty degrees."

I cracked a smile. "She does it all the time. Better to catch the neighborhood gossip. Oh, um...can I get you anything to drink?"

"I'm fine. Thank you."

The awkward silence that settled over us was painful, so I dove in. "I read the book. Well, the important part."

Alex settled back in a chair but maintained his perfect posture. "So you said. And what do you think?"

"It's quite the story."

"A story, yes. But like all stories, it's based in truth."

"Maybe. I want to ask you one thing."

"Just one thing?" he asked, shoving a lock of dark hair out of his face.

"Would you...would you take me with you when you fight the demons?"

Alex's whole body went rigid, and he stared at me, unblinking. "What?"

I took a deep breath. "I need to see you in action for myself. If I'm going to believe any of it, I have to."

"Then don't believe it. I'm not taking you anywhere near a cemetery right now. Do you have any sense of self-preservation?"

"Why do they come through cemeteries?" I thought of the man I'd spoken with before Halloween, how I'd likened him to a vampire. "And why can't I go, if I'm supposed to be a demon-hunting superhero?"

Alex raised his scarred brow. "That's what you got from what I just said? One," he held up a finger, "bringing you into a combat situation would put your life in danger. And you might have power, but you'd be a liability." He ticked off another finger. "And two, it would be breaking every rule in the book."

"According to you, my life is already in danger. What would you have me do instead?"

"Go to New Orleans. Meet with the Diurne Council and ask them for help."

"The what?"

"Diurne Council," Alex enunciated. "Our governing body." He shook his head. "There's so much you need to learn."

Meeting with strangers in positions of authority? No thank you. "So you can pawn me off and make me someone else's problem?"

"That's not what I said. But we have to do something about this. I have a job to do, and I can't spend every second watching you."

"I'm not a fucking child," I spat, clenching my hands into fists.

Alex massaged his temples. "I'm sorry. I didn't mean for it to come out that way. I haven't been sleeping much lately."

"Because of me. The problem."

"For Iznir's sake—we need to figure this out, not argue about it."

"I thought you could help me. But if you want to send me off to some council, then I'll take my chances here. Alone."

"That's not happening either." Alex stood, looming like a storm cloud.

My phone vibrated on the table, and I snatched it up. Walking into the kitchen, away from Alex's stare, I answered.

"How's the lake?" Bri said. "Do you need something?"

Yes. And no. "I'm...okay. Just wanted to let you know I'm home."

"Wow, you made good time."

I could hardly tell her that I'd traveled through some kind of tear in the space-time continuum. "There wasn't any traffic. Can I call you back?"

"Are you busy?"

I glared at Alex. "Job interview stuff. I'll fill you in later."

"Exciting! Can't wait to hear about it," Bri said, then hung up.

Alex and I stood on opposite sides of the room, facing each other. I leaned back against the kitchen counter.

"Friend of yours?" he asked, his tone steely.

I folded my arms. "Yes. She's a normal person, who doesn't know anything about demons or the forces of evil."

"Most don't," Alex replied.

I was ready to stun him with an excellent rejoinder when a succession of hard *thunks*, like knuckles rapping on a door, came from the center of the room.

I paused, not daring to move a muscle. "Did you hear that?" I whispered. Alex nodded, putting a finger to his lips, then walked toward me as silently as a jungle cat.

Thunkthunkthunk. It sounded like it was coming from underneath the floorboards, at the exact midpoint between us.

We both looked down at the same time. Then all hell broke loose.

The floor exploded and a shower of splinters rained down. I flew backward into the counter, my hip taking the brunt of the impact. My head snapped back into a cabinet, stunning me with pain. I righted myself, then lurched again when I saw what had burst from the floor.

The huge creature in the middle of the living room raised its head and scented the air. It was the same scaly beast from the Norton Cemetery, or if it wasn't it could have passed as its twin. Its teeth were sharpened into fine points that extended past its jaw, and its eyes were little more than gaping holes that extruded gray smoke.

Both the beast, and the chasm that had appeared where it exploded out of the floor, were between me and the front door. I had a mad thought that if I could slide around them, maybe I could go through the back and flee into the graveyard.

The creature hissed, the sound sharper than its fangs, then lunged at me. I fell to the ground, more by accident than design, but it missed me all the same. Although now I was underneath the beast, its body acting as a cage. It reared back, and I closed my eyes and covered my head as if that would protect me from being eaten.

The pain and tearing of flesh never came. I peeked around my fingers and saw that Alex had grabbed the creature by its serpent-like tail and dragged it away from me. He flung something from an open hand —the searing smell told me that it was burning—then leapt across the hole in my floor and grabbed my hand all in one swift motion, pulling us the few steps into my bedroom.

Alex slammed the door so hard that it rocked on its hinges. Then he ran his hand down the middle and there was a squelching noise, like a boot being pulled out of wet muck. He shoved me headlong into the en suite bathroom and shut us inside, then repeated the same motion on the door.

"What the *hell* is that?" I gasped, prone on the floor where I'd landed on a wet towel. My heart raced like it was trying to escape my chest and flee out the window. Which wasn't a bad idea, actually.

"That," Alex said, bending to pull something sharp and shiny from around his ankle, "is a demon. That seal will hold it off for a few minutes."

"Oh, *excellent.* Good to know I have an exact time frame for how much longer I'm going to be alive."

A series of loud bangs and hisses sounded, like the thing was battering down the bedroom door. "What are you going to do when it breaks the door down and eats us?" I said in a harsh whisper.

"You're going to stay put, and I'm going to unseal the other door and go deal with it."

Unsealing the door sounded like pretty much the worst idea in history. "You know what? I actually think we should just stay here. Maybe it won't be able to get through the door. Or, maybe it'll get bored and go try to eat some other people."

Alex gave me a look, like he couldn't believe I was being sardonic when a mythical creature was trying to kill us. He had a lot to learn about me.

"I'm going to go take care of this, and I'll be back before you know it." He placed his hand against the door, and it made that sucking noise again, then swung open. With the open bathroom door, we had a front row seat to the demon blasting into my bedroom.

It was coated in dripping mucous that left a trail all along the ground, like some kind of demonic slug. The demon hissed and opened its fanged mouth wide, liquid dripping to pool on the hardwood floor beneath it.

The creature lunged at Alex, but he was ready. He feinted right, and its scaly arm flew past him and went smashing into the wall. He pivoted, then the demon slowed, as if suddenly suspended in glue.

Alex raised his palms like he was pushing against a wall. The demon came unstuck and bunched up its coiled body to hurl itself at Alex. He reacted quickly, spinning and kicking out. Although the move looked like it should have broken Alex's leg off at the hip, the kick sent the demon flying into the opposite wall.

But then it flicked its tail, lightning quick, sweeping Alex's feet out from under him. Horror crawled up my throat anew, because the demon began to move *fast*, dragging its slick body across the room in a rapid crawl using scaly arms that were braided with ropes of bulging muscle.

The last scrap of my sanity fled, and I must have blacked out, because heat flashed over me like I'd come down with a raging fever. Something flickered in my peripheral vision. I inhaled sharply as I looked down and saw blue flames racing over every inch of my exposed skin. Another blink, and I stood before the demon, looking into the void where its eyes should have been. All I could think was that I wanted it far away from here, not to hurt me or Alex or anyone else ever again.

"Go to hell," I said, my voice strange and deep like the blackness at the bottom of a well. The words broke over the creature like a wave, and its scaly form folded in on itself like a vile piece of origami and vanished in a cloud of smoke and sulfur.

Alex was still on the floor, chest heaving and looking bewildered.

"Um?" I said, and sank to the ground, landing in a pile of rubble.

Alex was up instantly and at my side almost before I'd hit the floor. He didn't speak, but his hands shook ever so slightly as he performed a quick assessment, probing my neck and head. It was almost like a shoulder massage, and I leaned into his touch without thinking. He paused, but kept his hand in place that cupped the back of my head.

"Did it hurt you?"

I cleared my throat, testing out my vocal cords. "No." We had to stop ending up in situations like this, but I couldn't say that I minded when he played nurse.

"Sorry about that," he apologized. "I thought we had another thirty seconds with the door."

I let out a strangled noise that started as a laugh and ended somewhere between a sob and a gasp. I surveyed the wreckage that was now my bedroom. Furniture was smashed, books hung loose off of their covers, and shards of glass glittered on the floor.

"My floors," I said, sweeping up shards with my bare hands. Alex stopped me, taking hold of my wrists.

"Seph, stop," he commanded. "You're going to cut yourself." My fingers waggled uselessly. I seemed to be losing the feeling in my hands. How intriguing.

Alex looked around, like someone was going to appear out of thin air and help him deal with my shell shock. "We'll get this taken care of." His voice sounded muffled, like I was underwater.

"Oh, dear."

If anything was going to snap me out of my stupor, it was hearing Mrs. Parham's voice in my living room. Alex's head snapped around, and before I could register it he'd pulled me to standing and stepped in front of me. Mrs. Parham appeared in my room, surveying the disaster scene. "It did make a mess, didn't it?"

"M-Mrs. Parham?" I stammered.

"Hello, dear. I apologize for not coming sooner, but it seemed that your young man had things well in hand."

Alex was as taught as a bowstring, ready to fly. "What are you?" he said softly. Danger rang in every syllable.

Mrs. Parham smiled. "My name is Evangeline. I'm not only Persephone's neighbor, but was a dear friend of her father."

My body sagged, unable to take any more surprises. Alex caught me and pulled me tight against him. Then he set a blazing line of fire right through the middle of my bedroom. The flames licked tall and white hot, separating us from my neighbor, but didn't spread and engulf the room like I feared they would.

"No need for that, now," Evangeline said, her tone disapproving. "I would never harm her. I have been watching out for you for years, dear. I promised your father I would."

"What are you talking about?" I asked.

Evangeline looked at me with real grief in her eyes. "I lost contact with him soon after you were born, but I know he loved you. You are in danger, Persephone. There are many who wish you harm." She looked at Alex then, her gaze skewering him. "You must go, and quickly. There are more coming."

Alex's voice took on a deeper quality that echoed in my ears. "Tell me what you are," he demanded.

She didn't answer him, and turned back to me. "Be careful, dear. Trust your intuition. I hate to leave you, but it's not safe for me, either. Take care, Persephone." She added to Alex, "And protect her—please." Evangeline waved a hand at the flames, and before they flickered and died she winked out of the air into nothingness.

10

Alex was still holding me as he snapped his phone to his ear. "Meet us at Gravesville Historic," he barked. "With everyone. Call in the subs." Then he shoved the phone back into his pocket and half dragged, half carried me through the back door and into the cemetery.

"No," I shook my head. "Don't bring me back there." Dread gathered in my stomach, and for the first time in my life, I didn't want to step foot in a graveyard.

"Seph, you have to. I'm taking you somewhere safe. Davina, Hollis, and the rest of my unit are on their way," he said. "Someone is coming to clean up. No one will be able to tell anything out of the ordinary happened here."

I dug my heels into the soft ground, cold wind biting my face. The idea that no one would notice that there was a gaping hole in my apartment from a demon shooting through it seemed slightly unrealistic. "I'm scared," I admitted. I had reached my limit—there was no way I, on my own, could figure out a solution to the impossible problem I'd found myself in.

"They won't hurt you," Alex promised. "I won't let them." He brushed his thumb across my cheek, and warmth flooded my entire body. "I don't think you would, either. Seph...how did you do that? Where did that power come from?"

My feet stumbled across the ground as I allowed him to pull me along. "I don't know. All of a sudden I was on fire, then this feeling came over me. I'm not sure how to explain it." And I wasn't sure I wanted to discuss what happened. That I even *knew* what had happened. "Evangeline...you saw her disappear, right? Like, she was there...." Telling me that she knew my father. That they were friends, even. "Then she wasn't."

"I saw," Alex said grimly. "She's not one of us, so we'll be looking into her, too. I'm assuming you didn't know she's a supernatural."

"I didn't know anything about her until a few weeks ago," I answered.

"Here we are," he said, halting and propping me against a tall head-stone in the shape of a cross. "My unit will be here soon, then we can leave."

"You know, I'm normally able to walk." I experimentally pushed off of the grave. I stayed upright, saving me from further mortification. "Both of my legs used to work quite well."

"I'm sure," Alex placated, scanning somewhere over my shoulder. "You're very good at it."

An outright lie. "Where are we going? And how are we getting there?" I asked.

"New Orleans." He pointed behind me. "And like that." I turned and almost staggered again, but managed to keep my feet under me.

In the middle of broad daylight, a black hole—or a tear, really—hung in the air, suspended at waist level. And a foot was sticking out of it.

The foot was soon followed by a body, and finally a head emerged. The sandy-brown haired woman dropped to the ground, then stood upright. Her pixie haircut accentuated elfin facial features, her widely spaced blue eyes staring at me.

"Huh. You're taller than I imagined," she said, wiping her hands on denim-clad hips.

"Seph, this is Casey," Alex said. "And Sylvan, Sage, and Fern."

Three more bodies emerged from the hole. The first two had to be twins, as they were identical except for their hair; one had an undercut with the top part worn in a bun, and the other's was cropped close to their head. It was the same color—blond, almost silver, and their eyes were a pale, pale blue, like the surface of a lake at dawn. Another woman with dark skin and teal braids that brushed her elbows stood hipshot, her large eyes alert.

"And you already know us, of course," Hollis twanged. Davina followed close behind him, then closed the hole in the air like she was drawing curtains.

Their expressions were all smooth, with watchful gazes. This was one of the more bizarre experiences I'd had in my life—okay, the *most* bizarre—and they were all acting like it was business as usual. Which, maybe it was. That was a terrifying thought.

The twin with the cropped hair darted in the direction of my apartment, moving faster than I would have thought possible.

"Headquarters?" Davina asked, looking to Alex for confirmation. He nodded, then she performed the motions I'd seen Alex make before, when we'd been fleeing the creature from the Norton Cemetery. This time, because I wasn't in fear of my life, I watched closely.

Davina looked like a mime, both hands probing carefully as though searching for something in the air. After a moment, she stopped, the fingers of her right hand curling like a hook. She brought her other hand next to the hook and touched her fingers together. Then she pressed inward and drew her hands apart, straining with effort, as if making a hole in the sand and trying to prevent the grains from rushing back inside.

"That is so fucking weird," I breathed. "What is it?"

"A gateway. You'll get used to it," Casey chirped. Then she threw me a salute and stepped through, vanishing into the dark. The twin who had run into my apartment returned with my bag from the lake house slung over their shoulder, dropping it at my feet. They bolted through the black hole, the rest of them following. Only Alex and I were left standing amongst the graves in the weak afternoon light.

"Seph," Alex said. "Let's go."

"Mhm," I said, forcing the noise past my lips. The blackness looked suffocating, and my chest grew tight. "Okay. And how exactly do we...." I paused, searching for the right word, then gave up. There was no right word. "How do we?"

"It's as easy as breathing," Alex assured me. He hefted my duffel over his shoulder. "Just take my hand, and I'll do all the work."

I didn't remember my feet moving, but I found myself face to face with Alex, fingers intertwined with his. Our eyes locked, and I had to remind myself yet again to keep breathing. I didn't want to pass out now, not when I was on the verge of probably the most pivotal moment of my life. Alex tugged on my hand, and we stepped through the shimmering darkness, into the unknown.

I had the sense of being somewhere and nowhere all at the same time, of hurtling through an unfamiliar darkness at a million miles per hour while also standing completely still. I focused on Alex, repeating his name over and over in my mind like a prayer.

It could've taken ten seconds, or ten hours, but the pressure of Alex's hand on mine lessened and I dropped out of the dark, my feet hitting the ground with a thud. I staggered into something very solid before Hollis hooked my collar and pulled me upright.

It was warm. Much, much warmer than Gravesville, where I'd been just moments ago. Soft ground gave under my boots. The air smelled floral, and felt close and damp. This cemetery was in a grove of trees, their branches spread long and crooked like a spider's legs. They were draped with a silvery plant that looked like mermaid's hair.

The others ringed me, and without speaking they herded me through the gravestones. They moved with flawless coordination, anticipating each other's movements with Alex at the head of the formation.

"Where are we going?" I whispered to one of the twins who flanked my left side.

"Headquarters is through these trees," the twin with the undercut said, pointing.

More live oaks were ahead, and before long a stately mansion appeared through the forest. It was the color of sandstone, with a portico spanning the width of the central structure. Tall, wide windows were spread along wings that extended from each side. Patches of damp stained beneath the windows, evidence of recent rain. The building was a marvel of symmetry, standing like a monolith amongst the dark backdrop of the trees. Insects buzzed, a low drone in my ears that sounded like a warning.

Everyone stopped in unison, and I ran into Davina's back, getting a whiff of coconut shampoo. She turned around, arching a brow but giving me a tight smile. "Good luck," she whispered, then addressed the rest of Alex's unit. "Let's hit the mess."

I waited until they'd disappeared around the side of the mansion. "Where are they going?" I asked Alex.

"To see friends. We don't get to headquarters very often. And I'm taking you to the Diurne. Well, one of them—the others aren't in residence, currently."

Sweat slicked my lower back and hairline. I ran a hand through my waves, wishing for an elastic band. "When are we going back to Gravesville?"

"That depends on what the Diurne has to say."

Unease lurked in the pit of my stomach. "But I can still leave, right? They can't keep me here."

Alex's brows drew down, highlighting the tiny white scar running through one. "Do you want to be attacked and nearly killed again? Or do you want to be safe and get some answers?"

I gripped my wrist, then let go. My birthmark was no longer the source of comfort it had once been. It had betrayed me, tying me to some kind of supernatural order that I'd never asked to be part of. "But I have a life in Gravesville. And what if—" I paused, licking my lips. What I wanted to say was, *what if they murder me and bury me in a shallow grave?* Or, *what if they keep me locked in a dungeon and I never see the light of day again?* "What if they don't like me?"

He softened. "Don't worry about that. They'll like you." He walked up the wide front steps to the grand door, then stopped with a hand on the knob, looking over his shoulder. "Coming?"

"Shit," I said under my breath. "Yes, I'm coming."

———

The ceiling of the entryway soared above our heads, coming to a peak with a stained glass oculus set in the very center. Ivory plaster trimmed the walls in the shape of fleur-de-lis, and lush carpets patterned in emerald, ruby, and sapphire covered the wide-planked wood floors. To the unschooled observer—namely me—it looked like the home of a rich Victorian grandmother, and nothing like the headquarters of an ancient society of magical demon hunters.

Alex led me across the foyer to the great room, and we passed underneath chandeliers dripping with crystals that spread their glittering light in small pools. Shadows danced, featherlight, in the spaces between them.

"Is anyone else here?" I asked in a hushed tone. I wasn't sure why I was whispering, other than that the silence seemed so vast that I didn't want to be the one to disturb it.

"You'll see," he answered cryptically. We finally halted in front of a stretch of wall on the long side of the room that was settled between a set of twin mirrors. Their iron edges twisted and curled into shapes of vines and roses, so lifelike that it appeared to be a real garden arrested in dark metal.

He traced along the underside of the wall's wainscoting. With a soft *click* a door emerged and swung inward, revealing a dimly lit, sloped tunnel. The rough-hewn walls flickered with ominous shadows that caught the light from candles set into wall sconces.

"A secret passageway?" I asked in a voice thin as the lace curtains on the windows.

Alex turned his eyes heavenward. I would've called it an eye roll on anyone else. "The Aureum loves its traditions."

"Right."

He made a sweeping gesture. "Ladies first."

"Yeah, no thanks," I replied. "You go ahead." If this dank tunnel was any indication of what lay at its end, I wasn't eager to get there.

Voices floated down the serpentine tunnel toward us, but with the echo it was impossible to make out words. Alex started off and I followed close behind, never letting him get more than a step ahead of me. I stumbled on the uneven ground, and after steadying me he took my wrist in a firm utilitarian grip. I tried to ignore how my pulse hammered. We walked like that for a few more moments, connected in the dark by touch and the quiet sounds of our breathing.

Alex paused at the mouth of the tunnel, releasing my wrist. "Follow me," he directed. "And keep your eyes forward."

"What the hell?" I exclaimed. It was like we'd walked a circle, straight back into the entryway we'd just left behind. Even the oculus was overhead, showing a patch of blue sky. But we definitely weren't in the same place, because here, people milled about like industrious worker bees in a hive.

"It's a footprint, or an echo," Alex said, herding me through the crowd. They were all different ages and races, but two things unified them. Their clothes were overwhelmingly in dark shades, and they moved with a sinuous and fluid grace. "This area is the same as above, but there's an extension in the back that goes beyond the mansion."

No one paid much attention to us, although Alex nodded at a few people. Otherwise, we continued down ivory hallways with ornate crown molding on the ceiling and wide, polished wood floorboards underneath. Paintings lined the walls, depicting everything from land-scapes to mythology.

"Wait a second," I said. "This should all be flooded, shouldn't it?" New Orleans itself was below sea level, which was why they did most of their burials aboveground.

"Not if you use magic," Alex replied, not missing a beat as we proceeded deeper into the underground. Doors appeared every so often, and I wondered what lay behind them. He stopped in front of one and knocked three times.

"Enter," a deep voice called.

Nerves zipped along my bloodstream. "You're going to stay, right?" I felt too scared to care how childish I sounded.

Alex met my eyes. His were gentle. "I won't leave you alone."

The office we entered was surprisingly sleek and modern. I'd expected detailed woodwork and heavy velvet drapes, but everything was straight lines and clean angles. Including the glass topped desk behind which sat a man who bore an uncanny resemblance to Alex. They had the same jaw, although the older man's was beginning to soften with age, and the same thick eyebrows. His dark hair was gray at the temples.

I tensed as the man walked around his desk to meet us. He wore a gray suit with no tie, and a heavy signet ring embossed with a lily on the middle finger of his right hand.

Without sparing a glance for Alex, the man spoke. "You're here."

"Seph, this is my father, Councilman Edward Eames. Dad, this is Persephone Hart."

My chest clutched. *Fucking hell.* The council member was his *dad?*

Sweat prickled my upper lip. Alex hadn't thought to tell me that his father was one of the leaders of their magical society? I looked sharply at Alex, anger superseding my anxiety for the moment. His face was stoic, but I glimpsed a hand clenching and unclenching behind his back.

Edward nodded, not offering a hand. "Persephone is a powerful name. Not many would name their child after the goddess of the underworld."

"I prefer Seph." My voice came out somewhat strangled, like it had been squeezed through a tube.

"May I?" Edward asked, holding out an expectant hand. I looked around in confusion for a moment, before he clarified. "Your mark, Miss Hart."

"Oh." I hesitated, then slowly drew my sleeve back. Edward grasped my wrist. His hands were soft and smooth, a pencil pusher's. He bent over, running a finger over my birthmark.

"It is indeed the sign of the lily," Edward murmured, continuing to examine me. I shifted, wanting to rip my arm away. "And what's this?" He pointed to the faint scar on my palm from where I'd fallen in the graveyard.

"I fell. I, uh, do that sometimes."

Edward met my gaze. "There is something about you. Something certainly more than human."

Alex cleared his throat, then Edward's eyes flicked over to him. "Please, sit," Edward said, releasing me and gesturing to a set of clear plastic chairs that looked about as comfortable as a bed of needles.

Edward took his place behind the desk and steepled his fingers with a practiced air. "What else do you know?" he asked, addressing Alex in a business-like tone. I'd tugged my sleeves down over my hands, still feeling the imprint of Edward's touch on my skin.

"Nothing, yet, sir," Alex replied. "Only what I told you on the phone. Seph has been attacked by demons three times in the past two weeks, once right in front of me. She needs protection."

"And you have no knowledge of the Aureum, nor have you exhibited any power before?" Edward asked, his nut-brown eyes assessing me.

"No," I said. "I'm very boring. Or, I was."

"And what are the extent of your abilities?"

"I, um...can turn the lights on and off. Not on purpose."

The corner of Edward's mouth turned down, exposing a dimple. The same dimple that Alex had when he frowned. "Can you demonstrate?"

My heart skipped, and my stomach knotted. "Um...."

"Seph's power seems to be tied to her emotions," Alex answered, coming to my rescue.

"I see. And electrical disturbances are all that have occurred?"

I slid my eyes to Alex, chest tightening. Was he going to tell his father what had just happened at my apartment?

Not missing a beat, Alex responded, "Other than being down a light fixture, that's everything."

Relief coursed through my chest, followed by suspicion. Why had he lied?

"It is rare for a potential Guardian to come from outside the bloodlines," Edward said. "And your age...it is strange, but not out of the realm of possibility. What is impossible is that you should have access to your power without being initiated." At my blank look, he elaborated. "When our initiates gain their powers, they are able to see the supernatural world. But they cannot touch their magic until they undergo our initiation process and become novices."

"I understand," I said, although I wasn't really sure I did.

"You believe that your parents are human?" Edward asked.

"My mom couldn't be more normal," I said, picking at my cuticles. "Her family won't even celebrate Halloween, so I doubt that any of them are part of your, er—this."

"And your father?" Edward prompted.

Had Alex shared that my seemingly harmless neighbor was some kind of supernatural—had said outright that she and my father had been close, and had been keeping track of me for years? I decided to straddle the line between the truth and an outright lie.

"He hasn't been around for a long time. I'm not sure I'd even recognize him if we passed on the street." If he was even still alive.

Edward shifted back in his chair, but gave no indication he thought I was hiding the truth. "Miss Hart, has Captain Eames explained what it takes to become a Guardian?"

"No. Alex has been pretty busy trying to keep me alive," I said, my tone cooler than necessary. Even though Edward had been matter of fact, my hackles were raised, and I wanted to defend Alex. Though lord knew he didn't need defending, especially not by me. Alex's face was blanker than a fresh canvas.

Edward's eyes swept between us again. "He was right to bring you here, where we can watch over you while we seek answers."

"Seek answers?" I echoed, twisting my increasingly frizzy waves back. I would have given my pinky finger for an elastic band.

"Of course. There is a rhyme and reason to everything that happens in the Aureum. We leave no stones unturned, especially if it puts people at risk." Edward thrummed his fingers on his desk, the noise setting my teeth on edge. "Captain Eames and his team will be assigned to you for the next several days, while the other council members arrive and we make a decision."

"No," Alex growled. He made the word sound like a swear. The idea of having to babysit me had finally cracked his mask.

"Is that really necessary?" I asked, at the same time Edward said, "Yes."

"Dad—sir," Alex said, catching himself. "I can't stay here. We have a post to cover." His tone rode the edge of disbelief.

Edward lowered his voice, leaning forward infinitesimally. "Are you questioning a superior?"

Alex's lips turned into a thin line, but he lowered his eyes. "No, sir."

Edward sat back. "Good. You found Miss Hart, so it's natural that you will take responsibility for her while she is on Aureum grounds. Briefing another team would waste time and resources." Then he turned to me. "Miss Hart, while you are here you may avail yourself of the facilities, as long as you have an escort. We will reconvene with the rest of the Diurne Council in one week."

"But I can't stay here for a week," I protested. "What am I supposed to do?"

"Captain Eames's unit is at your disposal. I'm certain that something can be arranged to excuse your absence. Let Lieutenant De Silva know who to contact, and she will take care of it."

"Well," I said, fidgeting slightly. "Actually, I'm between jobs right now, so...it's fine, I guess. If it's only for a week."

"Excellent." Edward stood, buttoning his jacket in a smooth motion. "The captain will show you to our guest apartments. I look forward to speaking again soon."

11

___

I walked out of Edward's office on legs that shook like the high spin cycle of a washing machine. Behind me, the door snapped shut of its own accord. That was going to take some getting used to.

"So," I started, but I was speaking to Alex's broad back.

He was striding down the hallway already, then glanced over his shoulder. "This way." His tone brooked no argument.

I had the overwhelming urge to stomp on Alex's foot as soon as I caught up with him. The man was always dashing off somewhere without explanation. I didn't catch up with him, not until he disappeared behind an archway and opened another locked door, ushering me inside.

We were in an open plan apartment that had a small kitchen, living room, and behind a half wall, a bedroom. It was decorated in warm furnishings, with dark wood and terra cotta walls.

Alex ran a hand roughly through his hair, which on any normal person would have made it stand on end. But it only added to his maddeningly artful disarray, like he'd just stepped off a runway. I scowled.

"I know hanging out with me isn't your first choice, but you don't have to be rude about it," I said.

"*I'm* being rude? I've saved your life, what, three times now? Or is it four?" Alex said, looking very dangerous indeed. His eyes glinted, and the scruff on his face had an extra day's growth, covering his jaw in shadow. His resemblance to a pirate was more overwhelming than ever.

"All you need is a gold earring," I muttered sardonically.

His brows knitted. "What are you talking about?"

"Hm? Oh, nothing," I said, while I silently reprimanded myself for saying the quiet things out loud. "I'm a big girl, you know. I don't need to be watched."

"Yes, you do. It's not only for your protection, but for ours."

I folded my arms. "What threat could I possibly be to you?"

A muscle in Alex's jaw pulsed, and his face was the austere mask again, rigid and impenetrable. I took an unwitting step back, the space between my shoulder blades tight.

"This isn't a joke, Seph."

"Who's joking?" I countered. There was a sizzle and the smell of burning plastic reached my nostrils.

"Fuck," Alex snapped, yanking my arms away from my body and batting my sleeve that now had several holes burned into it. "This is exactly what I'm talking about. We don't know anything about your power. It's volatile, and someone could get hurt. You included. You are not made for burning."

Seething that I'd lost control again, I balled up my ruined hoodie and tossed it on a chair. "If you're so worried about me, then why didn't you tell your father? Also, thanks for the heads up there." I leaned against the narrow kitchen island, resting my weight on my forearms. Every moment of stress I'd experienced over the past couple of days had settled in my lower back.

A line appeared between Alex's brows, and he rubbed his lips together, like he was thinking. "Whatever happened back at your apartment...bad is an understatement."

"I don't know what's so bad about saving *your* life. That thing was going to eat you."

"I had it under control," Alex ground out, folding his arms and shifting into a wider stance.

"That's not what it looked like from my end."

He rubbed the line between his brows, squeezing his eyes shut for a moment. "I don't know how you manage to derail every conversation we have. The point is that if anyone else knows that you were able to take down a demon, on your own, without being initiated, you *won't* be allowed to leave. That kind of power out in the world, uncontrolled—it would be chaos. And...there is no need to form an association in the Diurne's mind between you and a rogue supernatural neighbor." Ah, Mrs. Parham. Her parting words echoed in my mind. *Protect her.*

Alex leaned on the other side of the island and rocked forward on his palms so that we were almost nose to nose. "I am trying to help you, despite what you might think of me. If we keep this quiet, then you and I can exist in peace for the week. No one else can know what you did if you want your freedom."

This wasn't the first secret I'd had to keep. Who would I tell, anyway? Everyone here was a stranger to me, but I saw the danger that laced their appraising stares and polite smiles that didn't quite reach their eyes.

And Alex? I wasn't entirely sure what to think about him yet. He was sort of a pain in the ass, but there was warmth underlying it. It was clear that he was a rule follower, but he was giving me the option to break them. Encouraging it, even. The question of why pecked me like an irritated bird, but it would be stupid to let this unexpected boon slip away.

I could last a week. If that was the price it took to keep me alive and figure out what the hell was going on, I could deal with it. Suck up my fear and bewilderment and skepticism, and get through whatever was coming from the Diurne Council. I would get the answers I needed, without being trapped forever with a bunch of supernaturals who could likely snap my neck like a twig. My heat beat pounded in my ears. Well, maybe I wouldn't be able to deny my fear entirely.

"Seph?" Alex prompted.

"Okay. I won't say anything. Do you need a pinky promise?" I stuck my pinky out, joking, but was surprised that after a second Alex took it. The feeling of his callused skin made warmth spread up my arm and down my—

"Well, that's that." I dropped my hand and stuck it in my back pocket. "Stronger than a blood oath."

The corner of Alex's mouth twitched, and his lashes fluttered in a way that made me wonder if he'd rolled his eyes, too quickly for me to see. "This is where you'll be staying for the week. You must be exhausted and want to rest," he said, emphasizing *rest*.

I ignored the implication. "Actually, I've got my second wind. What else is there to do around here?"

He gave me a long look, but acquiesced. "I'll ask Fern to show you around. Tomorrow, we get to work."

"On what?" I asked, but Alex was already out the door.

———

I'd been lazing on the overstuffed couch when the knock came—definitely not sleeping.

Fern's teal braids were piled on top of her head in a knot, and her large eyes were lined on the top lid in a cat's eye. "Hi, Seph. Long day?" Her voice reminded me of a pond's calm surface.

I nodded, shyness creeping into my throat. "Pretty long."

"But, you must be curious. Come on, I'll help you get your bearings."

We left my room and walked side by side as she showed me around different parts of the headquarters, including communal kitchen and dining areas, classrooms for the novices who were in training, a state of the art gym, and other residences. My head was on a swivel, full to bursting with the knowledge that I was surrounded by real life magic, despite it all looking so overwhelmingly normal.

"Fern, what's this room for?" I asked, as we walked back through a cavernous room near the tunnel entrance.

"It's kind of like an auditorium, or a meeting hall. If there are trainings or big announcements, even celebrations, that's where we meet. This is the Aureum headquarters for the entire southeastern United States, so it's used a lot."

"How many of you are there?" I imagined an army of leather coated demon hunters standing in formation, which was cool—in theory.

"About eight hundred in this region. In the whole US? Probably five thousand, total. The eastern seaboard has the most. More dense population, you know," she said. "And globally, there are about a hundred thousand of us."

"How do you keep all this a secret? A hundred thousand people isn't nothing. Especially when you're doing...the kind of work that you do."

She laughed again. "You mean, fighting monsters? We have our ways."

Fern led me back through the tunnel and up into the mansion. Her words echoed off of its rock walls, each reverberating loudly. "Our unit is assigned to Gravesville and the tri-county area. It's a good post. There's a lot of activity, as you can imagine, given the number of cemeteries."

"How long have you been there?"

"Three years." She held the door open for me as we exited the tunnel, then headed for a set of french doors that led to the grounds. The sun had passed its zenith, and shadows lengthened toward the house. The air was warm, but lacked the humidity of high summer, and smelled like magnolia blossoms. We walked away from the mansion toward the grove of trees that led to the cemetery we'd landed in. Away from prying eyes and ears.

"So, how does this stuff work? I mean, the portal things, and the guarding graveyards, and all of that. Why is it graveyards, anyway? Is there something about dead people that—"

Fern's soft smile stopped my babbling. "There will be time for all that. I don't want to overwhelm you. Now...can I ask you something?"

My shoulders inched toward my ears. I didn't want to be poked and prodded, and I was held to a promise not to speak about what had happened with the demon in my apartment.

She took my silence for agreement. "How did Alex end up finding you? We only got minor details, which is...unusual. Normally, he shares everything with us." She said it without a trace of anger or annoyance, more curious than anything.

This seemed safe enough to answer. "I'm not sure. Alex said he could...feel me? That I was sending off some kind of signal. Weren't you able to tell, too?"

Fern played with one of her braids, twirling it around her finger. "No, actually. None of the rest of the unit were. But now that you're here, I can sense there's something not completely human about you."

"Well, I do have this," I said, extending my wrist. "Everyone seems to think it makes me one of you." She scrutinized my birthmark, then pulled up her pant leg and pointed to a spot above her ankle. There it was, the same lily mark that I wore.

"We all have them, whether we're graveborn or chosen," she said.

"What's graveborn?"

"Oh—" Fern looked sheepish suddenly. "It's our name for Guardians who have magical heritage. Just slang, you know? But, even if you're not graveborn, you should have shown up on our radar when you were born. The mark is how the Aureum is able to track all potentials. It's like a homing device, or something. Anyway, once potentials from outside the bloodlines come into their power, we make contact with them. They're told the truth about what they are, and are offered the chance to join us."

"And if they don't?"

She tilted her head. "They usually do. But the ones who don't.... It's a hard life for them. They aren't quite human, but go on trying to fit into the human world. When potentials come of age, they begin to see the supernatural world. Think about it as a veil being lifted—humans can't see beyond it, but we can."

I nodded. Edward had said as much.

"The chosen ones who don't join us can't use their power, because they never go through the initiation. A lot of them end up anxious or depressed, suicidal even. I mean, what do you think would happen if you tried to talk to someone about seeing things no one else can see? They'd write you off as mentally ill, or throw you in a hospital. It's better to just accept it, even if you're not sure it's the life you want. Because the alternative isn't any better." Something in her placid expression twisted, but it was fleeting.

Words caught in my throat. Is that what would happen to me if I didn't become a Guardian? "That's bleak," I managed.

"Everyone thinks that arcana—magic," she clarified, "solves all of your problems. But really, it creates its own set of problems—sometimes far worse than being a regular person."

"Sounds like it." What would ten-year-old Seph think if she heard that magic wasn't all it was cracked up to be? The thing I wanted most when I was a kid was for my life to be different. To have a proper family, to not worry about keeping the lights on, to fit in one place, instead of the in-between space I'd always occupied. What if magic could've changed all of that? "I'm still trying to wrap my head around all of it. How do the Guardians who aren't born into this manage?"

Fern smiled, but it was tinged with sadness. "They get used to it. It's a culture shock, but we're all on the same team. You get a built-in community, a chance to be part of something bigger than yourself. Plus, magic is pretty damn cool."

She stopped by a bush with clustered pink flowers shaped like church bells. Some of the spent flowers littered the grass beneath it, forming a graveyard of blooms. She plucked a fallen blossom from the ground, then cupped it in her hand and blew gently. Brown turned to soft lavender, then purple, and the petals took shape again, becoming lush and fragrant. She handed it to me.

I studied the flower, looking for signs of decay, but there were none. It appeared the same as its live kin that hung on the bush. "That is amazing."

"You wouldn't be able to tell the difference between this and the others, now would you?" she asked. I had a feeling she wasn't talking about flowers anymore.

"No, not at all." I looked back at Fern. "Why are you being so nice to me?"

"Because Alex said you need help. And if he trusts you, then so do we."

"Just like that?" It was hard to imagine a world in which trust was given so freely.

She nodded. "Just like that."

"Well...thank you, anyway. I know this isn't your idea of a good time."

Fern snorted. "Are you kidding me? This is like a vacation. We have a week to relax and not think about patrols, recon, or demons. It's a gift, Seph. Really."

A gift for Fern, something bordering on disaster for me. My entire life had been turned upside down, flipped from dull mediocrity to crazed chaos. *But isn't it what you wanted all along?* an inner voice whispered.

I was saved from having to respond when my phone vibrated in my pocket.

"Sorry." I held up the phone, my stomach sinking. "Can I have a second?"

"Sure. But Seph? Don't tell anyone where you are, or who you're with."

With that warning ringing in my ears, I answered the phone. "Hi, Bri."

"Hey! I just left work. Want to grab a drink and we can celebrate your interview? Or, I can come over—"

I cut her off. "I'm, uh, actually out of town."

"What do you mean? You just got back," she said, some of the wind taken out of her sails.

"I'm—I decided to, um...." I racked my brain. "Visit my mom?"

"Oh." I wasn't imagining the hurt in Bri's voice. "Then what happened with the interview?"

"I didn't get the job. I think it's best if I, uh, spend some time at home for a while. My mom and Scott are going to help me with the rent for a bit, so, you know...I owe them." It was a struggle to say those last words.

"Oh," she said again. "Well...okay. They live in Virginia, right? It's not that far a drive. Maybe I can come visit."

Panic raced up my spine. "No, don't! I mean, they don't like visitors. Scott is kind of an asshole."

"Seph," Bri said. I heard the beep of a car locking in the background. "What's going on with you?"

"Nothing. Everything is fine." *Please don't push. Please don't push.*

"Look, if you need help, you can tell me," Bri said.

Lying to the Aureum was nothing to me. But lying to Bri? I felt hollow, like something had been scooped out of me and thrown in the trash.

"I don't need help," I said, as the desire for normalcy pushed against my chest. The desire to let my friend in on everything, to have her listen to all of the insanity that had happened to me. "I'm fine, Bri."

"You don't sound fine." Bri's steadfastness—which I'd always admired—made my throat tighten.

"I have to go," I said. "I'm...driving."

"Okay, then." Bri's voice was tight. "I'll see you later, I guess."

"You will. I'll talk to you soon. Promise."

I hung up the phone, a slick slide of guilt coating my insides.

Fern wandered back over. "Everything all right?" By the look she gave me, I imagined there was an unspoken question tacked on to that. *Did you keep your mouth shut?*

"Yes," I answered, pasting something that passed for a smile on my lips. "All good."

12

─────────

Davina appeared at my apartment bright and early the next morning. I was barely awake, chugging coffee when I opened the door to find her dressed in black, from her long-sleeved shirt down to her combat boots. At least my wardrobe would fit in here. She looked me up and down, then offered a feline smile. "Rough night?"

"Why are you here?" She brought out the bluntness in me.

"To bring you to the Library," Davina said, pushing her way inside. "Mind if I have some?" She nodded toward the overpriced coffee maker while taking a mug from the cabinet.

"Help yourself," I muttered. "What library?"

"*The* Library," she corrected, programming her coffee. "She's omniscient, and contains all of our knowledge—every book and grimoire and supernatural text your little heart could desire."

She? Davina had my attention. "I'll get dressed," I said, heading toward the bedroom.

"Take your time. Unsurprisingly, this stuff is much better than what we get in the barracks."

Moments later I reappeared, my face slightly pink from scrubbing. I wore my habitual black jeans and sweater with my hair pulled back into a knot.

Davina frowned slightly. "You're going to get hot in that."

"A demon destroyed my home. I didn't exactly have time to pack for the weather." Indeed, I had all of the ratty comfort clothes I'd brought to the lakehouse. I wondered briefly what had happened to my poor apartment—how long it had taken Alex's magical reinforcements to set things to rights.

"We'll get you some things," she decreed. "This way."

I followed Davina through hallways hung with paintings in gilt frames, twisting and turning until I had no idea which direction we'd come from. She halted at the threshold of an arched, wooden double door, its center embossed with a carving of a lily.

She pushed the lily, and the doors swung open. I let out an audible gasp, as I stood at the threshold of the most beautiful library I'd ever seen.

Dark wood shelves soared so high they appeared to go on forever, certainly far taller than should have been allowed given the confines of the underground space. The spines of thousands of books glinted in warm light thrown by wall sconces and lamps, which were set on small groupings of tables surrounded by worn leather furniture. Study carrels lined the wall to our left, made of the same wood as the shelves. Slightly tattered rugs spread across the floor, their corners overlapping irregularly.

I looked over at Davina, who grinned at me. "Pretty spectacular, huh?"

"Incredible."

We went up a set of spiral stairs to one of the upper levels. Alex was seated at a table, with a stack of books at his elbow. He rose and came to the railing to meet us. The gap between the long sleeve of his gray shirt and his wrist exposed an edge of dark, curling ink.

"Morning," Alex greeted us, the corner of his mouth twitching in what passed for a smile on him.

"Delivered safely, as promised," Davina said.

I didn't miss the way her long-lidded eyes swept over Alex. I couldn't blame her. He looked utterly delectable, his hair damp and curling slightly, the muscles on his lean body filling out his clothes.

"Should I stay?" she asked.

"No," Alex replied. "Check in with the subs. I'll find you when we're done."

Davina nodded once, then departed silently as a shadow.

"How was your evening?" Alex asked, his tone formal and distant.

"Fine," I answered. After Fern completed my tour, I'd returned to my room, eaten the ramen I'd found stocked in my little kitchen, then fell straight into bed. My sleep had been dreamless and restful, for once. "And...how was yours?"

"Busy. I'm not here often."

"Why not?"

"Because I'm in the field. This isn't only the seat of our government, it's where novices in the southeast region complete their training. I have some friends from my class who are instructors here now."

"When did you finish your training?" I asked, leaning against the railing, curiosity burning a hole in me.

"Six years ago," Alex answered. "Novices are initiated between twenty and twenty-one, then graduate three years later. After that, it's field work, bureaucracy, research, support staff—whatever branch they ultimately join—but no matter where Guardians end up, they go through the same basic training."

"What's the training?" I imagined magic wands and crystals, although I hadn't seen Alex use those. He was able to shoot fire with a spoken word, or the flick of a finger.

He crossed his arms, leaning a hip against the railing. "Everyone does theory, combat, and arcana their first two years. Third year is specialization and practicals."

"That's a lot of school." I had three years on the oldest of novices, which suddenly made me feel ancient and useless.

"Not as much as a four-year college," Alex countered. "And it's free. But you don't have to worry about that yet. What we have here today," he said, walking to the table and patting the stack of books, "is research."

At least it wasn't combat. Reading, I could handle. "What are we researching?"

"You. Or, your father, actually. I asked the Library for records of Aureum graduates dating back to the eighties. Do you know how old he is?"

I paused, and Alex looked at me expectantly. "Is this necessary?" I'd spent most of my life not thinking about my father, other than to curse him when my mom had a particularly bad week. There were days when I had to care for her like she was a sick child, bringing her boxed mac and cheese in bed while she stared listlessly at the wall.

"Aren't you curious about yourself?" Alex asked, sliding a weighty tome toward me.

Yes. But some stones weren't meant to be turned over. "Is there any other way?"

Alex's chest heaved in a silent sigh, and he leaned closer to me. "Do I have to remind you what's at stake?"

I recalled our conversation from yesterday with perfect clarity. *You won't be allowed to leave. That kind of power out in the world, uncontrolled—it would be chaos.*

The thought that I was some agent of chaos was laughable, until I remembered what had come out of me—the flames and the fury that had echoed in the deepest, darkest parts of myself.

"Fine." I opened the book. "His name is Zeke Hart."

We searched for over an hour, flipping through well preserved pages of Guardian graduates listed in alphabetical order. I'd gained a few paper cuts by the time I closed the last book. There were no Zeke Harts to be found in any of them, and I wasn't sure if I was relieved or disappointed. "Why can't you use magic to do this?" I griped.

"We don't use power for every little thing," Alex returned, snapping his book shut. "It's not a toy or a gadget."

"Okay, then." Maybe I'd touched a nerve, or maybe he was sick of me already, although we'd barely said a word to each other.

"I'll ask her for anything that might have your father's name," Alex said, as though I hadn't spoken. He stood, turning his gaze toward the ceiling. "Library—"

"Why do you keep saying she?" I interrupted, jumping up as well.

"Because this Library lives and breathes, just as we do. Except the books are her air, and knowledge-seekers are her sustenance. She contains at least one copy of every book that's been published since the beginning of written language."

Holy shit. For a moment I thought I could smell magic in the scent of the books, see it in the penumbra of darkness that hovered on the edges of flickering candles.

"Library," Alex said in a gentle voice. "I need birth records, please. From—" He looked at me.

"Gravesville," I answered. "Although I don't know if he was born there. But we'll have to go online to request those, then—"

He held up a hand. "Just wait."

We stood in heavy silence for a moment, then soft whirring sounded from somewhere beneath our feet—as if there was a large gear clicking within the bowels of the Library.

I waited for a book to come dropping from the invisible ceiling, when Alex turned back to the table that had our spent books spread across it. A thick file folder sat where there had been empty space a moment ago.

"Thank you, Library," Alex murmured, and I could've sworn the Library sighed with pleasure, the soft exhale tickling my ears.

"This is insane. But, no offense," I added hastily, in case she heard me. I stretched my arms overhead, yawning. "Can we take a break before we start again? My eyes are burning."

Alex's gaze was trained on my feet. "Fine. Are you hungry? We can go to the mess."

At the mention of food, my stomach rumbled. "Yes, but...is there anywhere more private? I don't want to—" To be seen and looked at and recognized as the outsider I was.

Instead of disagreeing, or calling me out on my cowardice, Alex nodded. "I know a place."

———

The place was enchanting, and most importantly, private. After disappearing briefly and returning with two brown bags, Alex led me to an immense weeping willow that was far from the mansion. Davina was right about the weather—a light layer of sweat coated me by the time we arrived, but the trek was worth it. The tree was next to a murky pond with jeweled dragonflies skimming across its surface.

We sat underneath the curtain of willow branches in companionable silence, shielded from the outside world. The light inside the canopy was greenish and shadowy. "How did you find this place?" I asked.

Alex swallowed a bite of his sandwich. "I grew up here, at headquarters. I used to come to the willow a lot."

"So you've really been in this world for your entire life. You're graveborn," I said, trying out the new terminology Fern had taught me. "What was that like?" When it came to Alex, I had an insatiable curiosity.

He shrugged. "I don't know how to compare it to a normal childhood. I still had to wait to come into my powers, just like those outside the bloodlines. But I learned the life and the rules from a much earlier age."

"This place, though. Even without being able to use magic, it's incredible."

"It has its perks. But the world becomes very small when you're confined to twelve acres," Alex said, his face smooth as he balled up the sandwich wrapper and shoved it into the bag.

"You couldn't leave?"

"We would go to other headquarters around the world, and spend time with other Guardians. What I mean is that...I haven't been around regular people very much." He seemed almost shy admitting it, looking up into the willow's canopy.

What would it have been like to travel the world? To have all of those resources at your disposal? Although, it seemed like we'd both grown up with different kinds of limitations. I wondered if that's why Alex was helping me now. Because he knew what it was like to be kept in a cage, albeit a gilded one.

I leaned back on the grass, pillowing my head on my arm. "I still don't understand what exactly it is you do, how it works. How much of what I read in that book you gave me is true?"

"Most of it," Alex said, drawing up his long legs and resting his elbows atop his knees. "At least, we think so. The first Guardians were gifted power from the ancient gods, pre-Mesopotamian civilization. It's been passed on through bloodlines, from parent to child—graveborn, as you've already learned apparently." He gave me an unreadable glance. "But other people with no blood relation can crop up. It's rare, but every now and then, we get someone completely outside of the bloodlines who's chosen by the gods. We intermarry with humans, of course, otherwise we'd die out. But they're bound not to give away our secrets."

Gods and magic. It was all beyond my wildest dreams. I had a hard time believing any deity would have chosen me for anything, let alone to fight demons.

"How about the other worlds?"

"There are an infinite number—we used to have people who cataloged them. But our focus is stopping what comes in from other worlds, not traveling to them."

"Have you been to one? Another world?" The words sounded strange to my own ears.

"No. No one but the highest of the high ranking, like my dad, would do interworld travel. We're bound to protect this one, and we have a hard enough time doing that without worrying about everywhere else."

"But in the story, it said that people from all over the worlds were chosen by Iznir to fight."

He shrugged. "That was millenia ago. Things change."

"If you were to go to another world...you would use a graveyard. Like how we got here."

"Yes. Cemeteries are spaces of transition," he said, answering my unspoken question. "The crossroads of life and death. Ritual burying, whether it's a body, or ashes, or just the memory of someone—it creates a powerful energy. And when you have loads of energy all swirling around together, like in a graveyard, it creates windows of possibilities—places where all of the worlds bump up against each other, like a giant net filled with balloons."

"Woah." Who could have guessed that every time I went to a graveyard I was surrounded by the multiverse?

We were quiet again, the flow of my questions stoppered as I processed everything Alex had told me.

He shifted toward me, his shirt pulling across the broad plane of his chest. "What happened to you before Halloween? The night I felt your power for the first time."

Could he still feel it? I pushed into a sitting position, skimming a hand along the silvery underside of the willow leaves. "I was at Gravesville Historic Cemetery. It had been a shit day, and...anyway, it was a normal night. Until...." My thoughts returned to the stranger, the dropped tarot card. "This weird guy showed up."

"What weird guy?" The tranquil atmosphere between us changed as Alex subtly straightened.

I chewed on my lower lip. "He was just taking a walk, like I was. We talked for a bit. Then I went home." Because that's really all that had happened, wasn't it? There was no nefarious undertone like I'd originally imagined.

"Would this have anything to do with that cut?" Alex said quietly.

The scar bisecting my palm was faint now, just a thin white line. Hard to believe it had bled so much.

"It was my fault. It was dark, and I tripped over a headstone." Embarrassing to admit, but it wasn't like Alex hadn't seen me fall before.

"Blood in the graveyard," Alex murmured. "Blood is a powerful magic. And when it's spilled in a place of transition...all sorts of things could happen."

"Do you really think that's it?"

"Tough to know for certain. But it's a theory."

"Wow. I guess being a klutz finally paid off," I said, more to myself than Alex, but he let out a short breath that might have been a laugh. My heart gave a slow roll upon seeing his close-lipped smile, brief though it was.

"Did anything else happen after the graveyard? Anything out of the ordinary? Apart from the attacks," he added.

It was more difficult to say what hadn't been out of the ordinary. "I've had some dreams. Nightmares. I walked out on my job. It seems like ever since that first night in the cemetery...."

"Seems like what?" Alex prompted.

"Like it's all connected." I played with a lock of hair that had escaped my bun. "Like a domino got knocked over, and everything else in my life fell down with it. And now I'm here."

"Like it's fate?" The probing glance he gave me turned softer. Warmer.

I shrugged, embarrassed. "Maybe. Oh, I just remembered. There was a ledger stone in the crypt that had my name on it."

Alex stilled. "What do you mean?"

"It was an epitaph. You know, here lies Persephone Hart, blah blah.

With my birthday and the date of the attack. There was another inscription, too."

"Do you remember what it said?"

I closed my eyes, willing the words back into my memory. "Let's see.... It would probably be easier for me to write it down."

Alex hesitated a beat, a flush staining his collar, then removed a scrap of paper and pen from his pocket and handed them to me. It was the receipt I'd written my phone number on.

I gave him a questioning look, but his features were written in stone. I scrawled the inscription on the receipt, as best I could remember, then passed it back to him.

He scanned it, his dimple flashing as he frowned. "If I cannot deflect the superior powers, then I will move the River Acheron," he recited. "More commonly translated to, if I cannot move heaven, I will raise hell."

I couldn't grow up with my name and not have a basic understanding of Greco-Roman mythology. The River Acheron, also known as the River of Lost Souls, was one of the rivers of the Underworld. The one upon which Charon ferried souls of the newly dead.

"That doesn't sound great," I said weakly.

"No. I'm not sure that it is." Alex's eyes were unfocused, like he was lost in thought. "Those attacks could have been random, but this...this was targeted."

Well, shit. "You think these demons are coming after me on purpose?"

"I can't say for sure, but it would be a hell of a coincidence." He moved into a cross-legged position, resting his hands on the tops of his thighs. "I'm going to teach you something."

"You are?" Excitement had my fingers tingling. "Even though I'm not initiated?"

"That ship has already sailed. It's too late to take anything back now. And...I would rather that you have some defenses, than none at all. No matter what happens at the end of the week."

I would also rather not become potential demon bait for a fourth time. "Okay."

Alex stood, offering a hand. He pulled me up, much harder than I'd expected. I flew smack into his chest. It was rock solid. He righted me, taking a step back.

"Sorry," I said, heat creeping up the back of my neck.

"That's all right. Guardians are much faster and stronger than humans. You'll get used to it."

I doubted it. "What am I learning?"

"What every novice learns in their first lesson. How to get in touch with the source of their power."

"It would be too much to hope that's easy, right?"

Another tight-lipped smirk. "We'll see how it goes. At the least it'll give you a feel for what your magic is like. Everyone has their own signature, or flavor, you could say."

Flavor. An image flashed lightning quick across my mind, of my lips tasting the smooth skin where Alex's pulse beat.

My cheeks flushed. I had no business thinking about that, none whatsoever.

Alex instructed me to take a ready stance, then hold my arms at my sides, palms facing out. Concentrating was difficult when my senses decided to go haywire. I could only think about his cedar smell, the feeling of being closed off from the rest of the world with just him.

"I want you to close your eyes. Go inward. Imagine you're walking a path. It can be anywhere you like. At the end of a path is a door," Alex said.

"Okay." I closed my eyes, breathing deeply. I could do this. My first lesson.

I was in a wildflower meadow. Sunshine kissed my skin with warmth, and the creamy scent of gardenia wafted through the air. Birds chirped and clouds scudded across the blue sky, pushed by a soft breeze. A worn dirt path in front of me cut through the meadow. I walked the path, meandering like a lazy river.

"Do you see the door?" Alex's voice seemed like it was coming not from a few feet away, but inside my head.

"Yes," I answered. There was a door just ahead on the path, like it was attached to a set of invisible hinges. It was black and shiny, like obsidian.

The birdsong in the meadow stopped, and the sky darkened. I stopped in front of the door, looking up as it loomed over me.

"Open it," Alex directed.

The handle, the same material as the rest of the door, was warm to the touch and smooth as glass. I let my hand rest there, as something reverberated in the middle of my chest. Something buzzing like the bees in the meadow, something that heard a call and wanted to answer it.

I opened the door.

A violent deluge of cold black water broke through, engulfing me before I even had the chance to scream.

13

———

I hadn't seen Alex in three days, not since he'd gathered me up, sweat-soaked and shaking, and brought me back to the mansion. After I finally told him what happened when I opened that obsidian door in my mind, his full lips had compressed into a thin line and his eyes hooded. He told me—no, ordered me—to stay in my room, until Fern showed up. I'd felt like a child, coddled and swaddled and soothed.

After that, Alex's unit passed me back and forth like a relay baton, never leaving me alone for a second until I was safely locked behind the door of my little apartment. I chafed at the constant company, spending more time in my room than not.

When the opportunity to rid myself of Hollis practically dropped in my lap, I took it. I didn't have anything against him. The Texan was actually growing on me, despite his corny jokes and cocky demeanor.

Hollis had coaxed me into the training room, where he was demonstrating how to bench press. The warehouse-sized space had sparring dummies, boxing rings, and a shooting range, along with yoga mats and intimidating exercise machines lining the walls. He hadn't believed I'd never worked out in my life, until I picked up a weight and almost dropped it on his foot.

I chewed my nails, staring into space while Hollis's voice droned in my ears. The feeling of that black water rushing over me, gushing up my nose and filling my lungs, kept flickering through my mind. I knew that the door, the meadow, all of it, was in my head—but it had felt so real, like I was actually drowning. And furthermore, I couldn't stop thinking about what might be beyond that unforgiving wall of water. About whatever was inside of me that was so dark.

"Are you paying attention?" Hollis drawled. "It's your turn next, and don't think I won't let this bar smack you in the head."

Sweat dampened the fabric of his shirt, his ample biceps flexing. With those sea-green eyes and easy laugh, I could understand why he garnered attention from the redhead in the corner. She was turning herself into a pretzel on a yoga mat, throwing obvious glances at Hollis.

"Friend of yours?" I asked, jerking my chin in her direction. Hollis sat up and lifted the hem of his shirt to wipe his face. I didn't think it was an accident that he flashed the redhead his washboard abs.

"Not yet, but I imagine we'll be acquainted soon." A slow grin lit his face, and the woman tossed her long hair before stepping into a fluid handstand.

"Why don't you go say hi? I don't think I'm the weightlifting type, anyway. More of an observer."

Hollis fake pouted. "What, you want to ditch me?"

"No, but I think you'll want to ditch me after you see that." I pointed. Hollis glanced over his shoulder, lips parting as the redhead opened her legs into a split while upside down.

"Go on," I encouraged. "I'm going back to my room."

"I really should walk you back," Hollis said, eyes locked on the redhead as she bent her spine in half. "Alex'll have my head if he finds out."

"Hollis, come on. What do you think is going to happen to me? I'm going straight back, I promise. It'll be our little secret."

"Well...all right, then. Meet you for dinner?" Hollis said.

"Sure thing. Go get 'em, tiger." I slipped out before he changed his mind.

Once I was out of eyeshot, I relaxed, rolling my neck and loosening my shoulders. The ability to wander without a companion hovering over me was glorious, and I drifted through the hallways of the mansion, taking care not to go around corners if I heard voices or footsteps. No one appeared, but there was one painting, wide and in a thick, gilded frame, that caught my eye.

It was my namesake. A toga draped artfully around the goddess of spring, a flower crown on her head. She stood across from Hades, who wore a red cloak and crown. His black horses gnashed their teeth and pulled a chariot that was meant to spirit her away to the underworld. Three nymphs in the background looked on in horror, while Persephone herself appeared wholly unconcerned.

I'd seen an image of the painting before, and had always thought that the goddess should be raging, or screaming, or crying—doing something to fight off her captor. But now, I wondered if she was resigned to her fate.

Or that perhaps she had sensed a seed of darkness laying dormant in her all along, and willingly walked into Hades's arms so it could bloom.

Voices echoed from around the corner. Startled, I turned, searching for a hiding place. I'd been so wrapped up in the painting that I hadn't noticed how close they were, and if I was caught—the last thing I wanted was to get Hollis in trouble.

Running down the hall on tiptoe, I pulled open a door at random and slipped inside. The room was pitch dark. I put my ear to the door, listening for the steps to fade while I tried to quiet my thundering heart. To my horror, the sounds were getting closer.

I dashed across the room, feeling around for—there. The protrusion of a doorknob bumped my hand, and I pulled. I wedged myself into the tight space and crouched in the corner, light flooding beneath the door as I eased it shut. My breath rattled in my ears, and I prayed that whoever had entered the room couldn't hear me.

The door squeaked closed, then I heard a woman's voice say, "So? Out with it."

"She could be a Watcher, Mindara." I recognized that voice. Ice gathered in my stomach, while heat flooded my face.

"Edward, you are an alarmist," Mindara said. "We hardly know anything about her. There is no reason to worry. Not yet, at least." The voice was firm, but there was a note of affection in it.

"There is every reason to worry. Creatures have sought her out three times now," Edward said. "With the last one, the pattern was the same. I reviewed the records last night."

A long sigh greeted his theory. "Yes, and a meteor could hit Earth at any moment and kill us all. We have precautions for this, Edward. The Aureum has not survived for millenia by accident. The Watchers are no closer to us than they were a thousand years ago. Surely you have confidence in the program?"

"Nothing is a guarantee," Edward said, his voice tight.

"There could be a thousand explanations for the attacks. You know how attractive demons find young power. They can't resist getting a taste. Miss Hart must be potent indeed, which, I shouldn't have to remind you, is what the Aureum needs. Our numbers have dwindled for too long."

"You would threaten the security of everything we've built for *that*?" Edward growled.

There was an icy silence. "You forget your place," Mindara said quietly. Goosebumps prickled my skin.

"I apologize," Edward muttered. "It was not my intent to question, only to protect what we already have."

"I cannot fault your passion or loyalty. But we will let the Diurne decide. Her examination is in two days. Then we'll see what nature of creature she really is."

My stomach dropped. Edward hadn't mentioned anything about my meeting with the Diurne including an exam.

"Yes," Edward said, although he sounded reluctant. "Yes, I suppose so. But, Mindara, if she is a Watcher?"

"Then we will take care of her. This conversation is over, Edward." I heard fabric rustling and the shuffle of feet, then the click of a door closing.

I counted to two hundred before cracking open the door of my hiding place. The light was still on, illuminating an empty sitting room with a plush chaise longue and floor-to-ceiling bookshelves.

Without stopping to think, I darted into the hall, head down, until I reached the safety of my room. My body felt electrified, like I'd just touched a hot wire. The conversation had only been a few minutes, but it seemed like I'd been in the closet for hours. What was a Watcher? What exam—

A knock sounded on my door and I flinched. Had anyone seen me scurrying back to my room like a dog with its tail between its legs?

Slowly, I walked to the peephole from where I'd been pacing in the kitchen. It was one of the twins, the one with the short hair—Sage. They wore standard Guardian black, with thick platform boots. Silver rings climbed both ears, and their hair appeared freshly shorn. I opened the door.

"Hi," I said, slightly out of breath. Be normal, I urged myself. Not like you were just eavesdropping in a closet.

"Hi," Sage echoed, in a voice like a bell's clear chime. They held up a stack of books. "I brought some things for you. I thought you might be bored."

"Oh...thank you," I said belatedly, looking at the books.

"Alex told me you like to read," Sage added, still standing on the threshold.

"He did? Sorry, come in."

Sage followed me inside, leaving the stack of books on the kitchen island. The titles included some of my favorites. How had Alex known?

"How are you getting along?" Sage asked, looking far more at home in the guest apartment than I felt.

Trying not to have a panic attack. "Great."

It felt like Sage's glacial eyes could see right through me. "Are you sure about that? You don't feel like it."

"Feel like what?" I crossed to the couch where I'd dropped my hoodie and shrugged it on.

"You're nervous about something. I'm a reader," Sage elaborated. "Not like these." They gestured at the pile of books. "But here." They pointed to the center of their chest. "I sense emotion in others."

I wanted to curse whatever had put Sage in my path. Exposure of my innermost thoughts and feelings was my worst nightmare. "Sounds handy," I said.

They smiled. "It can be."

Silence spread across the room. "How would you feel," I asked, "if all of a sudden you woke up one day and were changed? And the world that you knew didn't exist anymore?"

"I would feel shocked. Devastated, even. At least that's what it was like for me," Sage said.

"What do you mean?"

"I'm like you, Seph. Well, both Sylvan and I are. We're the only ones in our unit who come from outside of Aureum."

"Oh. I...I didn't realize."

"That's okay." Sage gave another gentle smile. "We were happy, before we were chosen. We were both in our second year of college—I was studying biology, and Sylvan was an art major. I had a girlfriend who I loved, and a great group of friends. And then...." Sage paused, a faraway look in their eyes. "Strange things began happening to us. I thought I was having a psychotic break, because I started to see things that I knew other people couldn't."

"What kinds of things?"

"Things that scared me. A bat the size of a Great Dane, flying around the laundry room of my dorm. Tentacles snaking out of the drain in the bathroom sink. A ghoul lurking in the corner of a lecture hall."

"Jesus," I said. "That sounds terrifying."

"Well, it wasn't all bad. I saw good creatures, too, like fairies. They wouldn't have hurt anyone."

"Fairies? Wait, no—nevermind. What happened after you started seeing all that stuff?"

"It was a few weeks until Noriko came to us. She's on the Diurne. She told us about the Aureum, and how we'd been chosen by the gods to protect the world. I thought it was a load of garbage, but...."

"But it was an explanation," I finished. "The only explanation."

"Yes, it was," Sage nodded. "Still took a while to accept, but once I saw the magic, I couldn't unsee it."

"Did you ever get attacked by any of those creatures? Did they try to...hurt you?"

"Not at all. They were more scared of me than I was of them, I think."

I hadn't seen any ghouls or fairies. My encounters had been with demons, and they *had* tried to kill me.

"What about Sylvan?"

Sage laughed, a wind chime dancing in the breeze. "He thought we were having the same nightmares, that it had to be a twin thing. But he was excited when Noriko showed up. Sylvan adjusted to the change much more easily than me. You'd think that already being different would help me acclimate more, but if anything, my identity made it more difficult to accept. I've had to try hard all my life to get other people to accept who I am, and I was tired of fighting that battle. I didn't want another one." We were silent for a moment. "You'll be okay, Seph. Alex won't have it any other way."

I scoffed. "He made it clear he would rather be anywhere but headquarters, chaperoning me."

"It's good for him to slow down. As captain of the unit, he's constantly on the run, cleaning up all of the messes and taking care of us. I imagine it's like herding a particularly feral group of cats."

The image made me crack a smile. But I wasn't part of Alex's unit, and he wasn't obligated to clean up my messes. I didn't belong to him. "He seems so controlled, like he knows exactly what he's doing all the time."

Sage smoothed a hand over their silvery hair. "In the technical sense, we aren't fully human. But we aren't robots, either. I assure you that the heart which beats in his chest is one hundred percent fallible." Sage leaned closer. "I'll let you in on a little secret. Eameses are not allowed to fail. It's all bullshit, of course. Alex's mom finally got the message and left Edward when Alex was a novice. His sister, Sophie, went with her."

"That's awful." I wasn't surprised about Edward—I barely knew the man, but he had an edge that made it seem like he was difficult to satisfy.

"Would you do it again?" I asked suddenly. "If you had known what you do now when the Aureum came to you. Would you join them?"

Sage gave me an inscrutable look. "My answer shouldn't impact yours."

Dropping onto the couch, I pulled a blanket over my lap. I wanted to burrow into its soft folds, to hide under all of that fabric for eternity.

I didn't want Sage to feel my cowardice. I didn't want any of the Guardians to. But fear leaked out of me like a sieve, and I didn't have to look at them to know that they felt the cold burn of it. It was always there, buried like the seed of darkness I'd imagined Persephone harboring, clogging my throat and stifling my breath. It kept me away from the world, and the world away from me.

"Seph," Sage said. "It's normal to feel scared. I was terrified when I found out. But I can't tell you what to do. You have to make the choice on your own. Although, I think you could fit here, too. If you want it."

Did I want it? This strange world where magic was real, and power hummed in the veins of the gods-touched. I'd felt power like a flaming brand when I faced the demon that had threatened Alex, but it had gone dark since. The black wall of water rose in my mind again.

"I don't know," I whispered. "I don't know what to do."

"Trust your gut," Sage encouraged. "You'll know what choice to make when the time is right."

The only problem was that I'd spent my entire life ignoring my gut. "Did you have to do an examination when the Aureum found you?"

"An examination? No. Just my initiation ritual," Sage replied.

So it was just for me. The thought of being scrutinized and laid bare before the Diurne was terrifying. What if they found out I'd self-immolated and toasted a demon? What if they locked me up forever? I didn't know who in the Aureum I could trust—clearly not Edward, and my faith in Alex had yet to be proven.

Somehow, surrounded by all of these people, I felt more isolated than I ever had.

Sage's overture of friendship was kind, but I reminded myself that they weren't my friend. None of the Guardians were. "Thanks for the books." I stood, wrapping my arms around my waist.

"You're welcome," Sage said, a flicker of regret in their eyes. They walked to the door, turning back while their hand rested on the knob. "Remember to listen to your gut, Seph. It won't lead you astray."

I nodded, as the door clicked shut behind Sage and I was alone again.

14

———————

Time was up. I got out of bed, neck knotted with tension. My thoughts ran wild, worrying about the upcoming examination and the thousands of ways it could go wrong.

I watched the magically-induced sunrise from the window in my underground apartment. The clouds were pink and gold, while a corona of light filtered through the live oaks. Mist snaked across the roots of the trees like seeking fingers. I wanted to run through them, to ride the mist all the way up into the clouds.

Instead, I showered and dressed, avoiding looking at myself in the mirror. I needed fresh air, to get aboveground for the first time in days. Not that I was considering running.

With dripping hair and coffee in hand, I opened the door. Straight into a solid wall of muscle that smelled like fresh cedar aftershave.

Stumbling back, I dropped the mug. It shattered with a loud crack, hot liquid spilling all over the floor. "Shit!" I hissed.

I dove to pick up the shattered pieces, but Alex had already bent down, sweeping the pieces into his hands. The habitual lock of hair that curled over his forehead was damp. Our eyes met over the puddle of coffee, and he extended the mug to me. It was fully repaired, not even a crack to show it had been in pieces seconds ago. The spilled coffee had vanished.

"Thanks," I said, still crouched. He stood, towering over me for a moment before extending a hand to pull me up. Hesitating only for a second, I took it.

I didn't realize how much I missed him being around until that moment—that maybe part of the reason I'd been so on edge was because he'd practically disappeared. And I wasn't sure how to feel about that.

"Sorry. I didn't mean to scare you," he said. There were bluish circles beneath his eyes. I probably had a matching set. It seemed that neither of us had slept well.

I went to the coffee pot, taking a moment to collect my fragmented thoughts while pouring a fresh cup. "Oh, it's fine. Starting the morning with a near heart attack always gets the blood pumping." Leaning against the counter, I faced him again. He was wearing his ghost smile.

"Where were you headed?" he asked.

"Outside," I answered, gripping the mug tighter. "Did you...did you know I was going?"

A muscle in his jaw jumped and he ran a hand over his scruff. "I can feel you, remember?"

"Right." I hesitated, gnawing my lip. "Can I ask you something intrusive?"

He arched his scarred brow. "You can ask, and I'll consider answering if I can have some of that." He pointed to the coffee maker.

"Fair enough," I mumbled, pouring him a cup and handing it over. "So...when you feel me. What's that like?" I'd been curious about it ever since he'd first mentioned it. Wondering if it was at all like the strangely intense attraction I felt to him.

Alex drank deeply, his face half-hidden by the mug. He placed it on the counter, his face blank. "That is intrusive."

"Oh. Sorry," I said, inwardly cringing.

He shut his eyes briefly, and they were friendlier when he opened them. "Let me start over. I brought breakfast. I...thought we could walk to the willow."

That brought me up short. "What kind of breakfast?"

Alex retreated to the hallway, then returned, carrying a brown paper bag. "Banana chocolate chip muffins. Freshly baked."

I shrugged, trying to pull off nonchalance, then the scent of warm gluten hit my nostrils and saliva pooled in my mouth. "Okay."

The fresh morning air was chilly, making me wish I'd brought a jacket. Still walking, Alex shrugged out of his and held it out to me. It was made of dark, buttery leather. I shook my head. "I'm fine."

"Just take it," Alex snapped. Then he pressed his lips into a thin line, like he was harnessing another retort.

"Okay, then." I put it on and the smell of the woods enveloped me. Images of tall cedars and juniper berries clouded my mind, and I had to stop myself from sniffing like a deranged bloodhound.

We were silent after that, but I was hyper-aware of Alex's presence. I watched him out of the corner of my eye, the sinuous and powerful way he walked, the confidence he wore like a second skin.

We reached the pond, where the whiplike branches of the weeping willow draped artfully in the still air.

"So, where exactly have you been?" I asked, picking at my muffin.

He exhaled, long and slow, and the bag crinkled under his fingers. "In meetings, and other incredibly boring things."

I toed the marshy ground. "Look, I get it. I wouldn't want to be responsible for some half-baked supernatural, either."

"That's not it. Being responsible for other people is what I do. I brought you here to apologize."

"Oh." It was hardly an elegant reply, but he'd surprised me again.

"This...*you* are unfamiliar territory for me. I've been trying to find my footing, but I keep misstepping. So, I'm sorry." Alex said, his eyes holding mine. "I regret anything I did that made you feel like you're a problem. You're not."

He seemed sincere, the sharp planes of his handsome face softening. I remembered Sage's words from the other day—*I assure you that the heart which beats in his chest is one hundred percent fallible.*

"Why have you been avoiding me, then?" I didn't add deep down what I wanted to accuse him of—that I'd asked him to stay, and he'd left me. I'd been in good hands with his unit, but they weren't the man who had held me up when my legs couldn't support me. Who had saved my life, when I didn't know I needed saving.

Attraction wasn't trust, but this thing between us...well, I didn't know what it was.

Alex scrubbed a hand through his damp hair. "I pushed you too hard the other day. I thought I should give you time. And...that you might not want to see me."

"No," I said quickly. "I mean, you didn't push me too hard. I wanted to do it. You couldn't have known."

The corner of his mouth twitched. "You know, you haven't just broken the rules by manifesting your power. You've obliterated them."

"Is that a compliment?" I asked, finally taking a bite of my muffin.

Alex breathed a laugh, then looked startled that the sound had come from him. "I'm not sure." He sobered, and I wondered what emotion creased his brow. "You can joke, but the danger isn't over. I'll rest easier when you get through the Diurne's questioning without revealing the strength of your power." He paused. "You know, I've kept looking for your father this week."

My heart stuttered, but I asked anyway. "What did you find?"

Alex slowly shook his head. "I checked birth, death, marriage, and graduation records for the entire state of North Carolina. There were no Zeke Harts born before 1980, and even that would be assuming that your dad was a teenager when he had you."

"How can there be nothing?"

Alex looked like he wasn't sure if he should apologize or not. "I can keep searching. He's out there, somewhere. He has to be. We'll find him."

I looked out over the pond. Water bugs skated across, a hundred ripples forming on its surface. I didn't need or want my deadbeat dad taking up space in my brain when I had a more pressing issue to address. He was a problem to be dealt with later, if at all. "Tell me about the Diurne."

Alex accepted my change of subject without question. "It's made up of seven council members. They're elected every five years, but there are no term limits," he replied, like he was reciting from a textbook. For all I knew, he was. "All of the council members were high ranking in the Aureum before they were elected, and represent each of the seven regions. They create our laws and make decisions through majority vote."

"Democratic of them," I said through a mouthful of muffin.

"They were inspired by the Concilium Plebis. Some Guardians back then were part of it."

I choked a bit. "Really?"

Alex nodded. "The Aureum loves tradition, but we've always held progressive ideals. Our history is so interwoven with people from varied places and cultures that diversity is our norm. Our power and our mission bind us together."

"I guess fighting against the forces of evil would do that," I admitted.

"It does. The Diurne will do their best to convince you to stay. We need more Guardians," Alex told me, his expression earnest. "There aren't enough of us anymore to keep up with the demons crossing over."

That's what Mindara said, but I couldn't tell Alex about my sojourn into eavesdropping. "What happens if I leave? If I don't join?" All week, the question had been circling in my head like a bird of prey.

Alex's eyes tightened slightly, and the nostrils of his fine-boned nose flared. "I can't know the future. But if I had to guess, nothing would change. Demons would probably continue to hunt you. And I don't know if you could survive it."

The assessment wasn't condescending or contemptuous. Alex was right. I didn't know what the hell I was doing, and couldn't reliably defend myself. If I was given the choice, I could walk away from the Aureum, from him—or I could stay, and learn to use the power I'd been given. I could step into a new life, and maybe even find out the truth about who I really was. Although I had a feeling, deep in my bones, that it would cost me somehow. No truth was free.

"What do you think I should do?" I looked at Alex, at the lithe power practically coming off of him in waves. It made something beneath my skin hum and flutter. He rubbed a hand over the shadow of a beard on his jaw, staring out over the pond. Then he met my gaze, the corona of gold in his deep green eyes almost glowing.

"Stay."

My breath hitched, and lightning shot down my spine. I only realized Alex was inches away when I had to raise my chin to look at him. I could have sworn electricity crackled in the space between us.

"Alex." Davina's smoky voice came from behind us. Where the hell had she come from? I shifted away from him, putting more space between us and tucking away the butterflies winging around my belly.

Alex straightened, shuttering his eyes as his stoic mask dropped into place. "Yes?"

Davina wore skintight workout attire that accentuated her curves. Her hair was pulled back into a sleek ponytail. "It's time for Seph to meet with the Diurne. How are you feeling?" she asked me. I was surprised to see concern and a measure of kindness in her dark eyes.

I swallowed, my throat dry. "As ready as I'll ever be."

"You have nothing to worry about," she said. "You coming, Eames?"

"Right behind you," Alex answered. I shrugged off his jacket and handed it over. He hesitated, then took it, slipping it back on. I didn't look at him again as we started toward headquarters, but felt him at my back, steady and noiseless as a shadow.

After entering the mansion, we went down the tunnel and through the underground complex. Davina stopped in front of a door that had lilies carved into the lintel.

"Good luck," she whispered to me, just as she had on the first day we'd arrived at Aureum headquarters.

I nodded, not trusting my voice.

"Give us a second," Alex told Davina, his eyes still on me. She left on silent feet, then we were alone.

Alex and I were so close that I could see the pulse that beat in the hollow of his throat, the muscular line of his neck and jaw. "Lock your door," he said, urgency lacing his tone.

"What?"

"Keep it locked, Seph. Nice and tight. They won't be able to see what's inside of you." He took my hand, squeezing, like he could impress the knowledge into my skin. Warmth raced up my arm where he touched, and his eyes flashed. Then he, too, was gone, and I was left staring at the long, empty hallway.

"Enter," a voice called through the door.

Steeling myself, I turned the handle and crossed the threshold. The room was grandly appointed, with a coffered ceiling inlaid with gold. A rug in brown and dusty rose tones spanned the entire length of the room, and crystals dripped from a three-tiered chandelier on the ceiling.

Edward and six strangers, middle aged and older, were seated behind a long table trimmed in gold leaf, facing me like a panel of judges.

In the center was a small woman dressed in a red presidential pantsuit. She sat as though she balanced a crown on top of her cap of black hair, her expression as regal as the immaculate pearls that hung around her neck. Edward was to her right, along with another man who wore a grave expression, and a black-haired woman who looked at me with curiosity. To her left were three more people, a tall man with dark skin and a shaved head, a blond woman, and another woman whose gray hair unfortunately resembled a helmet.

There was something vaguely familiar about the woman in power red, with her even features and bronzed skin. She smiled at me, and it was how I imagined the big bad wolf looked when he was dressed in the grandmother's clothing. "Welcome, Miss Hart. Please, do be seated," she said.

I recognized her voice right away, and for a moment was back in a dark closet with my heart beating out of my chest. This was the woman who had been talking to Edward about the Watchers. I walked slowly to the fainting couch that was positioned in front of the long table and perched on the edge.

The woman in red spoke again. "Miss Hart, my name is Mindara De Silva. As you may have gathered by now, we make up the Diurne Council, the Aureum's ruling body in the United States. To my right is Councilman Eames, who you already know, Mathew Carter-Moore, and Noriko Kimura. To my left is Lamont Roderick, Estelle Mallory, and Ana Lucia Rodriguez Perez." Each of them inclined their heads in turn, murmuring greetings. The feeling that I was in front of a firing squad increased with each introduction.

I nodded, still not trusting myself to speak. Sweat gathered around my hairline, and my head buzzed like it was filled with angry bees.

"How have you been finding headquarters?" Mindara asked.

My first attempt at speaking was little more than a wheeze. I cleared my throat. "It's very nice."

"I'm glad to hear it." Her voice was warm, but her eyes were impassive. "I apologize for the formality, but we hope to make this as quick and painless as possible. We have a few questions for you, if that's all right."

And if it wasn't all right? As soon as I had the thought, Mindara gave her wolf-smile again.

"Yes," I said in a low voice. "That's fine."

"Excellent. Let's begin with the events of October the twenty-eighth."

Mindara questioned me about my work, family, habits, friends, and even my medical history. Some of the other council members chimed in to clarify or ask their own questions. I answered them, my skin sticky with sweat, while trying not to give too much away. Apparently, talking to people as little as possible for most of my life had been great training for an inquisition.

After an hour, the questions let up. None of the council members acted as if any of my answers were cause for concern. The blond woman on Mindara's left stood. She wore all white, a starched shirt and wide-legged pants that appeared effortlessly chic.

Edward cleared his throat. "If you don't mind, Miss Hart, we have one more request for you." My heart beat thickly, like my blood had turned into cement. "There is an examination that the Diurne performs on initiates we believe to have special abilities. It is...invasive, but not painful. We are simply checking on the viability of the source of your arcana. If you agree, then I believe the Diurne is prepared to offer you a place among us. To become a full-fledged Guardian."

Edward must have thought that the carrot he dangled would have me jumping to agree. I looked at all seven of the council members, their expressions blank—bored, even. I wondered if it was a Guardian trait, or part of their training.

I could say yes—could agree, and put myself at risk for failing the examination, for the Diurne discovering my abnormality. But I would have a chance at a different future, one where I had power beyond my greatest imaginings.

Or, I could say no. I could walk away from all of it, return to my normal life and do my best to dodge demon attacks and stay alive. I teetered between the two, feeling as though I might be torn in half.

"Miss Hart?" Edward prompted. The blond woman flexed her fingers.

Now or never, said my heartbeat. *Now or never. Now or never. Now or—*

"Yes," I blurted, my fingernails digging into my palms, creating little half moons. "Yes, I'll do it." There was no time to recover, to think about what I'd just said, before the blond woman approached me.

"Wonderful," Edward intoned. "Councilwoman Mallory will perform the examination."

"Please stand," the blond councilwoman directed. Her voice was mild as a summer breeze, her dark brown eyes unassuming.

What had Alex told me in the hallway? I pressed my hands together, like he'd squeezed mine. *Lock your door.* If Alex, with his intimate knowledge of the Aureum and the Diurne, thought it would be bad if they got through…well, I'd just have to keep them out.

I stood, facing Councilwoman Mallory so that we were in the center of the room. She grasped my hands. Her skin felt cool and papery. "Close your eyes, Miss Hart. I'll do the rest."

My eyes fluttered shut, and I found my door again, down the winding meadow path to where it stood like a foreboding statue.

Part of me didn't want to go anywhere near it, wanted to run back down the meadow path and put as much space between it and me as possible. I pushed aside the disquiet and stood with my back to the door, defending it. The Diurne couldn't find that dark wall of water.

I waited for something to happen, but the sky stayed clear and the flowers in the meadow danced happily in a light wind. Was Alex wrong? Maybe the councilwoman was doing something else entirely, and it had nothing to do with my door.

Fog descended on the meadow so gradually that I didn't notice until the air began to turn gray. Then a cold mist prodded me, wrapping around my ankles and tugging hard. I backed up, flattening myself against the door. "Go away," I commanded, voice trembling, although I wasn't sure who I spoke to.

The mist floated around my body, pressing, seeking the gap between me and the door. I focused all of my might on keeping it closed. I envisioned thick chains wrapped around it, with padlocks and harsh spikes. The cold brush of metal against my back had me inhaling sharply, and chains clinked as I shifted. But the fog continued to work on the door, to rust the chains and probe for weaknesses.

The hinges trembled. Sweat poured down my face as I gritted my teeth. The pull was too strong. My door squeaked open a finger's width, the sound like nails on a chalkboard. Water sprayed through the crack and I shoved up against it, blocking the gap with my body to keep everything from spilling open.

I wasn't enough. The councilwoman would breach the door, and they would know. They would see everything, and I might be consumed by whatever waited behind it. Terror curled through me like the mist, and the sound of my pulse thudded in my ears. I had to protect myself, to stay hidden, small, invisible.

But if I was invisible, the fog would cut right through me. What if I could become as solid as the bedrock under the soil? To be strong and tall like a spreading oak, to anchor my roots into the ground so that no one and nothing could touch me.

Scorching heat raced along my face, and for a moment I feared that I was aflame again. But the heat hadn't come from me. It was the sun, blasting through the meadow, its rays cutting through the mist like a hot knife through butter.

I blinked and the fog was gone, along with the sensation of pressure along my skin. My door was shut tight again, no sign of water escaping. I loosed a small sigh as I blinked my eyes open.

Estelle scrutinized me, her mouth drawn at the corners. She released my hands. How much had she been able to sense through the crack?

"Is it...done?" I asked. Adrenaline raced through me, and I wanted to shake, to collapse, while I waited for her verdict.

"Yes," Estelle answered. She turned away from me and faced the Diurne. "Miss Hart's arcana is not nearly as strong as would be expected for an initiate. I am surprised that she has been able to do anything at all. A fluke, perhaps."

Thank you, sweet baby Jesus, and Buddha, Krishna, Ishtar, Allah—

"Well then, Miss Hart. I have only one question left for you." Mindara paused, perhaps enjoying the drama. Now that the examination was over, I wanted to wipe the wolf-smile off her face. "Will you stay with us, and become a Guardian of the Aureum? Will you take your oath, and pledge to use your arcana to protect the powerless and vulnerable? To honor your power, and the responsibility that comes with it?"

This was the real choice. Could I leave my old life behind, and step into the unknown?

Pain stung my palm as I remembered that first night in the grave-yard, when I'd fallen and my blood seeped into the waiting earth. That was really the moment it all began. The spark that lit the fuse, and resulted in me standing on a cliff, at the edge of something extraordinary. At the strange hour, in the space between day and night, I'd felt the itch under my ribs, the feeling poking at me like a pebble stuck in a shoe.

For once, I peeled back the layers that covered the feeling and looked it dead in the face. And what I saw there left me breathless.

Yes, its teeth were sharp and bared, like a predator's; yes, the way its hands reached out, grasping, like they wanted the world and everything in it, spelled danger; and yes, the wild eyes that were endless pools of longing terrified me.

But desire had a name, and it was mine.

I met every one of the Diurne's waiting gazes as I gave my answer.

PART II

"I could tell you my adventures—beginning from this morning," said Alice a little timidly; "but it's no use going back to yesterday, because I was a different person then."

— LEWIS CARROLL, *ALICE IN WONDERLAND*

15

———————

"Hold still, will you?" Fern held a pin between her teeth, then jabbed it through the fabric of my dress. I fought the urge to shift my weight again.

I stood in front of a three-sided mirror that had magically appeared in my apartment this morning. Fern crouched at my feet, hemming the gown that I was to wear for my initiation. "Why can't I just wear pants?" I asked for the third time.

"Because it's tradition." She ran a finger across the hem, and the fabric tucked into a clean line, like it had been sewn with needle and thread. "Plus this dress is amazing, and you look hot in it."

Fern wasn't wrong. The dress was black as a raven's wings, a beautiful confection of silk and lace. I traced the lines of the fabric that hugged my body, highlighting curves I hadn't known I possessed. The gown's neckline buttoned around my throat, but the material that covered my décolletage to my neck was sheer, creating the illusion that the delicate swirls of applique lace were painted on. The sleeves of the dress were long, ending in a V-shape at my knuckles.

"There, that should do it," Fern said triumphantly, standing fluidly. When I'd made the decision to join the Aureum only a day ago, Alex and his unit had dropped their facade of normalcy. Their full, extraordinary selves shone through, and I had to wonder how I'd ever believed they were only human. "You can take it off now. I'll have it ready for you by tomorrow afternoon."

The Aureum was pulling out all the stops in their rush to initiate me. Casey told me that this year's crop of first year novices had their initiation ceremony three months ago. I, of course, was a different case altogether. I'd pleaded with the Diurne to allow me to skip the public spectacle, but they wouldn't take no for an answer.

"Every novice since the establishment of the Aureum has undergone a public initiation ceremony and celebration," Edward informed me, somewhat sternly. "You will receive the same honor, despite your circumstances." Apparently, the Diurne's evaluation had been enough to dissuade his suspicions about me. But I still felt uneasy around him, and didn't push the subject.

There was also the matter of the initiation ritual itself to get through. "I still don't know what I'm choosing for my sacrifice," I fretted to Fern when I was back in my jeans and t-shirt. The skin around my thumb bore the marks of my stress.

Fern put the gown inside a garment bag, then draped it over her arm. "You have a whole day to decide. The gods will honor whatever you choose. This sacrifice...it's meant to be difficult—it's the first challenge you'll face as a novice."

That's what I'd been dreading. I couldn't think of anything I owned that was valuable enough to sacrifice. A book, maybe? But most of my belongings were still in Gravesville.

"What if I'm not cut out for this? I mean, I'm already old compared to the other first year novices. I'll be practically geriatric by the time I've finished my training."

Fern laughed, sweeping her teal braids behind her shoulder. "Oh, please. When your arcana and potentia—your enhanced physical abilities," she explained at my confused look. "Anyway, when they manifest after your initiation, you'll all be on the same playing field. Age is just a number."

"Isn't that what old guys use as an excuse for dating people twenty years younger than them?"

She blew air out of her lips. "Has anyone ever told you you're impossible?" There was a smile somewhere under the exasperation.

"Often," I replied. Her comment turned my thoughts to Bri. Bri, who I needed to call and break the news to that I wasn't going back to Gravesville. I would have to make up some story, lie to her. Again. I didn't even know when I'd be able to see her next. There was only one more night for me to have the conversation I'd been avoiding.

"Go relax," Fern said, smoothing a hand over my arm. A sense of ease floated its way into my chest. "I'll see you in a bit."

I nodded, holding on to the false sense of comfort she'd given me, and made my way back to my room. The Diurne's offer to join the Aureum, my acceptance, and now the initiation, were all happening so fast that my head was spinning. I had to think about how to tie up the threads of my old life so that I could begin my new one. It wasn't like I'd never see Bri or my mom again—but when I did, I would be changed.

There were still so many questions swirling around me: about the Watchers, my father, my power. Part of me knew there was no better place to answer them than with a magical library at my disposal. Just as soon as I tackled what I dreaded most—calling Bri.

I changed into my most comfortable sweats when I got back to my room, then did the dishes that were piled in the sink. After that, I cleaned the bathroom, bedroom, and reorganized the dresser. When I ran out of distractions, I pulled out my phone and stared at the lock screen. It was a photo of me and Bri at the beach, posed cheek to cheek. One weekend we'd driven all the way to the Outer Banks for a night only, swimming and soaking up the sun until we were more salt than anything.

Taking a deep breath, I called.

"Seph!" Bri's voice came through clear on the other end of the line. "How are you? How's your mom's?"

I was glad she couldn't see my wince. "I'm good. Actually, better than I've been in a while."

"Oh, really? The restorative powers of Scott's awkward stares must be strong."

A laugh escaped, then I bit it back. "Never underestimate the powers of a mediocre white man."

"Exactly. But really, how is it up there? I miss you a ton. Watching *Buffy* alone isn't nearly as satisfying without your commentary."

Stabbing pain erupted in my chest. "It's fine. I've been busy."

"More job applications?" Bri asked.

"Applying for grad programs," I answered. This was the easiest lie I'd come up with that would give me an excuse to disappear for three years. "You finally beat me down. I'm taking your advice, exploring my potential." I hated using words that she'd meant with sincerity against her.

"That's...that's great!" she said. I knew Bri too well to hear anything but false cheer. "Which program?"

"I'm applying to a few. Business," I said. "There are some programs that have rolling admissions, so I should be able to leave soon."

"Oh. Well—I'm happy for you. But, business? Do you think you're maybe rushing into it?"

My stomach clenched. "It's the right time. I'm unemployed, and my mom and Scott are co-signing a loan for me. I don't have many options right now."

"Seph," Bri said, slow and deliberate. Then she paused, as if weighing her words. "It sounds like you're running away from something."

I forced myself to laugh, and it sounded robotic. "What do you mean?"

"You came back from the lake house early, and you've been avoiding me ever since. Tell me what's going on," she demanded.

"Nothing is going on," I said, injecting lightness into my voice. "I—"

"I thought we were too good of friends for you to lie to me," Bri said, her voice turning frosty. "What the hell is happening to you? Are you in trouble? Look, I can help if you need it. There are safe places I can take you."

It was my turn to feel confused. "What safe places? What are *you* talking about?"

Bri was silent for a moment. "Seph, just trust me. If there are people —things—that are threatening you, I can help."

Confusion stunned me. "What would be threatening me? Bri— what do you know?"

"You tell me your secrets, and I'll tell you mine," she countered, in a tone I'd never heard her use before. "If you trust me enough to let me help you, I will."

"What secrets?" Questions that I hadn't cared to think about because Bri and I didn't pry into each other's histories came bubbling to the surface. "Where does your money come from, Bri? Why did you have a random, uber-fucking-rich lake house available for me to use at the drop of a hat? Where do your parents live?" I demanded. "If we're both keeping secrets, then you need to respect mine."

"I have *tried* to let you in. I left the damn door wide open, but you won't step through. I've tried to be there for you, to have a real friendship with you. But you're too terrified of being abandoned to actually care about anyone," Bri snapped.

Twin arrows of hurt and guilt stuck in my chest. "Bri, no," I croaked. "You are my friend."

"I wanted to be. But you won't let me." She sounded sad now, and tired. "You know what, Seph? This conversation is pointless. And if you actually decide to give a shit, you have my number."

The line went dead.

I was frozen, hunched over like there was a gaping wound in my middle. When I tasted hot, salty tears, I realized that I was crying. Then I curled up on my side where I'd been sitting on the couch, and closed my eyes.

Sleep didn't feel that different from waking. I laid there, either with my eyes closed or staring as the shadows on the wall ebbed and flowed, until I heard a knock. After the knock sounded for the third time, I rose mechanically from the couch and opened the door. Fern, Sage, Casey, and Davina were on the other side, holding the black dress and a few other canvas bags.

Casey blanched when she saw me. "Holy shit, Hart. What happened to you?"

Without answer, I left the door open and returned to the couch, curling my legs up beneath me.

"Did someone die?" Casey asked, taking a seat across from me. Fern followed her, and Sage knelt beside me. Davina hovered in the kitchen.

"Seph, it's time to get ready for your initiation," Fern said softly.

Fuck. The initiation. "What time is it?" My throat was dry and my voice cracked. Davina brought me a glass of water, and I gulped it down even though it hurt.

"You have to be ready to go in two hours," Davina said. "Is this something we can fix by then?"

I shook my head, unable to say the words aloud. I didn't know if it could be fixed, ever.

"Then you need to button it up, sweetheart," Davina commanded. "You've got over a hundred people expecting you to be presentable."

"Davina," Sage scolded. Their hand was on my shoulder, and I knew they sensed everything I felt. "Be gentle. She's clearly gone through some kind of shock."

"No, she's right." I stood, rubbing my stinging eyes. I couldn't take Sage's sympathy. Davina's directness felt better. Taking a deep breath, I shoved every feeling I wasn't willing to name inside of a box, then locked it and threw away the key.

I'd made the choice to give up my old life. I needed to stand by the consequences of my actions, whatever happened. "Can you make me look not like shit within the next couple hours?"

Fern eyed me for a moment, then nodded. "Of course. Let's get to work."

———

I wasn't sure how four hardened warriors had become my fairy godparents, but apparently Guardians had all sorts of talents. By the time they escorted me outside, each wearing a gown with the exception of Sage, who had on an incredible silver suit, I was different. I didn't at all resemble the hollow-eyed woman who'd looked like death warmed over that they'd started with.

Fern had braided my hair into an elegant bundle, with curling tendrils escaping to brush the nape of my neck. Davina had applied an expert hand with my makeup, turning me into a striking creature with dewy skin, smoky eyes, and beestung lips. Even Casey had given a snort of appreciation when I'd appeared in my gown. I walked on Sage's arm, trying not to totter in my heels as we walked from the mansion onto the pitch-dark grounds.

The irony was not lost on me that it was the best I'd ever looked, and the worst I'd ever felt.

During my insufficient hour of initiation prep from two days ago, I learned that the ceremony would be held in a separate, larger graveyard on the property than where we'd come through from Gravesville.

Small spheres of light had been enchanted to hang in the air like stars, illuminating the cobbled path we followed through the live oaks. The thick scent of honeysuckle filled the air, slightly cloying but not unpleasant. The air was moist but cool, and I was grateful for my long sleeves. I couldn't help but think of a funeral procession as the five of us walked down the path.

My entourage stopped in front of a set of tall iron gates that savagely speared the air. The motif in the metalwork was a garden, with lilies heavily featured. Through the gates was a crowd of people standing amongst the gravestones, split in two by a path leading to a large white mausoleum built in the same neo-classical style of the mansion's facade. More spheres of light dotted the air, providing a soft glow to the whole scene.

My hands shook as I thumbed the tiger's eye pendant I'd insisted upon wearing. I never took it off anymore, though I knew my attachment to it was silly. Sweat dampened my brow. "I don't think I can do this," I whispered. We stood in a circle, my back to the gates. I still didn't know what I was going to do for my sacrifice—I'd been catatonic during the time I was supposed to have made a decision.

"You can," Sage assured me. They brushed a hand down my arm, and I noticed some of my dread evaporate, like they'd siphoned it away. Then they opened the gate on silent hinges, and took their place among the audience.

"I don't know what the fuck to do." Panic rose, threatening to choke me. "Help me."

"I wish I could, Seph. But it has to come from you. You'll figure it out," Fern said with confidence.

"You can always give your blood," Casey suggested. She reached under her dress and pulled out a knife, offering it to me hilt first. I stared at her, nonplussed.

"Casey, get lost," Davina shot. "Go ahead, Fern. I've got this."

Fern glared at Casey. I heard Casey's muffled, "*What did I say?*" as they walked away.

Davina brushed an invisible piece of lint from my sleeve, then looked me in the eye. "Whatever happened to put you in this state, use it. Turn your pain into your offering. And no matter what, don't let them see you sweat," she instructed. Then she unfolded the cloak she'd been holding, and draped it around me, pulling up the hood so that it hid my face. "Now knock 'em dead." With that, she gave me a little push, and I stumbled through the gates.

Shuffling toward the mausoleum, I kept my gaze trained on the flagstone path. The low murmurs fell silent, and even though I refused to look at the crowd I sensed that all eyes were on me.

When had breathing become so difficult? It hadn't been a problem until a few weeks ago. After what felt like both a year and five seconds, I reached the steps of the mausoleum. I stood at the bottom, while another cloaked figure, who I knew from the rehearsal was Lamont Roderick—a Diurne councilman—stood at the top. He held a large book open in his hands.

When the air was completely still again, he spoke. "Initiate, kneel."

Obeying him, I carefully knelt, but trod on the hem of my dress and fell the last few inches, landing on the heels of my hands. *Fucking hell.*

"You, Persephone Hart, have come to sacrifice, to pay your debt to the gods, and to honor the dead who have walked this path before you," Lamont said, his voice ringing with gravitas. "You have come to hallow this ground, and journey from unsworn to oathbound. Do you accept this of your own free will?"

Last chance to back away. But I wouldn't. Becoming a Guardian meant protection, and strength. It meant purpose.

I nodded, still looking at the ground. When silence reigned, I peered at Lamont and saw his expectant look. "I mean, yes," I said in a hoarse whisper. My heart thumped against my ribs wildly, looking for a way out. Every limb felt like it was on fire.

"We call to the goddess Iznir, and her followers. Observe the sacrifice of your daughter, Persephone."

This was the point where I was supposed to walk up the sweeping stairs to the wide dais of the pale stone mausoleum where Lamont stood. I rose on trembling legs, taking every step slowly. Black spots flooded my vision, and I blinked rapidly to dispel them.

Lamont stepped away from the mausoleum's doors, into the shadows. "It is time to present the sacrifice."

Sweat beaded my brow, as I felt the pressure of everyone's eyes on my back. But my mind was blank, and no thunderbolt of inspiration struck me. I clutched at the tiger's eye pendant reflexively.

I couldn't do it. I would have to run from the ceremony, shame like a noose around my neck, and head back to Gravesville. To return to my normal life, except without Bri. I would be jobless, friendless, and still so damn alone.

Davina's words echoed in my mind. *Turn your pain into your offering.*

Pain, at least, was something I had plenty of.

Tears welled, then slid down my face like rain on a windowpane. The agony of old hurts burned in my chest, seeping into my limbs like melted wax. I was drowning, my breath coming ragged. I dropped to my knees again, banging them hard against stone, but I couldn't feel anything except for the deluge of pain sweeping through me.

Heat flashed around my ribs, then I felt a lump of something hard digging into my side.

With numb fingers, I reached for the lump, which was in a hidden pocket in the cloak's lining.

A jet-black stone the size of a peach pit, cut with the many facets of a diamond, nestled in my palm. Light sparkled across the gem, making visible a strange symbol scratched into the surface. It was a sort of triangle, with three spirals connecting in a center point. The stone pulsed, hot in my hand, like it had its own heartbeat.

I clenched it, the ridges digging into my skin. What strange magic had put this in my hands?

Still kneeling with my head bowed, I placed it at the threshold of the mausoleum's doors.

Blue flame spontaneously erupted, encircling me and the glittering black stone. The onlookers gave a collective gasp. Heat flared at my back, but I stayed kneeling, hunched over myself. There was nothing left. I was empty.

"You have suffered indeed, daughter." The voice was female, strong and cold like a north wind.

I raised my head to see a woman standing inside the circle of flames with me. Black curls hung to her waist, a circlet of pure light atop her head. Her dark eyes glittered like the stone she held aloft in her smooth brown hand. The woman's features were honed like a knife's edge.

"Who are you?" I croaked.

"Iznir, Mother of the Chosen. But you knew that. Persephone," she said, turning my name into something sacred. She came closer, and I stood, putting us eye to eye. "You were born under the rose moon on the solstice, your father's daughter. You were already marked with power when I chose you for my own."

My voice came from outside of my body, and it seemed like I was standing apart, watching myself speak to this illusion of a goddess. "Why did you choose me? Marked with what power?"

The goddess's rosy lips curved in a benevolent smile. "You can save my Chosen who have strayed, and restore balance to the worlds." She traced the inlaid symbol on the black stone. "The Triskele. You give me your past, present, and future." She closed her hand around the stone. "With this sacrifice, my power now runs in your veins alongside your own. Use it wisely, daughter. Keep your own counsel. I appear only to you this night." She reached out and gently held my wrist, and my pulse jumped under my birthmark.

Then I blinked and she was gone. The flames died instantly, leaving me standing alone amidst a soot-stained circle, heart thrumming like a wild thing.

Lamont's eyes were wide, and his knuckles were white where they gripped the book. He came forward. "The sacrifice has been accepted," he proclaimed to the crowd. Then Lamont turned to me. "Place your hand upon the book and repeat after me."

I did as he bade, surprised to find that my hand was steady. My mind was fixed on what the goddess had revealed to me, although I wondered if I conjured her out of some sort of delirium.

"I, Persephone Hart, swear to uphold the tenets of the Aureum: to use my power to defend the gateways of the world; to protect human life at all costs; and to be loyal to the Aureum and my brother and sister Guardians."

I repeated the words quietly, but my voice didn't waver. Lamont drew back my hood, then removed the cloak. He gave me a nudge so that I faced the crowd of Guardians. They stood like statues, their grace and power arrested in cold marble.

"Please join me in welcoming our sister, Novice Hart!" Lamont called, clapping. Others picked up the applause, until it echoed around the cemetery. Hollis whistled, its shrill shriek piercing the air.

I walked down the steps of the mausoleum, head held high with the words of the goddess ringing in my ears, out of my old life and into the new.

16

———

Whispers followed in my wake as I broke away from the crowd, heading deeper into the graveyard. The congratulations and subsequent stares were too much. Everyone tried to get a look at the strange new novice, like I was a zoo animal. Even though we were outside under the stars, it felt like all the air had been sucked up. I needed to breathe.

Picking up my skirt, I disappeared into the trees that were draped with thick, trailing moss. Magnolia blossoms glowed pale white against the darkness, sitting upon heavy skirts of branches. It had to be closing in on midnight, and fatigue weighed heavily on me.

I made slow progress because of the dark, but when I could no longer hear the sounds of revelry, I stopped and leaned against a mausoleum that was dappled with lichen. Carved into the door was a relief of a weeping woman, shrouded in her grief. The cool dampness of the rock seeped through the fabric of my gown.

I had seen a goddess. *The* goddess, Iznir, who granted Guardians their—our—power. What had she meant about bringing balance to the worlds—about all of it? I puzzled over her words, until rustling sounded from the trees.

Out of the shadows emerged a tall, lithe figure. I tensed, holding my palms flat against the mausoleum, until a small sphere of light appeared in the person's cupped hands and illuminated their face.

It was Alex. Of course, he was able to track me down—he could feel me. I relaxed my shoulders, then my whole body went rigid again as he approached. Because holy hell, the man looked like sin wearing a suit.

Alex's black brocade jacket glistened with the slightest sheen of silver threads. His white shirt was open at the collar, exposing the muscular line of his throat. I traced that line with my eyes, all the way across his firm jaw, to the scruff that highlighted his cheekbones, and landed on the wicked curve of his mouth. He'd combed his hair back, but the habitual piece that hung over his forehead had escaped. It brushed his scarred eyebrow, and he flicked it back with a toss of his head.

"You're missing your own party," Alex stated by way of greeting. The ball of light he'd been holding floated upward to hang around the lowest branches of the trees.

I blinked away my blatant stare. "That's the point. I hate parties."

"Well," Alex said, coming to rest against the wall next to me, "so do I. But don't tell anyone."

"Another secret?" I said lightly. "You seem to make a habit of involving me in them."

Alex studied me, his lips parting slightly. "I do. I'm not sure how that happened."

"Oh, it's not just you," I said, leaning back and looking up at the forest canopy. "People always end up telling me stuff. Not because I want them to. They think the quiet girl won't talk."

He quirked a brow. "Quiet? You don't seem quiet to me. In fact, you usually have a smarta—a smart response ready for everything."

"Yeah, well." I shrugged. "There are exceptions to every rule."

"Well, you are exceptional. That's obvious." He said it matter-of-factly, but heat still crept up the back of my neck.

"Can I tell you a secret?" I asked softly. The darkness and seclusion loosened my tongue, and it seemed like whatever I said would be absorbed into the night and disappear with the rising sun.

Alex inclined his head, shadows shifting over the planes of his face. "It only seems fair. A secret for a secret."

"All I've ever wanted is to be normal. To be so regular that no one noticed me. At least, I used to," I admitted.

I expected Alex to be mocking, or to tell me how idiotic that was.

Instead, he hummed in agreement. "I understand, more than you know."

"Really? But you're...." I waved at his general being. "You know."

He gave a low chuckle. "What's that?"

"Oh, come on. Don't make me say it."

"I'm certain I don't know what you mean," he said, but his eyes were teasing. Alex seemed freer here. Even his posture was more relaxed, like the bonds that held him with militant precision had gone slack.

I sighed, regretting opening my mouth in the first place. "You're so sure of yourself. This is your birthright, and you've always known it. You've never had to question what you are, or where you come from."

"No," Alex agreed. "I know exactly where I come from, and what's expected of me. But it isn't always what I've wanted. The pressure of carrying on the family legacy used to strangle me. I almost ran away, once."

I turned to him, my eyes in line with his chin, and tipped my head back. "No way."

He nodded. "I was fifteen and decided I'd had enough of being a councilman's son. All I'd ever wanted was to be a scholar. Instead, I was forced to learn diplomacy at my father's knee, to attend meetings and learn politics and train for ten hours a day. But my mom stopped me from leaving, convinced me to come home before my dad got wind of it." He started to pick at this thumb, then slowly lowered his hands to his sides. As though it was an old habit he was still trying to break.

I felt a pang of empathy for teenage Alex. I could just see him, a gangly adolescent with a defiant curl to his lip. I understood what it was like to suffocate under the weight of a parent's shortcomings.

"Where would you have gone?"

"Hm? Oh, anywhere would've done. Anywhere that wasn't home. Anyway, that was a long time ago." He gazed down at me through dark lashes. "What about you? What were you like at fifteen?"

My instinct was to clam up, and I ducked my head. Alex reached out and hesitantly skimmed my knuckles with his fingertips. Still looking down, I opened my hand for him. He took it and squeezed, his calloused palm sending flutters straight to my belly.

"Come on, Seph. A secret for a secret. Besides, I'm leaving tomorrow."

I jerked my head up. "You are?"

"Now that the week is up and you've been initiated, there's no reason for my unit to stay. You'll join the other novices and begin your training, and we'll return to Gravesville."

No. No, no, no. Suddenly, I was desperate to keep him with me.

"I was a dork when I was a teenager," I said abruptly. "Or maybe more of a pariah. Even the nerds avoided me."

Alex arched a brow. "I have a hard time believing that."

I scoffed. "I went to school with the exact same kids from kindergarten until high school graduation. When everyone was five years old and formed the opinion that I was a freak because they couldn't pronounce my name, it stuck." That, and the cast-off clothing a kind teacher donated to me.

"I don't think I'd use the word *freak* to describe you."

"Then how would you?" I asked with a boldness that shocked me. I was balanced on the thin edge of a knife, waiting to see if he would return the terrible wanting that raced along my skin.

"Well, you're quick. Funny. Brave." I shook my head and began to protest, but he laid a finger on my lips to stop me. Chills alighted down my spine. "I'm not finished."

I nodded, my entire existence distilled into one single touch.

He smiled, the first real smile I'd seen on him. It was brilliant, like the sun had just dropped into midnight and illuminated every shadowy corner. "Where was I? Oh, yes. Extraordinary. Bewitching." Time slowed as the last word hung on his sculpted lips. "Beautiful."

Something golden and euphoric ran through my veins as Alex gripped the hand he still held and drew me toward him, tracing the finger on my lips down to the pulse that flickered below my jaw.

His warm breath whispered against the shell of my ear, goosebumps alighting on my skin. "You asked me what it feels like—this connection I have to you." He drew a sharp breath. "It feels like you're the center of gravity. Like you're a fire, burning hotter than the sun, and I'm a moth drawn to the flames." His voice grew thick, shaky. "It would be better for both of us if I left right now."

There was a long moment where the sounds of our breathing mingled in the night air. "You should tell me to go," he said with finality.

I pulled back, looking squarely into those forest shadow eyes. If this was our last moment together, I would be greedy. I would take everything he offered, and bare my body and soul in return. It was selfish, and stupid, but I couldn't find a damn to give.

"Stay," I whispered.

Alex's mouth parted, in surprise or desire, then he threaded one hand into the mass of my hair and spread the other across the small of my back. He pulled my hips snug against his, and I let out a muted gasp.

His eyes slowly lowered to my lips, then he kissed me. He felt so incredibly soft, but hard, too, and when he traced his tongue across the seam of my mouth, I opened for him. An ember of heat gathered low in my belly, stoked by the pressure of his mouth and light nips that had me arching toward him. I threaded my hands through the mink softness of his hair, dragging him closer.

"This damn dress," he said huskily, kissing down the line of my neck. I arched to give him better access. His hand moved from my hair to the clasp, and he flicked it open. Then, he trailed a finger down the column of my spine, buttons falling open. "Has been driving me crazy." He molded my ass, pressing me against the wall of the mausoleum so that rough stone scraped against my bared skin.

"You can—thank—Fern," I gasped, running a hand underneath his shirt. I felt hot, smooth skin over tight muscles, and I couldn't get close enough to him. Alex seemed to feel the same way, and he tightened his grip, sending spirals of pleasure to my core.

He chuckled low in his throat, and the ember that had been burning sparked into a conflagration, lighting me up from the inside out.

Our hands streaked over each other, parting flesh, tearing fabric, until my dress hung around my waist and his shirt billowed open. He palmed my breast, brushing his thumb over the peaked nipple. I moaned, low in my throat, and kissed him fiercely.

It was like I was blind and deaf and dumb to everything except for him, my head buzzing and filled with pure Alex. So when he reared back, it took me a moment to realize what was happening.

"What are you—" I skidded three feet away from him, like a giant hand had knocked me back. The buttons on the back of my dress had done themselves up, and a quick pass of my hand told me that I didn't have a hair out of place.

Alex stood like an iron pillar against the wall of the mausoleum, all of the ardor he'd exhibited a moment ago replaced by blank coolness.

"Hollis," he said. I squinted, and a blond head appeared out of the darkness. Hollis wore a navy suit with a turquoise bolo tie. He was only missing a ten-gallon hat.

"Hiya, cap. Seph," Hollis said, nodding to me. "You're missing your party."

"Yes, we've been over that," I said through gritted teeth. Cooling sweat dampened my skin, and I shivered. I still felt like I'd been smacked in the face with a two by four, and was trying to come to terms with the fact that Alex's mouth was no longer attached to sensitive parts of my body.

"Well, Councilman Eames sent for you, Alex," Hollis continued, adjusting his bolo tie. His gaze moved between us, assessing, but he didn't comment further.

Alex jerked his chin in acknowledgement. "Walk Seph back?"

"Course," Hollis agreed.

Alex looked at me impassively. I wondered if he could read the emotion in my eyes and the plea in my mind. *Don't leave.* Something fleeting crossed his face, then he inclined his head infinitesimally and melted into the shadows.

I released the breath I hadn't realized I was holding. Damn Edward, and his terrible sense of timing. And Hollis, too, for that matter.

He took my elbow, walking at a leisurely pace. I wasn't in any hurry to return to the party, so I let him guide me slowly through the headstones.

"So," Hollis said, breaking the thick silence. "You don't seem like you're enjoying yourself."

Well, I had been—but I didn't want to discuss the mind-blowing kiss I'd shared with Alex. I was no blushing virgin, and had fumbled in the dark with sweaty boys who wouldn't acknowledge me in the light of day. But that kiss—I rubbed my lips together, trying to reclaim the taste of him.

"No," I answered. "I'm not."

"Well, try to enjoy yourself now, because the next few months are gonna be exhausting. Living in the barracks, sleeping in a twin bed, no privacy—I'd give my left arm to go back," he said wistfully.

"We are very different people."

Hollis gave a low whistle. "That's for sure. But you'll bond with your year of novices quicker than two ticks on a boar."

"Thank you for that image," I said acidly. Then I stumbled over a root, and would have gone flying had Hollis not caught me.

"Your balance will improve when your potentia comes in. Should be anytime now, since you're official," he assured me.

Something akin to a growl worked its way up my throat. "Why aren't you tripping?"

His smile was pale against the gloom. "Honey, we don't need light to see in the dark."

"Call me honey again, and you won't see anything at all," I muttered.

He chuckled. "I heard that."

"Is there *any* privacy around here?"

"You can make your own, if you try hard enough."

I was decidedly silent after that, and we made swift progress toward the floating lights that illuminated Guardians in their slick suits and clinging gowns. Hollis led me over to where Fern stood near a raised tomb, champagne glass in hand, chatting with a group of Guardians. He gave me a bright smile, and I glowered.

"I think I'll be going now," Hollis declared, edging away from us. "See ya, Seph."

The crowd of Guardians dispersed, finding other people to gossip with.

Fern lifted a brow and sipped her drink. "You made Hollis nervous. Congratulations. That's not easily done."

I pressed the spot between my eyes, where a headache was brewing. "I didn't mean to. I get prickly sometimes when I'm stressed. This whole initiation has been...."

"Over the top? Archaic? Intrusive?"

"Something like that," I agreed. "What was yours like?"

"The same, except less fire and about forty novices."

"Was it really that...unusual?" I grimaced. I wanted to ask if Iznir had appeared during Fern's initiation as well, but the goddess's words echoed in my head. *Keep your own counsel. I appear only to you this night.*

Fern smoothed a hand over her braids that were pulled up in a sleek twist. "Usual, unusual. Who are we to question the gods? The important part is that you found your sacrifice, and it was accepted. I knew you could do it."

"Have they ever rejected anyone?" I asked, snagging one of the champagne glasses that floated by on a disembodied tray.

"Very, very rarely. I think the last time was decades ago. The gods know what they're doing."

Fern's confidence somehow made me warier. Who could I trust here? The Guardians who milled around in their finery, with their affable demeanors and jovial laughter, suddenly seemed sinister. I was a garden snake in a den of vipers, and would do well to remember it.

Just then, a flash of sequins caught my eye. It was Davina, who wore a glittering black dress that plunged in a deep V almost to her navel. Eyes followed her as she swayed across the open space toward Mindara, the short councilwoman who'd conducted my inquiry.

"Holy shit," I murmured. Davina was wearing the dress before, but my nerves had been so severe I hadn't really noticed.

"Mhm," Fern said, finishing off her drink. She waved a hand and the empty glass floated away. "She can't help showing off. None of us can, really. When we let off steam, we don't do it halfway."

Davina and Mindara exchanged a formal air kiss. They shared an uncanny resemblance. Then, realization dawned on me. "They're related."

"Yeah." Fern gave me a confused look. "You didn't know? Mindara is Davina's mom. She grew up here, same as Alex."

Of course.

"Are there any more surprise parents on the Diurne?" I asked, still watching mother and daughter chatting.

"Noriko Kimura has a son who's a second year novice. Yuto. He's... right over there," Fern said, gesturing to a muscular young man with a floppy haircut. He stood in a knot of other Guardians who looked around his age. As if he heard Fern—which he very well might have—he looked over his shoulder at me with open curiosity. I hid behind my glass.

"The Aureum isn't immune from nepotism." She sipped her champagne, and I thought I saw her lips move again.

"What did you say?"

She blinked. "Hm? Oh, just that when Alex leaves his captaincy, Davina will take his place and have her own command."

"Leaves his captaincy?" Alarm bells rang in my head.

"He's being groomed to take over for Edward one day. He's got a few years left before he moves back to headquarters and becomes some kind of command administrator."

"So his whole life has already been decided for him."

Fern opened her mouth, then closed it again. She sipped from her glass. "It's the way things are, Seph."

"How about you, Fern? Did you have a choice?" I drained my champagne, clutching the flute in a death grip. Was it alcohol, or Alex's kiss that had decimated my filter?

She gave me a long look. "I did what was best for me. You made the same decision."

And somehow, I had gotten myself mixed up in a whole mess of complications. But it was too late to turn back now.

"I think it's time for me to go." I turned to leave, but Davina called my name. She approached us, a midnight jewel.

"Seph! Well done, you," she said, squeezing my arm.

I forced a smile, while my stomach felt slick with unease. "Thanks. I'm going to turn in. I appreciate everything you've done for me. Both of you. Will you tell the others?"

Davina laughed, low and rich. "You won't need to say goodbye."

The unease turned cold. "What do you mean?"

"I just heard from my mom. Our unit is going to be in and out of headquarters for the next three months, getting you up to speed before you join the other novices. Think of it as private tutoring. The unit will rotate between Gravesville and here, so that we can cover you *and* our post. Isn't that exciting?" Davina's eyes glittered like her dress.

"But...that can't be right," I said, more to myself than Davina or Fern. "Alex said you're going back tomorrow."

"For now, I'm taking the twins and Hollis. Alex, Fern, and Casey will stay here with you. Then we'll swap on and off, mixing it up a little." A smile lit her blood red lips. "This is going to be fun."

I was frozen to the spot like someone had glued me there. Alex, who had just kissed my brains out—who thought he was leaving—was going to be here for the next three months, acting as my teacher. My face burned at the things I'd said, the way I'd exposed myself to him. And this, all while I had been tasked by the goddess to restore balance to the worlds, in addition to pursuing my own secret investigation into my parentage.

"Yes," I choked. "Fun."

17

─────────

"No, no, you're doing it all wrong," Casey said, hands on hips as she looked down her upturned nose at me. I lay prone on the training mat, breathing hard. We were in an offshoot room from the main gym that had an exercise bar running along its length, and floor to ceiling mirrors set on cream walls.

"I figured I wasn't supposed to end up on the ground," I muttered. I took the hand she extended and got to my feet, rubbing my ass where I'd landed squarely on it.

"Have you ever done physical activity of any kind?" she demanded, looking me over with an air of resignation. We'd begun only ten minutes ago, and she seemed ready to throw in the towel.

"Yes," I said defensively. "I had to do PE like everyone else."

"And beyond that?"

"Does taking walks count?"

"Iznir's tits," Casey swore. "We have a lot more work to do than I thought. No wonder they want to get you trained up before you join the other novices."

In the two days since my initiation ceremony, when I'd learned that Alex's unit had been put in charge of my supernatural education, I'd been more physically and mentally exhausted than I ever had in my life. I'd spent most of my time in the Library with Fern, but this afternoon was my first combat training session with Casey. Alex had so far managed to avoid me.

I cringed thinking about our next encounter. The last time I'd seen him, we'd been wrapped around each other like ivy on a tree, hands in places that made my body burn with the memory. And if I couldn't keep my mind off of him and on my training, I was in trouble.

"Hello?" Casey snapped her fingers. "Where'd you go?"

"Ah, nowhere. I'm here. Show me again."

She walked me through the steps of basic self-defense, such as how to set my feet properly and make a fist. I was so unbelievably out of my depth it was laughable. Casey was, in fact, laughing at me.

"I didn't know ankles bent that way." She flashed me an impish grin, her incisors charmingly crooked. "You defy physics, Seph."

Even I had to laugh at that. "When does it get easier?"

"Your potentia should be coming in any day now. For me, it was about three days after my initiation. One second, I was sparring normally with a training dummy, and the next I punched a hole through it." Casey smiled again, reminiscing. I was glad we were on the same side.

"Let's move on to laps. No, sprints. No—"

"I'll take it from here, Case."

Every nerve ending in my body fizzled with electricity, and I turned slowly to see Alex standing behind us, arms folded, face impassive.

Casey nodded, turning to leave without question. "Sure thing. See ya, Seph."

I watched her leave the room, then stared through the empty door. I could be professional. I could speak to Alex like a rational adult, and—

"How have you been?" Alex asked, and damn if his voice didn't hit me like an arrow to the heart. When he spoke, I saw sunlight piercing through the mist, bringing light everywhere he went.

He seemed tired, his skin slightly sallow and his cheek dimpled in a frown. But his posture was still immaculate, his dark hair tousled.

"Better now that I don't have to run sprints," I said, digging my nails into my palm. "And...how have you been?"

He studied me before speaking. "Fine. Look, I meant to see you earlier. I just—"

"It's fine," I cut in. I couldn't bear to listen to excuses. "Don't worry about it." I was fine, he was fine, we were all goddamn fine.

"I've been thinking about what happened. About you," Alex said, starting to come closer, then seeming to think better of it. "But personal feelings aside, you have to understand that what we...that it can't happen again. I'm going to be teaching you, and it's far too complex to get involved. Guardians working together on a combat unit are never allowed to have...relationships. It gets in the way of the job."

I nodded, my heart sinking. "Right. Makes sense."

He rubbed his lips together, his cupid's bow going taut. "Seph, I'm sor—"

"Do not," I said, holding a hand up and giving him a sharp look, "apologize." I couldn't stand it if he was sorry about the way he'd held me in the graveyard. Because after so much heartache and confusion, it'd made me feel human. Alive.

Alex didn't look away. His voice was soft when he answered. "Okay."

"So, did you want something?" I asked, because if I couldn't be blunt with the man who had put his tongue inside my mouth, who could I be blunt with?

"Yes. I wanted to show you the Oratory," he explained.

"You want to...take me to church?" I asked, wrinkling my forehead.

"Not exactly," Alex answered, leading me out of the room and down another endless hallway. "Like most things around here, the name is left over from tradition. In medieval times, Guardians used churches, mosques, temples and the like, as centers for their own rituals and arcana. It made sense at the time since most of the burials were done in the churchyards or adjacent land."

"Why couldn't you build your own places? Seems like it would be easy, given that you can just poof," I gestured, drawing my fingers together then apart, "anything into existence."

"More often than not, it was just easier to sponsor the building of religious sites—anonymously, of course. It wouldn't exactly have been conducive to secrecy to create 'The Aureum Center for Arcana,' given humans' fear of anything supernatural."

We stopped at an arched wooden door that soared above my head, its twin halves coming to a point in the center. I'd passed it before, but had never stopped to examine the carvings covering the golden wood. Angels, devils, and all manner of mythical creatures cavorted beside each other, etched in such detail that I was able to make out their individual facial expressions.

"That's incredible." I traced the outline of an angel's wing, the worn wood slippery. Then, to my shock, it fluttered softly under my finger. It happened so quickly that I thought I'd imagined it, but when I looked at Alex in question, he nodded.

"Wait until you see inside." He placed a hand on each door panel, and they swung smoothly inward.

Even the Library paled in comparison to this place. Golden light suffused the room, spilling out of candle-lit sconces that cast fluttering shadows on the walls. Crystals, mirrors, and bowls of hammered gold lined a series of open shelves. Towers of books were strewn about, their cracked spines giving away the fact that they were well used. The air smelled spicy and fresh, like a pine forest covered in frost.

My eyes darted from marvel to marvel, trying to drink it all in. "Please tell me those aren't rubies," I said, turning toward the dark glittering stones inlaid in walls made of river rock.

"Then I won't tell you," Alex said, unable to keep the grin out of his voice.

"You've been holding out on me," I accused, walking toward the great stone hearth that was the focal point of the room. Dried herbs hung from the wooden mantle in bundles, and the blazing fire added warmth and wood smoke to the already cozy space.

"It's time to begin your formal arcana education." Alex picked up a book, stroking the cover with fondness. Firelight played across his face, highlighting the hollows and smooth lines.

Heat sparked in my belly, crackling like the fire in the hearth. I turned toward it, letting the warmth wash over me.

"So this room is for learning magic?" Even if Alex hadn't given me a little background earlier, anyone would have been able to feel power as soon as they stepped across the threshold. My fingertips tingled in recognition, and I crossed my arms, tucking them safely away before I lit something on fire.

"Arcana. But it's basically the same thing, yes."

"From what I've read, that's central to the Aureum's principles. All of the world's creation stories, mythologies, beliefs, even religions—the details are different, but they all contain similar threads."

"You've been doing your homework," Alex acknowledged. "There are endless ways to work with power. Some use words or magical artifacts. Some use conduits like wands, or cards. And some don't use anything at all except the energy inside them." His words were soft and measured, almost hypnotic.

He waved toward a shelf, and a glittering crystal flew through the air toward us. He caught it in his outstretched hand, then tipped it into mine. "Guardians all have power sources that connect to particular objects or themes. Things like that. You'll see what I'm talking about in a minute. But, what it really comes down to is desire. Tap into it, and let the arcana flow through you to shape the world to your will."

Desire. I swallowed down my own desire that left my throat dry.

"Then why is my power so erratic?"

"Because it's ruled by your emotions," he explained. "You feel angry, you explode the lights. You feel scared, you defend yourself by becoming an electric force field. When you're able to control your feelings, you can manipulate your power to comply with conscious thoughts instead of emotional urges."

Alex crossed his arms and leaned against a scrubbed wooden table piled with more books. "Order and rules are what we live by, and if they're not followed, our whole system could collapse. So now, you'll start to learn the rules."

But I had already broken the rules, so thoroughly that I wasn't sure I could place the shards of them back together. I took a deep breath and nodded. "Okay."

"First off, there are some things we can't use arcana for. The first is healing mortal wounds. The second is killing. And the third is bringing back the dead."

"So, life and death, basically? But don't you kill demons?"

"Demons are spirits, which technically can't die. They can be temporarily incapacitated, contained, or sent back to their own worlds. And they can be controlled, but only if you learn their true name."

"What's a true name?"

"It's their secret name, the name that describes their...essence. Demons guard them fiercely, for obvious reasons. Learning a true name isn't the most effective way to fight a demon, because it takes too much time and energy to figure out when containing or banishing them does the job." Alex scratched his wrist, lifting his sleeve and exposing lines of ink. "But to answer your initial question, no, we can't use arcana to take a life. Although, that wouldn't stop me from stabbing someone in the heart, as long as I didn't use my magic."

"Good to know," I muttered.

"Also, there's an energy cost to using arcana," he continued, fully in teacher mode. His eyes lit up, like he was really enjoying it. "The more you use, the longer it takes to replenish, and the more energy it saps. You can run out, and it can take awhile to replenish, so you need to keep an eye on that."

"Got it. Energy sapping," I repeated.

"Now, let's go back to your door," Alex said, gesturing for me to sit at the table next to him.

I sat reluctantly, facing Alex. "I'm not sure that's a good idea," I said, wiping already sweaty palms on my pants.

"We have to start somewhere," he countered. "You'll be okay, Seph. I'm right here. I won't let anything happen to you."

Even if I didn't fully trust Alex, I trusted that he wouldn't put me in harm's way. I nodded my agreement.

"Close your eyes," he instructed. "Go to your door."

I did as he asked, finding the obsidian door in the unsuspecting wildflower meadow. It loomed large and solid, the sun a glare on its glassy surface. My heart rate picked up. In the dream place, I closed my eyes and folded in on myself, the memory of the examination overtaking every thought.

"You're safe," I heard Alex say in my mind. I felt pressure on my hand, somehow both inside and outside of myself. Then there was a presence beside me, warm and solid, and I opened my eyes to see Alex. His shocked expression mirrored my feelings, but he really was in the meadow, the light wind ruffling the ends of his hair and light glinting on the dark silk of it.

He released my hand abruptly, looking around. "This is where your door is?"

"Why? What's wrong with it?" I retorted.

"There's nothing wrong with it. It's just different than mine. And

I've never...I've never been inside anyone else's head before." He admitted this last part almost shyly.

"Oh. Why not?" I wound my waves into a knot to prevent them from blowing into my mouth.

Alex scratched his jaw. "I didn't know it was possible."

"Great. Another freakish anomaly." I turned toward the door. At least Alex's presence had taken my mind off of what waited behind the obsidian monolith. And, it was reassuring to have him there, like he was a talisman against the dark.

"Not freakish. Extraordinary." Alex cleared his throat and smoothed his expression. "Shall we?" He gestured toward the door.

"You're coming with me?" I asked.

"Would you prefer to go alone?"

Definitely not. But still.... "It almost drowned me," I said, as my stomach tied itself into intricate knots.

"You don't have to be afraid of yourself," Alex murmured. "Not here."

"What'll I do if it swamps us?" I approached haltingly until I could reach out and brush the smooth stone with my fingertips.

"Ask it not to."

"It can't be that simple," I returned.

"Desire, remember?" The corner of his mouth pulled into a half-smile. "Whenever you're ready."

Instead of menacing, I tried to imagine the door as friendly. Protective, even. That it just wanted to keep me safe. I laid a hand on the knob, and felt the slight thrum begin in my chest until my whole body was alight with it. The call, the yearning, intensified. *Don't crush me*, I said in a silent decree. *I just want to see what you're hiding.* Then, breath held, bracing, I inched the door open.

There was no crushing wall of icy black water. A small wave lapped over my feet, then dispersed. I looked over my shoulder at Alex, and he nodded in approval. Opening the door wider, I stilled at the view beyond the threshold.

The sky was a charcoal sketch, with broad strokes of black and gray in clouds that undulated like ocean waves. Flowers the color of moon-dust spilled over hills covered in downy grass. Bone-white trees speared bare, gnarled branches into the air, witches hands' that cupped the darkening welkin.

But the crowning jewels of this eldritch landscape were the two rivers that cut through the valley between hills, twining and crossing like the roots of a tree, one black and one gold.

"Goddess alive," Alex whispered. He was braced in the doorframe behind me, so close that it seemed I could hear the beating of his heart.

The magic that pulsed through my veins felt like a velvet sweep of lust, heady and brilliant. My blood thrilled, and I itched to fling myself over the hills and find the heart of the lush darkness.

"It's amazing," I whispered. I couldn't believe I'd been scared of this place, not when for the first time in my life I felt at home. I could make a life here, amongst the dark skies and bright flowers that dotted the ground like constellations.

I followed the pull toward the rivers that wound sinuously as serpents. When I reached the mossy bank where there was a confluence of black and gold, I knelt and dipped a hand below the surface. Instead of water there were individual threads, spinning out endlessly in either direction, hundreds of them in just a handful.

"What is this?" I wondered, letting the black and gold strands run through my fingers like droplets. They behaved like water, fluid and light, and as I manipulated them I felt echoing tugs inside me.

"That's your power source," Alex said, kneeling next to me, although he didn't touch the river of threads as I did. "But there's two of them, the black and the gold. There should only be one."

With this sacrifice, my power now runs in your veins alongside your own. Iznir herself had said as much. I was a Guardian, but I was also something else entirely, something that had been a part of me from birth. The goddess had chosen me for a reason, and she'd commanded me not to tell anyone what I'd been tasked with. Watching Alex, so earnest and with clear curiosity shining through his scholar's gaze, my heart broke a little. He wanted to keep me safe, for me to trust him. But I couldn't.

"I don't know," I shrugged, standing. "What's through your door?"

Alex looked taken aback for a moment. "I—it's usually personal. But since I've seen yours, it seems unfair to have you at a disadvantage." He hesitated, then spoke. "It's light. When I walk through my door, I can see it in every color, every spectrum and hue and brightness. It's like I'm harnessing the power of the sun."

It made such perfect sense that Alex was made for the light. And I, apparently, was made for the dark.

"What do I do with it all?" I asked, surveying my kingdom of perpetual twilight.

"You'll learn to work with it. To use it, and pull the strings of power so you become the master of your world." Alex's eyes burned with a strange light as he spoke, and I wondered if the untamed energy that flowed through me had spread to him like contagion. Electricity crackled in the space between us, and lightning jumped from cloud to cloud overhead.

A smile curved my lips as I smelled ozone mixed with some rich floral scent—vanilla, or jasmine. I felt glorious, magnificent, enchanting. Right. Perhaps the seed of darkness I'd considered from Persephone's painting was both terrifying and beautiful.

Wind picked up, tossing Alex's hair, and he smiled that breathtaking smile, the one that made my heart ache. Hunger and fierce wanting curled through me, sending long, fluid pulls to my belly.

I'd felt the hardness of his body under mine, the nimbleness of his deft fingers as they plied my skin, the power and heat of his lips on me. I wanted him. All of him.

As if he was reading my thoughts, his eyes turned dark, reflecting the storm above. They weren't controlled, or kind, or curious—all of which I'd seen before. They held a barely restrained intensity, something untamed in its sensuality that promised oceans of pleasure, should it be unleashed. His lips parted, and the pull in my belly became a liquid tug, urging me toward him.

"Seph," he breathed, his voice rough as if it had been dragged over a bed of live coals.

My heart raced, and we were reaching for each other when lightning struck the ground between us.

He disappeared before my eyes, then with a shock like being doused with cold water, I came back to the Oratory.

We were still seated across from each other, but he was decidedly not touching me. I tried to quiet the sound of my panting breath.

Alex cleared his throat, standing and knocking his chair over in the process. He righted it quickly. "Well. That was good, for your first time. We can finish there for today." I blinked, feeling whiplash from the sudden change of scenery. "I'll be going back to Gravesville tomorrow with Fern and Casey, and Davina and the others will swap with us. Keep spending time in your power source—alone," he added.

I was surprised at the fierce protective surge I felt at the thought of someone else knowing what was behind my door. And I didn't want Alex to get in trouble for helping me keep the twin power sources a secret.

"Okay," I agreed. Then, trying to sound casual, asked, "When will you be back?"

"In a week," he said, not meeting my eyes. Then, softer, "Take care of yourself, Seph."

I watched him leave, the figure in black who had almost succumbed to the intoxicating feeling of my power. That made two of us, at least.

18

———

My days fell into a routine as the weeks passed. Before my hated combat training, I spent the first half of my day with the Library, where I threw myself into the study of demons and magical lore. I became familiar with her quirks—that she was often tired first thing in the morning and needed some time until her invisible gears were up and whirring, and that she didn't mind if you scattered crumbs around but became infuriated if you tried to use a cell phone.

She learned to anticipate my needs, leaving materials in what had become my habitual study carrel on the third floor. Alex's unit tasked me with learning the names and features of demons listed in grimoires with odd titles like *The Sacred Magic of Abramelin the Mage.* I'd begun to see texts from magical sourcebooks, ranging from Sumerian to Slavic to Elizabethan, in my sleep.

Sylvan was supervising me today, although we weren't the only ones camped out in the Library. Novices scattered around in cliques, engaging in the covert studying and overt flirting of undergraduates everywhere. I knew they were curious about me, and I'd even exchanged shy smiles with a few of them. But I wasn't looking forward to the end of my three month catchup period, where I would be joining their ranks. Already I was closing out my fourth week, in what seemed like no time at all.

And...I still hadn't been able to continue the search for my father. I wouldn't have had to hide it from Alex, but he was never in the Library with me since he was supervising my arcana education.

Yawning, I stretched my arms overhead. Sylvan looked up from where he worked in a sketchbook. "Tired?" he asked, setting down his pencil.

I nodded, then glanced at a wall clock. "I have fifteen minutes before I'm supposed to meet Davina. I think I'm going to try to take a power nap."

Sylvan nodded, flexing his graphite-stained fingers. "If your body is telling you to rest, you should rest. Want me to walk you to your room?"

"Sylvan," I admonished, adding a smile for good measure. "I know my way around by now. You don't have to be my bodyguard anymore."

"All grown up?" He grinned back. "Okay, Seph. See you tomorrow."

We walked to the ground floor together. "Oh, I have to...pee," I finished, darting into a side hallway where I knew a bathroom was, before he had a chance to protest. I hurried around the corner, then waited for Sylvan to leave. When the coast was clear, I went back to my carrel on the third floor.

A man scanned the shelves to my right. I waited until he moved on before whispering my request. "Library, I need anything else you have on Zeke Hart."

There was a soft *plunk* behind me. I peered over the top of my study carrel and saw the paperback on an adjacent table. I looked around for passersby, then quickly fetched the book and brought it back to my desk.

My fingers stilled over the pages. I knew this book. I'd never read it, but its cover that displayed the wrought iron gates of Gravesville Historic Cemetery was familiar. It was on the shelves of every tourist trap and bookstore in town.

An Unabridged History of Gravesville, NC: America's City of the Dead, by Laurence Zollicoffer.

"What the hell?" The floor rippled, as if the Library shrugged; *you asked for it.*

"I don't need this. I know where he used to live. Library, I said Zeke Hart." I took care to enunciate his name.

There was no answering whir, no grumble or thump that indicated she was about to produce something. "Did you hear me?"

This time there was a clunk, then a book appeared on the table. I picked it up. The title read, *Nothing Left To Give*. It was a thriller, with a cover illustration of a hand holding a bloody knife.

"Hilarious," I muttered. "Is there really nothing left?"

She sighed, the sound like wind blowing through tall grass.

"Okay, fine." I wracked my brain for any other search term that might work. Alex had already looked up my mom's hometown, and her married and maiden names. There was a marriage certificate between her and my dad dated 1994, but that was all.

Frustrated, I kneaded my forehead. There had to be something else, something related to him, no matter how obscure, that might inadvertently lead me to some kind of evidence that the man existed.

"Oh," I breathed, when it came to me. It was obvious, really—why hadn't I thought of it before? "Library. I need information about the Watchers."

I waited one minute, then five, then ten. "Okay, you don't know what that is, either. Got it." Gathering my bag, I was ready to leave when something appeared on the table. It wasn't a book, a binder, or even a newspaper. It was a photograph, roughly the size of a playing card.

The photo was a black and white headshot, showing a young woman with short, coiffed waves, and a brilliant smile. Her neck was a long, graceful stem, and just beneath her collarbone was a smudge that I recognized as a lily birthmark. She wore a slim chain necklace with a delicate cameo pendant, and a collared dress. *Cora Roth- Class of 1918* was printed in bold typeface on the bottom of the photo's white border.

"Who is she?" I asked, more to myself than the Library.

"Who's who?"

I spun around, hiding the photo behind my back. Davina tilted her head, her dark eyes curious. She was at the top of the stairs, hopefully too far away to notice the photo. Curse her supernatural hearing.

"No one," I blurted. "Just talking to myself."

She tossed her hair over one shoulder. "You're late for combat."

Damnation. I slid the photo into my back pocket, then grabbed my bag. "Sorry. I got caught up."

"I can tell by the lack of books." She arched a singular brow.

"It's my fault," a deep voice said behind me. A shadow emerged from the stacks. It was the guy Fern had pointed out to me at my initiation celebration, one of the other Diurne nepo babies. "I distracted her. We were discussing...gateway theory."

Davina's eyes narrowed. "Sure, Yuto. Second years aren't even close to touching gateway magic."

"A man can dream, can't he?" Yuto gave a charming smile, his teeth white and even. "Anyway...see ya, Seph." He winked at me and disappeared back into the stacks. I wasn't sure whether to feel relieved or creeped out that he'd come to my aid out of nowhere.

"Whatever," Davina said, sharing an exasperated glance with me. She waited until we were out of the Library to speak again. "I'm friends with his older sister, Akira. Yuto is the annoying little brother who's too young to be your friend, but too old to be cute."

"Where's Akira?" I asked, grateful for the subject change.

"Stationed on the west coast, in the bay area."

"It must be hard to keep up friendships being so far away," I noted.

Davina grinned mischievously. "You forget that anyone is just a gateway away."

"Oh, right." Another Guardian passed us in the hall, and I waited until they were out of earshot to continue. "What did you mean about second years not touching gateway magic?" I actually had read the theory, courtesy of the Library. There were lots of arrows and diagrams and something about physics, which I'd spent several years trying quite hard to forget about.

"You don't learn gateway theory until third year, and even in the first year after graduation you're supervised every time you open one. If you do it wrong, you can end up with half of you in one place and the other stuck in the vacuum. I'll tell you what my instructors told me—do not fuck with gateways until you're trained," she warned.

"Wouldn't dream of it." I breezed through the open door of the training center, meaning every word. I wasn't keen on losing a limb to the all encompassing nothing-and-everything feeling of a gateway.

Guardians sparred on the mats, ran on treadmills, or otherwise engaged in acrobatics that made me dizzy. I went to my usual training mat in the far corner and dropped my bag, shucking off my sweater. My sore muscles protested at the motion as I exposed my bruise-clad arms.

Even after a month, my supernatural strength and speed hadn't manifested. Alex assured me it would be any day now, and I tried to ignore the worried bent to his mouth. What use was a demon hunter who couldn't keep up with the demons?

"We're using the target room today," Davina said, bending to loop my backpack over her shoulder before she led me through the training center into an offshoot room. The room's walls were plywood, and there were red bull's eye circles painted on them in regular intervals.

She dropped my bag along the wall, then reached behind her back and produced two short knives in each hand. The blades had wicked points and were only slightly longer than their handles. "If you can't use your body as a weapon yet, you can learn to use actual weapons."

"You want to give me a sharp implement?" I asked, not able to fully mask my horror.

"I won't let it get out of hand," she assured me. She passed me one of the knives, handle out, then floated it out of my reach before I could take it. "See?"

"Sure," I said, although it didn't provide too much comfort. She floated the knife back into reach. The hilt felt unforgiving and rigid in my hand.

"These are throwing knives." Davina tossed hers into the air, caught it by the handle, then flicked it so quickly that the knife became a blur until I heard a thud. It was embedded in the center of the bull's eye, buried to the hilt. "You don't have to be strong or overpower your opponent to use these. You just have to be quick and accurate, both of which I'm certain you can manage."

"You have a lot of confidence in me."

"Why shouldn't I?" After adjusting my stance and giving a demonstration, she said, "Okay, your turn. Remember, this is only your first try. The goal isn't even to hit the target today."

I gripped the knife as she'd shown me, not too tight or too loose. I eyed the red circle and lined up my arm. On an exhale, I released the knife, watching it spin end over end until it hit the farthest edge of the target, blade quivering.

Disbelieving, I turned back to Davina. "Did you see that?"

She gave me an appraising look. "Not bad, Hart. Not bad at all. Let's go again."

She put me through my paces until I consistently hit the target. I still bounced a few knives off the wall, but most of them stuck in the outermost edge of the red ring.

I was damp with sweat and my arm was more sore than ever when we stopped, but I felt a glow of satisfaction that I hadn't experienced with combat training. My time spent studying grimoires was easy and even enjoyable, and I'd made some slow progress with practicing arcana —at least, I was easily able to get through my door, now. But my natural clumsiness and human reflexes hadn't lent themselves to punching and flipping.

"I want you in here practicing daily," Davina instructed as we crossed back through the training room. "And take these." She handed me her belt with the four blades tucked into sheaths.

"I never thought I would appreciate someone giving me weapons, but thank you," I said.

"Once you've mastered those, I'll give you an enchanted dagger. Imagine impaling a demon with a flaming, cursed blade." Her smile was sharper than the knives she'd handed over, and she became the sly huntress again, her eyes darkening and her sleek hair hanging around her face.

"That sounds...interesting," I decided. Or horrifying.

I paused to pull my sweater on, and when I reemerged I spotted Edward approaching us from the open doors.

"Lieutenant, Novice Hart," Edward said, straightening the cuffs of his charcoal suit. He wore a white shirt and a gray tie, with black shoes that looked like they cost more than a mortgage.

"Councilman," Davina answered. She'd grown up with Edward, was close friends with his son, and she still maintained the stiff formality that I'd come to associate with the Diurne.

They both stared at me when I remained silent. "Oh, hi. Councilman," I added belatedly.

"I've come to check in on your progress," Edward said. "It's been a month, and I understand that your potentia has yet to manifest."

As if it was something I could control. A sudden spurt of embarrassment made my cheeks burn. "Not yet."

"Seph has been making progress, Councilman. It's all in the report," Davina said.

I looked sharply at her. "Report?"

"Of course. The Diurne keeps files on all novices. We want to be certain you're up to scratch when you join the other first years."

Fucking hell.

They were still watching me. Cora Roth's photograph in my back pocket burned like a hot coal. I'd foolishly let my guard drop over the past month, had begun to trust that I was safe here. What if Yuto had overheard me ask the Library about the Watchers?

"I don't think Seph is ready for that," Davina said, answering some question of Edward's that I hadn't heard.

"If Novice Hart isn't prepared to demonstrate the progress you mentioned, perhaps we need to rethink this plan," Edward said in a pleasant voice that held a threat just below the surface. "We pulled your unit for a specific reason, Lieutenant. But if it's all a waste of time, you can return to Gravesville, and we will place Novice Hart with a different team. Captain Villanueva might be a good fit."

Davina's expression flashed with disgust for the briefest of moments. Who the hell was Captain Villanueva to provoke that response? "No, Councilman. That won't be necessary. Seph?" She turned to me, her back to Edward, and mouthed, *say yes.*

I nodded shortly, anxiety tickling my sternum. Edward gestured us toward the mat, several sparring Guardians pausing to watch.

Davina stepped onto the mat in a ready stance, regret marring her lovely features. Dread gathered in my stomach. I was nowhere near ready to fight someone as skilled as Davina. She was going to destroy me.

I approached the mat, holding my fists ready like Casey had taught me. We circled each other, staring, until Edward called, "Now, if you please."

Davina advanced on me, throwing an exploratory hook. It came slow enough that I had time to duck out of the way and dance back, trying to stay light on my feet so I didn't trip. My goal was to divert and defend. There was no way in hell that I could hit Davina hard enough to hurt her.

She swiped and kicked until I was at the very edge of the mat, cornered with nowhere to go. When I was truly pinned, Davina stepped back and lowered her hands.

"What is this?" Edward demanded. "You haven't done anything but dance in a circle. Get back on that mat, Lieutenant."

"Sir, I—"

"That's an order," Edward said. His finery did nothing to mask the savagery in his eyes, and a cold chill ran down my spine. The crowd was silent, their stoicism fanning the flames of my fear.

Davina hesitated, then walked back to the mat. She wouldn't look me in the eyes. We squared up again, and this round it didn't take her any time at all to strike. She jabbed out, catching me on the chin. My head snapped back, but I didn't fall. I feinted when she struck again, but she hooked my leg and took me down to the mat. I landed with a heavy *thwack* that knocked the air out of my lungs.

"Again," Edward ordered.

I got to my feet, still winded. Davina landed a kick on my thigh, spinning me like a top. When my back was to her she struck me hard between the shoulder blades. I fell to my knees, skinning my palms.

It happened over and over, until I swayed like a drunk and tasted blood. It ran down my chin, dripping onto the ground. Every part of me throbbed with pain, but it wasn't enough to drown out the humiliation that burned like a brand. There was murder in Davina's eyes when she turned to Edward.

"Again," he commanded.

"She's concussed," Davina protested. "This isn't fair."

"Fair?" Edward stepped onto the mat. "What isn't fair is that scores of demons and monsters infiltrate this world every single day. That innocents die at their hands, and that each one we let get away spreads evil like an infection." He looked me square in the eyes. His glistened with ice. "Tell me, Novice Hart. Do you think the enemy will go easy on you? That they won't do anything in their power to leave you bleeding on the ground? This is what you signed up for. Kill, or be killed. *Again.*"

Davina was going to kill me. There were only so many hits I could take before I would fall down and stay there. But some stubborn part of me that wanted to prove Edward wrong forced me to my feet. No matter what he said out loud, he didn't think I belonged. If it had been his choice alone, he would have sent me packing to become some demon's midnight snack. Despite his claim about wanting to save innocents, I had a feeling he didn't think that applied to me.

And *fuck him*.

So I got up, and when Davina punched me in my swollen cheek, I dug deep. Some part of me went to my door and threw it wide open so that the twin rivers, dark and light, almost blew it off its hinges as they gushed out, threading into my muscles and snaking through my veins like some kind of benevolent parasite.

I absorbed her blow, staggered back, then, feeling the golden and black threads wrapped around my limbs, kicked out. My foot caught Davina in the ribs, sending her careening backwards. Her open mouth and wide eyes fueled my assault, and I advanced, battering and twisting and fighting like hell, all controlled by the strings of power.

She backed up, out of the circle, and we danced a vicious waltz around the training center, leaving a path of ruin in our wake.

That I posed a real challenge seemed to have awakened Davina's predatory instincts. She moved like smoke on the wind, and while I battled brutally to keep up with her, she was lethal grace. Our skin slid slickly against each other when we made contact, and I tasted salt and iron. My world narrowed to the smell of sweat, the burn of muscles, and the sheer ecstasy of my magic.

Even though power fed my strength, I began to tire. My stamina was nothing compared to Davina's, who likely could have kept up her assault all day. I stumbled, and when she landed a kick I fell to my knees. My hand brushed the knife belt at my waist. I didn't have enough time to think if I should—I just acted.

The blade went sailing out of my hand, wide of Davina. She ducked and charged, but I loosed another that missed her again, then another, until I was out of weapons and she was on me, twisting my arms up into a vicious hold, her knee on my throat.

I was gasping, bloody, my clothes torn and every muscle screaming in pain. Davina looked down at me, her lip bleeding and her hair snarled. Her expression was ruthless, cold and calculating. Then she blinked, snapping out of it. "Well done." She removed her knee from my throat, then held out a hand to pull me up. I was reaching for her when she stepped back, face clouding.

Footsteps rang across the silent space, so loud they could have been gunshots. They stopped, then a shadow loomed over where I lay on the floor. Edward's face was cold, his mouth twisted.

"That was pitiful and inadequate. Sloppy and unacceptable." He tossed a knife on the ground by my head, where it clattered in my ear. I flinched at the sound, and his lips thinned. "You need to do better, Novice Hart. The Aureum demands nothing less." With that final parting line, he turned on his heel and left. The crowd who had been gathered dispersed, filtering out of the training center.

Hot tears of humiliation gathered in the corners of my eyes. I blinked furiously, but they overflowed my lids and soaked into my hair. How could Alex, who was pure light, have come from such a prick? I had done my best with what I had, and it wasn't enough.

"Come on." Davina knelt, helping me up. I clutched my ribs, which throbbed as if they'd been pounded on by a hammer. "Don't listen to him," she said in a low voice. "You kicked ass. Seems like he wanted to force your abilities, and it worked."

I stopped, thunderstruck. "That's what this whole fucking charade was about?" I ground out. It hurt to speak.

She shrugged. "It's likely. And you can't say it wasn't effective."

Rage licked up my spine, and a lightbulb shattered overhead, the song of raining glass slicing the tension. "You people are fucked up."

"Hey," she snapped. "I wasn't the one who decided that was a good idea."

"But you did beat me to a pulp on his orders."

"That's right. It was an order. And I have to do what he says. So do you."

I gritted my teeth. "This is wrong."

"No, Councilman Eames is right," Davina said. "It's child's play compared to what's out there. You have no idea what you're up against. If you don't train harder, run faster, and think smarter than them, you'll end up in the ground. We lose a dozen Guardians a year to those monsters. And if they win, we're all fucked." Her cheeks were scarlet, her teeth bared in a snarl.

I wanted to tell her I'd already faced down a demon and won. That as the flames licked hot down my arms, I'd sent it back to hell, or wherever it had come from. But I bit my tongue. "I'm done."

To her credit, Davina didn't coddle me or make noises about my injuries. "Fine. I'll see you in a week." With a sweep of her long hair, she limped away. I allowed myself the smallest bit of satisfaction.

Grimacing against the pain in my ribs—and the rest of me, for that matter—I sifted through the mess we'd left to find my bag. It was shoved halfway under a squat rack, the strap hooked around a weight. I hauled the plate off of it, then checked the contents. My notebook and phone were still intact, thankfully. Then I felt for Constance's pendant, and breathed a sigh of relief that it still hung around my neck. All that was left was the photo of Cora Roth. Where had I put it? I searched my backpack before remembering it had never made it there. It was still in my pocket.

Heart hammering, I slid my hand into my back pocket, but there was only the feeling of smooth denim. I checked all of my pockets, my bag, my shirt, but came up empty. I spent the next half hour searching every inch of the gym, becoming increasingly frenzied. When I turned over the last mat and looked in the last corner, I had to admit that the photograph was gone.

"Fuck!" The word rang around the empty room, mocking me. Not only had I been publicly humiliated and had my ass handed to me, but the one clue I'd managed to get my hands on—the one that I was supposed to be keeping a secret—had disappeared.

That photo of Cora Roth was out there somewhere in the wrong hands.

19

———

The morning after my public bout with Davina, I expected the aches and rainbow of bruises on my skin. What I didn't expect was Alex appearing at my door, looking like he could shoot lightning bolts from his eyes. But his rigid jaw softened as his gaze roved from a livid mark on my temple to the way I favored my right ankle.

"What are you doing here?" I yawned, rubbing sleep out of my eyes.

"I just got back from Gravesville. I heard it was bad, but...not this bad." The line of his mouth became grim.

I grunted in response, then limped to the kitchen. Pouring a mug of fresh-brewed coffee, I hissed as the hot liquid touched my split lip. "Fuck, that stings."

Alex followed me in, seating himself at the tiny island. His tall frame dwarfed it. "That fight should never have happened. I'm so sorry."

"What are you apologizing for? You didn't use my face as a punching bag." I wasn't even angry at Davina anymore. She'd only been following orders, barbaric as they were. Alex, Davina, me—we were just cogs in the Aureum's machine.

"From what I heard, you gave as good as you got." He scrutinized my swollen cheekbone, not managing to hide his wince.

I shook my head. "I'm betting Davina doesn't look like this."

Our eyes met across the table, and my stomach did its usual flutter that happened whenever he was near. Alex cleared his throat. "Any sign of your potentia manifesting?"

I huffed out a breath. "I don't think Edward scared it out of me, if that's what you mean. But I felt something different. Instead of having to go to my power source, it all came spilling out of me. It felt...." Better than the silence of a graveyard, or the smell of a secondhand bookstore. Better than a hug from Bri, or Alex's smile. "Good."

The corner of Alex's mouth pulled up. "Yeah. It does. As you get more familiar with it, the connection to your arcana grows. It sounds like you're ready to start with simple tasks—lighting candles, elemental manipulation. But we can give it a couple of days, until you're better." He hesitated. "Actually, if you want...I can heal you. I'm not great at it, but I could take the worst of the pain away."

"If it'll stop me from walking like I have a stick up my ass, I'm in."

Alex shook his head and blustered a laugh. "I could probably do that, yes. I just have to make contact with the...affected area."

"Oh." I chewed on my lip. "Uh...sure."

He came to my side of the island, moving slowly as though to give me plenty of time to adjust to his presence. I stared at the hard plane of his shadowed jaw. He had the slightest dusting of freckles underneath it, pale brown against white skin.

Pushing his errant lock of hair back, he asked, "Are you sure you want me to?"

I mentally gritted my teeth against the pull of need in my center. "Alex, I could barely get out of bed this morning. I can deal." *I can deal with your hands on my skin, knowing that I can't have more than that.*

His lids lowered, hooding his eyes, and he nodded. He raised a fingertip to my cheek, pressing lightly. I cringed, but the discomfort was soon replaced by warm tingling. Sighing, I leaned into Alex's touch. He drew his hand away, and I straightened, conscious that I'd been on the verge of purring like a cat.

"Anywhere else?" he asked, when he was finished tending to the other bruises and cuts on my face, and my injured ankle. I'd almost swooned when he knelt in front of me and slid his deft fingers up the hem of my sweats.

"No, I'm fine. Thanks. If your healing skills are amateur, the professionals must be able to bring back the dead."

"No one can bring back the dead." He sidled back, surveying me. "Your ribs."

"What about them?" I washed my mug in the sink, then placed it on the drying rack. The movement caused much less pain, for which I was grateful.

"Your breathing is shallow."

Thrice-cursed supernatural hearing. "They might be bruised."

"Let's see. Come on, don't be stubborn."

Muttering about pushy magic users, I raised the hem of my sweater to reveal a patchwork of purplish-blue bruises covering my torso.

Alex sucked his teeth. "This might be broken." He traced a finger along a particularly brilliant streak, and I spat a string of curses. "Inventive," he said, arching his scarred brow. "I've never heard some of those."

"I read a lot," I grunted.

"Move here," Alex said, positioning me in front of him. "So I can do both sides at the same time. All right, hold on. This may hurt." More gentle than a whisper, he skimmed his fingertips slowly up my left and right sides, from the curve of my waist to the band of my sports bra. I couldn't help the little groan that escaped my lips as the pain eased.

"How's that?" he asked. Was it just me, or did his voice sound rougher, lower?

I turned around, not realizing how very near we were. I inhaled his cedar scent, and my breath caught in my throat, as if to keep that part of him close. His eyes were darkest emerald, ringed by the black sweep of his lashes. I wanted to brush them with my lips, to trace the line of his fine-boned nose.

"It's great." I pulled my sweater down, covering the now yellowed bruises.

"Right." He rocked back on his heels. "Will you be up for training tomorrow?"

"Yeah. I'll be fine." Physically, perhaps. Emotionally, I felt like the wreckage of Pompeii.

"Okay, then. I'll see you." He turned to leave.

"Alex?"

I scrutinized him, and he stood there patiently, letting me. He'd come to check on me. He'd healed my wounds. He was keeping my secrets. Over the past weeks he'd somehow slipped into the place of my closest confidant. I realized, with surprise, that I trusted him.

Even more than trust, the feeling was like an invisible tether that led me straight to him. A connection that had grown from errant weed to solid oak while I hadn't been looking.

Maybe it was time to ask for help.

"Can you keep another secret?" I asked.

He paused. "I...yes," he agreed. "What is it?"

"Do you know what a Watcher is?" I observed him closely for a reaction.

The corners of his mouth drew down, exposing his dimple. "A what?"

"A Watcher."

"Do you mean someone is watching you? Where is this coming from?"

"No. It's just something I overhead."

"Overheard from—nevermind. Did you ask the Library?"

I smiled faintly. "Yeah. She gave me a photo, but I...misplaced it." I explained about Cora Roth, who was part of the graduating class of 1918. "But please, don't tell anyone. I think it might be related to my dad."

"I won't. But I can help you search."

Warmth and light surged through my whole body. "Thank you."

Alex nodded. He walked out, then paused in the doorframe and looked back. "Just so you know—if it had been me yesterday," he said, voice low, "I wouldn't have done it. No matter the consequence."

Then he was gone, like a phantom chased away by the dawn.

"Oh, shit." I slumped, burying my face in my hands.

Should I have chosen to acknowledge the feelings that hid in my deepest shadows, I might have admitted that I wanted Alex with an ache that set my bones on fire. I might have said that the invisible tie that bound us was threaded with desire so heavy it snatched the breath from my lungs. I might have believed that the moment the lines of our stories crossed was the best and worst thing that ever happened to me.

But he'd been right, all those weeks ago. I was not made for burning, and whatever was between us would only ever live in the dark.

"Don't try to think too hard about it. In fact, don't think at all." Sylvan held me with his glacial gaze, settling into a cross-legged position on the grass. His silvery hair was pulled back into a bun, and his sharp cheekbones gave him more than a passing resemblance to a Norse god.

He decided that arcana practice would be outside today, so that we could 'connect with the earth and all of her living creatures.' I liked Sylvan's bohemian manner, but my patience was running thin. After weeks of failing to manipulate my power, I wasn't sure how sitting in the cold grass would help.

"Okay. Not thinking," I said. I dropped down across from him, arranging my long legs so that I mirrored him.

"Now, close your eyes. Feel your door. Let your door feel you."

Oh, for Christ's sake. Finding my door was easy, but getting the power to rush through as it had the day I brawled with Davina had proven challenging. Well, not only challenging—impossible.

I returned to the familiar cold, unyielding obsidian. It opened for me, and I saw the dull glint of black and gold threads coursing through their rivers, the overcast sky and the twilight with its lavender tinge. Euphoric energy rushed through me, but when I tried to pull the rivers out of the door, they remained stubbornly immovable.

"I don't think this is working." It really only felt like I made progress when I worked with Alex, anyway. But as soon as he left, my control would disappear, too.

"That's all right." Sylvan laid back on the grass, staring up at the solid gray clouds. The air was still and thick, but managed to hold a chill.

Giving up, I laid down beside him. "Why can't I do it?" Edward's threat rang in my head every time I tried to pull on the flowing black and gold threads of my arcana. *Kill or be killed. Do better.*

"Your power responds only when it has to—when your emotions are so heightened that it's forced. You need to start a conversation with it. To build trust with yourself."

How could I trust myself when I felt so out of control? So powerless?

A white-winged butterfly flitted around Sylvan's head, maybe drawn by the bright shine of his hair. He lifted a fingertip, and the butterfly alighted on it, wings fluttering. "Animals don't try to fight their nature," he observed, as the butterfly took flight again. "They just exist, following their instincts."

I'd been fighting my nature as long as I could remember. Staying silent when I wanted to rage and shout. Shoving people away when it would have been a benediction to let someone else fight for me. "Isn't there some kind of shortcut? *Magic For Dummies*, or something?"

Sylvan smiled, the curve of his lips poetry. "Lean in, Seph. Lean into what you've got."

I released a slow breath, fighting the urge to scream.

"I can sense your restless energy," he observed, still looking at the sky.

"Are you a reader, too?" I asked.

"No. But I have eyes. Let's go work some of it off."

We went to the training room. It always reminded me of my humiliation at Davina's hands, and a layer of unease settled over me.

Sylvan set me up with a sparring dummy. He coached me through hits, and I was reminded again that despite his gentle nature, he was as deadly as any Guardian.

"You're getting better. But put some feeling into it this time. Use your anger."

"I thought I wasn't supposed to let my emotions get the best of me." Alex told me as much, the day he'd introduced me to the Oratory.

Sylvan gave a knowing nod. "That works for some people. It doesn't work for you. Now, envision this is someone you really, really don't like." He tapped the center of the dummy's chest. "And hit it here."

Clark's face flashed into my mind, along with Edward's. "I think I can do that."

"Good. Now go."

I punched the dummy, satisfied when it rocked back on its stand. Despite not having supernatural muscles, my form and strength had improved over the past months.

Sylvan folded his arms. "Come on, Seph. You can do better than that. Tap into your rage."

"What happened to not trying too hard?" I lifted a brow.

He smirked. "It's already there for the taking. You just have to decide you want it."

Before I could bark a retort, Alex and Hollis walked into the training center. They raised a hand in acknowledgement, then went to one of the open mats and began to spar.

Hollis flowed and crashed like an ocean wave, bobbing fluidly and lashing out aggressively. Alex, on the other hand, struck like lightning, there one minute and gone the next. The dull sounds of flesh striking flesh sounded, along with their grunts and pants.

What was so appealing, I wondered, about two men fighting? The round ended in a stalemate, and they stripped off their shirts before beginning again.

It wasn't just the shining, sweaty skin, rippling abdominal muscles, and hard biceps that made me stare. Both of their arms, from wrist to shoulder, were covered with black tattoos.

The tattoos were of lettering that curled and looped into intricate illustrations and patterns. It was extraordinary work, like each told a story that only the wearer could decipher. I gaped at them, wondering how I'd missed it before. But Guardians were always covered in long sleeves and pants. I'd thought it was some kind of unspoken uniform, but perhaps it was habit from hiding their ink while amongst humans. Because those would definitely get them noticed.

"They are beautiful, aren't they?"

Sylvan's voice snapped me out of my daze. "Um. Well—I'm supposed to be hitting something, aren't I?"

"I don't think this is going to help your concentration," he said, sotto voce. "Why don't you go practice on your own? Remember, use your anger."

I fled the gym, decidedly not looking at Alex and Hollis and their deadly, thrumming power that acted on me like an aphrodisiac. Why wasn't everyone screwing, all the time? I understood the rules about not dating within units, but it had to be hard to resist with all of the raw sexuality floating around. God, I didn't need to think about Alex and screwing in the same sentence, be—

"Novice Hart."

Startled, I lifted my gaze. Edward strolled down the corridor, coming from the opposite direction.

"Hi." I ducked my head and made to pass him.

"Shouldn't you be in training?" His tone was inquisitive, his brown eyes friendly. He sounded different from the man who'd thrown a dagger at my head and told me to kill or be killed.

Yet, sirens went off in my brain. I clutched my tiger's eye pendant. "I'm practicing on my own for a while. Sylvan thinks I'm ready for more independence." It was an utter lie that I told with a straight face.

"Well, that's good news. Very good. And, how are you doing otherwise? Missing your family?"

"Um—no, not really."

We stood in silence for a moment, and I gnawed my lip. "I should go, get started."

"Wait," Edward said, holding a hand up. "About the other week. I may have been too harsh." His countenance was open, sincere. "I worry, you see. I want to be certain that every novice has the skills they need in order to advance and thrive. Your safety is paramount to us, and with your special circumstances.... Anyway." He gave a rueful smile. "Please forgive my exuberance."

Anyone might have welcomed an apology from a member of the Diurne Council with open arms. For someone so high ranking to ask a common foot soldier for forgiveness could be viewed as admirable.

But that person wasn't me. I'd spent too many years being condescended to by powerful men, and the words coming from Edward's mouth smelled of bullshit and falsehood.

I showed my teeth when I gave my most poisonous smile, and employed one of my mother's favorite weapons. "Well, bless your heart. How thoughtful of you."

And there it was in Edward's eyes. The snapping rage, the flare of contempt that flashed for the briefest of moments before he masked it. I brightened my smile, letting him know that I'd seen the slip. That I wouldn't forget it.

He didn't stop me when I walked past him, throwing the bolt on my door as soon as I got back to my room. My breath came rapidly, and I poured myself a glass of water, chugging it down to wet my dry throat.

"That was very, very stupid of you," I said aloud. No one answered, except for the sound of blood rushing in my ears. I walked into the bedroom, fully intending to bury my face in a pillow and scream, when I stopped cold.

Something was different.

I turned a circle, taking in the room. The queen-sized bed was still a rumpled mess, as I'd left it that morning. My books were stacked in a haphazard pile on the white desk, the old band t-shirt I slept in on the floor. But there was a tingle at the base of my spine, a whisper of doubt.

Nothing was out of place—but something was missing. My black duffel that had been with me since the lake house wasn't next to the closet, where it had lived all this time. I walked over, staring down at the empty space on the red rug.

"What the hell?"

There was no sign of it in the closet, bathroom, or living area. The studio apartment had to be less than five hundred square feet; there weren't many places it could be. Giving up, I kicked the bed in frustration. Pain sang up my stubbed toe, and I dropped to the ground, cursing. On my hands and knees, I spotted a black handle.

"How'd you get under there?" I extracted the bag, rifling through it. It held a pack of extra hair elastics Fern had given me, a bottle of lotion, and the Magician tarot card I'd picked up in the cemetery months ago. I rooted around, finding the lotion and hair elastics, but no tarot card. I searched again, going through every nook and cranny, even shaking the bag upside down. Nothing fell out except for some lint.

I combed through the entire apartment, but the Magician was gone. I sank onto the couch, interlacing my fingers and holding the back of my neck to release the tension that curled up my spine. Where the fuck could it have gone? I'd seen it when I arrived, nestled in a pocket. It couldn't have just sprouted legs and walked away, like....

Suddenly, Edward waylaying me in the hall took on a whole new meaning.

The bastard didn't want to apologize—he was distracting me. Distracting me, while someone searched my room.

Edward hadn't bought my act. He was still suspicious that I was a Watcher. Hell, maybe he'd even grown doubtful of my abilities, despite Alex covering for me in his reports on my arcana training.

What did a Guardian do if they caught a Watcher? Or someone who they suspected was one? *Then we will take care of her*, Mindara had told

Edward as I listened from the closet. I had no doubts as to what that meant. My arms and legs went numb, but my chest and stomach were filled with leaden weights.

I had to leave. To get the hell out of here, and find somewhere to lay low for a while until I figured out a plan.

Opening drawers at random, I scooped out armfuls of clothes and threw them into the duffel. I'd cleared out half of my room when I slowed.

Maybe this wasn't such a good idea. I had no plan, no place to go, and no money. If I ran now, they would surely catch up with me. I would be like a child, packing my bag after a tantrum and only making it to the end of the driveway.

All of my eggs were in the Aureum's basket, and the basket had been thrown into a dumpster. I'd broken my number one rule: not to rely on anyone but myself.

Sinking to the floor, I clenched my hands to stop the tremors that wanted to wrack my body. I needed to think. I scrubbed my hands through my hair, willing a solution to come to me.

I replayed the conversation with Edward again, and his sham of an apology made my gut burn. The thought of us making small talk was laughable. And when he'd asked about my family? That was—

Genius. Edward had given me a way out.

The Diurne wouldn't deny me a visit to my mom, would they? After all, I was bound to be tied up once training started—from what I'd gathered, novices got breaks few and far between. Once I got to her house, I would find a way to disappear.

A lump appeared in my throat at the thought of leaving Alex. At leaving the rest of the unit behind, as well, but particularly him. His kind heart, his curious mind, and especially his smile. This was more than I had allowed myself to feel in so, so long.

My heart cracked, but I let the pieces fall and shatter. I rose from the floor, straightening my spine. I would do whatever was necessary to survive.

I always had.

20

I bided my time over the next couple of days. I didn't want to appear too eager to leave and set off any alarm bells. No, it was better to take some space and let Edward think I didn't notice that someone had searched my room and taken the tarot card.

Nothing in my routine changed. I still went to the Library and worked on memorizing grimoires, I made frustratingly slow progress with arcana, and spent my afternoons getting beat up in the training room. At least now I could hit near the center of the target when Davina drilled me with throwing knives.

Disentangling myself emotionally from Alex and his unit was proving to be an issue. Part of me wanted to laugh with them, to nurture the budding relationships that had begun to flourish. But the other part of me knew it would hurt that much more when I left.

Worse, they'd picked up on it.

"What's up with you?" Casey asked, eyeing me over her caesar salad. "You're quieter than normal."

We were at dinner while the others were off on their own—punching things, if I had to take a guess. I picked at my veggie burger, tossing bits of bun onto my plate.

"Maybe you're just loud."

"Nope. Well, yes." Casey fished all of the croutons out of her salad and placed them in a pile, scraping lettuce out of the way. "But that's not it."

Damn it. She was more perceptive than I gave her credit for. "I'm just tired. Probably due to my puny human weaknesses."

Casey polished off her pile of croutons and began attacking a plate of chicken tenders. "Well, you're not going to like what I say next."

On high alert, I abandoned my veggie burger. "What?"

"The whole unit is practishing a drill in the shemetery tonight. You hafta come," she said through a mouthful of tenders.

"Everyone's here?"

She swallowed. "Yep. Special occasion. See, you can't say no."

I groaned. "Can I be given an exemption? I'm not part of the unit, anyway."

"It'll be good practice for you. Come on, Seph. Don't make me order you."

She met my glare with a grin.

It was late evening by the time we left the mansion, and the insects had started up their night sounds. Rain spit, dampening my eyelashes, and fog drifted around the trees. The smell of night blooming jasmine tickled my nose, musky with just a hint of sweetness. We'd come to the end of the grove of trees at the back of the property.

Low stone walls bordered the graveyard, enclosing mausoleums that loomed like hulking sentinels. Black walls rendered them almost invisible in the dark, but I was able to mark them by the little white flowers that bloomed at their feet. This was the cemetery we'd landed in after fleeing Gravesville.

"Where is everyone?" I peered around in the dark, but my human eyes weren't able to discern anything. "Casey, I swear, if this is a prank—"

The others filed out from around a mausoleum, and Fern's white teeth shone as she spoke. "Surprise!"

"Gotcha," Casey said, slapping me on the back and knocking me a step forward.

"What surprise?" I asked. Suspicion filled me, and I cast a wary eye over the group. Alex stood in the back, his face masked by the gloom.

"We're showing you a good time," Hollis drawled. "It ain't all work and no play around here. We didn't want you to get the impression that protecting the world from dark creatures is a drag."

"That's right," Sylvan piped up, clapping Hollis on the shoulder. "We're taking you out."

"No one ever forgets their first time out with these fools. For better or worse," Sage sighed.

Hell in a freaking hand basket. "I'm actually pretty tired—"

"Oh, come on, Seph. Don't be a party pooper." Davina swaggered to the head of the group, slinging an arm around my shoulders. I made a concerted effort to relax them. "We all figured you could use some fun. We'll only be gone for a few hours."

"Where exactly are we going?" I asked with trepidation.

"You'll see," Fern answered cryptically. Her hands spread over the air in familiar movements.

I stepped back. "Oh, no. I'd rather not." Especially not after Davina's warning about splicing myself between dimensions.

"It won't hurt you, Seph," Sylvan added. His eyes twinkled.

"That's what you say now," I muttered.

"You've already done it twice before," Alex said. "And it wasn't so bad, was it?"

Had it maimed, bloodied, or terrified me? No, no, and yes. My new litmus test for safety was rather depressing.

At least the outing would give me a few hours away from headquarters. And it might be the last time I would spend with the unit all together before I left for good.

"Okay, fine. But you have to hold my hand."

Hollis winked and linked our hands, raising them above his head like I'd won a prize fight. I was going to miss his goofiness.

Fern continued to rake her fingers through the air, looking for that undefinable snag that would tell her she'd found the correct gateway. "Ah, got it." She pulled her hands apart, revealing a length of midnight silk against the mist. "All right, everyone in the pool."

I moved aside to let the others pass. When everyone had gone through, Hollis squeezed my hand. "Ready?"

Nodding, I took a deep breath. Before I had time to think anything else, he yanked me forward and through.

I was full and empty, hot and cold, frozen and boiling. Then I spilled out not onto the dewy grass I'd expected, but soft, silty sand.

Hollis pulled me upright. The Guardians were silhouetted in the dark alongside swaying palm trees. Just beyond them was the sea, shining in the light of a waning crescent moon. Waves crashed gently on white sand, and the unmistakable smell of saltwater carried on a light breeze that cut through the wet heat.

"Where are we?" I asked, awed.

"Welcome to Gold Cay," Davina said. "The Aureum's own private island."

"You have a *private island*?"

"This is one of them," Alex said. "It's our own paradise, out of the way of human eyes."

I spun in a slow circle. To the left and right were unbroken sand and water, and behind me was a well-worn path through scrubby vegetation. Lights twinkled beyond the wall of tangled green leaves and twisted bark, signaling some sign of habitation.

Hollow sadness filled my stomach. "I don't know what to say."

Sage gave their tinkling bells laugh. "Come on, Seph. We'll show you around." They threw their arm around my waist, leading me down the path toward lights in the distance. Simple grave markers were scattered around either side of the path, the pale shadow of them like ghosts.

"Gold Cay was a pirate stronghold in the seventeenth century. There have always been Guardians here, but the island came into our possession about a hundred and fifty years ago. Some make their homes here permanently. And, it just so happens that Gold Cay isn't plottable on a map or visible to anyone except those brought directly through a gateway," Sage explained as we walked.

We approached a low slung building of whitewashed stucco with wide, open windows that captured the cross breeze. Music with thumping bass pumped out of them into the humid heat. Broad-leafed tropical plants crowded against the outer walls as if they were trying to get inside, and brightly colored planters held blooms of fuschia and vermillion that speared into the air.

Other Guardians on holiday, or perhaps just partying for the night like us, crowded the interior. Dark wood contrasted with the same white washed walls from outside. A teak bar spanned the room, dominating the space. Behind the bar were shelves mounted all the way to the ceiling filled with hundreds of glinting glass bottles.

"Eames!" a voice called from the crowd. A woman with dark hair cut into a razor sharp wedge greeted us. Her breezy blue dress fit exactly with the island theme.

Alex stooped to give the woman a brief hug, looking at her with genuine pleasure. "Hey, Laila."

"So this must be the famous Persephone, eh?" Laila asked, making no secret of giving me the once over.

"The one and only," Casey said, elbowing her.

Laila laughed, bold and unapologetic. She held out her hand. "Pleasure to meet you."

"Same," I managed to get out. "And, it's just Seph."

"Right," she answered, giving me a wink. Then, she addressed Alex. "So, this is what it takes to get you to come back to my bar?"

"Laila, you know I'd never leave if I didn't have to."

Never leave? I stopped my eyes from narrowing, but I couldn't prevent the curl of jealousy in my stomach.

"What can I do to make it up to you?" Alex asked, all quiet charm.

She looked at him speculatively for a moment, then laughed again. "You can spend your money. *Lots* of money."

"Done."

Drinks flowed, music played, and laughter swirled around the room. The scene could have been from any bar anywhere in the world, except for the people in it. The Guardians took no lengths to hide their supernatural qualities here. Power spilled from them like the liquor Laila poured, and they appeared to almost glow under the dim lighting. It was hypnotic, mesmerizing, and I wanted to gulp it down in one swallow.

Except that I couldn't, because within a matter of days I would be gone.

I tried to play the part, debating literature with Sylvan, while Fern and Hollis danced around the room. He more than made up for his lack of rhythm with enthusiasm.

The others played a drinking game the likes of which I'd never seen before, as it involved levitating beer and pouring it into a partner's waiting mouth without spilling a drop. Their shirts became more beer soaked the longer the game went on.

Someone tapped me on the shoulder when I went to the bar for another round. It was Yuto, the novice who'd covered for me with Davina in the Library. He had a coy smile waiting for me.

"Hi," he said, extending a hand. "I don't think we've formally met. I'm Yuto."

I set my drink down on the wooden ledge of the bar carefully, given the tequila shot I'd taken with Sage and Sylvan ten minutes ago. "Seph." His grip was light and friendly, and was it my imagination that his hand lingered in mine longer than necessary?

"So, how's your private tutoring going? I have to say, the other novices are anxious for you to join us."

"Are they?" I picked up my beer and took a pull. The cold glass sweated in my hand, a respite from the heat. "I can't imagine why."

His grin turned lazy as he circled a finger. "You've got that air of mystery going for you."

I didn't know what to say, so I busied myself with taking another sip. Somewhere in the back of my mind, a little voice warned me to slow down.

"But, I don't think you're a mystery. I've figured you out."

A warning shiver ran down my arms, despite the crush of bodies around us. "Oh?"

"You've got Eames wrapped around your finger. The rest of them, too." He leaned against the bar. "I can't blame them. From what I've heard, everyone likes you."

"You don't know me." The words came out colder than I'd intended, but that didn't deter Yuto. In fact, his smile grew sharper.

"But I'd like to." He traced a finger down the back of my arm, watching my reaction.

Keeping my gaze steady on his, I took a step back. "I don't think so."

"Oh, don't be like that." He leaned in to whisper in my ear. "You wouldn't want me to tell everyone your secret, would you?"

This time, I couldn't help but show the alarm that coursed through me. My eyes widened, taking in his smug expression. "What secret?"

"Why don't we get another drink, and we can discuss it?"

I was saved from having to answer when Alex appeared beside me. I didn't have to look to know it was him. I smelled cedar, and felt a tug in the center of my chest, drawing me toward him.

"Kimura," Alex said evenly.

"Eames," Yuto replied. His mouth flattened.

"Enjoying yourself?" Alex sipped his beer, flicking his eyes away like he was already bored with the conversation.

"I was," he answered. "Seph and I were in the middle of something." He looked at me lasciviously, as if I was in on his little game.

"That was just ending," I replied. I pressed an elbow into Alex's side in a silent plea. He put a casual arm around my shoulders, his weight comforting.

Yuto gave me a long look, his pique palpable. "I'm sure we'll talk again soon."

Without answer, Alex steered us away from the bar and out through the main doors.

"Thanks," I exhaled. "He—"

Alex held a finger to his lips, then motioned me away down another sandy path that was lined with low bushes. We finally halted after several minutes.

"Supernatural hearing," he explained. "This is far enough."

"Right." The humidity made my hair curl wildly, and I tucked a wayward lock behind my ear.

"What did Yuto want?" Alex looked guarded, his eyes hooded and mouth drawn.

Waves crashed on the shoreline on the other side of the dunes as I warred with myself. Even though I trusted Alex, there was still a part of me that wanted to keep my mouth shut and make myself small.

"Seph, what is it?" Alex's voice caressed me like a soft breeze. "I see your gears turning." I looked askance at him. "You get this little line right here," he said, touching the space between his brows.

Oh, this would hurt in the morning. But what was another twist of the knife to an already open wound?

"Yuto threatened me." I was barely able to hear my own voice over the booming surf. "He said that he'd tell everyone my secret."

The silence between us turned heavy with fury.

"What?" Alex's voice was unnervingly soft.

"I don't know what he meant by it. But I think he was watching me in the Library the other day when I asked her about the Watchers. And...." I looked up at the star-studded sky, breathing in the salty sea air.

"Seph." Alex placed a hand on my shoulder, the gentlest touch. "You can trust me."

"I know," I whispered. Swallowing, I continued. "Someone searched my room the other day. They took something."

He didn't ask me how I knew, or if I was sure. "What did they take?"

"A card. It was tarot—I found it in the cemetery. The night you first felt me."

Alex's face was drawn, hard. "I don't know what's going on, but we will figure this out," he promised. "I won't leave until we get to the bottom of it."

My throat ached, but I swallowed it down. "That's not your choice."

He bowed his head, and I wondered if he was feeling the weight of the Diurne Council, of his loyalty to the Aureum. Of his legacy that was both promise and burden.

"Alex, I need to go home."

His head snapped up. "Why?"

"Not for good," I lied, digging my nails into my palm. "I haven't seen my mom in a long time. I need to make excuses, wrap up loose ends. I wasn't able to do any of that before I left."

"And you want to go now?" Was that a hint of suspicion?

"It's perfect timing," I said quickly. "I can ask about my dad, see if my mom can share anything that might help lead to him." That, at least, wasn't a lie. I was intending to demand answers from my mom—she owed me after a lifetime of silence.

"I can ask the Diurne for permission," he said, running a hand through his hair. It had grown out, the curl more pronounced now than when we'd first met. "It might go better coming from me."

"Thank you."

Alex took a step toward me, his gaze intent. "Seph," he started, but was interrupted by a whooping holler and a scream.

Hollis blew past us, followed by the rest of Alex's unit, yelling about moving the party to the beach.

I felt a tug on my hand, then someone was pulling me along toward the ocean like demons were on our heels. Music and laughter streamed into the air, a bright spot on the sober turn the evening had taken.

If it was indeed my last night with the unit, I would surrender to their exhilaration and take joy where I could.

Things got somewhat blurry after the mad dash to the beach. Someone started a bonfire out of thin air, then a handle of bourbon was passed around. Everyone took a turn slugging from the bottleneck, Hollis in particular taking an extra long pull and smacking his lips appreciatively. In the light of the dancing flames, the Guardians looked like young gods who had come down from Mount Olympus to fraternize with mortals.

They regaled me with tales of their own novice days, of mishaps and triumphs and first kills. That last part I wasn't so keen on.

"So, you've all been together since you were novices?" I asked, taking another ill-advised pull from the bourbon.

"No," Fern said, shaking out her braids. "I'm from the Mid-Atlantic region, Casey is from the Midwest, and the twins are from the PNW."

"You know I'm from Texas. Everything's bigger," Hollis slurred. Fern pushed him over, and he landed in the sand with a heavy thud.

"And Alex and I are from the Southeast. The best!" Davina declared, throwing her arm around Alex and laughing.

Hollis made a raspberry sound with his mouth, having pulled himself back into a sitting position. "Too much talkin' and not enough swimmin'."

I imagined it was the bourbon that thickened his accent until it dripped like honey. He ran toward the water, pulling his clothes off so they dropped like a breadcrumb trail, until he was only clad in boxers.

While I fully expected him to be laughed off, the Guardians followed suit and began to shed their clothes as well, then dove into the water, sleeker than seals. I stood on the beach, open-mouthed in shock, while they crashed around like children in nothing but their underwear. There wasn't a hint of self-consciousness in the way they moved, untroubled and so sure of themselves.

Alex was the last to follow, throwing me a glance before he pulled his shirt over his head and tossed it to the sand. He had a trimly muscled frame, with a dusting of hair scattered across his chest. It started again below his navel, leading downward, framed by taut abdominals.

Then he plunged into the dark water, cutting through the waves like he was a dolphin instead of a man.

The Guardians called out, shouting for me to join them. I shook my head, content to watch, until Hollis charged out of the water like a rambunctious golden retriever, threw me over his shoulder, and tossed me in, kicking and screaming.

"You motherfucker!" I spluttered, laughing. I splashed him, and he bobbed under the surface.

The water was warm, coating my lips in brine and making my eyes smart. I ducked under, holding my breath and striking out from the shore until my muscles burned. It was quiet underwater, the lack of sound more unnerving than the chatter of human voices for once. I broke the surface and drew in a deep lungful of air to find Fern beside me.

"This is nice, isn't it?" she said, swimming lazy circles around me.

"Very nice."

"Can I tell ya somethin'?" she asked, her words slurring. "A secret."

"Uh-huh," I answered. Treading water was more difficult after the bourbon, beer, and tequila.

"I wanted to change the world." Her eyes lost their tipsy glaze for a moment, focusing on me. "To help people."

"Aren't you doing that already?" I asked.

"Yeah," she said, dipping her chin into the water. "I fight evil bastards, so...s'not so bad."

"No...I guess not."

Apart from Fern's sudden angst, they all looked so carefree. Davina frolicked like a mermaid around Alex and Hollis, her long hair fanned around her like seaweed. Casey created a little water tornado that she sent racing toward Sage. Sylvan bobbed on his back, staring up at the stars.

I turned back to Fern. "Hey, are you all right?"

She held a finger to her lips. "Watch this." She disappeared under the water, and a moment later Casey gave a blood-curdling shriek.

"Damn it to all of the *hells*, Fern!" A chorus of laughter sounded, and after a moment Casey joined in.

I realized I could pick out all of their individual sounds in the cacophony, like music notes in a song. They were each unique, but formed a beautiful harmony together.

And then there was me. I floated on my back, looking up at the crescent moon, wishing more than anything that I could be one of them.

21

———

Rain poured from the heavens, spilling down the neck of my shirt. The wet material clung to me as I dashed back to the car from the gas station, cutting across the path of the headlights. Panting, I deposited an assortment of sweets into the center console.

"That's a lot of candy. For breakfast," Alex observed, turning on the windshield wipers as he pulled out of the lot.

"I don't know what you like, so I got a few." Selecting a Twix, I peeled back the wrapper and took a bite. Sweet chocolate and gooey caramel melted in my mouth, and I hummed in satisfaction. "Damn, that's good."

Alex blindly grabbed a pack of M&M's and tore the wrapper open with his teeth, spitting out the paper and pouring a few candies into his mouth. "Cars are so slow," he complained, crunching. "Especially when it's raining. Humans completely forget how to drive."

I had to agree. Although the Diurne approved the request to visit my mother, they'd ordered us to keep a low profile. Which meant we were traveling by car and forbidden from using magic except for emergencies.

If they thought the length of the drive would deter me from leaving, they were dead wrong. So, we were on a road trip from New Orleans to my mom's house in central Virginia. It would take us fifteen hours and three minutes, and we hadn't quite made it through the first hour yet.

The argument I'd prepared for traveling alone had died on my lips when the Diurne decided Alex would accompany me. I still had a chaperone, even now. And would have to spend the next fourteen-ish hours plotting a way to throw him off my trail.

I ignored the dull ache around my ribs that throbbed whenever my mind strayed to the idea of leaving.

Alex fiddled with the radio of the Audi. Smooth voices with non-regional diction flowed out of the speakers.

"NPR? Are you trying to fall asleep at the wheel?" I turned the dial, landing on an indie rock station.

"I like to be informed about current events," he said, but his voice held a teasing edge. "So, you haven't said much about your mom."

"There's not much to say," I answered.

My mom and I had a tenuous relationship at best. After she'd met her new husband, she snapped out of her depressive state. I never wanted for anything after they got married—food was always on the table, and I had a healthy allowance. But she could never make up for the years when she hadn't been up to the task of mothering. When my younger half-sister had been born, I'd stepped out of the family fold even further, letting my mom focus her attention on the baby. It was better for everyone that way.

Alex nodded. He, of all people, understood my silence. "It'll be worth it, if she can give you answers about your dad."

"I guess so."

Dredging up long forgotten memories of my father would certainly cause my mom pain. She was always so careful to avoid all mention of him. He was less than a ghost in our lives, because even that would require some kind of pale imprint, a trace left behind. My mother had scrubbed away the memory of him as efficiently as the houses she used to clean for a living.

Alex let the subject drop. "You know, I never asked what your life was like. Before the Aureum."

"There's not much to say about that, either."

The sound of tires on wet pavement *shhhd* under the faint music of

The Strokes' *Reptilia*. "I want to know you, Seph." He sounded almost shy.

"You do know me. We've been together almost nonstop for the past couple of months." Except for those weeks when Alex went to Gravesville, and I missed him horribly.

"We've got…" he checked the GPS. "Thirteen and a half hours to do nothing but be stuck in this car. Might as well make a little conversation."

"What about you?" I asked, desperate to take the focus off me. "If you didn't have to kick demon ass, what would you do instead?"

He chuckled humorlessly. "No one's ever asked."

"Well, I'm asking."

"If I could do anything?"

"Sky's the limit."

He reached for a KitKat, crunching into it. "I'd study."

"Study what?"

"Everything." His eyes brightened at that, a faint smile curving his lips.

I believed him, that this dangerous man only ever wanted to use his curious mind. "You should."

The corner of his mouth pulled down briefly, flashing his dimple. "You know that's impossible."

"Nothing's impossible! Look at me. A few months ago, I was one of the most boring people alive. And now I'm some kind of multiracial magical being destined to—" I clamped my lips together. I'd almost said, *destined to save the worlds.* "To some kind of ineptitude, because I can't make my power work. You know, I was reading in the *Grimoire of Armadel* about summoning demons for—"

"Hold on. One, you're not inept. We just haven't figured out exactly how your arcana works yet. And two, did Fern not talk to you about summoning?"

"Should she have?" Not only did grimoires identify the names of demons and list their attributes and weaknesses, they also told the reader how to summon and bind the spirits listed amongst their pages.

"Gods and angels. I can't believe I didn't mention it. It's just that—"

"Training novices isn't your normal job. I know."

Alex inclined his head in acknowledgement, eyes glued to the road. "Guardians never, ever summon. Summoning is dark magic, only used by people who want to gain power by making deals with demons."

"This seems like it would have been important for me to know."

"It is." His jaw went taut. I was sure that Alex was mentally castigating himself for the oversight. "The Aureum's goal is to rid this world of demons, not invite them in. Most of the people who wrote these grimoires were humans who stumbled upon the occult. We had our hands full trying to prevent them from summoning. Then, we had to get rid of whatever they had managed to bring in before they wreaked havoc."

"Okay, no summoning the hell-beasts. Got it."

I fell asleep somewhere in the middle of Georgia, lulled by the rain. But it was clear again by the time I woke, with bright, sunny skies pouring through the car window. My face was squished against my hand, cradled against my headrest. I wiped gummy drool surreptitiously from my chin.

"Where are we?"

"Just crossed over into Virginia. We should be at your mom's in about three hours."

I had slept hard, dreamless, and, apparently, for hours. "Sorry," I yawned, stretching like a cat. "I don't usually sleep in the car." I rolled the window down, letting the cold air wake me up.

"And you said NPR was boring." The radio twanged out some kind of country melody. I winced and changed it, landing on an eighties station. I was delighted when Alex began to sing along to *Higher Love*.

"Wow." I gave a slow clap when he finished. "That was incredible. But a little pitchy."

"The eighties was the best decade for music. That's the hill I'll die on." Cranking the volume to full blast, Alex looked over at me and arched a brow as he started on *Sweet Child O' Mine*. We sang together in a horrific duet, laughing so hard we lost our breath.

We talked about everything under the sun—our likes and dislikes, books, music, politics—and as we reached the Redfield county line I wished we could turn around and drive back to New Orleans. Just so that I could have another fifteen uninterrupted hours with him, the world reduced to just the two of us in our happy little bubble.

My mom and stepfather lived in a cookie-cutter development on the north side of town. It wasn't my childhood home, but where they'd moved after I left for college, while my sister Claire was still in middle school. The rows upon rows of identical houses, with everything managed by the HOA down to the height of their bushes, always made me feel like I was in an alternate reality.

"This is...nice," Alex commented, as we passed yet another McMansion on a postage-stamp yard.

"That's an interesting way to say soul-sucking." I stared out the windows. Anxiety was a long rope coiling in my stomach.

We crawled down blandly named streets at a snail's pace. "Turn left at the end of Maple Court, then it's on your right," I instructed. The car slowed as we approached my mom's house. I sat unmoving, looking at the plastic evergreen wreath that graced the farmhouse style front door.

Alex turned to me. "Are you ready?" His eyes were the dark green of leaves in late summer, and I saw myself reflected in them. I appeared completely normal, not at all like a wayward child full of lies and secrets, coming to interrogate her mother before disappearing into the darkness.

"Not even a little bit. But I have to do it anyway."

Alex took my hand and squeezed gently. "Families are hard."

I leaned my head back against the seat. "This sucks."

"It does, but I'm here for you. Should we come up with a code word in case you need me to step in?"

"What, like code red?"

"Maybe something more subtle, like.... Twizzlers." He held the empty wrapper aloft, and the scent of fake strawberry wafted over to me.

My heart gave a painful throb. "Twizzlers it is."

"Excellent. And you remember the cover story?"

I nodded. Alex was posing as my boyfriend, new enough that it wasn't strange I hadn't told anyone about him yet, but old enough that we were beginning to make introductions. It hadn't been my idea.

"Let's go, then."

We walked to the wide front porch. I let the silver knocker fall three times. After several long moments, the door swung wide, revealing my mother. Her expression changed from polite curiosity to shocked surprise.

"Seph?"

"Hi, mom."

"Oh, sweetheart!" she gasped, reaching out and pulling me through the doorway into a bone-crushing hug. "What a surprise!"

My face was buried in the silk of her tastefully highlighted blond hair, so I couldn't answer. Our relationship may not have been the easiest, but I knew my mom loved me. We wanted to understand each other, but were so different that it was difficult to bridge the divide between us.

"Hi, Mrs. Tedford," Alex said, stepping forward and extending his hand smoothly. "It's nice to meet you. Sorry to spring this on you, but Seph wanted it to be a surprise. I'm Alex, Seph's boyfriend."

In a move worthy of Houdini, he extricated me from her embrace, replaced her bereft hands with his own in a firm handshake, then wrapped his free arm around my shoulders and pulled me to his side. I snaked my arm around his waist, hoping we were convincing enough. Lisa Tedford had the keen eyes of a hawk, and the instincts of a hunting dog on a scent trail. I added a too-bright smile for good measure.

"We were, um, passing through," I said. "We're going to DC to visit Alex's family and he wanted to meet you."

My mom blinked her round blue eyes slowly. She looked from Alex to me, eyes widening. "You two are...together?"

"Yes," Alex said, his grip tightening around my shoulders.

"Well, please excuse my manners and come inside. It's a pleasure to meet you, Alex."

She led us from the wide foyer down the hall to the open plan kitchen and living room. White and beige dominated, with pops of winter decor, like little trees covered in fake glittery snow. Very *Southern Living*.

"Alex, you make yourself comfortable. Seph, a little help in the kitchen, please? We'll just be a minute." Her eyes were overbright and moving fast toward madness. I braced myself for the interrogation. Alex sent me a grimace, then made a swift exit to the couch. Coward.

"Seph, I didn't even know you had a boyfriend," my mom said in a hushed voice, as she pulled plates and cookies out of cabinets with frenetic energy. "You couldn't have given me even a little notice? Make some coffee," she snapped, pointing to the machine.

Oh, hell. It was going to be worse than I'd anticipated—and I'd anticipated her reaction to be just shy of nuclear.

"Sorry, mom," I mumbled, grinding the coffee beans for longer than strictly necessary. "I just thought it would be nice that I was bringing someone home."

My mom stopped mid-charcuterie assemblage and turned to me. Wait, when did she have time to cut three types of cheese? The woman was unstoppable, I thought, not without a little fear.

"Oh, Seph," she said, pulling me into another suffocating hug. "I don't mean to act like this. I'm thrilled, of course, just a little taken off guard. I feel like I've barely heard from you over the past few months, and then you show up here out of the blue. Everything's all right, isn't it?" She blinked guilelessly.

Things were the furthest from all right they'd ever been. But she always wanted everything to be okay, everyone to be happy—I didn't think she could handle the truth. No, I knew she couldn't.

I looked straight into my mom's faded denim eyes and gave the most genuine smile I could. "Yes, everything's fine."

My mom scanned me, gnawing on her lip. For a second, I thought she'd point out the lie and ask me what was really going on. Instead, she squeezed my hand and returned my smile. "Good, honey. That's good. Now, let's go and bring this to that handsome boyfriend of yours."

We made small talk, sipped coffee, and ate cheese and crackers. Alex lied through his teeth very effectively, all soft charm. He had a younger sister in grad school at Northwestern, studying social policy. His parents were from DC, his mother a doctor and his father a business owner. He was raised there, then went to NC State for college and studied criminology. He'd landed in the Gravesville police department afterward, and hadn't looked back since. I noted that in the fictional version of his life, his parents were still together.

My mother made all the appropriate noises, expressing her pleasure at the upstanding young man I'd brought home. "How did you two meet?" she asked, fiddling with the tray that didn't need to be straightened.

We'd come up with a story for this, as well. I was about to tell her that we'd met on a dating app, the simplest explanation, when Alex cut in.

"I was on the job." He gave a quiet smile. "I went into Whitlock and Williams looking to question someone, and met Seph. She seemed so annoyed that I interrupted her. You should've seen her glare," he said to my mom conspiratorially. "But...she was so beautiful. I couldn't take my eyes off her." He was looking at me, and I took a hasty gulp from my mug to cover my flushed face. "The rest is history, as you can see. It was fate, I think, that brought us together."

I choked on my coffee while my mom gushed and made cooing sounds. Did he really think it was fate, or was it another convincing lie?

"That is so incredibly sweet," my mom smiled, wagging a finger. "I have a good feeling about you two."

"Me, too," Alex said, laying a hand on mine and squeezing.

Part of me wanted desperately to believe him. In a parallel universe, where he was actually the NC State grad, where he was my real life boyfriend instead of this utter farce, we could be happy together, live a normal life. We'd get engaged after an appropriate length of time, have a big, fussy wedding with his mom the doctor and dad the businessman in attendance, then buy a house and have two kids and a golden retriever.

But, another part of me chimed in that if that were the case, there would be no Fern, no Hollis, no Davina, or anyone else. There would be no magic, no wonder, no mystery, and the world would be that much emptier because of it. My reality had become painful and messy, everything I'd always tried to avoid. And yet—even though I was running from one of the only good things to ever happen to me, I was glad that it had happened at all.

It was at this moment, when Alex had lulled my mom with adorable meet-cutes, that he pounced. "Seph hasn't told me much about her father," he said.

The temperature in the room dropped twenty degrees. My mom froze, her mug halfway to her lips. She looked at me, eyes widening. I shrugged, giving her a *you're on your own, kid,* look.

"I...we...." She cleared her throat. "Her father and I split up when Seph was very young. There's not much to say."

"That's what Seph told me," he said, nodding in agreement. My mom's shoulders lowered a fraction of an inch. "But, selfishly, I just want to know a little bit about the man who helped produce such an incredible woman. She really is one of a kind, isn't she?" He sent me another look, this time with some mild heat behind it. I fought dual urges to both throw myself into his arms and send a swift elbow to his ribs.

My mother gawked. She was trapped by good manners, hoisted by her own petard. "Well, when you put it that way," she managed. "I don't have much to say. But there is a box in the basement with a few things that you could look through, some items that he...left." She swallowed audibly. "I thought...that Seph might want them one day."

My jaw must not have actually hit the floor, because my mom and Alex were still acting normally. "You did?" I had no idea that my mother had been toting around a box of his things for the past twenty-six years. I'd always been too afraid to ask, but to think she'd had his stuff all along and never even mentioned it? Angry heat suffused my cheeks.

My mom twisted her wedding ring. "Well, I didn't know what else to do with them, Seph. Alex is right, you ought to know a few things about your dad."

Except that she'd done her damndest to pretend I'd been born from immaculate conception and there hadn't been a father to begin with. But of course, if *Alex* wanted to know, then she would give it up.

"Well, Scott should be home from the club soon," she said, foregoing subtlety in changing the subject. "Please tell me you'll stay. I'm making chicken and dumplings for dinner, your favorite."

"I—I'm not sure. Alex's parents are expecting us," I managed to grind out.

"They'll understand if we stay for a night—or two," Alex asserted. He rested a hand on my upper back, massaging my rigid muscles with his thumb.

Shaking my head, I got up and walked to the basement, avoiding my mom's apprehensive gaze.

22

———

"I can't believe she kept his stuff." I switched on the bare lightbulb in the unfinished part of the basement that was used for storage. The floors were bare concrete and the air was musty with the scent of neglect.

It was the only place in the house that wasn't organized to within an inch of its life. Dusty boxes were stacked on metal shelves and spread all over the floor with no sense of order. It was a perfect representation of my mom's preferred method of dealing with problems—out of sight, out of mind.

"People hold on to things, even if they hurt them. He may have left, but he's still the father of her child."

I scoffed. "He literally left her a note saying not to go looking for him." Despite my mom's absolute repudiation of my father—or maybe because of it—I was eager to see what he'd left behind.

We sifted through the mess, coming across long-forgotten treasures amidst the junk. Photos of me as a toddler, chubby cheeked and curly haired. A trophy for reading the most books out of the whole school during my fifth grade year. The only award I'd ever won, whereas we came upon two boxes of Claire's gymnastics trophies.

"Hey, I think I found it," Alex called from across the room.

He held a shoebox, the lid already removed. As soon as he set it down on an old patio table, I hurried over and peered inside. I wasn't sure what I expected, but I supposed it would've been too easy for it to contain documentation of my dad's whole life story and family tree.

The box was almost bare, holding only three items. I pulled them out one by one and laid them on the table.

The first, a thick envelope, yellowed with age and creased to softness. The second, a delicate silver ring braided with vines and leaves that looked so realistic, it was hard not to believe I wasn't touching a living thing. The third was a black and white photograph, unframed.

The photograph had been the clue that this was the box we were searching for. It showed four people, arms linked around each other like they were old friends.

I picked out my father immediately. The resemblance between us was undeniable, and the breath caught in my chest as I looked into an almost exact copy of my own eyes. My father's hair curled around his angular face, and apparently I inherited my height from him, too. He was at least a head taller than the rest of the group.

"Here, sit down." Alex's voice was full of authority. "You're white as a sheet." He shoved the chair underneath me, and I fell into it heavily, my bones turning to liquid. Because it wasn't just my dad staring back at me, smiling a wide smile. Evangeline was there, too, her head thrown back in laughter.

She looked much younger in the photo than she did now, her hair dark instead of white, and the crow's feet and lines around her mouth were traced lightly instead of etched. I wondered if grief had done that. She had one arm wrapped around my father, and on the other side of her was, I assumed, her husband. He held her waist with loving ease, in the way of couples that have been together for a long time. Uriel, she'd said his name was. The man had a close-lipped smile, but his eyes were full of mirth.

The fourth person in the photo stood on my dad's other side. He wore a mischievous smile, like he'd been the one to tell the joke that had everyone laughing. His hair curled to his shoulders a little wildly, and he wore a hoop in his right ear, lending him a piratical air.

The group stood in front of an old-fashioned storefront, like something from the early twentieth century.

I was stunned. Evangeline had said she'd been close with my father. Now, I held the proof in my hands.

Alex leaned in closer, gripping my shoulder as if he thought I'd fall out of the chair. He pointed at Evangeline. "I didn't recognize her before, but that's your neighbor, isn't it?"

I licked my lips, trying to wet them, but my mouth had gone dry. "Yes, it's her. She was telling the truth."

"So it seems," Alex murmured. "Do you recognize anyone else?"

"I think this is her husband," I said, pointing to the man on Evangeline's other side. "I'm not sure who the other guy is."

"How about these?" He gestured to the ring and the envelope. "Any sense of what they are?"

"There's only one way to find out." I reluctantly put down the photograph and emptied the yellowed envelope. A thick wad of folded pages fell out. I picked one at random and started to read.

Dear Ezekial,

Congratulations! What exciting news about the baby. And expected on the solstice, no less! There is no doubt that your daughter will be powerful— I'm sure you all will have your hands full. Please share our well wishes with Lisa. You are greatly missed, but we know that you have built the life you've dreamed of, with the woman you love, and now have a child on the way. It's what you always wanted.

We do not mean to disrupt this joyous time, but would feel remiss not mentioning Lucas. He has been unlike himself these past few weeks, taking foolish chances and making mistakes. Just yesterday, he was perilously close to being followed back after crossing over from the other side. Do not fear, the seam is still hidden from the Golden Ones, but his actions put us all at risk. Will you appeal to him on our behalf? He listens to you far more than his old school teachers.

With all of our love,
* Evangeline and Uriel*

. . .

Numbness settled into my face, and thoughts flashed through my head, so quickly that I barely grasped one before another took its place. Alex knelt down beside me, worry creasing his forehead. "Seph?" he asked gently.

"They're letters. Alex, I think something happened to my dad. And it has to do with the Aureum."

"What? Why?"

I showed him the letter, pointing out the phrase *Golden Ones*. "That has to be a reference to the Aureum, don't you think?" Aurum was gold in Latin.

"Maybe," he said, standing as his eyes flicked over the rest of the letter. He frowned. "Well, now we know for certain that your father was —is, a supernatural."

My world shifted yet again, and I was struggling to make sense of it. I finally had details about my father's life. He had family, friends, a home he'd left behind. *We know that you have built the life you've dreamed of.* What if my father hadn't abandoned us? What if something happened to him, and he was taken away, or forced to leave? What if the anger and hurt I'd carried around my whole life like an invisible wound wasn't justified?

"Why has your mother never told you about this before?"

"I'm sure she hasn't read the letters." Out of sight, out of mind. It hit me that maybe she couldn't bear to look at the daughter who so resembled the man who hurt her.

"And you don't think he ever told her what he was?"

"He must have kept that part of himself hidden." Secrets, so many secrets. "My mom is...normal. Very, very normal. Maybe he was afraid of telling her—afraid she'd leave him."

"There might be more clues in the rest of these," Alex said, gesturing to the pile of letters on the table. "We need to go through them." But he looked to me, waiting for my assent. I nodded slowly. Desire to devour the letters on the spot warred with the part of me that'd put up an iron barricade around my dad's memory.

"Seph, Alex! Dinner's on!" my mom called down the stairs. For a few minutes, I'd forgotten where we were.

"Coming!" I yelled back. Like I really was a teenager again. I blew a deep breath out of my lips. "Alex?"

"Yeah?"

"Twizzlers."

He reached out to help me stand, his sure grip on my elbow. Holding on. "Got it."

———

Dinner was a thoroughly awkward affair. Claire blatantly stared at Alex throughout the whole meal, her fork missing her mouth several times. Alex kept up a stream of conversation with my mom, while my stepfather, Scott, shoved food into his mouth as fast as possible before retiring to his office—most likely to drink whiskey in silence. He was as different from my dad as could be, in looks, at least. Everything about him was a mousy, colorless beige, while my dad had practically leapt out of the photograph, despite it being black and white.

My thoughts swirled. I was facing a devil at the crossroads. Part of me wanted to stay in the center of it forever, to remain frozen in inaction and not make any choices. But if I did that, then I'd be at the mercy of whichever lurking beast came for me first.

"Seph, honey?"

"What?" I snapped, looking up from my almost untouched food.

My mom flinched as if I'd struck her. "I...I was going to ask about this business program Alex was telling me about. It sounds like a very smart choice." She nodded and smiled, praising me for my pragmatism. That was how it had always been—do the smart thing, even if it had nothing to do with what I actually wanted.

Well, I was tired of doing the smart thing—of pretending that things were okay, of living like a ghost, afraid to leave a trace of myself on anyone or anything.

"Yes," I said, stabbing a dumpling, the fork scraping along the bottom of the bowl. "It'll keep me busy. And I won't be able to visit often—flights are expensive." I shoved the dumpling into my mouth and choked it down.

Her smile faltered. "Of course. I understand."

"Thanks for dinner. I'm heading up." I stood abruptly, and even Claire tore her gaze away from Alex to look at me through narrowed eyes. She was my mother's clone, with her blue eyes and blond hair, and indifference to anything that inconvenienced her.

"It's only eight o'clock," Claire said, probably disgusted that her older sister was so lame.

My mother stood. "Sweetie, your sister is tired. She's had a long drive. I'll put the linens out in the spare room for you all."

"Um—" I blinked at Alex. He looked back, raising his scarred brow. I realized the downside of posing as a couple was that we had to *act* like a couple. Which included sharing a room. We hadn't intended on staying the night here when we came up with the plan. However, with the emotional rollercoaster I'd been riding, I just wanted to lie down and fall into oblivious slumber.

"Right. I know where you keep everything." I left the formal dining room, walking upstairs and turning right at the landing.

Since I'd never lived full time in the house, whenever I visited I slept in the guest room. The walls were nondescript eggshell, with a few bland watercolor landscapes hung on them.

I turned as the door clicked open and Alex appeared, holding a stack of towels and some chocolate mint candies that hotels used during turn-down service. "From your mom," he said, depositing them on the bed.

The fact that she was treating me as an actual guest after how I'd acted at dinner shouldn't have hurt, but it did. "She likes you. I think she'd try to marry you herself if she wasn't with Scott."

Alex sighed. "I doubt that. Although I get your feelings about him. I'm surprised that someone like your mom is with...him."

"She feels safe with Scott. He has enough money to provide for her, and is boring enough that he's not going to take off."

"There's comfort in predictability," he said.

"Oh, I know." It's just that lately, I'd developed a taste for something else.

My eyelids were heavy, and my whole body ached from the long drive. But my muscles went taut as Alex stepped away from the door, closing it softly behind him. Oh, right. We were supposed to be sharing a room. All night. Just the two of us, in a ten by ten space that felt tighter than a broom closet.

"I can find somewhere else to sleep tonight. If I leave out the window, your mom will never know the difference in the morning," he said, gripping the back of his neck. His bicep flexed under his long sleeves. I stared fixedly at the window.

If I was smart, I would have said yes. With Alex gone, I could sneak away in the middle of the night and be out of state before sunrise. He wouldn't feel me for hours if I left when he was asleep, giving me the head start I needed. I was certain I could figure out a way to dull the tie between us. Somehow.

But selfishly, I wanted him to stay. I just couldn't bring myself to do the smart thing.

"No, that's okay. It's just one night." I turned my back to him, busying myself by rifling through my dad's letters. "I'm going to look through these, see what I can find."

Alex walked over, taking the envelope and setting it on a dresser so new it could have been straight out of the box.

"Hey—"

"The letters can wait until morning. They're not going anywhere. And you need rest. You look dead on your feet."

"Just what every person wants to hear," I mumbled, pushing my hair out of my face. My scalp was greasy, and I needed a shower.

"That's not what I meant," Alex murmured.

I looked up at him. He looked back, and there was nothing chaste in the way his eyes skimmed over my mouth. If I leaned just an inch closer, our lips would align. I swallowed. It was the graveyard all over again, except now I knew the taste of him, knew the feel of his hard body beneath my fingers. A shiver ran down my spine, but I was hot, like my core was molten and sending out licks of flame into my belly.

I might have been burning alive from the inside out. My lips parted, and his eyes turned almost black, his pupils dilating. Alex seemed to be fighting some internal battle, and I was rooting for his common sense to lose. I had already made my choice.

Then he took a step backward, putting about a foot more space between us than a regular person's stride. Disappointment and frustration doused the fire inside me.

"I'm going back down for a bit. I need to call the unit, check in." He walked to the window and locked it. "I'll grab a blanket and sleep on the floor tonight." Then he left without looking back.

My wanting had been so fierce that I thought I might spontaneously combust. But, Alex stepped back. He'd made clear that what was between us was impossible. Sure, his control slipped, but it had been a long day for both of us. I would take a long, hot—or cold—shower, and go to sleep.

Hair wet, I pulled on a t-shirt and got in bed. I plumped my pillow aggressively, punctuating each punch with a sharp exhale. There was a smell of singed fabric, and a tiny burn appeared in the white cotton.

"Shit!" Dropping the pillow on the ground, I stamped out the smoldering flame then kicked it under the bed to hide the evidence. How embarrassing would that explanation be? *Oh, nothing to worry about Alex, I just set fire to this pillow because you won't jump into bed with me.*

I turned off the overhead lights, leaving a lamp on for him even though I knew he didn't need it. I suspected he was purposefully waiting until I'd fallen asleep before he returned. Closing my eyes, I tried not to relive the scene with Alex by thinking about what was in those letters. It didn't work, but eventually I found my brain quieting. I really was tired to the bone.

Right before I drifted off, the door creaked open. I kept my eyes shut, not wanting to give away that I was still awake. Alex paused beside me, and I worked to keep my breathing deep and even. Then there was a soft weight on my head as he brushed my tempestuous waves away from my forehead and tucked them behind my ear.

"Sleep," he murmured. The last thing I remembered was the warm, comforting pressure of his hand on my cheek.

23

"I've got something," Alex said. He sounded cautious, but I caught the note of anticipation beneath.

That morning, I'd woken to a cup of steaming coffee under my nose, courtesy of Alex. He'd already woken and dressed, then left again after I was awake to give me time to make myself presentable.

It was Thursday, so the whole household was either at work or school—or pilates, in my mom's case. After sleeping for ten hours and with the weak, late January sun shining, I felt more optimistic than I had last night.

Settling into the deep sofa in the living room, Alex in the armchair across from me, I almost felt at ease. Almost.

Most of the letters I'd read so far were fairly boring, day to day stuff. *This is what I did today, how's so and so doing, blah blah blah.* However, they seemed intentionally so, like the writers didn't want to give too much away. They were all from Evangeline and Uriel, or Lucas. The earliest I'd found dated two years before my birth, which seemed to be when my father had come to Gravesville.

"What?" I practically sprang over to him, looking over his shoulder at the letter.

"It's from Lucas. This part, here." He moved his finger along the page, highlighting the passage.

. . .

Ezekial, you have mentioned no news of the mission in your recent letters. I sense that with the passing months, you are less likely to return to us. With each tether you create to the other side, first your wife, and now your unborn child, you grow farther and farther from Canhaben, until we are but a speck on the horizon. Meanwhile, I am stuck in Jupiter's musty book-binding shop while you waste your chance at glory. Admit you have turned your back on us, and that you will no longer fight for the freedom of your people. The Watchers will remember this.

"The Watchers," I breathed. Cora Roth's photo flashed through my mind. The back of my neck prickled in warning. "So my dad was one of them? And maybe Evangeline too, and Lucas."

"But we still don't know what a Watcher is," Alex said, staring at the letter. "And what's Canhaben?"

"I haven't heard of that before. But Edward mentioned some kind of program." I cupped my face in my hands, blocking out the room while I recalled the conversation I'd eavesdropped on. "And Mindara said that the Watchers were no closer to the Aureum than they were a millenia ago."

"You spoke with my father about this?" His tone held shocked disbelief.

Oh, shit. "No, I overheard him and Mindara talking about it. About me." I uncovered my eyes. Alex was angry, the set of his full lips a thin, hard line, his jaw clenched.

"Gods, Persephone." He ran both hands through his hair, looking up at the ceiling. I could see him grasping at the tether of his control, and it was slipping away from him rapidly. "That's how you found out about the Watchers? And you didn't think to let me know?"

"I barely knew you back then. It was during my first week at headquarters."

That had been the wrong thing to say. "I thought you trusted me. But you've been holding this back the whole time?" His voice was stiff, and I knew it was to cover the flash of hurt that flared in his eyes.

"I did tell you about the Watchers. Eventually. Can you blame me for not wanting to say where I heard it? From the moment I met your father, I knew he was suspicious of me. And apparently he's been digging up dirt for months now, even after my initiation."

Understanding dawned on Alex's face. "He's the one who ordered your room searched. *Fuck.*" He jumped up and began pacing. I'd never seen him this way before, had barely ever heard him curse.

"Are you okay?" I approached him as I would a startled animal.

He breathed deeply, nostrils flaring. "Give me a minute." His eyes shut, and I watched a battle play out on his face. When he opened them after a few moments, they were the clear, calm green I remembered. "What else did Mindara say?"

"That Edward was wrong. That there was no way I could be a Guardian *and* a Watcher."

"All right. That's good, at least. Did they say anything else about this program?"

"No, nothing."

Alex looked aggrieved. "*Why* in the name of gods and angels have I never been told about it? If Edward is in charge, I should have known."

"You said it yourself. The Aureum holds its secrets close, and the Diurne are the ones who gatekeep the flow of information."

"All right. Edward suspects you, but doesn't have any proof. So he goes looking for some, and finds the tarot card. But that means nothing." I noted that Alex had reverted to calling his father by his first name, and the way he said it was edged with frost. "You are not a threat, Seph. We'll make the Diurne see it our way."

I took a deep breath. "Is there anything else in the letters you read?"

"No," he said with a shake of his head. "It seems Lucas was a bit of a hothead, putting that into writing. The others were careful not to mention anything directly."

"I noticed that, too." But something was niggling in the back of my brain, some sense that I was overlooking a vital piece of information hovering just outside my range of vision. "Can I see the letter again?" Alex handed it to me, and I scanned it in its entirety.

There it was. A seed of hope sprouted in my chest as it finally hit home.

"Jupiter's bookbinding shop."

Alex's brow knit. "What about it?"

I bounced on my toes. "Jupiter's Books and Stationery was stamped on the back of the tarot card."

"The card you found in Gravesville?"

"In the cemetery," I finished. "Holy shit. When I was asking the Library about my dad, she sent me a book about Gravesville. I didn't think it meant anything, because I already knew he'd lived there. But what if she was trying to tell me something else?"

Alex's eyes were wide, his lips parted. Excitement coursed through me, like bubbles fizzing in a glass of champagne. Both of us flinched when the front door opened. I scooped up the letters and stuffed them back into the aged envelope.

"Seph, I'm home!" My mom appeared around the corner with a gym bag slung over her shoulder, wearing tasteful workout attire. Her blond hair was clipped up, and she held a canvas bag in each hand. "I went to the farmer's market and picked up a few more things for you all. Alex, do you like fish? I was thinking we could have seafood tonight."

"Mom, wait." I went into the kitchen, while Alex disappeared upstairs. My mom was already unloading the grocery bags with efficient, practiced movements. "We're not staying tonight."

She paused with a bag of apples halfway to the counter. Her face fell. "What do you mean? You just got here."

"Alex's parents are expecting us," I said, repeating our cover story. "We have to leave. I'm sorry."

She pursed her lips, applying herself to the task of washing fruit. "Well, I understand. If you've made a commitment, you should stick to it."

"Mom," I said gently, drawing her away from the sink. The fine lines around her eyes deepened, making her look older than her fifty-two years. With a pang, I realized that I was the same age as she'd been when I was born. "I'm sorry I've been distant. But why did you keep dad's stuff from me?"

Her eyes clouded with sadness. "Because I didn't want him to take you away from me, too."

"That never could have happened."

"Maybe it was wrong of me. But once I finally put it away—put him away—there didn't seem to be any point in bringing it all up again." She sighed. "Despite your father being a complete jackass, he gave me you. I will always be grateful for that. And I'm sorry, because even though it's the last thing I wanted, it seems that I've let him come between us anyway."

The admission was far from perfect, but it was a start. And she had kept his letters for me, in the end.

Alex came back downstairs with our backpacks. "Ready to go?"

I nodded, and he walked out to the car. My mom and I followed behind him.

"It was great to meet you, Mrs. Tedford," Alex said, extending a hand to shake.

"Oh, it's Lisa." She pulled him into a hug. "Don't be a stranger, now. Bring my girl back soon." Our eyes met over my mom's head.

"I'll do my best," he replied. Then he started the Audi and waited for me, the engine idling.

My mom opened her arms, and I stepped into them. "I hope you found what you were looking for," she whispered into my hair.

I breathed in the scent of her gardenia shampoo and sank into her embrace, finding a sliver of comfort in her softness.

She pulled back first, holding me at arm's length and looking me over. Something passed through her eyes, quick as a breath, then disappeared. "Please call when you get there. Or text me, at least."

I nodded, then got in the car. She waved us off from the front porch, her lips compressed into a worried line.

———

"We're going back to Gravesville the normal way," Alex said, turning north on the highway. He'd shrugged on a weapon harness that bristled with knives. I prayed we didn't get pulled over.

"What happened to no magic? And you're going the wrong way. Hollywood is south." Hollywood Cemetery was one of the largest and most prominent graveyards in Virginia. The sprawling park-like grounds were vast and beautiful, even on a barren winter's day. But that was south, in Richmond.

Alex shook his head. "No, it's too conspicuous. There's another place closer that's quieter. We're less likely to attract attention there, just as a precaution. And, I really don't give a shit what Mindara said. We're doing this our own way."

We took country roads, where the land sloped gently and spread into farmland. Pines and the naked boughs of maples neatly bordered fields of cows cropping grass, along with the stubble of harvested cornfields.

After half an hour, Alex pulled the car off onto the flattest stretch of road he could find, given there was only a ditch instead of a shoulder. "We'll leave the car here and walk the rest of the way."

"Won't an abandoned car on the side of the road be conspicuous?" I imagined that wasn't a frequent sight for folks who lived in such a rural area. He solved the problem by running his hand over the car so that it blended with the trees like camouflage.

"Come on, this way. It'll be a few minutes walk."

I slung my backpack over my shoulder and fell into step beside him. We stuck to the cover of the trees. "And where are we, exactly?"

"Scotchtown Plantation."

As promised, about ten minutes later we came to a clearing in the trees, through which I spotted a plain yet sizable colonial style building in the distance. Alex halted and put his backpack down. "Why are you stopping?" I had expected us to continue on toward the grounds around the building, where the cemetery was likely situated.

Alex gave me a quizzical look. "We're here."

"What?" I looked around at the bare, leaf covered earth. There were no markers of any kind, not least the grand headstones or mausoleums I expected from a plantation family's graveyard. "There's nothing here."

Alex placed his hands on my shoulders. "Close your eyes," he instructed.

"I don't—"

"Trust me."

I did as he asked, my eyes fluttering shut although I felt absurd. "Reach out with your mind. Let your senses sink into the ground, and tell me what you find there," he instructed.

I breathed deeply, feeling the air move through my lungs and out my nostrils. I imagined the moist, cool dirt, and all of the microscopic organisms that made their home there. I thought about the texture of earth falling through my fingers, of the sound it made when it hit the ground. The organic smell of living things was pungent in my nostrils. I saw layers of soil, from rich humus to red clay. And then there were the bones.

My eyes flew open, but the image was imprinted upon my vision. A small skeleton, wrapped in the embrace of a larger one, nestled directly below where we stood. "There are bodies here," I breathed, stepping away from the spot.

"This is an enslaved people's graveyard," Alex explained. "Unmarked and lost to time. They're all over the South."

Horror mingled with sadness, tightening my throat. "The people who own the land don't know it's here?"

"Either they don't know, or have willfully forgotten."

"But, that's...." Terrible seemed too tame a word.

"People will go to untold lengths to hide their bad acts. Sometimes it's ignorance, and sometimes they just want to cover up the truth."

"Well, why don't you tell someone else? A historian, or a researcher? Let someone know there are people here." These people, whoever they were, had families that would be looking for them. Who wanted to remember them. They had been degraded and tortured in life, and now the insult continued in death.

"It's not our place," Alex said softly, regret in the downturn of his mouth. "We don't get involved in human affairs."

"You do when it's convenient for you. Don't you think this is important?"

"Of course I do. But there's nothing to be done about it right this second." His eyes scanned the clearing over my head. "We need to get a move on."

I fumed. "Alex, we have to do *something*. If we ignore it, that makes us complicit." I tried not to let the insidious idea that had wormed its way into my brain take root—that he didn't have to care, because of his white skin. But it was there now.

"No, it does not. The only thing we have to do is get back to Gravesville, before the Diurne figures out we're not where we're supposed to be."

I shoved away from him, feeling frustrated and powerless to my core. We could come back, couldn't we? After all of this was over. We would come back and make it right. I was about to demand it, when a wave of greasy nausea rolled over me. I stopped in my tracks and bent double, clutching my knees.

"What is it?" Alex's alarmed voice was in my ear as he supported my waist. My legs had gone boneless.

While we were talking, my mind had continued to reach into our surroundings, not stopping at the field of buried bones. It operated in the background on autopilot, outside of my conscious awareness, but something it came across had just triggered the sick feeling in my stomach. It felt wrong and out of place, like a rotten smell amidst a field of flowers.

Closing my eyes again, I focused on the nausea to trace the thread back to its source. Then, I vomited spectacularly, pitching up the morning's breakfast. Alex pulled me into his arms when I finished, soothing me, but every muscle in his body was rigid.

"Something's coming," I rasped. That feeling of wrongness was a demon, a disgusting, vile beast not of this world. It couldn't be anything else.

Alex moved in front of me, shielding me with his body as searched the clearing. "How long do we have?"

"I don't know," I said, wiping my mouth on my sleeve. I'd reflexively recoiled from the demon, and dropped the thread of connection. "But it's bad."

Alex looked torn. He half turned, spreading his arms as though preparing to open a gateway, when a light breeze stirred the trees. Leaves rustled dryly, then fluttered to the ground like raindrops. The wind picked up, and it grew ice cold claws that tore at our clothes.

The choice had been made for us. It was too late to run.

"Stay behind me, and if something happens, go straight back to the car and head for Gravesville. Call Fern and tell her you're there, and she'll come get you." He said all of this as if we were discussing where to go out to lunch, not making emergency plans in the event that he was incapacitated by a fucking *demon*.

"No. I won't leave you." I wouldn't. I'd made my choice.

"We don't have time to argue. Please, just listen for once."

I reached for his hand and squeezed. "No."

He heaved an exasperated sigh, and a nervous laugh burbled from my lips. That is, until the demon reached the clearing.

It came on the cold wind, more impression than solid form. Fallen leaves swirled into the air and coalesced into a vaguely human shape, with arms and legs and a long torso. It didn't look terrifying, exactly, until it shot a blast of arctic air in our direction that turned into razor sharp icicles.

Alex threw us to the ground. We rolled, and he shot white fire at the icicles. They melted and reformed into a pool of ice that was smoother than glass. The breath was knocked from my lungs, and while I gasped and coughed, Alex had already thrown another assault at the demon.

The demon moved like smoke, simply vanishing and reappearing at will, almost lazy in its movements as it sent various forms of icy terror hurtling at us. Alex had drawn a circle of fire around me that seemed impenetrable to the wraith's attacks. The fire didn't even give off heat, but it kept the demon at bay while he worked to capture it.

It was a battle of fire and ice, and soon the clearing filled with smoke and vapor that mingled into one large cloud, so that it was almost impossible to see what was happening.

I desperately wanted to help, but knew I was more of a liability than an asset in this fight.

A resounding crack split the air as a deadly icicle collided with a tree, burying itself halfway into the trunk and splitting it up the center. The icicle had been headed for Alex, and although he deflected it at the last moment, he'd been hit. He grunted, a short gasp of pain. Blood welled from a gash in his forearm.

Air, leaves, and fallen branches whirled and whipped around Alex, trapping him inside of the maelstrom like a firefly stuck inside a glass jar. Then, the demon disappeared, the leaves that gave its shape fluttering back to the ground.

"Alex!" I screamed, trying to make out his form amongst the detritus of the tornado. I rushed forward but couldn't get past the circle of fire. I was trapped.

The need to help him burned through my chest and spread to my limbs, consuming me until I felt hotter than the sun. I jumped over the flames, and they parted below me. Hitting the ground hard on the other side of the circle, I sprinted toward Alex.

I was inches from the tempest when frosty fingers wrapped around my ankles and pulled. Falling, I took the brunt of the impact on my forearms. The demon dragged me on my belly, away from Alex, icy needles of pain climbing from my ankles up my legs. I kicked wildly, trying to wrench myself away, but nothing happened. I was frozen.

Fear burst its dam, flooding me. My wheeling eyes slid to the demon. It had crystallized into a solid form, taking the shape of a man with a bird's face. Arms slid from underneath ragged, leathery wings, and scaly talons were in the place of feet. The creature was horrible, monstrous, boring into me with eyes so pale they were more white than blue.

I tried to recall the molten feeling from only moments ago, pushing it from my chest out into my limbs. The demon shuddered and gave a terrible cry, clicking its beak. Then pain sliced through my skull like a hot knife, and everything went black.

24

———

A cloud of breath hovered above me when I blinked my eyes open. I felt a bone deep chill, like I'd been dunked in an icy lake then rimed in frost. My body shook violently, a clattering sound echoing through the dark room. Straining to raise my head, I made out the glint of manacles clamped around my ankles.

I was stretched out on a high, rectangular stone platform, hands chained behind my head and feet spread apart. A single lightbulb hanging from the ceiling illuminated the space.

The cold seeped into my brain, scattering my thoughts. At least I was still alive—for now. And Alex—was he?

Fear flooded my already racing heart, and I fought against the bindings, yanking and bucking like an animal in a trap. The chains held steady, and an electric shock zipped through me as though I'd been poked with a cattle prod. I stopped struggling.

Closing my eyes, I went to my obsidian door. The meadow was burned and barren today, as if a wildfire had torn through it. When I pulled on the door, it stayed shut fast. I banged on it with my fists, kicked it, and bloodied my fingers prying at the edges. I screamed in frustration through chattering teeth.

Panting, I laid back against the hard platform. Yelling wasn't going to help anything. I needed to focus. Lifting my head again, I looked around the small room. There were no windows in the dark stone walls that were coated in a layer of pale slime. A second rectangular platform to my right was stained with dark splotches. Chains were bolted to the floor in each of its corners, the manacles laying open on the platform. I couldn't see the wall behind my head, but those to the left, right, and center were empty, save for a single closed door. The air smelled of mildew and rot, and something faintly metallic.

Somehow, the chill deepened, and wind whistled through the room. I tried to shrink away, but was held fast by my bonds. There was a noise like a breeze rustling dry grass, and the bird-like demon materialized out of thin air.

Its wings were gray and leathery as an elephant's hide, torn and moth-eaten. The beak was long and tapered to a sharp point, like it was made for carving. Terror surged through me, snatching my breath away.

The demon clicked its beak. "She smells of bloodwine and deathsmoke. She lays a scent trail brighter than the eyes of Baal Zebub." Its voice screeched like a hawk's. Then it made a keening noise, and I realized it was laughing.

"What do you want?" My voice was rough, and my throat ached. "Why did you take me?"

"Master sends Ventusiel to catch the witch. Ventusiel is of the wind, and the ice, and of death. He is master's most trusted servant." He tilted his head, looking at me from round eyes with scaly lids. Despite the threat, the demon sounded childish, like he was searching for praise on a job well done.

"Who is your master?"

Ventusiel didn't answer, but stepped behind me, taloned feet clicking against the floor. I twisted, trying to follow the demon with my eyes. I heard a soft clink, like metal touching metal. "Ventusiel will hold her until master comes, he who commands a thousand legions. Ventusiel and the witch will play a game."

A racking chill ran through me, rattling the chains.

The demon came back into my range of vision, holding a serrated blade in a taloned hand. My insides melted like candle wax, and suddenly I didn't feel cold anymore. "W-What game? Shouldn't we wait for your master?"

Ventusiel bobbed his head from side to side. "No, no. If she doesn't want to play the game, she will be punished."

"Okay, okay. I'll play the game with you." Anything to keep that sharp knife away from me.

The demon clicked his beak rapidly. "Ventusiel will ask questions. The witch will answer. If the witch lies, she will get the blade. Ventusiel always knows a lie." He puffed his chest proudly. "That is why master gives Ventusiel the job."

I took a deep breath, flexing my fingers and rolling my ankles. My hands were going numb. I needed more time, time to try and get into my damn locked door. "That's very impressive. I can understand why your master relies on you." He preened, shaking out ragged wings. "Can I ask something before we start the game?"

Ventusiel nodded. "Ask one question only, witch. Ventusiel wants to begin."

"When I answer, can I ask you a question in return? It only seems fair." I held my breath, waiting for the demon's reaction. I was counting on his childlike logic to agree. If I'd angered him, I imagined I'd be getting acquainted with the serrated blade.

Ventusiel tilted his head, blinking rapidly. "She answers a question, she asks a question?"

"That's how games work," I said through frozen lips. "Right? A truth for a truth."

The demon drew the blade across a talon. The screeching noise it produced sent a shiver down my spine. "Fine. We begin."

I exhaled slowly. All I had to do was answer correctly, and I might be able to get some information that would help me escape. And buy myself time. Because if Alex was still alive, he would be able to find me.

"What is the witch's name?" Ventusiel demanded.

An easy one. "Persephone."

The demon gestured to me with the knife. "She asks."

"Why did you take me?"

"Ventusiel says already."

Fuck. Apparently I needed to be extremely careful when wording questions.

"My turn. Where is the Golden Ones' lair?" he asked.

The Golden Ones. "Do you mean the Aureum?"

Quicker than a blink, Ventusiel sliced the blade across my upper arm. I cried out as blood spilled out of the three-inch gash. "Not an answer," the demon squawked, glee in his eyes. "If she does not answer, maybe Ventusiel will pluck out the eyes and eat the insides."

"New Orleans," I choked through the pain that radiated up my arm. "Their headquarters is in New Orleans."

Ventusiel nodded. "Truth. She asks a question, now."

"Why does your master want me?"

"My master, the lord of abundance, makes a deal with the master of the Golden Ones. He gives my master the witch, and the witch will be bound in another world."

He spoke in such a casual manner that my reaction seemed out of place. Fear, rage, and desperation flooded my system, and I saw red. I didn't hear Ventusiel's next question, and got a slice across the thigh for it. The pain almost didn't register.

"Listen!" he squawked. "Ventusiel says, where does the witch keep her power?"

That was not a question I wanted to answer. What if he was trying to get inside of my power source? And what would happen to me if he did? "My power doesn't work the right way. I can't use it."

"Lie!" the demon cried triumphantly. Reaching for me with taloned hands, he grasped the center of my shirt at the neck and tore. It ripped down the middle, and I shrieked, flailing. The demon pressed the tip of the knife under my collarbone, cutting a jagged line from shoulder to shoulder. A bloodcurdling scream tore from me, and I saw stars.

Ventusiel inhaled deeply, the tiny slits on top of his beak flaring. "Bloodwine," he repeated. The edges of my vision were still gray when he dipped his beak into the open wound, lapping at my blood with a proboscis-like tongue.

It was as though he'd shoved a flaming poker into my flesh. Nausea rose, and I arched away from him, retching. Vomit spilled down my cheek and splattered to the floor. Hot bile burned my throat, and by the time I'd finished, Ventusiel had stepped back. His beak was coated in a slick of my blood.

"The witch tastes good," he crowed, shaking out his tattered wings. "She tastes *good*." He bent to drink again, but gave a pained hiss when his beak closed on my tiger's eye necklace. Using the knife, he cut it off my neck and flung it into the corner. Then he bent to the gash on my leg, his long, thin tongue protruding.

I am going to die.

Images flashed before my eyes like a highlight reel—sunset in the graveyard, Bri having breakfast in my living room, the lakehouse, Alex's serious eyes watching me, laughing with the other Guardians, my mom standing on her doorstep, watching us leave.

Love, sorrow, and grief twisted tightly inside of me like strands of a rope. Then something shifted, like a weight being released, and my door blew open so hard it rocked on its invisible hinges.

The rivers of my power, light and dark, flowed under my skin, tangling with my emotions. The threads were as pliable and strong as spider's silk. And they didn't just wrap around my muscles, like when I'd fought Davina, but burrowed inside of me such that my magic and my body became one and the same.

Suddenly colors appeared brighter and the world seemed sharper. Smells, sounds, touch, taste, sight, all became more potent than they'd ever been. Pain screamed through my bones, and the scents of rot and blood that had been strong before became nauseating.

Power surged through me, and on a cry, I ripped my chains from the floor with a screech of metal. Scorching heat chased the chill out of the air.

Ventusiel shrieked, scrambling backward, attempting to take flight in the low-ceilinged room. Shouting, I swung the chain links that were still attached to my wrists. They twisted around the demon, bringing him crashing to the floor. Rage clawed at my chest, and flames sprang to life on my skin. I walked to where he lay in a heap, trying to free himself of the heavy chains.

"You dumb motherfucker," I hissed.

Ice crystals, sharper than needles, flew at me. I brushed a hand through the air, flames melting them instantly. Bending, I grabbed the demon's throat and squeezed, pinning him to where he lay. Ventusiel squawked and coughed, but I didn't release him.

"I have a message for your master. Tell him to get fucked, and if he ever tries to come after me again, he'll be the one in chains."

I let go. With one final, earsplitting cry, Ventusiel faded then disappeared.

After ripping the chains from my manacled hands, the iron bracelets still stuck fast, I ran to the wall behind the raised stone platform. Torture implements covered it from floor to ceiling. Saws, knives, and other horrific bits of metal glinted dully. I had my power, still gushing through me like a swollen river, but I needed a weapon. I grabbed two daggers with rusted handles, shoving one through a belt loop and holding onto the other. Patting my pockets, I noticed that my phone was gone. Shit.

Running again, I was halfway across the room before I slowed. I was forgetting something, but I didn't know what.

Cursing myself for a fool, I went back and scanned the wall from floor to ceiling. Everything was rusted, dark metal, or leather. There, in the corner—my necklace. Maybe it was still a silly trinket, but it had done something to Ventusiel when he touched it.

Stooping, I picked it up. As my fingers closed around the bloody chain, something white glinted on the rack and caught my eye. I moved aside a braided leather strap. Behind it swung another necklace, mother of pearl cameo against onyx backing.

Untangling it from the hook, I shoved both necklaces into my pocket and ran.

The door was locked, but I simply melted the doorknob and kicked it open. Beyond was a set of stairs. I bolted up them, half expecting someone to come after me, but the house appeared empty. There was another door at the top of the stairs, unlocked, and I threw it open.

A thicket of woods lay beyond an overgrown yard, tangled with vines and choked with weeds. A driveway, potholed and more dirt than gravel, led into the forest.

I followed it. My legs were strong, and my breath remained even despite my sprint. It seemed like it would be hours before I tired.

I ran for miles, but there was nothing along the road except for fields and woods. No houses or cars appeared. If I could just get to a phone, or someone could tell me where I was, I could go back to Scotchtown and get Alex. If he was still there.

Dread gathered in my stomach, and I ran faster, the manacles still attached to my wrists clanking. Moments later a shadow passed over-head, and I looked up.

Something akin to exultation swamped me, and I stumbled, falling to my knees as if in supplication. Alex had arrived, but in a way that I never expected.

He circled in the sky above me on iridescent wings that shifted from blinding white to soft gold in the light. His eyes were wild and dark, his face haggard. Without landing, he skimmed the ground and scooped me into his arms, flapping mightily so that it only took a second before we were level with the treetops. Flat farmland spread beneath us like a patchwork quilt.

"Seph," he breathed, burying his face in my hair, while he crushed me to his chest. "Thank all of the gods, you're alive."

I should have been crying tears of joy and relief. Instead, I blurted, "You have...wings?"

"I've been flying for hours, following your trace. Twenty minutes ago, it was like a bomb went off over there." Alex jerked his head, indicating the direction I'd come from. "What happened to the demon? How did you escape?"

"He's gone. I'll tell you everything, I just...wow." Above, blue sky faded into quiet darkness, while below us the sun was setting. The clouds turned to pink, the last rays of light gilding them. Violet and lavender swept in, washing the world in a tenderness that made my heart ache. The wound on my chest throbbed, as if reminding me that this peace couldn't last.

Alex's arms tightened around me. "It hurt you." His shadowed jaw was rigid, but he softened his gaze when he looked down at me. "I'll take care of that, soon as you're safe."

"Where are we going?"

He angled downward, and we descended, circling. Hundreds of graves dotted the ground beneath us, symbols of death that felt like hope. Alex beat his great wings to slow to a hover, then touched down softer than a falling snowflake. He set me on the grassy ground.

"Gravesville. The subs are staying at the house, but there's another place that's well protected. Then I can contact the Diurne, and—"

"No!" They couldn't know that anything was amiss. Edward couldn't know.

Alex's face settled into lines of confusion. "Why not?"

"We can't trust them. Ventusiel, the one who took me—he said that the master of the Golden Ones made a deal. That the demons could have me, if they took me to another world and bound me."

"What the fuck?" Alex growled, lines appearing between his brows. "The Diurne would never make deals with demons."

"Never say never." I drew the delicate cameo pendant from my pocket, holding it aloft so that it dangled between us. "This belonged to Cora Roth. I recognized it from her graduation photo. It was in the basement where I was chained up and used as a fucking knife sharpener." My chest wound seared in pain at the mention of it. Alex took a step toward me, but I moved away. "Maybe the Diurne used a demon to get rid of her—the same demon."

A battle played out on Alex's face. He'd been brought up in this system, had lived and breathed the Aureum's tenets since birth. Yet, as much as I cared about him, I would leave him here and now if he didn't believe me. The stakes had changed, again.

He walked away, tucking his glorious wings against his sides. I was certain that he was going to leave, or turn me in, or—

His fist drilled into a tall headstone, shattering it to pieces with a sharp crack, while his harsh breath punctuated the twilight stillness.

I flinched, retreating until the back of my knees ran into a tomb. Alex turned toward me, and there was such potent rage in his eyes that fear trickled down my spine. The danger I'd always known was lurking under the surface of his usual mild-mannered self had emerged. He looked like a wrathful god, powerful and terrible all at once, spreading his wings so that he was cloaked in shadow.

Alex advanced on me, stalking silently like a jaguar on the hunt. My muscles tensed, taut as a bowstring. I brought my fists up, ready to defend, but knew I was outmatched by a thousandfold.

He reached me, eyes hooded and wickedly sculpted lips drawn. Then, he bowed his head so that his dark hair shadowed his face. "When you were taken, when I thought—" He faltered, then started again. "When I thought about what could have happened to you, it felt like part of me died. I won't let anyone harm you again, demon or man. I won't betray you. I'll stay for as long as it takes until you're safe." Alex looked up, meeting my eyes, and suddenly I felt lighter than air. "And after that, if you'll have me."

His beauty was breath-stealing, all-consuming, maddening, the planes of his face stark and haunted and hopeful.

And I wanted it all. His sunlight and his shadows, his rage and his peace, his lethal power and the safety of his embrace.

Moving into him, I linked our fingers and tipped my face up to meet his burning green gaze. "I'll have you."

The corners of Alex's mouth pulled up and he bowed his forehead to mine. Our breath mingled, and he skimmed a hand along my ribcage. I winced as the shiver that rolled through me tugged on the torn skin of my wound.

"We need to get that taken care of," he said in a low, uneven voice.

"It doesn't hurt." That was a patent untruth, but what was pain compared to the feel of his hands on me?

He pulled back, assuaging my noise of protest with a stroke of his finger along my lips. "Part of taking care of you is not allowing you to roam around with an untreated flesh wound."

"Well, when you put it that way." It both thrilled and terrified me that he would take care of me. "Wait—your arm."

Blood from the gash in his forearm had dripped down to coat his hand in a sheen of sticky red.

"I can't even feel it." Alex took hold of the iron still on my wrists, and the manacles dropped onto the dead grass. "I have a safe place where we can stay in Gravesville. It's a bolt-hole on the edge of town we use for emergencies. Or, when my unit gets sick of each other and needs space. We're still supposed to be in Virginia—no one will know we're there."

I chewed my lip. "You're sure?"

"Positive."

"Okay. Let's go."

Dropping my hand reluctantly, Alex made quick work of opening a gateway. When he reached for me again, I held on tight. Not because I was afraid any longer, but because the weight of his calloused hand in mine made me feel brighter than the sun.

As one, we stepped into the darkness.

25

The moon glowed like a beacon by the time we made it to the old gas station on the outskirts of town. Its light threw shadows across our path, turning every rock and tree into a crouching demon.

I wasn't expecting a mansion, but I hadn't realized the safe house would be so...dingy, was too kind a word.

The dilapidated gas station appeared abandoned, with weeds sprouting through fist-width cracks in the concrete, and shingles missing so that the roof resembled a checkerboard. The windows were spiderwebbed with cracks, and a sign proclaiming the place *Handee Mart* listed to the side.

"This is it?"

"Not everything is as it appears," Alex answered. Hands still linked, we picked our way across the debris-strewn parking lot.

With a snap of his fingers, he unlocked the door of the gas station that was smeared with substances I'd rather leave a mystery. Where I was expecting to see dust and grime was a simple cottage interior. We were in a living room of sorts that had tufted leather couches and a long wall of built-in cabinetry. Warm wood and pale walls provided quiet comfort.

He closed the door behind us, murmuring quietly over the lock, and the door changed from grimy glass to burnished mahogany.

"This is insane. Or genius—I'm not sure which."

"It can be both, as long as it serves its purpose. Wait here, I'm going to add an extra seal to the windows and get something to clean your wounds."

He strode from the room, and I went into the kitchen to scrub the filth from my hands. "Why does the house look like such a wreck from the outside?" I asked when he returned a few minutes later carrying a white plastic case.

"We don't want humans wandering around here and blowing our cover," he replied, gesturing for me to sit. "If all they see is an abandoned gas station, they won't want to stick around. Even if they look inside the windows, they'll only find trash and filth. And, we add an extra layer of magical security. The building is technically condemned, although we keep it off the city's demolition books year after year."

Alex sat beside me on the leather couch, pulling a brown bottle and a roll of gauze from the first aid kit. "I'm going to clean your wounds before I heal them. I'm no expert, as you know, but it should be enough to close the skin." The corner of his mouth drew back, flashing his dimple. "I'm afraid you might have a scar." It appeared he'd taken care of his own gash when he'd been retrieving the kit. The skin under his tattoos was shiny and raw, but closed.

I shrugged, wincing at the movement. "It won't be my first."

"Where else are you hurt?" His tone was measured, but I didn't miss the way his jaw ticked.

I extended my left arm, then pointed to my thigh where the fabric of my jeans gaped. Congealed blood coated the gash, and my pants were stiff with dried blood. It was swollen and hot, probably due to the sprint after I'd escaped the house.

"Do you want to...remove your clothing? So I can see properly." The tips of his ears reddened, and I smiled at his sudden shyness. It made me feel reassured as I shimmied out of my jeans. My top was destroyed already, so I ripped the remaining few inches of fabric that held it together and shucked it off. My bra looked as though it had recently featured in a slasher film.

"So, what was your first scar?" Alex asked, surely trying to distract me as he opened the bottle of hydrogen peroxide and applied it to the gauze.

"Falling out of a tree when I was five. I had to get three stitches on my elbow. Shit!" Stinging pain shot through my chest as Alex dabbed at the wound.

"You're doing great," he encouraged. "That sounds like an inconvenient place to get stitches."

"It was," I said through gritted teeth as he moved on to my arm, cleaning the blood away as he went. "Oh, mother*fucker*. That hurts."

"Hopefully the healing won't be as bad?" he suggested.

I shuddered. "What about you? What was your first scar?"

He tapped the thin white line that ran through his eyebrow. "Fighting a lesser water demon. I was ten, and my father thought I was ready to start playing in the minor leagues, so to speak."

I looked up from where I'd been tracking his progress on my thigh. "What? You were a child. You didn't have any power yet."

"No," he agreed, getting another piece of gauze. "And after it almost ripped my face off, Edward refused to have it healed. My mom put her foot down and took care of it, but it left this scar. Dear old dad said it was a good reminder for me to never drop my guard."

"That's barbaric," I asserted, horrified.

"Yeah, it was. Okay, I think we're done here." He bundled the bloodied pieces of gauze together, setting them aside. "I need to concentrate for this next part. Tell me if it hurts too much, and I'll back off."

I nodded my assent. Alex was so gentle as he traced the lines of my wounds, the tip of his tongue caught between his teeth. I experienced a surge of hatred toward Edward. He'd done everything in his power to turn Alex into a hard, unfeeling bastard. But it hadn't worked. His light shone too bright to be extinguished.

My skin knitting back together didn't hurt, exactly. It was more of an itchy tingle, slightly uncomfortable, although not as bad as being cut in the first place. When it was finished, Alex sat back, face paler than normal.

"Are you okay?" I asked, running my fingertips along the line of raised skin on my chest. It felt tight, but the pain had already quieted.

"Never better."

I reached out tentatively to stroke his jaw. This new space we occupied was uncharted territory, and I didn't want to screw it up. Alex nuzzled me, his stubble scraping pleasantly along my palm.

I wasn't sure if it was because of the promise he'd made under the velvet twilight, or that I'd decided to let him in, but I felt different. Like the invisible thread of attraction that pulled me to him had grown fibers of steel cable, binding us fast to each other.

"Do you feel that?" I whispered.

"I thought it was just me." His gaze swept over my throat, my mouth, my cheeks, before finally resting on my eyes. "You feel...different. Changed."

I was. Irrevocably. "What did I feel like before?"

He sighed softly. "Like fire and honey. It doesn't make sense, I know. But now it's like...." He tilted his head, searching. "The blue part of a flame. Moonlight, and the darkness between stars."

"Does that scare you?"

He tilted my chin up. "I'm not going to run. Remember?" I nodded, eyes on his. They had gone soft, the corona of gold a faint glint instead of a sunburst.

"Seph, I've wanted you from the first moment I saw you. You were like a goddess, with that powerful, pissed off look in your eye. Like you couldn't wait to get rid of me." He drew a hand languidly down to my hip. It felt like a firebrand, an arrow straight to my center. "But I couldn't leave you alone. Because I'd felt your power wake up, so you were already inside of me, you see." His eyes darkened, the pupils dilating as his lips parted. "And I haven't been able to get you out since." He closed his eyes for a moment, drawing a deep breath. "I haven't wanted to."

"Oh," I said hoarsely. All of my nerve endings were aflame, begging for him to touch me more. "That's good, then." Swallowing, unsure, I brought my hand to cover his where it rested on the flare of my waist.

Alex slowly drew me to him, close enough for our breath to mingle. "Is this what you want, Seph?" he asked, his eyes searching mine.

I ran a tentative hand over his chest, feeling his heart thundering against my palm. He pressed his lips together on a muffled exhale, and I sensed that his tether was close to snapping again. He wanted me as badly as I wanted him. But I knew that if I said no, he'd back off without question.

"Yes," I whispered. "This is what I want."

There was a fraction of a second where we stared at each other, like Alex couldn't believe what he'd just heard.

Then he pulled me in fiercely, and we came together like two waves crashing, with deep, frantic kisses and demanding hands. We were standing, and I was tearing off of his shirt, soaking in the feel of ridged muscle over warm skin. Heat sparked low in my belly, spreading into a wildfire that lit me up from the inside out, consuming everything in its wake.

Alex shuddered as my teeth scraped along his neck, and power surged in my blood, black and gold threads reaching out and binding us together. My feet came out from under me as he swept me into his arms, dashing down a hallway with supernatural speed.

A small part of me wanted to run as far and fast as I could, away from the overwhelming sensations and feelings that were crushing me. But the bigger part that just wanted him, wanted this, shoved it out of the way and ran full tilt, flinging me over a cliff with no parachute.

He kicked open a door and carried me inside. I had the sense of dark walls and the moon shining through an open window. The room was spare, unlike the great room, but it was neat as a pin.

"Sorry," Alex murmured. "It's not the most romantic setting."

I exhaled, the sound catching in my throat. "All I see here is you."

It was true. Alex was everything to me, his presence making up a hundred percent of my world in these precious moments. I was immersed in his scent, cedar and something uniquely Alex, the heat of his body, the desperate want in his eyes. I couldn't care less if we were in a burning building—the only thing I'd think about would be him.

He kicked the door shut and turned, pinning me against it. My knees were weak, but I clung to him. His hands stroked down my waist, cupping me, burying his face in the column of my throat.

"Ow," I gasped. His weapon harness was still strapped on, pressing into me. He shrugged it off impatiently and it clattered to the floor. He kissed me, brushing his tongue along the seam of my lips. I opened for him, and he slipped his tongue into my mouth. Pools of heat washed over me, and I responded in kind.

"Seph," he murmured, saying my name with the reverence of a believer. He dropped his head and his teeth skimmed over the swell of my breast. With his solid weight against me, I felt like my namesake, the goddess who had power over two worlds.

I reached down, raking my fingers over the ridges of his abdominals. He shivered, and I felt stronger than I ever had in the sparring ring.

He shifted and grabbed my wrists, holding them in one hand as he pulled them above my head. I let out a gasp of held breath, startled by the sudden movement. Goddess, he was fast.

I wriggled my bound hands, desperate to touch him, but I was caught in the iron grip of a god.

"My turn," he whispered. A slow smile lit his face, not the small, reserved one he usually had, but a lazy grin that liquified my core. He swept me up again, then lowered me onto the bed.

He traced slow patterns across my skin, the roughness of his calluses sending waves of pleasure flooding through me until I was gasping to keep my head above water, wiggling underneath him to try and sate the need that bundled in my core like a pile of smoldering kindling.

His eyes traced a trail from my panties to my bra that left me gasping. "I don't think you need those anymore," he murmured, and then I was only wearing my skin. He took me in slowly, and without any other options, I stared back at him, feeling a boldness that was stranger than magic. His lips parted on a hard exhale, and his eyes gleamed.

I shivered and gripped his arms, feeling his muscles bunch beneath my hands. I followed the band of his triceps, running my hands over the lines of script tattooed on him. Up close, I recognized English, French, Arabic, and German, among others. The writing curled and twisted into fantastic shapes, creating stunning portraits with words.

"What are these?" I'd been curious, of course, but never brave enough to ask.

"Protection," he murmured, his lips doing interesting things to my neck, making it difficult to speak.

"From demons?" He didn't answer, intent on his task of turning me into a quivering mess. "Alex?"

He pulled back reluctantly. "Tradition says that if you mark yourself with the names of the demons you fight, they can't come back to harm you."

"Does it work?"

"I've never had to find out."

There must have been more than a hundred names tattooed on him. His lethality was branded into his skin, a sign of his power. But when I looked into his eyes, I didn't see the warrior. I saw the scholar, the leader, the protector. The man that frustrated me, challenged me, wanted to protect me. Who had shown me things I could never have imagined in my wildest dreams.

I took his hand and drew it toward me, then dipped my head, keeping my eyes on his as I pressed my lips to one tattoo, then another, and another, until he covered me and I couldn't think of anything except the hard feel of his body against mine.

If my body was a living flame, then he was the oxygen that fed the fire. His lips closed over my breasts, using teeth and tongue to create the sweetest agony. I sunk my hands into his dark curls as pleasure sang through me to the point of pain. He traveled downward, using those clever fingers and pliable mouth so that I was helpless, completely at his mercy. And when he lapped at the very center of my desire, I fell apart.

"Yes," he breathed, trailing upward until his lips brushed the shell of my ear. "You. Are. Beautiful," he said, punctuating each word with a nip to my earlobe, my neck, my shoulder.

I didn't have any words, just lay there gasping as the riptide of feeling pulled me under.

While I caught my breath, his callused hands played along my rib cage, the curve of my waist, my breasts, until the fire that had been banked surged again and his clever fingers found me wanting.

"Now," I managed. "Alex, please."

He rose over me, that wicked pirate's grin curving his mouth, the look in his eyes telling me that he would like nothing more than to bury himself inside of me to the hilt until he forgot his own name. I was more than obliged to help with that, and sank my teeth into his shoulder to tell him so.

On a groan, he parted my legs with his knee, guiding himself in, then rocked his hips into me, his eyes going dark as he watched me go wild. I bucked under him as he stroked me to the edge, slowly at first, then building until I knew I would come apart at the seams and there would be nothing left of me, until I felt so full that I couldn't take anything else but still somehow needed more.

Alex shifted and drew one hand to the small of my back, pulling me tightly to him. He thrust harder, stroking longer, and when he groaned my name I let go, going blind as I fell. He exhaled roughly, then, riding my wave of pleasure, fell after me.

He rolled us over so that I straddled him, and I slid down boneless until my nose nestled in the curve of his neck. We lay there quietly, and I listened as his racing heart quieted to a steady beat.

He drew his hand up, brushing my back, igniting little shivers all over again. I felt flushed and sated, wondering absently if I'd ever get used to his touch. My head was filled with an unfamiliar fog of pleasure, one that I never wanted to end. The humming of the thread had quieted, but I felt its presence in the center of my chest, stronger than titanium yet light as a feather.

"Do you see, now?" he murmured.

"Hmm?"

He shifted me so that we faced each other. I splayed my hand on the hard plane of his chest. He looked the same, but there was some imperceptible change in him, a lightness around the corners of his mouth.

"I've never felt like this before. This...wanting. Thinking about you all the time, even when you're not around. Wanting to be better because of you, for you. I hope that I can show you what you mean to me."

Heart in my throat, I nodded. "You did. And you can show me again later, if you want."

He smiled his heartbreaking smile, his eyes crinkling at the corners, and my heart just flopped at his feet for the taking. I was gone for him, and whatever happened now, there was no taking it back. I knew that he was more than capable of destroying me. I just stopped giving a damn. Because the thought of having Alex terrified me, but the thought of being without him was unimaginable.

He kissed me deeply, his tongue sweeping across mine, sending heat racing to my belly. Then, he rolled me on top of him, and I inhaled sharply as his hard length pushed against my thigh.

"How about now?" he asked, quirking his scarred brow.

I bit my lip, thrilling at the way his green eyes flared with gold, and dove into him.

There was nothing between us now, no pretenses or facades. We were just two people, skin to skin, not caring about a thing in the world except for each other.

26

A faint clicking noise woke me. No sign of dawn's light filtered through the window in the dark room. Alex sprawled beside me in bed, his arm underneath my head serving as an exceedingly comfortable pillow. I sighed, ready to roll over and go back to sleep, when I heard footsteps in the hallway.

Alex's eyes flew open instantly when I brushed a hand over his chest. I put a finger to my lips and pointed to the door. He rose silently, slipping on his pants and padding out of the room on bare feet.

I searched for my clothes before remembering they were shredded and covered in blood. Whatever was out there, I was going to have to face it stark naked. Wrapping the soft comforter around me, I got out of bed and stood in the doorway.

The sound of low conversation came from the living room. The words were muffled, but the tone was strained. I took a step into the hall when the most curious sensation tickled my brain. It was a voice. Alex's voice. *Stay put, please. It's Davina.*

I peered around, but Alex was most certainly not in the vicinity. What the hell? And what was Davina doing here? I retreated back into the room, turning on a lamp and searching for something to replace the comforter I wore like a dress.

Eventually I found a pair of sweatpants and a t-shirt in the closet, both too big for me, but it was better than nothing. By that time Alex had returned. His hair was rumpled, his lips lightly swollen from our exertions that had ended only hours ago.

"How did I hear you? And what's Davina doing here?" I whispered, trying to smooth my bedhead.

Alex drew me in and dropped a lingering kiss to my mouth. I wanted more than anything to bury myself in his arms, but he released me with a regretful look. "You heard me? Good. Since I've been through your door and into your power source, I thought I might be able to send a message."

"Well, it worked. But what about Davina?"

He ran a hand through his hair, making it further stand on end. "Apparently her mother mentioned something to Edward that concerned her, and she tracked me down. Even if the other Guardians can't feel you, they can still feel me."

"I didn't realize all of you are connected like that." Although, hadn't Fern mentioned something months ago about their lily marks acting like a homing signal? Tension curled around the back of my neck. If Alex was with me, it would be like a flashing neon sign pointing to my location.

"It's usually helpful, but proving pretty inconvenient right now."

"What did Mindara tell her?"

His mouth thinned. "That I might be returning to headquarters without you."

Learning Edward wanted me gone was one thing—proving the rest of the Diurne was in on it was another. Blood drained from my face in a rush, leaving me lightheaded.

"Davina is worried," he assured me. "There's no way she's in on whatever deal they made with Ventusiel's master."

"Alex, I don't know about this." She *had* beaten me to a pulp because Edward commanded it.

"She would never," he promised. "I trust Davina with my life. I've known her since we were both in diapers. Despite what our parents have done, she believes in the Aureum. She wouldn't go back on everything we stand for—dealing with demons and trying to kill Guardians? It's madness."

He appeared so earnest, so sincere, that I believed him. When it came down to it, I trusted Alex, and if he said he trusted Davina, it was good enough for me. "Okay," I agreed. "So now what?"

"It's time to come up with a plan." He cupped my face, kissing me again swiftly. I flushed with pleasure, still barely believing Alex had switched from friend to lover in the space of a night.

We met Davina in the living room, where she sat straight as a ruler in a wingback chair. Her hair was tied back, the long, sleek tail hanging over her shoulder.

"Seph." Her voice went lax with relief. Before she jumped up, catching me in a strong hug, her gaze halted on my flushed face. Oh fuck, where had our clothes ended up last night?

I hesitated before putting my arms around Davina, making eye contact with Alex over her head. He nodded in reassurance.

"Hi, Davina." I pulled back. "So...Alex told you about Ventusiel." It wasn't a question.

She shook her head. "I can't believe it. I'm so glad you're okay. When I think about what could have happened...." Anger replaced the sympathy in her gaze. "I just can't believe it," she repeated.

"Start to." I drew the neck of my t-shirt down, exposing the raw pink line of the scar that ran below my collarbone from shoulder to shoulder. "I've got a couple more of these."

Her eyes narrowed on the wound. "I do, Seph. You have to understand that this goes against every principle we've ever been taught. It's wrong, and we need to make it right."

"That's what we're going to discuss," Alex said, arms crossed. He was all business again, the competent authority that he used to command his unit settling around him like a cloak. "We believe Gravesville holds the answers about Seph's father we're looking for."

"What makes you think that?" Davina asked.

"Information her mother shared," Alex stated. "Our plan was to come here anyway, before we were ambushed and she was taken."

So, he was choosing to omit the letters, and the photograph with Evangeline. Not that I minded—I would rather have kept that information private.

"They'll come for you," she said. "If you're not back by tonight, they'll send Guardians."

"Then we need to hurry. I want the rest of the unit here as soon as possible. We're going to search Gravesville Historic Cemetery."

"We are?" I asked, looking from Davina to Alex.

"That's where you found the tarot card from Jupiter's Books. We'll start there, and hope something will point us in the right direction."

"What tarot card?" Davina said, her brows drawn down.

"I found one in the cemetery, the night Alex felt my power for the first time. We learned it might have come from someone connected to my father. And, a few days before we left headquarters, it was stolen from my room."

"Iznir's tits," she muttered.

Her use of Casey's familiar swear made me smile grimly. "Exactly."

"We better get started," Alex said. "The clock is ticking."

———

Alex trussed me like a Thanksgiving turkey, strapping all manner of dangerous objects to every limb and beneath my clothing. Davina had hunted up some of Sage's clothes for me, which were much closer to my size than what I'd been wearing.

My eyes met Alex's as he slid a weapons harness over my shoulders and belted it. There was concern in them, the corona of gold flashing in the green. "You all right?" he murmured, tightening the harness.

"As I can be. I'm not sure why you're turning me into GI Jane," I complained, loosening the strap he'd just tightened.

"You need to be prepared for anything." He tightened the strap again, then tugged a jacket over me, hiding the harness from view. "You're strong, and smart, and can take care of yourself. But having a few extra daggers never hurts."

His eyes lifted to a point over my shoulder. Fern, the twins, Casey, and Hollis appeared in the doorway as silently as a warm wind. They were dressed in all black and bristling with weapons, like a goth swat team.

"I can't believe you got abducted without me!" Casey walked over and slapped me on the shoulder. "Why is she getting to have all the fun?"

"Goddess help me, of all the idiotic things to say," Sage muttered, enfolding me in a brief embrace. They drew back and stared at me for a long, unnerving moment. "You're okay." Their eyes narrowed. "More than okay, actually. And your potentia has come in."

"Hot dog!" Hollis called. "Good timing, too. We ready to get this show on the road?"

"Leaving now," Alex said, adding one last palm-sized cylindrical object to his belt that he'd informed me earlier was a salt bomb.

We trooped out of the door, standing on the cracked asphalt of the parking lot as dawn's first rays peeked over the horizon.

As one, seven pairs of wings unfurled, the breeze it created blowing my hair back. Nonplussed, I stared. "So, all of you have wings. This is a thing."

"You have them, too," Fern smiled. "Or, you will, eventually." Hers were the blue, green, and yellow shades of a peacock's feathers, coordinating perfectly with her teal hair.

I came to my senses, looking around in a panic. "Someone's going to see you!"

Sylvan chuckled. "No, we're invisible. Or, if not completely invisible, well camouflaged. It's about manipulating the wavelengths of light around you."

Alex picked me up, scooping beneath my knees and holding me tight to his chest. Then, with a mighty flap of his wings, he rocketed into the sky. I let out an involuntary whoop, turning to see the other Guardians flanking us, three on each side.

The flight was over almost as soon as it began. I wished I'd had more time to see Gravesville from above, all of the cemeteries spread out to create great swaths of nature amongst the city. After a few minutes, we touched down softly just inside the tall iron gates of Gravesville Historic Cemetery. It was exactly as I remembered, and I felt comforted that at least this little slice of my life was unchanged.

Alex set me down carefully. "Okay, Seph. Show us where you found the card."

I led the Guardians just over the treeline, where I'd spoken with the strange man who'd borne more than a passing resemblance to a vampire. The early light had already clouded over, leaving the sky dense and gray. Snow clouds, my mom would've called them, looming like a heavy iron fist.

"It was around here." I recounted our conversation from that night.

"Sounds like he might've thrown a little something of the magical variety your way to keep you talking," Hollis speculated. "Are we thinking this guy was a demon?"

"He seemed...human. Every demon who's come after me has felt different—cold, or nauseating. Maybe he was using magic, but it wasn't anything like that."

"Okay," Alex nodded. "Let's do a grid search. We're looking for any artifacts or traces of supernatural activity—more tarot cards, lingering spells, power echoes, anything like that. If anyone unfriendly shows up, send out the emergency signal. Davina, Fern, and Sylvan, go east. Sage and Casey, west. Hollis and Sylvan south. Seph and I will go north."

Everyone dispersed, taking off at speed. Alex and I split off from the group once we cleared the grove, heading north towards Angel's Rest. It was named for statues of the seven archangels, each standing before their own altar tomb. The raised tombs were arranged in a half circle, with Azrael, the angel of death, in the center.

We silently scoured the ground and examined headstones. Alex formed a tiny, glowing blue sphere of light in his hands, then sent it ahead of us. *It's like a metal detector for arcana*, he'd explained earlier.

I stopped over a bare patch of dirt behind a mausoleum. Crouching, I ran my fingers over the hard, cracked earth. The branches of a massive spreading oak scratched the building's roof, singing a winter song. I shivered, the cold air sharp in my lungs.

Alex knelt next to me. "Did you find something?"

The dirt was chalky against my fingers and bone dry. I stood up, brushing my dusty hands against the knees of my jeans. "Maybe. Why isn't any grass growing here?" I stared at the ground, walking along its perimeter.

Tiny snowflakes began to fall, landing upon the yellowed grass like powdered sugar. Alex sighed. "Snow. Just what we need."

"Actually, yes." I pointed at where the snow disappeared about a foot above the bare patch, as though it was being siphoned away. I crouched again, running my hand along the circle's edge. When I pulled it up, minute white crystals coated it.

Alex took my hand, examining it like a specimen under a micro-scope. He popped my index finger into his mouth.

"What are you doing?" I gasped, both alarmed at his lack of hygiene and the lightning bolt of pleasure that shot straight to my center.

"Sodium chloride. It's harmless table salt. Whoever was here, they laid a salt circle. And that only means one thing."

"Well, don't leave me in suspense."

"Summoning."

An image popped into my head of the stranger's long fingers spreading the salt in a circle, his accented voice chanting the words of a dark incantation.

Alex brought a cupped hand to his lips and whispered into it. He opened his hand and blew across it. "I just called the rest of the unit."

Sure enough, they came running toward us a few moments later from all corners of the graveyard, tiny snowflakes sparkling in their hair like diamonds.

"A summoner?" Davina's voice cracked like a whip. "How could we have missed that?"

"It happens," Fern stated, crouching and running a finger along the circle's perimeter. "The boundary enchantments would have caught anything he managed to call, anyway. If only we had the damn tarot card, then we could try and open a gateway with it."

"If only, but that's not an option. Search every blade of grass in Angel's Rest." Alex checked his watch. "Quickly."

My stomach twisted with anticipation. "Is there anything else I can do?" I asked Alex, as the Guardians dispersed. Not having a great hold on my magic left me feeling useless.

"Use your senses, like you did at Scotchtown. Anything feels off, let me know." He squeezed my hand, then walked toward where Fern and Davina inspected a mausoleum.

I closed my eyes, breathing deep and even. Ever so slowly, I began to feel the world around me. The earth was sleeping, quiet with winter's hibernation. But I heard the scolding call of a bird, and bare branches rubbing against each other. I smelled the snow, earthy and crisp, and woodsmoke.

There was something ahead of me. It had a gentle rustling feeling, like water burbling in a brook. I opened my eyes. The feeling emanated from the large oak I'd noted earlier. I hurried toward it, calling out to the others.

I was feet away from the trunk when my toe caught a root as thick as a python that breached the ground in a wide and solid arc. Tripping, I caught Alex's look of horror as my pinwheeling body crashed into the oak tree.

Except, I didn't feel the crush of pain I'd been expecting. I passed through the tree altogether, like the gnarled bark and graceful boughs were an illusion. Alex reached for me in slow motion, his arms flung out, fingers grasping at a sleeve that wasn't there. My own reaching arms were as slow as a fly trapped in honey, and I could only watch as the tree closed around me before I was flung into darkness.

I saw and heard nothing, and only had the rush of wind on my skin to tell me I was falling, down, down, down. I thrust my arms out to stop my fall, but they were trapped against my sides, only moving a scant inch or so. Claustrophobia descended over me, and a scream caught in my throat along with the rest of my breath. Similar to going through a gateway, time and space seemed not to matter. I could have been falling for a second or a year.

Then, suddenly, the ground was underneath me. I landed on my feet, for a moment at least, until gravity and the realization that I wasn't dead caught up with me. Dust flew into the air, engulfing my face in a cloud. I coughed, sitting back on my heels and wiping gritty particles out of my watering eyes.

Tall shelves jammed with books lined the walls, and narrower bookcases were crammed tightly together around the space, creating odd angles. There were a few windows placed haphazardly around the shelves at differing heights and in off-kilter shapes. It smelled of old paper, and a sense of vellichor filled me.

Heart thumping, I pressed the wall behind me and pounded on surrounding bookcases, pulling out books at random in search of some kind of mechanism that would take me back to the cemetery. Plaster had flaked off the ceiling in great patches, but there was no human-sized hole that I could have fallen through.

Perhaps I could send Alex a mental message, the way he'd done with me earlier. As I thought of him my chest lurched, and I realized it was the tug of the thread that lived just under my ribcage. It dragged, like there was an anchor on the end of it, but far, far away.

Alex, if you can hear me, I'm okay, I thought in the direction of the pull. *I'm in a...library? No, a* bookstore.

A frisson of excitement coiled in my belly. *Come find me,* I urged.

I set off into the warren of stacks, trying to stay in a straight line so I could trace my way back. It was impossible. Inevitably, I had to weave around oddly placed bookcases and backtrack when I hit dead ends. It didn't help that everything looked the same, either. All the books were bound in dusty leather or muted cloth, with no new fiction or paper dust jackets to be found.

Curious, I stopped and pulled a book from the shelves at random, opening it to the title page.

A Treatisse on Daemons of the Twelfthe Hour
J. A. Greer

I flipped through the book's brittle pages, stopping here and there at illustrations of the 'daemons' referenced in the book's title. The images showed beings that looked like men, but had steely eyes and teeth too sharp to be human. This was a grimoire.

Definitely magic, then. I closed the cover and slid it back home.

After several dead ends and an increasing sense of worry, I turned the corner of a particularly high row of shelves and stumbled into a door. It looked as old as the rest of the place, with a large brass knocker in the shape of a...a triangle, with three spirals connecting in a center point. The Triskele.

Heart thudding loudly in my ears, I jiggled the handle, but the knob held fast under my grip and refused to budge.

"Well, shit. Of course it has to be locked," I muttered. Alex's words from earlier popped into my head. *You are strong, and smart, and can take care of yourself.*

It was then I remembered that I had supernatural strength and could just kick the door down. A moment later the wood around the lock splintered with a resounding crack, and it swung open.

Darkness permeated beyond the door, but my enhanced night vision illuminated the room. I crossed the threshold. The air smelled of glue and sawdust, of mustiness with something sharp cutting across it. It wasn't altogether unpleasant. Low wooden tables were organized in neat rows along opposite walls, various sharp-edged tools scattered across their surfaces.

I picked up a long-bladed knife, its wide metal tip blunted into a half circle. In hindsight, I appreciated all the weapons Alex had saddled me with.

A creak sounded to my left, and I whirled around, unsheathing a knife from my harness.

"Who's there?" I called, trying and failing to keep my voice level. Cold sweat beaded at my hairline, sending a chill through me. "Show yourself!"

A vaguely human silhouette stepped out from around a corner.

My chest tightened, but I managed a hoarse whisper. "Who are you?"

"I should be the one asking you that," said a voice with a lilting, musical accent. "You're in my shop, after all. Trespassing, one might say."

Slow recognition built, and the hairs on my arms prickled with awareness. "Are you Jupiter?"

"Who's asking? And to hells with it, let's have some decent light."

Oil lamps set into the walls flared all at once. My eyes smarted at the sudden bright burst, and I blinked rapidly.

I could see all too well now, and held my breath as I assessed the man standing before me. He was thin and lanky, maybe an inch or two taller than me. Appearing roughly my age, he wore dark, homespun clothing that looked like it was from a different era, as if he was cosplaying a Victorian lamplighter. It was neat but had clearly seen better days, judging from the patches and lines of stitching. His features were vulpine, the line of his jaw sharp and eyes that were long lidded and tilted upward slightly at the corners. His full mouth twisted into a frown.

There was no doubt this man was the stranger from the graveyard. One of the long-bladed, blunt-tipped knives dangled loosely from his hand.

I pinched the tip of my dagger, ready to throw it. Blue flames sprang up on my skin, bringing the smell of ozone with them.

"Hold on, now. No need for that," the man said warily. "I'm not going to harm you."

I didn't drop my stare, every nerve ending in my body alight. "I know you."

The stranger's brow knit, and he scowled. "Do you, now? I don't think I've had the pleasure."

Why was he lying? "What do you know about the Watchers?" I shot off.

His frown deepened. "And what would that be to you?"

"Were you summoning, that night we met in the cemetery?"

The stranger cocked his head and let out a quiet sigh. "Ah, I see. You've met my brother."

"Brother?" Confusion wedged in, replacing some of my wariness.

"My twin. Penn is his name," the stranger said. "I'm Simon."

I studied Simon. His head of rich chestnut hair was cut short, not like the man from the graveyard, but he could've gotten a haircut. His eyes were gray as a storm cloud, with flecks of yellow in the iris, as though they were streaked with lightning. Unfortunately, they gave nothing away.

"Seph," I replied.

"Bless you," he said, showing no recognition at all.

Somehow in the middle of all the anxiety and tension in the room, I wanted to roll my eyes. "It's my name," I clarified.

"Ah, sorry. Pleased to meet you, Seph." He sounded anything but, like he was just as annoyed and baffled as I was tense.

A moment hung in the air where we said nothing, but continued to take each other's measure.

"That means you're from the other side, then. I could've guessed. Your clothes." His gesture encompassed the whole of me. "What are you, some kind of witch, then?"

I didn't correct him. "How do I know you're not lying?"

He laughed shortly. "Not going to take my word for it, eh? I imagine you're no one's fool." I watched him in silence. "All right, then. I'd best show you."

The knife slid in my damp grip. "I'm not doing anything until you tell me what I want to know."

Simon let out a long suffering sigh. "I just said I'd show you, didn't I?"

"Why don't you drop that knife?"

"What, this? It's only a bookbinder's knife. Too dull to slit your throat, if that's what you're wondering."

He threw the knife on a table with a clatter, then turned on his heel and stalked off. I had no choice other than to follow him through the swinging doors, or be left behind.

The flames died on my skin. "What is this place?" I called, hurrying after him.

"It's a bookshop. Surely, you figured that out? You'd have had to come through the stacks to get here," Simon replied.

"So this really is Jupiter's Books and Stationery?"

"The one and only," he muttered darkly.

We climbed a rickety flight of stairs that twisted and turned like a vine climbing a tower, and bypassed several landings that had doors heading off into other directions. There was an air of decay about everything, from the creaky floors with finger-sized gaps between the wood planks to the cobwebs that hung from the ceiling like bits of frosting.

Simon didn't stop until we reached the very top of the stairs. He pulled an old brass key with large, square teeth out of his pocket and inserted it into the lock of a gnarled and pitted wooden door. The hinges squeaked in protest as it swung open into another small room.

The space reminded me of a sepia photograph, dusty and from a bygone century. A heavy typewriter sat on a wooden desk, its keys so worn from use that the letters had almost rubbed off entirely. More spiderwebs strung the rafters, and I sneezed from the dust rising from the rug under Simon's footfalls. He pushed through another door.

The place was like a rabbit's warren, with alcoves and hallways stashed where they didn't seem to belong. The books upstairs looked much newer than those in the labyrinth of the stacks below, and glass cases held sleek fountain pens on display behind their doors.

Simon finally stopped, pointing to a large oil painting that hung on the wall behind the counter. It was at odds with the rest of the shop, gleaming like a new penny. The frame was a magnificent piece of art itself, polished to a mirror-like shine and carved with fanciful swirls.

It was a family portrait. An adult man and woman stood in the background, with three children arrayed in front of them. The man and boys were wearing suit coats and bow ties, and the woman and girl had on high necked dresses with long sleeves, their hair neatly parted and pulled back.

The little girl looked to be around four or five years old, her face cherubic and framed by blond curls. The two boys had to be around middle school age. I recognized the sullen set to Simon's pointed chin immediately. The other boy had his exact same face, but his eyes gleamed with mischief, whereas Simon's held resentment. The boys bore a strong resemblance to their mother, except that her hair was a true, blazing red.

When my eyes finally alighted on the father, my heart simply stopped for one painful moment. I'd seen that face before, albeit with a different expression. He was solemn here, but I recognized that the mischievous glint of the son's eyes had been inherited from his father. This man had to be Lucas, my dad's friend.

"See? I'm telling the truth. There are two of us."

He sounded smug, but his voice was faraway in my ears. I felt like I was back in the passage in the oak tree, in free fall and powerless. I didn't notice Simon had opened the front door of the shop until a blast of cold air hit me.

Outside the open door, the sky was an overcast band of every shade of gray imaginable, from silver to graphite. It was impossible to differentiate between the layers of cloud cover and the smoke billowing from tall brick towers in the distance. The air smelled like a mixture of smog and oil, so thick I almost choked on it.

A tall clock tower in the center of the city loomed high above cramped buildings that were shoved together like rows of crooked teeth. The tower was in disrepair, streaked with orange rust and missing one of its hands, while the other teetered drunkenly. In the far distance, a railroad track circled the city, a line of rusty train cars parked like forgotten toys.

"Welcome to Canhaben," Simon said, smiling grimly. "We're delighted to have you."

PART III

"That's very curious!" she thought. "But everything's curious to-day. I think I may as well go in at once." And in she went.

— LEWIS CARROLL, *ALICE IN WONDERLAND*

27

So, this was Canhaben. My father's world, where the other half of me was from. If I'd ever imagined what it would be like to discover my heritage, it wouldn't have been this—covered in layers of dirt and grime, wrapped in a musty wool blanket while the son of my father's estranged best friend made me a cup of tea.

We were in the storeroom of Jupiter's. Simon had made it as habitable as he could, dusting off a chair and wiping a dirty mug with the hem of his shirt. I hadn't yet shared our fathers' connection.

"So, what was your twin—"

"Penn," Simon interjected, sliding a steaming mug toward me across the table. I took it, fearful it would taste as stale as the rest of the place.

"What was Penn doing in the graveyard on the other side?"

"What did it look like?" Simon eyed me over his tea, taking a deep draft.

"I didn't actually see him doing anything. But he left behind a card with Jupiter's Books and Stationery stamped on it. I followed the trail here."

"You some sort of detective, then? Your...choice of accessories would suggest otherwise."

My hand went to the trio of knives at my ribs. "Let's just say that I have them for a good reason."

"Course you do."

We eyed each other across the table. I broke the silence first. "I'm looking for information. I could make it worth your while if you tell me what I want to know."

He found that funny, letting out a dark laugh. "Make it worth my while? That's a good one."

"Isn't there anything you need?" I looked pointedly at the decrepitness of...everything. "Money, maybe?"

"Look...Seph, right? You're new here, so I'll forgive your ignorance. This is a dying world. And there isn't a gods-damned thing anyone can do about it. So I suggest that you shove off, back through the seam to the other side, and go on your merry way."

Confusion made my thoughts spin. "What do you mean?"

The yellow in Simon's gray eyes flared. "Exactly what it sounds like. The light's gone out of the world, and she's gasping for air as the last of her life is belched out into a mass of smoke and decay. You saw what's out there. Soon, the whole thing will crumble to dust, taking all of us poor sods with her."

"How is that even possible?" That was horrible, but gave me an inkling of why my dad might have left Canhaben in the first place.

"It's our fate," he said, jerking a shoulder. I would have bet that his nonchalance was practiced.

"That's pessimistic of you."

"Optimism was bred out of the family ages ago. It doesn't do to look on the bright side if you're from Canhaben. There are no silver linings, no windfalls, and not even a speck of good luck to be found at all." He smiled again, but it was all sharpness and no warmth.

It seemed like if I was to get anywhere with this ornery man, I had to lay all of my cards on the table. "Simon, I haven't been completely honest with you."

He showed no surprise. "We all have secrets. Gods know I have plenty of them."

Bracing myself, I drank some tea to wet my throat. The mint and honey flavor was a pleasant surprise. "My full name is Persephone Hart. Zeke—Ezekial Hart was my father."

Simon stared at me for a long moment, then pushed back from the table, his chair emitting a loud squeak. "You're joking."

I shook my head. "No. And I know he was friends with your dad. I recognized him from the portrait."

Simon's entire demeanor changed. He smiled, a real one this time. It softened his hard edges. "This is unbelievable. How is Ezekial? He left here before I was born, so I never met him. Wish I had, though—dad always had great stories about him."

Oh. My stomach fluttered with some unspoken feeling. "I can't tell you. I don't know him, either. He left me and my mom when I was a baby."

His brows drew down in confusion. "What? There's no way the man my parents talked about would have done that. They were best friends, you know."

"That's what I thought, too. I found some letters that your father wrote to mine, after he left for the other side."

His eyes lit. "Do you have them?"

"No, they're back home. Sorry."

Simon stilled for a moment. "That's all right. It's just that my father is gone too, you see. He died."

"Oh. I'm so sorry," I said weakly.

Simon waved a hand. "It was a long time ago. It's just, the only thing I have left from him is this place. It would be nice to have something else, aye?"

I understood that all too well. "I'll bring them to you, if I can."

"Cheers."

We stared at each other, absorbing the strange and unfamiliar ties that bound us. In another life, I might have grown up with Simon, been friends with him. Instead, he was as alien to me as Canhaben.

"So that's why you're here, then," he said, breaking the silence. "You want to find out about your dad? Why haven't you come before?"

"I didn't even know Canhaben existed until recently."

"Your mum didn't tell you?"

"She didn't know, either."

Simon scratched his head, disturbing the chestnut strands. "Gods," he repeated. "You must feel like you've been dumped on your head."

I exhaled sharply. "Something like that."

"It might have been better that way, that you didn't know. There's nothing here for you, Seph." There was a pleading note in his voice. "You're better off going back to the other side, back to your life."

"I can't do that." Not only because I was being hunted. "Put yourself in my place. Wouldn't you want to know, even if there was nothing you could do to change it?"

"No. If I was in your place, I would go home and forget about Canhaben."

"Look, Simon," I implored. "If I don't get some questions answered, I don't think I can go back home at all."

"You in some sort of trouble?" His eyes narrowed slightly.

"Frankly, yes. A lot of it."

"Right, then. I'd be an arse if I didn't help out the daughter of my dad's best friend, wouldn't I? What do you want to know?"

"For starters, what was Penn doing in the graveyard?"

Simon turned his back to me, walking to the tiny stove. "D'you want more tea?"

"I'm fine." I waited impatiently for him to complete the process of boiling water in the dented kettle, shaking the loose tea leaves into a little pouch, and finally submerging it into his mug. His hands were flecked with paint.

"Are you going to tell me?"

He settled back into his chair with a heavy sigh. "Story time, eh? Right. Long, long ago, the world of Canhaben wasn't like it is now—it was an important place, a center of commerce and innovation. Many creatures, mortals, immortals, and beasts alike, would come from other worlds to trade with us. There was a lot of back and forth in those days, and the policy among most of the worlds was to keep their borders wide open. That is, until the evil ones came." He paused to drink his tea. "Murderers and foul creatures they were, spreading across worlds like rot. This went on for a time, until the Golden Ones showed up to hunt them."

The Golden Ones. The Aureum. I sat up straighter in my chair, hanging onto Simon's every word.

"We're not sure where the Golden Ones came from, only that they had human form but were blessed with more strength, speed, and power than a mortal could ever hope to possess. They drove back the evil, but in doing so closed the borders of the worlds to keep the bad from spreading." Simon cleared his throat, then sipped from his mug. "Ever since then, we've been slowly fading out of existence. The commerce dried up, and so did the spark that keeps this place alive. It's happened to other places too, worlds that have already gone still and cold. So you see, this is how we learned that when the worlds aren't connected to each other, they die. Like a plant that's been kept from water, soil, and sunlight, we will wither away into nothing."

Simon reached a hand out, but drew back. "Seph, are you well?"

I'd momentarily forgotten how to breathe. The world coalesced to a single point, and it was almost as if Iznir appeared in the middle of the shabby floor as I recalled her decree. *You can save my Chosen, and restore balance to the worlds.*

"I—I'm fine," I choked. "There must be a way to keep the bad stuff out and the borders open."

"Not that anyone has found thus far," Simon said, with a shake of his head. "Over time, the seams of the worlds can become weak from rubbing against each other, and you get a split here and there. That's the only reason Canhaben is still holding on. For the time being." His dull acceptance made it seem like it would be happening sooner rather than later.

"The oak tree," I murmured.

Simon nodded. "It goes into the stacks, coming through that wall. It's the only seam we've got."

"So Penn was trying to escape?"

"No. He's trying to save us, the bloody fool. I've always said he's got more nerve than sense," Simon murmured, almost as if he was talking to himself. "He thinks spirit calling will open the borders again."

Spirit calling. Was that the same as summoning?

"Know any spirit callers, do you?" Simon asked, drumming his fingers on the table.

I licked my chapped lips before I answered. "No."

"I can tell what you're thinking. And no, he's not some kind of evil sorcerer."

I opened my mouth, ready to retort, but he held a hand up to silence me. He went to the bookcase on the far side of the room, pulling out a weighty tome. He slid it across the table to me.

"What is this?"

"Open it," he commanded.

I did as he asked, opening to the title page. It was the *Ars Theurgia-Goetia*. I'd studied it back at Aureum headquarters.

"I know what this is."

"Then you know the purpose of a grimoire is for summoning and working magic. Those lot, the Golden Ones, tried to ban summoning. But it's not all about conjuring evil or destruction. If you've read grimoires, you know there are good or neutral spirits—demons—as well, those that teach magic and help people."

"But all demons are bad. I mean, they're...demonic. Soul sucking devils that are hellbent on human destruction."

Simon clucked. "I didn't take you for a bigot."

"I am not a bigot!" I protested. "It's just true. I've seen these creatures with my own eyes. They've attacked me." The scar on my chest pulsed faintly.

Simon heaved an exasperated sigh. "Of course some demons are bad. Just like anything else in the worlds, there is darkness and light, and all manner of shades in between."

I flipped through *Ars Theurgia*. The Aureum insisted on the fact that any demon could cause chaos and destruction, that their very natures were evil at their core.

"Not all beings who conjure and trade in magic have innate ability," Simon continued. "They need rituals, words, movements, objects, relics, and elements to work with power. And sometimes, that means calling on creatures who are naturally powerful already. Penn is trying to keep this world alive, foolish and useless as his efforts may be."

If what Simon said was true, then by trying to keep my world safe from demons the Guardians were suffocating every other world. I imagined a glass dome placed over a candle, its flame snuffed out because it was starved of oxygen.

In *Ars Theurgia*, my fingers stilled on a page that depicted a demon with a woman's head and the body of a snake. *Hidriel, a Wandrng Prince. Very courteous and willing to obey; they delight most in or about waters.*

"Fine. Say this is all true—"

"It is," he interrupted. "Sorry. I don't talk to people much. It's just me here, usually."

I thought about the family portrait hanging in the other room. His twin was clearly still around, but he hadn't mentioned the little girl or his mother. "Where is he? Penn, I mean."

Simon shook his head. "Your guess is as good as mine."

"You don't know?"

"He comes and goes as he pleases. He's the younger of us by ten minutes, and certainly acts like it."

"Okay. So, what does all of this have to do with the Watchers?"

His eyes flickered, then the long lids shuttered. "All that's not enough to make you want to leave yet?"

I snapped *Ars Theurgia* shut and pushed it into Simon's chest. "I refuse to accept that. What if we can help you? I have friends who are powerful." *And part of the problem.* "They can help solve this. There's a path forward, you just haven't found it yet."

"No, there's not." Simon's eyes held sadness, but he was resolute. "There's nothing left to do for this world but to let it go, slowly and quietly, in the way that all worlds die. Soon there will be no one to remember us. And if no one remembers, you cease to exist."

That chilled me to my core. Watching your own end slowly coming had to be torture, the most painful of deaths. I wouldn't accept that it was Canhaben's fate, or anyone else's.

"I'll remember."

We stared at each other, and Simon looked away first. "Fine. I'll take you to the edge. Maybe then you'll finally get it through your head there's no chance of saving us."

"What's the edge?"

He raised his finely arched brows. "The edge of the world."

I paused, thinking I'd misheard him. "Come again?"

"Aye, it's exactly what it sounds like. It's the edge of Canhaben, where it's crumbling away to dust."

"I don't believe you."

Simon rifled through a closet, moths flying out like he'd disturbed a whole extended family of them, and handed me a worn coat. "Come along, then. See for yourself."

The coat was too large, but I pulled it on over my jacket and hugged it tightly against the cold as we left Jupiter's.

Tiny flakes of snow swirled in the air, never quite making it to the ground. The few people on the streets walked hurriedly to their destinations with their heads down, collars pulled high.

The scene was so different from home, but familiar at the same time. Buildings crowded together like they, too, wanted relief from the cold. They had once been grand, but were now faded like old memories. I covered my nose and tried to breathe through my mouth to avoid the oil and ash smell.

We passed an outdoor market, and curiosity got the better of me as I paused at a stall. An old and diminutive woman was selling what I thought were blankets, but turned out to be clothing, the fabric so patched and stitched that the tattered pants and shirts resembled quilts.

"Three for a pound of meal!" she cried over and over. "Four for a pound and a half!" She turned her grizzled smile on me, tongue poking out through the gaps of missing teeth.

"Care for one, love?" she asked, scanning me up and down. Her eyes narrowed when she took in my crisp jeans. "What's that you got on there?"

"Bugger off," Simon growled, taking my elbow and pulling me away.

"Simon," I said under my breath. "Why are there still so many people here? Aren't they trying to get away?"

"If more than ten people go through that seam, in say, a day, it'll collapse. And it becomes more unstable the more it's used," he said. "The time for leaving was long ago." Looking straight ahead, he took a left down a cobbled street that had an ominously steep incline. A crooked street sign read *Lychgate Road*. We climbed the hill, my calves burning with the effort.

At last, we reached the top. Headstones, crypts, and mausoleums spread as far as the eye could see in every direction. There were even areas where the stone effigies were piled on top of each other in heaps, as if they'd run out of room and had no choice but to go skyward. Trees and vines also vied for space, their dark canopy providing a backdrop to the chaos.

Not only did the cemetery look wild, but there was an energy surrounding the place that made the hair stand up on the back of my neck. "Is this it?"

"You'll know when we get there," Simon said, starting down the hill.

The paths that wound through the jumble of gravestones resembled spreading roots. Some were long and some were short, with tracks branching off to form a wild tangle. A ditch filled with brackish water cut through the graves, winding parallel to the bottom of the hill then disappearing from sight.

I picked my way down carefully, shuffling sideways at points because it was so steep. When I finally met Simon at the bottom, he started off again without another word. The air felt sticky, as though any words that were spoken would be caught and arrested mid-speech.

I traced the sloped tops of graves, running my fingers through the snarl of vines and weeds that wrapped around them. Some had inscriptions that were easy to read, and others were blank, the names lost to time. The cemetery of this dying world should've been cold and dead, but instead it felt agitated as a caged animal.

We crossed a rickety bridge over the fetid ditchwater. The longer we walked, the more deteriorated the path became. Chunks of crumbled rock crunched underfoot, and the wind picked up. Soon it was whipping my hair into knots, and I had to bow my head into the gale to keep going.

The long, patchy grass was brown and dead. Small fissures zig-zagged across the dirt, crossing and twisting over each other until the ground turned into a mosaic of cracked earth and small craters. The wind howled even harder, blowing dust in my face and making my eyes tear up.

I spotted Simon just a few feet ahead of me, and when we drew level it was like I'd hit an iron wall. Understanding that I couldn't move forward anymore, I cupped my hands around my face and peered through the dust.

The ground fifty yards ahead was broken off into a jagged and crumbling line, like the teeth of the old woman who'd stopped me in the market. And beyond that, there was...nothing.

It was the absolute blackness of outer space, but without the brightness of stars. The wind was so loud I almost couldn't hear myself think. Simon's face had gone totally blank, devoid of emotion. It was an awful, terrifying scene, something that should have repelled me and filled me with horror.

But I wasn't afraid.

Instead, I felt a prickling at the back of my neck that spread through my arms and legs, all the way down to my fingertips and toes. I crackled with electricity, blue streaks of current flying over my exposed skin like shooting stars, and I felt so full, so powerful, so *alive*.

Striding toward the edge, I broke past the invisible barrier. I glanced back at Simon, who was still stuck behind the wall, yelling at me, but the wind stole the words right out of his mouth and tossed them away into the abyss.

There was such energy here, and the darkness pulsed with it. Couldn't he feel it? How the earth jostled and vibrated, trying to pull away from the void while the endless chasm crept forward anyway, devastating everything in its path. How the blackness beyond the edge was drawing everything toward it, like a magnet.

This world didn't want to die, that much was obvious. It was fighting like hell against the dark. But it was weak, and as I stood on the very end of the edge, a section next to me crumbled away and dropped into the darkness like a calving iceberg.

No. I felt the loss of that patch of earth as keenly as if my own arm had been severed. I didn't want the chasm to take another bite, to claim one more part of this place as its own.

I threw out my arms toward the falling clods of earth like I was going to gather them up. They stopped, floating on the air like a cloud, weightless, although I felt the chasm clutching at me, dragging.

Come back, now.

The loose soil and grass flew upward and sealed itself against the area from which it'd fallen. I sighed, uncurling the tension from my ribs. *That's better.*

Then, the wind buffeted me, knocking me off balance. I dropped to the ground, my energy draining like water disappearing from a bath. Crawling on my hands and knees, I made my way back to the line of demarcation.

Simon wasn't the only one standing there. Alex and the rest of the Guardians had arrived, and were trying to penetrate the invisible wall.

Simon was yelling and gesticulating wildly, with Sylvan attempting to placate him.

After I dragged myself across the border, Alex pulled me upright, cradling me to his chest. I leaned into his solid warmth, my vision fizzling. Strong arms scooped under my legs, carrying me back toward safety.

28

"How did you get through?" I mumbled into Alex's neck. I didn't know if he could hear me through the howling wind—I couldn't even hear myself. My chest felt hollow, like I'd left a piece of myself behind in the void, but my vision cleared.

His arms tightened around me. "We had to blast through that oak—magically speaking, it's fine, we stitched it back up. But, there's a hole in the wall of the bookstore. I followed your trail here. What were you thinking, Seph?"

I winced as I caught Simon's furious yelp even over the roaring wind. "You can put me down, I'm fine."

"No." Alex's tone was fierce, but there was fear in his eyes.

I turned his face toward me. "I can walk on my own. Please."

Mouth a grim line, he stopped. I slid out of his grasp, fighting not to sway as I turned to Simon. I had to shout to make myself heard. "These are the friends I was talking about. The ones who can help you."

Simon shook his head, curling his lip in anger. "I want them out. They can bloody well come back where they came from."

He stalked away, and the rest of us followed silently, the Guardians throwing me pointed glances that I didn't answer. He led us through the graveyard, taking side streets, until we entered Jupiter's through a door in a back alley.

"Can we please sit down and talk about this?" I asked, trailing after Simon. He walked into a kitchen, throwing his coat onto an iron peg mounted on the wall. The kitchen, like the rest of the house, had seen better days. Scars and burn marks covered the counters, and grease stains splattered the wall behind the stove. At least there were no spiderwebs.

"Talk about what? The fact that the bloody cavalry has broken into my home?"

I put a hand on his arm, and he stilled. "I have things I want to tell you, Simon. And I'd really like to get some answers from you. This isn't a joke to me. This is my life. I would not ask you to do this if I didn't have to," I begged.

Whatever he saw in my eyes had his shoulders lowering. He blew a long sigh through pursed lips. "Fine. Sit."

The Guardians arrayed themselves on one side of a trestle table, and Simon sat on the other. I put myself at the head, hoping to play the neutral party.

I gave Alex and the others a rundown, introducing Simon and sharing what he'd told me about his dying world.

The situation quickly devolved after that.

"Seph, you really believe this joker?" Hollis's usual jovial tone dripped with derision.

"Hollis," Alex cautioned. "We are guests in Simon's home."

"I'm just saying that it's his word against thousands of years of history," Hollis stated, leaning back in his chair.

"Shall I speak slower so you can understand?" Simon asked pleasantly. He was enjoying needling the Guardians far too much.

"Even talking about this is treason," Davina interjected. Her tapping foot under the table betrayed her nerves. "Our oaths say—"

"Sweet goddess, everyone knows what our oaths say, Davina," Fern said over her, rolling her eyes.

Sylvan jumped in. "Don't talk to her like that."

"Everyone, stop," I ground out. Between the arguing and the magnetic feeling of the void still tugging at me, my head was on the verge of exploding. I sighed heavily, and the fire flickered and died as though a gust of wind swept down the chimney. "Sorry."

Casey snapped her fingers, and the flames jumped to life again. Simon looked shocked at such casual use of magic.

"It's okay, Seph. You're right," she said. "Arguing is getting us nowhere."

Most everyone had the good grace to look ashamed that Casey, of all people, was the voice of reason.

"You lot saw the edge," Simon said. "What more evidence do you need?" Silence answered him. "What Seph did—I've never seen the likes of it. No one can pass through the barrier, let alone put pieces back together."

Alex caught my eye and his voice sounded in my head. *Ask him about the Watchers.*

In front of everyone? I sent back, envisioning the message traveling down our link. Fatigue clouded my focus, and I wasn't sure he'd receive it.

There's nothing else to lose. Davina's right. Just by being here, discussing this, is breaking our laws. The rest of the unit already have enough information to turn us in to the Diurne. But they can't do that without implicating themselves. The skin under his eyes tightened. Although we'd only been separated for a few hours, Alex looked almost as tired as I felt.

I nodded at him. The conversation had only taken a few seconds.

"Simon." I turned to him. "Can you please tell us about the Watchers?"

"The what?" Sage said.

Simon's face went blank again. He kept his eyes on me as he spoke. "If I were to say anything, I would need some kind of guarantee that you won't bring down an army on Canhaben."

"Why the hell—" Hollis started, but Alex cut him off.

"You have my word," he replied. "And I represent my unit."

"Sorry, mate. Not good enough," Simon declared. "I'll take a blood promise, or nothing."

Everyone around the table looked startled. Alex was unphased, his mouth set in a cool line. "No problem. I'll do it now."

"You trust this bloke?" Simon asked me, as though Alex wasn't sitting right across from him.

"Implicitly," I answered, while in the same breath I thought, *What the hell is a blood promise?*

 Alex assured me.

"Alex, don't," Davina warned, placing a hand on his arm. He didn't say a word, only stared at her hand until she removed it.

Simon left and returned with a yellowed piece of paper. Alex sliced his palm with a knife from his belt and dipped his finger into the pooling blood. He touched the blood to the page, and words sprang from it, a sanguine promise. Alex folded the paper and handed it to Simon, who scanned, then pocketed it.

"All right, then. That's sorted." He took a deep breath, and began. "Almost since the beginning of humankind, there have been Watchers." Everyone sat up straighter, leaning in toward him.

"Legends say immortals were sent from the world of the gods—or, *a* god, depending on who you ask—to explore the worlds of men. In truth, they were sent to conquer the humans, who were seen as lesser beings. So two hundred of them went, led by the immortals Asael and Shemihazah. In your stories," Simon said, giving me a pointed look, "they are known as the Grigori, or the Watcher angels.

"But the Grigori didn't conquer the humans—instead, they joined them, building lives and teaching the people the ways of immortals, mating with the daughters of man. Their children were half human, half immortal, and with their supernatural lineage and knowledge of the secret arts, became a powerful force in their own right. The powerful gods who had sent them down didn't like that at all, not one bit. The Grigori were supposed to do their bidding, to colonize the mortals and subjugate them, not join with them and give away their secrets. So, the gods came down to punish the Grigori and destroy the Nephilim."

"Nephilim?" I interrupted.

"The part human, part immortal offspring. They could turn into giants and had all sorts of powers, so the legend says. That rubbish in the stories about them being evil—well, maybe some of them were, but not most. Most were good folk who helped the children of men, tried to improve upon their lives a bit, you know.

"And so the gods, they hunt down the Nephilim. A lot of them were destroyed, captured, or banished to other worlds. And even then, some of the survivors chose to go into hiding, to find their own corners of the worlds out of sight of the gods to conceal themselves. But, survive they did. Their lines even prospered, what with the knowledge from the immortals they passed down generation to generation, and their supernatural blood, although diluted, still ran strong in their veins.

"These survivors, the sons and daughters of the Nephilim, are known as the Watchers, not only because of their lineage from the Watcher angels, but because they watch and wait in hiding for the day they will be able to walk freely again without being hunted."

"Hunted by who?" Davina asked, gaze calculating.

"A few creatures. But mostly, the Golden Ones. Or, should I say— you lot."

The deafening silence that followed thundered in my ears.

"That's right. I noticed your mark right off," Simon told me, gesturing on his wrist to the position of my birthmark. "Yours too, blondie," he said to Sage. Sage's was on the side of their neck, exposed by their cropped hair. "The Golden Ones have been trying to exterminate the Watchers for millenia."

"But why?" My stomach fluttered, and my chest tightened.

Simon shrugged. "Damned if I know. It's just the way it's always been. And you haven't been content just hunting Watchers. No, you've got to destroy our worlds, too. I s'pose that's a more efficient way of killing." He said all this with an indifference that lodged a shard of ice in my heart.

"If—let's say this is true," Fern started. "Then the Aureum has been sponsoring genocide. That goes against everything we've ever been taught. Our oath to the goddess is to save lives, not murder."

"Well, you're only murdering certain people," Simon corrected, folding his arms. "Which leads to the problem of you." He nodded toward me.

"What about her?" Alex's voice was dangerous in its softness, inviting Simon to see what would happen if he took a shot at me.

"Well, she's clearly one of you. But she's also a Watcher. So, I'm not sure how that squares."

I felt the moment all the Guardians's heads swung in my direction. Their gazes bored into me, pressure dancing along my skin.

"How do you know that?" Davina demanded.

"Because Ezekial Hart is a Watcher. Canhaben is one of the worlds that was populated by Nephilim after they went into hiding. Almost all of us who live here have their blood."

There it was. Confirmation. I knew my heart was pounding, but I couldn't feel it. I couldn't feel anything.

Casey whistled softly, breaking the hush that had fallen. Standing stiffly, I left the room. No one followed me.

I walked the gloomy, maze-like halls of Jupiter's until I was thoroughly lost. Eventually I came upon a long room that had the feel of a woman whose beauty had faded with age. It was worn, like the rest of the manse, but a specter of its former splendor lingered.

I stopped underneath a wide chandelier that dripped with emerald crystals and sat on the begrimed floor, wrapping my arms around my knees.

Watchers, Nephilim, Grigori—I was on a carousel that was spinning too fast, and I couldn't jump off without breaking a leg.

Footsteps sounded, then Alex appeared at the end of the room. He was paler than usual, although I wasn't sure if it was just the dim lighting. "Can I sit?" he asked. I nodded, and he folded his long legs on the floor beside me.

"You know, this changes nothing. It just confirms what we thought."

"Doesn't it?" I met his eyes, and they appeared black in the light. "Your unit is involved now. Even if you've agreed to help me, they didn't sign up for all this."

"That's true. They have a choice. If they want to return to the Aureum, I won't stop them. But I will take responsibility for Simon's secret. I won't expose Canhaben."

"So you believe him?"

"About the Watchers?" Alex considered. "It fits. There's lore that explains it."

"What lore?"

"That the Nephilim aren't just human-angel hybrids. That they're the first demons."

"Oh, fuck." I dropped my head into my hands. "Now I have demon blood?"

"There's still a lot we don't know," Alex answered swiftly. "And if you do, then so does Simon. But, it's the only way that Guardians going out and hunting Watchers would make sense. We take down other supernaturals that threaten humans, but at our core—we're demon hunters."

Alex and I looked at each other for a long moment.

Hunter, and hunted.

———

We returned to the kitchen to find Simon and Hollis at each other's throats.

"You lot go around filling people's heads with the idea that all demons are the spawn of evil, when in fact there are millenia of evidence proving that's false," Simon shouted.

"And what about the evidence proving it's true?" Hollis spat back.

"Your lot's propaganda at its finest," Simon replied with disgust. "You have the influence and resources to shape world events and create the narrative you want people to believe. It's all about power and control. Meanwhile, the ones who are innocent end up suffering and hiding in the shadows."

"Hold on," I said, stepping between the two men. "Can we agree that you are both a product of your upbringing and leave it at that?"

"Don't ruin our fun, Seph. This is better entertainment than *Real Housewives*," Casey chortled.

Hollis turned to Casey, snapping his teeth. "No one asked you."

"Listen up," Alex said in a mild voice. His unit instantly quieted. Davina and Fern turned their attention to him where they'd been speaking in low tones across the room. The twins walked over from the flickering hearth.

"Obviously, everyone knows the truth about Seph by now." Alex placed a hand on my shoulder. "She's both a Guardian and a Watcher. Her father is from this world, and her mother from ours. But she took her oath, just like we all did. Graveborn or not, it doesn't matter. She's part of the Aureum, but the Aureum has tried to harm her." His eyes scanned every watching face. "We swore loyalty to each other. Whatever happens next, I'm staying with Seph." Davina inhaled sharply, and Hollis kneaded his forehead. "I'm giving you all a choice. You can stay with us—or, you can return to the Aureum. I won't hold it against you if you choose to leave. But know that if you go, you will not share any of the information you've learned today. If you do, that blood promise will kick in, and it won't turn out great for me."

A hard weight settled in my stomach. So, Alex had been counting on his unit's loyalty to him to keep them in line. "I won't ask you to give up your lives for me. I would never expect it."

Fern was the first to speak up. "I'll stay."

Some of the weight lifted. "Really?"

"It's not even a choice. I believe Simon, and if there's a chance to save innocent lives, to right some wrongs—I'm in."

"Me, too," Sage added. "I'll stay."

Sylvan held his twin's hand. "If Sage stays, I'm staying."

Casey shrugged. "I go where the fight is, and it sounds like the fight's here."

Hollis and Davina looked at each other, then at Alex. "Cap, you know I'd follow you anywhere. I just don't know about all this. About him," he said, frowning at Simon.

"You don't have to declare yourself now, Hollis," Alex said.

"I...I'm not sure, either." Davina's dark brows were drawn down, and she rubbed her lips together. "Can I have some time?"

I wasn't sure if anyone else noticed it, but I caught the flash of anguish in Alex's eyes. "Of course. Why don't you sleep on it?" Then, he turned to Simon. "I'm afraid I'm going to ask to impose on you a little longer. What we need is time," he said. "Learning about her Watcher side might be the key to Seph figuring out her arcana. She needs to work on mastering that, so she can be ready for what we're facing. And, we need time to regroup and figure out how we're going to deal with the Diurne. Will you allow us to stay here while we do that?"

A wave of surprise washed over me. Simon's face soured.

Alex caught my look. "What else could be safer for you than hiding in another world?"

"He's right," Simon said with some reluctance. "That seam is the only way in or out."

"And," Alex added in an undertone, "if we stay here, you can learn more about your dad."

He wanted to hide me away, just like the Nephilim in Simon's tale.

But he had a point—it seemed like I would be safer here, for now. "Okay."

Simon massaged the bridge of his nose. "It's not like I don't have the room, I suppose."

"Thank you," I told him. "You don't know how much this means."

There was something in Simon's storm cloud eyes I couldn't decipher. He blinked and it was gone, replaced with begrudging acknowledgement.

"You can't go wandering around, though," he warned. "You've got to stay in the shop. If people knew that your lot was here, there'd be a riot."

"That won't be a problem," Alex answered firmly.

"Please tell me you have indoor plumbing," Casey chimed in. "I cannot piss in a bowl."

Simon looked ready to have a coronary, his face purpling. But he unlocked doors and shepherded the Guardians around, providing them with bread that was on the staler side and blocks of hard cheese.

"We'll compensate you for the food," Alex said, once it was only the three of us left.

Simon waved him off. "You're all right. My mum would wring my neck if she knew I was taking a stranger's coin for a little hospitality. Speaking of, you can have these." He pointed to two doors side by side, one of which was ajar. Through it I saw a large painting of the woman with the red hair from the family portrait upstairs. She lounged in a green field, a book in her hand and a secret smile on her lips.

"I'll leave you be. Washroom's at the end of the hall." He pointed down to the right. "Sleep well."

"Thanks," I said, covering my mouth as a yawn sneaked out.

Giving a stilted nod to Alex, Simon left.

Once he was out of sight, Alex came up behind me, putting his hands on my shoulders. I leaned back into him, and he wrapped his arms around me, dropping his head into the curve of my neck. "Separate rooms?"

I appreciated that he was willing to give me space. I turned into him, framing his shadowed jaw in my hands and leaning in for a kiss. "I'll take my chances with you."

29

The sleep I so desperately craved escaped me. I tossed and turned, lost in images of the howling void. But even more than that, I couldn't stop thinking about how I'd felt standing on the edge. Electric, and alive, and vital. It would be a terrible idea to go back there, surely. But that didn't make the thoughts go away.

I finally rose an hour before dawn. Alex looked so peaceful in sleep, his brow smooth and lips slightly parted. But the shadows under his eyes told a different story, so I let him rest.

Retracing our route from the bedroom level to the kitchen proved challenging. Jupiter's seemed to be a shop in the front, with living areas and inventory kept on the lower levels. I got turned around in the labyrinthine layout, but eventually stumbled upon a kitchenette off one of the landings. My stomach growled, reminding me that yesterday's bread and cheese hadn't done much to fill me.

A little gas stove with a dented teakettle on it squatted in the corner. After rummaging around in the cupboards, I found a tin of tea and a few mugs amidst the cobwebs. Maybe it would dull the edge of my hunger. I sniffed the tin dubiously. I'd prefer coffee, but it was better than nothing. I didn't think too closely about how long it had been sitting there before I filled the kettle and lit the stove.

I sidled up to the counter to wait for the water to boil when Simon appeared in the doorframe. His hair was mussed, his clothes rough but tidy with his tweed vest and tarnished watch chain.

"Morning. I hope I didn't wake you," I said.

"Not at all." He cleared his throat. "Couldn't sleep."

"Oh. Same." We stood in the quiet for a beat until it was broken by the whistling kettle. I fixed my mug then hesitated. "Do you want some?"

"Please," he said. I poured him a cup and pushed it toward him. The mug's heat brought welcome warmth, bolstering my nerves. I felt awkward, unsure of what to say.

"All right?" he asked.

"Yes, thanks," I said automatically. I took a breath. "Actually, no. A lot on my mind, you know?"

"I can imagine." Another pause.

"Is that painting of your mother? In the room where I slept last night," I blurted.

His gray eyes skimmed over me. "Aye."

"Oh." I took a sip of my tea. It tasted bitter and stale, but I swallowed anyway.

"Ada was her name."

I hesitated. "Was?"

"She's gone now, too."

"What happened to her?" That was intrusive, but Simon didn't shy away, instead looking at me head on when he answered.

"She tried to save us, like a bloody fool." His words were tinged with regret and love, twin arrows that pierced my heart. "That's what they've all done, everyone in the family. My mum, dad, sister, they've all gone and wasted their lives trying to save this cursed place." He shook his head.

"Like Penn?"

Simon nodded. "Yes, idiot that he is. He'll be back, then hatch another harebrained scheme that will fail miserably."

"Don't you even want to try to save yourself?"

"I'm not a martyr, Seph. I'm a pragmatist. And I'm not about to risk my skin fighting a losing battle." His jaw was set, his knuckles white on the handle of his mug.

"How much longer?"

"Who knows? It could be a week, a month, a year, a hundred years. There's no rhyme or reason to it. Sometimes it'll take twenty feet in a day, sometimes a foot a year."

"Sounds scary."

He shrugged. "I try not to think about it too much."

How could he not? Even now, the specter of the black chasm lurked in the back of my mind.

"Just because you pretend it's not there doesn't mean it's going to go away." This was clearly the wrong thing to say, because Simon slammed his mug down on the counter, splashing liquid. I flinched.

"I fucking well know that, don't I!" he exploded. "We can't leave because of your bloody boyfriend and his bleeding knights. They've kept us trapped in here like rats in a cage, and now we're all paying the price." His chest heaved with the force of a freight train barrelling down on me. "Don't come in on your high horse like I've just decided to give up, all right? If there was any hope, I'd have some. I don't imagine you'd feel optimistic if almost everyone in your family killed themselves for nothing."

Shame flattened me like an ant crushed under a bootheel. I wanted to crawl into one of the cabinets and hide. Simon was right. I had no room to lecture him about how he coped. The desire to help was stronger than ever, and I felt a fresh ripple of anger at the Aureum.

"Sorry," he said, rubbing his temples, the fight gone out of him like a popped balloon.

"No, you're right. I'm an idiot. I want to make this right, but I don't know how."

He shook his head. "You're all right, Seph."

I paused a beat before I asked him the question that had been circling in my mind all night. "Can you tell me more about my dad?" I didn't have any right to make more requests of Simon, but I couldn't stop myself.

"Like I said, I never met him," Simon replied, seeming grateful for the change of subject. "But he was my dad's best mate from childhood, knew each other from their nursery days, you know. I wish I could tell you more."

I recognized Simon's wistfulness as someone else who had lost a parent. This was a connection we shared, something that joined us even though we were almost complete strangers. And I liked Simon. Even though he was prickly, I accepted it because I could be, too. I felt a pang as I realized how lonely he must be, how little human contact he seemed to have.

"That's okay. What about your parents?"

"Mum and dad were the best," he said. "It wasn't all doom and gloom, you know. Things started getting worse about ten years ago. The edge was receding faster all the time. There have been food shortages, sickness. You've seen the air out there, as well. Not exactly paradise."

"No, I suppose not." Poor Simon. It seemed like death and decay haunted him like a vengeful ghost.

"What's your life like, back on the other side?"

"Well, up until a little while ago, it was pretty...boring," I decided. "I wasn't really an exciting person. I did the whole nine to five thing, you know, working for the weekend. But I was okay with that. Or, I thought I was. Things in my life had a kind of order. And now...."

"It's pure mayhem?" Simon suggested.

I gave a wry grin. "Essentially, yes."

Lifting his mug, he came closer. "Selfishly, I'm glad our paths crossed."

"I am, too," I answered, somewhat surprised to find it was true.

There was a light knock on the wall, and I turned to see Davina standing in the door. "Morning," she said. "Mind if I borrow Seph?"

Simon's lip curled, but he picked up his mug and walked out. "She's all yours," he said as he passed Davina.

She came in, folding her arms across her chest and leaning against the counter next to me. "How'd you sleep?"

"Fine," I lied. "You?"

"Not much, actually. I'm trying to figure out what to do." Her eyes were puffy, and her skin held a sallow tinge.

My throat tightened. "I'm not sure what you want me to say."

"I don't want you to say anything. I just wanted to ask you some questions. About what happened when you were taken by the demon."

Tension gathered in my shoulders. "I really don't want to talk about it." I'd seen Ventusiel's face in my dreams, felt as his proboscis tongue entered my body through my wounds. I didn't want to relive it while I was awake, too.

"I wouldn't ask if I didn't feel like I had to. I just want to know exactly what it said to you about the Aureum."

"Didn't Alex already tell you?"

"I need to hear it from you." Her dark eyes were intent on mine, probing.

I sighed. "The demon said that his master made a deal with the master of the Aureum. That they would hand me over if the demons agreed to bind me in another world."

"You don't think it was lying?" She twirled a lock of her hair. I'd never seen her fidget before.

I thought back to the demon's childish sense of fairness, of his adherence to the rules of the fucked up game. "No. I don't."

"If I stay, it'll mean giving up everything I know. It would mean forsaking my family, my future."

I set my mug down with a decisive clatter. "I'm glad you have a choice. I wish I had one, too."

"Seph—"

"I can't help you, Davina."

I left her there, a tear threatening to roll down her lovely cheek.

———

In the end, both Davina and Hollis chose to stay. I was shocked when Alex told me later that day, as I rifled through Ada's closet.

"I was sure Davina was going to leave," I told him, holding up a moth-eaten, collared smock. "She didn't sound very enthusiastic about staying when we talked this morning."

"She spoke to you?" Alex asked. He rubbed his jaw, his stubble turning into more of a beard with a few extra days' growth.

"Yeah. She wanted to know exactly what Ventusiel said to me about the Aureum. As if I needed to relive it again."

"Cut her a break, Seph. This was an extremely difficult decision for her."

I hung up the smock and turned to Alex. "Her mother might have ordered my murder, Alex. I'm having a hard time scraping together sympathy."

"She's sacrificing a lot."

I scoffed. "Yeah, well, so am I. I've already given up my life twice, Alex. The one I thought I wanted, and the one I actually wanted. And that doesn't even mention what happened to my dad, who was probably being hunted by the Aureum. Maybe they did something bad to him. And now they're after me."

Alex's eyes slid away from me, and he rubbed the crease in his brow. "I realize all that, Seph. I'm just saying, it's complicated for Davina."

And for him, I remembered. I had one foot in two worlds, but so did Alex now. Softening, I reached for him, but he turned and walked out of the room.

"Alex," I called. He didn't turn around. "Well, shit." *Nice going, me.*

I left too, heading for the stacks downstairs. All the way there, I wrestled with my feelings. It wasn't that I blamed Alex for anything. I was grateful for him, and cared about him more than anything. I just didn't know if we'd ever be able to come to terms on this. Our loyalties were too divided. *Hunter and hunted*, I reminded myself, then shook off the thought. Alex wouldn't betray me, even if we didn't agree.

Sage and Sylvan waited for me by the door with the Triskele, the one Simon had told me was a Watcher symbol. I'd recruited the twins to help me do some research. We were trying to figure out how to stop the edge of Canhaben from crumbling into the void. And while we were at it, to find out exactly what the void was.

There were thousands of books in the stacks. The three of us stood in a line, facing down the overwhelming mass of them. And this was just a tiny fraction of the whole subterranean archive.

"This is a disgrace to libraries," Sage admonished. "Our Library would burn itself down out of shame if it got to this state."

"I'm not sure that this library has sentience," I answered.

"Of course it does," Sylvan said. "It's just sleeping."

"I'm sorry, what?" Sage and I both turned to stare at him.

"I thought you knew." He shrugged. "The whole house is in a sort of...slumber? Trance? I can hear it breathing."

"Interesting. I wonder if that has anything to do with the edge," Sage said, tapping their chin.

"Even more reason to figure this out. But how do we find what's useful without going through each book by hand?" I wished for our Library more than ever.

"Magic." Hollis stepped around a corner, hands in his pockets. Simon trailed behind him.

"Oh—hi," I said, taken aback at the sight of them peacefully coexisting. "I didn't know you were coming."

"It's my house, isn't it? I go where I want," Simon retorted.

"And I want to help," Hollis stated. "It's a way that we can give back to these folks what we've taken from them. Fact of it is, it's our responsibility."

"Well said." Sylvan grinned, patting Hollis' shoulder.

"Excellent. The more hands, the better," Sage said. "We need keywords."

We brainstormed, ending up with the words *edge, void, world, gateway,* and *Canhaben.*

Sage raised their hands, then paused, turning to me. "Why don't you try, Seph?"

"I'm not sure that's a great idea. There's a lot of flammable material down here."

"We've got you, Seph," Hollis encouraged. "Go to your power source. You can do this."

Simon watched, curiosity on his face instead of the open disdain he usually wore around the Guardians.

"Look, I'll show you." A book flew from a shelf into Sage's waiting hand. "I see my power source as a mountain. I think about what I want, then I pull strength from that—it's like, if I can shift the right stones, in the right order, my desire becomes real."

My instinct was to conceal, but the Guardians knew almost everything now, anyway. "But I have two power sources."

Sage's pale eyebrows rose. "Really?"

"They're rivers. One black, and one gold."

"That'll be the Nephilim in you," Simon interjected. I'd almost forgotten he was there. "And the other bit. Makes sense you would have one for each."

"No wonder we weren't making any progress," Sylvan said. "I wish I'd known this sooner, Seph."

"But we understand why you couldn't tell us," Hollis added. "Good thing is that now you don't need to hide it anymore."

Warmth spread through me. No, I didn't need to hide from them anymore. And it felt damned good.

"Go on, Seph. Try it," Sage encouraged. "Send your rivers out into the world and see what happens."

I closed my eyes, not needing to go to my door anymore to find my power. It was there, ready and waiting beneath my skin. How would I need to manipulate the rivers to make my desire real? The gold and black threads pulsed. The gold, so light and bright, and the dark so shadowed and weighty.

The gold threads felt friendlier. I imagined directing them out into the stacks, whispering the key words down the thin strands. Some unseen force tugged on me, and my eyes flew open as I lost my balance.

A veritable tidal wave of books flew through the air. Sylvan had to throw up an invisible shield to cover us, straining with the effort. Finally, the last book bounced off and flopped to the ground.

"Well...you did it," Hollis said, straightening.

"Sorry." Heat flushed my cheeks.

"We'll work on it," Sylvan promised. "Maybe Simon can help too, since he's the resident Watcher expert."

Simon gave a noncommittal shrug, but I noted the interest in his eyes.

I surveyed the pile of books. "Well, at any rate, this is going to take us forever."

Sage's eyes lit up. "The answer is here somewhere. We'll find it." They rubbed their hands together, diving in.

30

Simon and I were in the ballroom practicing levitation. Assorted objects sat in a pile on the far side of the room, and he'd tasked me with moving them using my power. I was supposed to be placing them at his feet, where he stood some ways to my left. So far, I'd managed to pulverize a tin kettle and smash some lovely teacups when they dropped out of midair like stones.

I winced. "Don't you think I should practice on something less breakable?"

He shook his head. "Nah. None of this is getting used, anyway. Try again."

This time, I closed my eyes, picturing the rectangular silver tea tray in my mind. I dipped into the river of power that flowed at a languorous pace today, and envisioned the tray flowing with the threads. Then, a thought about the Diurne finding us, kidnapping me, and killing all of my friends intruded into my thoughts. The tray clanged to the floor.

Sighing, I put my hands on my hips. Until Simon picked up a plate and flung it at my head, frisbee style. Reacting instinctively, I flung up a hand and the plate shattered, pieces crashing to the ground.

"What the hell was that for?" I cried.

"Proving my point that you can do this," he answered, folding his arms. "When you're not thinking too hard, and you're threatened, your power reacts to protect you. You need to let your guard down."

"I'm trying."

"No, I'm not certain you are. Have you been working with your black river?"

I scowled. I'd been practicing arcana and combat with almost every Guardian, plus Simon, daily, on top of spending time in the stacks researching. Things were still somewhat tense between me and Alex after our discussion in the closet a few days ago. He was spending his time trying to figure out how to gather evidence against the Diurne, slipping into bed after I'd fallen into deep sleep.

The very last thing I wanted to do was touch those pulsing threads of darkness. They had a different feel from the golden river, something more chaotic and wild.

"That answers that, then," he muttered. "Why, Seph?"

Shame trickled down my throat. I didn't want to admit that I was afraid. "I just...it doesn't feel friendly, like the gold."

"You have to accept both parts of you. Not just the Guardian side," he admonished. "How do you ever expect to master yourself if you're ignorant?"

His words stung, but they were true. Simon had been a great teacher so far. He was a veritable encyclopedia of magic, although his abilities were limited to small things, like turning the lights on and off. He claimed that he'd gathered his knowledge by slowly working his way through all the books contained in Jupiter's.

"You're right. I'm acting like a coward."

"Nonsense," he said brusquely. "You've got more guts in your little finger than most people have in their whole bodies."

"Well...thanks."

"I know what you need." Simon's long-lidded eyes considered me. They were more on the blue side of gray today, and I'd noticed the color appeared to change with his moods. Blue meant happy, yellow angry, and green sad.

"What's that?"

"To connect to your Watcher heritage. Come with me."

Our lesson forgotten for the time being, Simon brought me to a part of the house I hadn't been to yet. We descended through the stacks, down, down, until we must have been deep underground.

"Remind me again why you have a dungeon?" I asked. The walls changed from plaster to rough cut stone, and my breath puffed out in a fine vapor.

"I'm not entirely sure," he responded. "My four times great-grandmother built the house and opened the shop. It was she and her sons that made the business successful."

"She's Jupiter and sons? That's badass."

He chuckled. "I suppose. She was quite the woman, or so I've heard. But, as you can see, things changed. As Canhaben decayed, the family got smaller and poorer, and the house has been falling into disrepair for a number of decades. It's impossible to keep up on my own."

"And why doesn't Penn help you?" Simon's mysterious twin still hadn't reappeared.

He gave a one-shouldered shrug. "It's his way. We're very different. Never had the closeness you would expect twins to have. I'm content here, tending to the books. He would drive himself mad within the hour. He's not the type for quiet. Right, here we are."

We stood outside a medieval door made of thick wooden planks held together with iron bands and bolts the size of silver dollars. Simon drew the latch back, and it gave way with a little protest and rusty scraping.

The room was similar to the Aureum's Oratory, except more in keeping with Simon's house. Every surface had the ever-present dust and sense of neglect. It smelled of soft, rotten wood, and something sharp and skunk-like.

"Good god." I covered my nose with my sleeve. "What is that?"

"Hellebore," Simon said, and even he seemed affected by the stench. He wrinkled his nose. "You get used to it."

"What's it for?"

"Poison." He sounded almost cheerful.

"Oh, god, Simon," I groaned. "You're growing poisonous plants in your basement? This is why no one wants to hang out with you."

"Funny. It's helpful to have if a demon gets out of hand. The poison affects them, marginally, causing a slowing of the reflexes. It could save your life. Here," he said, crossing the room to a set of open shelves mounted above what I could only describe as a miniature laboratory setup. Metal holders and glass beakers were haphazardly scattered around, and wheels and levers poked out of odd places. He plucked a corked glass vial from the shelves, handing it to me.

I examined the jar. A label was affixed to the outside with *black helle-bore* written in neat script. "Gee, thanks. No one's ever given me a present that could kill me."

Simon's eyes flashed the color of the ocean on a sunny day. "You're welcome, in advance."

I made a noncommittal noise, slipping the bottle into the pocket of my borrowed trousers, an old pair that Simon had outgrown. I could only wear the same pair of jeans so many days in a row. Simon had offered me his sister's dresses that were still hanging in the closet of her room, but I declined. I wasn't really a dress person, and I just couldn't bring myself to wear his dead sister's clothes.

More dull glass bottles sat on the shelf from which Simon retrieved the hellebore. Dill, lavender, oregano, yarrow, poppy, wormwood, aconite, calamint, parsley. Apart from the poison, these were herbs that could be found in any natural remedy shop.

"Did you know that parsley is the herb of the dead? It's dedicated to Persephone," I said, running my finger along a dusty label. "The Greeks used to say that it grew so slowly because the seeds had to travel to hell and back first." I might not have liked my name, but I knew all of the goddess-related trivia.

"Aye," Simon said. "We have those stories here, too. Some of your fairytales are quite good as well." His voice came surprisingly close to my ear, and when I turned around he was standing far nearer than I'd thought. I took a step back, bumping my hip into the low counter.

"We still follow the old ways and plant it on the graves of our dead," he explained.

"Oh." I thought about Simon planting parsley on the graves of his own family, and cast around for something else to say. "Do you use it for summoning?"

He held my gaze for another moment, then gestured to a breakfront cabinet. It held mirrors of all shapes and sizes, shells, bowls, what looked to be animal bones, feathers, an assortment of jars, and to top it all off; a grinning human skull. *What the fuck, Simon?*

"We use herbs for spirit-calling, but that's not one of them. We're after the living, not the dead."

I moved out of range of the skull's eyeless sockets. "So, how do you do it?"

Simon folded his arms. "I don't mess with it myself, generally. But it's not hard, as long as you know what each demon requires to be summoned. Some can only be called at certain hours of the day, and some will only appear in a mirror, or must be held in a vessel. Oh, and you'll never want to be without this." He pointed to a jar of white crystalline flakes. "Salt is the most effective protection we have against demons."

"I still can't believe that something so simple and common can be so powerful," I observed, picking up the jar and giving it a quick shake. The flakes clumped like snow.

"The most powerful things are usually simple. Creatures, including us and your lot, complicate the dickens out of our power. In reality, you don't need all the fancy trappings. Clear intent is the most valuable tool you possess."

I looked from the salt to Simon. "You're a good teacher, you know. Why don't you help other people with this stuff?"

His lids shuttered. "I told you. I don't mess with magic any more than I can help. It's caused enough chaos in my life."

"But you're helping me."

"That's different."

I laughed. "Come on, Simon. That's not true."

"I'm paying back my debt to your father, that's all."

"How can you be in debt to someone you've never even met?"

He leaned back against the counter next to me, looking straight ahead at the decrepit wall. "Your dad saved mine's life. If he hadn't done that, I wouldn't be here. Though, to tell you the truth, it only staved off the inevitable."

"How?" My voice was high, strained with the want of collecting any drop of information about my father, the stranger. Through Simon, I was getting to know him. And I didn't hate what I'd heard.

"A spirit calling gone wrong. My dad was the cocksure type, thought he was invincible and could do whatever he wanted without consequence. He got in over his head with a powerful spirit, one of the bad ones. Your dad had told him not to, said he wouldn't have any part of it, but he came right in the nick and stopped the demon from topping him." Simon gave me a significant look. "We repay our debts around here. You never know what having an open favor could cost you someday."

I mulled that over. "So when will you consider the debt repaid?"

His brow wrinkled. "I'm not sure. I guess when I'm confident you won't get yourself killed as soon as you leave."

"That might take a while."

"All the better for me, then. It's nice to have some company around here," he said.

"Ah, so you do admit it," I teased.

"Well, you're all right. It's them others I'm not sure about."

"Simon." I turned to him. "They're not going to do anything bad, I swear. They're good people, not like…."

"The whole rest of them?" Simon answered for me.

"Well, I'm not sure. Some of them, definitely," I said, thinking of Edward. "But I think there are lots of Guardians who wouldn't agree with what their council has been doing."

"Seems like they've got you in enough trouble," he grumbled.

"Yes. But…as much as I hate to admit it, I think we're supposed to be here. Like, fate, or something," I said, feeling mild embarrassment.

"You're meant to be hunted by a bunch of pompous, stuffy, controlling, heads-up-their-arses dictators?"

He had a point. "That we're meant to change them. But, there's still one piece of all this that doesn't add up."

"*One* piece?"

I'd been thinking about this ever since Simon explained about his dying world. "Well, if they shut our world off from all the others, won't we die, too?"

We were both silent for a moment, considering.

"They've got to have a way around it," Simon said. "You talked before about that demon telling you this Diurne business set him on you. Sounds like they're in league together."

The weight of it all pressed down on me, tightening my throat. If we were to have any chance of succeeding—of surviving—I needed every advantage I could get.

"Simon, I'm going to push your debt further," I said. "If you teach me to summon, I'll owe you."

He rubbed the back of his neck and blew out a breath, hesitancy written all over him.

"Please. I'm begging you. I need this." Not only did I need it, but I wanted more than anything to keep the people I cared about safe. Like Alex said, I was strong and smart. I just needed to prove it to myself.

"Don't make me regret this."

"I won't, I swear."

"All right, then," he said, pulling bottles off the shelves and setting them on the table. "This is the first part of your education. Herb lore." He launched into a lecture, explaining each of the 'cornerstone herbs' he'd pulled. Watching him go into teacher mode made me smile, because he really was good at it.

"What's got that look on your face?" he asked suspiciously, breaking off from discussing the merits of using vervain versus St. John's Wort to ward off curses.

"Nothing," I said, my smile growing. "Just happy to be here."

———

I didn't exactly keep my summoning practice a secret from Alex. I just very carefully didn't mention it.

We were in the oneiric landscape behind my door, sitting on a hillside covered in downy grass and tiny flowers that gleamed like pearls. The sky was a softer, lighter gray today. It was a welcome respite from Jupiter's dreariness, which was grating on everyone.

Alex and Simon had argued about letting the Guardians out to roam the city. They were used to prowling graveyards in search of demons to pulverize, and being cooped up made them irritable and sour.

"If you're found out, there'll be a lot of uncomfortable questions. Folk here aren't exactly thrilled with your lot, given you're killing us off," Simon told us, with a scowl that would have given children nightmares.

So, we continued on as we were, all hoping that the next breakthrough—whether from my magic, a plan for how to move forward, or figuring out what was going on with the edge—was around the next corner.

I ran my fingers through the grass, enjoying the low hum of power thrumming in my chest. "So, you wanted to talk about something?"

Alex sat with his long legs sprawled in front of him, propped up on his elbows. He straightened, flicking a lock of dark hair out of his face. "I've been thinking a lot these past few days. About you, and me, and... all of it."

"Me, too." I'd wanted to address the tension between us, but—I didn't know how to. What if I screwed things up even more?

His green eyes turned so serious as he beheld me. "The fact of it is, there will always be a part of me that is loyal to the Aureum. It's what I've known my whole life, what's shaped me. It's the world I belong to."

I stiffened, but stayed silent.

"But I am loyal to the Aureum—not the Diurne. I think that's why we technically haven't broken our oaths and lost our power, because at heart, we still believe in the mission of saving people—not just *some* people. That's what's important."

I released the breath I'd been holding. "Of course. Alex, I would never doubt that for a second. I just wasn't sure if...if I make sense in your world. I'd understand if you wanted to keep me out."

He shook his head slowly. "I don't want to keep you out. It's just...." Rubbing his lips together, he tried again. "I don't exactly have a template for how to have a healthy relationship. I can be closed off, and secretive. I'm not perfect. But right now, you're one of the only parts of my world that makes sense. I never want to keep you out."

Warmth coursed through me, spreading under my skin like magic. I'd never had these feelings for someone before—this bone deep connection. And I never wanted it to end.

"I don't want to keep you out, either."

"Let me do what I do, and you focus on getting as strong as you can." He stood, holding out a hand for me. "Come on, I want to show you something."

We walked through my obsidian door together, and came back to reality where we were seated on the floor of our room.

He went to the chest of drawers that sat flush against the wall, opening the topmost one and removing a paper. "I had Simon draw something up for you," he said, turning and handing it to me.

"What's this?" It was an ink drawing composed of script, the letters looping and intertwining to form beautiful artwork.

"You've fought two demons and won. They're for your protection tattoos. If you want them, that is. I understand if you don't." Alex looked slightly bashful, his eyes holding tentative hopefulness.

I planted a soft kiss on his lips. "Of course I do. They're beautiful. Thank you."

He smiled, one that transformed his whole face, his eyes crinkling in the corners. A deliciously light sensation spread through my limbs. "I wasn't sure if you'd want to. But, I think it's important to honor your Guardian side, too," he said.

I looked at the drawings again. I saw perfectly the story of my encounter with both demons worked into the design, written in English, Latin, and maybe Gaelic. Flames were heavily incorporated, and I recognized a Triskele, too. I laughed softly at my previous insistence that I wasn't meant for burning. It had become my specialty.

"I think it's important, too."

For once, I could read Alex's emotions like they were written in the pages of a book. His eyes were bright with pleasure, the smile still hanging around the corners of his mouth. "So you like the design? You don't want to change anything?"

"No, not a thing. And I have to say, I'm pleasantly surprised that you worked this out with Simon. It must have taken some planning."

"He's a grumpy bastard, but you can't deny his talent."

"True. Thank you, again." I raised my chin for another kiss, and he grasped it, grazing my lips softly before he slipped his tongue into my mouth. I made a sound low in my throat, pulling him closer. The press of his body against mine made my power go from a slow drift to a flash flood. But he pulled back, planting a kiss to the tip of my nose.

"Are you ready?"

I felt a little slow and dreamy from the kiss. "For what?"

"Your tattoo. There's no time like the present," he said, flashing his pirate's grin. "There would usually be pomp and ceremony, but under the circumstances...."

"Hm...." I said, running my hands up and down the corded muscle of his forearms. They were very distracting. "Will it hurt?"

"A little. We don't take the pain away. It's part of the process. But, if you want me to, I can."

"What, and wimp out? Casey would never let me live it down."

"No one has to know."

"I won't cheat. How is it done?"

"I'll imprint it onto you, with arcana. It won't take long, and will be instantly healed after."

"Convenient," I murmured. "Okay, then."

Alex positioned me on the bed and rolled up my sleeve. He sat next to me, laying my left arm in his lap. Then he pressed the page with the drawing to the inside of my forearm, and I felt a brief flash of heat. The drawing remained after he peeled the page away, transferred to the skin. It wasn't reversed like I'd thought it would be, but appeared just as the original art.

"Is that it?"

"No. The hard part comes next. Are you ready?" I swallowed and nodded. "Last chance for me to numb it," he offered.

I shook my head. "I'm ready."

Alex placed his hand on the transferred drawing, and it took everything I had to keep from shrieking. It felt like *fire*, like someone had taken a soldering iron to my skin to trace the image. I gripped the sheets with my free hand, willing myself not to move.

I chanced a look down and saw the lines of the image thicken slightly in concert with the burning sensation. Then, almost as soon as it began, it was over. The burning became a slight sting, then faded entirely.

"That fucking *hurt*. But it looks beautiful," I said, admiring my new ink.

"I'm sorry," he murmured, taking my hand. "And it does. It suits you."

"Does it?"

"Absolutely." He reached up to tug the elastic out of my hair, where I'd pulled it into a knot on top of my head. My hair cascaded down in a cloud, almost reaching below my bra line. It was usually never this long, given its unruliness, but a haircut had been the last thing on my mind these past weeks. I went to tuck it behind my ears, but Alex captured my wrists and leaned into me.

"You're beautiful. Incredible. Powerful." He planted each word in my skin with his lips and I felt the truth grow from the seeds.

Then, he drew a line with his nose to the hollow of my throat, leaving shivers of pleasure in his wake. "Did you know this little spot here drives me crazy?" he said. "I think about it all day long. It's maddening."

Heavy lust swept through me as I watched him watching me. It shocked me, time and time again, that Alex had chosen me.

"I know what you're thinking," he murmured, lifting his head from his slow worship.

I was loath for him to stop. "How?"

"You're tight right here," he murmured, touching the point between my shoulder blades, spanning his hand there. He massaged the spot, and I groaned softly. "And, I've been in your head. I know you."

Fear and delight shivered down my spine at his words.

How many times do I have to tell you that you are worth it? That you are the most stunning, bewildering, extraordinary person I've ever met? You shatter me, Persephone.

I felt the truth behind his words, resonating along the tether, filling my heart to the very brim. It was painful, but perfect.

"Maybe one day, I'll believe you," I whispered, watching the deep green of his eyes flicker in the candlelight. "You have to know that you're the same to me. Alex, I—" I stopped, the words caught in my throat. There was no doubt I was in love with Alex. But saying it aloud would make it real, and I was raised at the feet of a woman who'd been scooped hollow by love and shattered into irreparable pieces.

No matter how much I wanted Alex in my life, I was terrified that if I gave my heart away, it would be thrown out and left for dead.

The worst and best part about it was, Alex understood. He, too, bore the scars of a home filled with silence. And yet, here he was, risking it all for a feeling. Maybe, if we let each other, we could heal our wounds together.

"I know," he said. Then he kissed me with such desperation that it was almost violent, and I welcomed his pain, matching it with my own.

We stripped each other bare, reveling in life-giving touch, fabric rending under our hands. He covered me entirely, his need frantic and whipping a hurricane of wanting that pooled in my center. I returned it, using teeth and tongue and lips to tell him a story of how much I needed him. He flipped me, turning my back to his front, and pulled me against him, filling his hands with my breasts.

One hand trailed toward the apex of my thighs, caressing and kneading. Then he slipped a clever finger inside me, humming with pleasure at the slickness he found there. He stroked and rubbed, teasing me, inciting a slow burn that consumed me whole.

When I couldn't wait anymore, couldn't take even a millimeter of space between us, he drew my hips back, filling me with his length and shooting me over the edge. My head fell back against him and he feasted on my neck, breathing my name as he set a fierce pace. One hand worked the bundle of nerves at the apex of my thighs and the other snaked around my waist, holding me tight to him.

We fell apart and put each other back together again. This was a language I understood, and I tried my damndest to show him the words that I couldn't say. He responded in kind, and when my blood sang and his eyes went dark, we collapsed into each other, a protection against our own demons.

31

My power grew slowly, in fits and starts. I was getting to know both sides of my magic—the gold and the black—but was still nervous about the savage pleasure that coursed through me when I grazed those dark threads. It made me feel...monstrous, in a way. Thorny, and sharp, and hot enough to burn.

Working with that part of me always put a cloud of irritability over my head. It came out when I was sparring with Fern one afternoon, my hits more brutal than intended.

"You're out of control," she said, after she'd taken me to the ground and pinned a gentle forearm over my throat. "When you're out of control, you make careless mistakes."

Panting, I shoved her off and rolled to my feet. "I'm sorry. I just feel...." Itchy. Uncomfortable. Restless. We hadn't made any progress with our search into the void, either. I felt as if everyone's eyes were on me, watching and waiting for me to do something—anything. "Pressured."

"I understand that, Seph. More than you know." She used the hem of her shirt to wipe sweat from her brow. "I grew up in an area where I was one of the only Black kids in what felt like the whole town. And even on the unit, before you came, Davina and I were the only people of color. We can't make mistakes, not like the other Guardians. They preach equality, but there's bias in the Aureum, just like everywhere else. Magic folk aren't immune."

I nodded. That's how I'd felt, too, even in my own household. The other part of my identity—the one that came with the brown skin and curly hair I'd seen in the photo of my dad—wasn't something others understood. I barely understood it myself. No one had ever taught me.

Fern flowed to the ground, folding into a cross-legged position. "That's one of the reasons why I was so quick to stay in Canhaben. In the beginning, you think being in the Aureum is some kind of grand adventure—you feel like a hero, or if you're graveborn, like you're following in your family's footsteps, doing your duty. But once you've been in it a while, you start to see the cracks. Small things here and there, and then they become bigger and bigger, until it's too late and you've been swallowed whole. You were stuck the moment you swore your oath, and there's nothing you can do about it now except keep on going, otherwise you've wasted your whole life."

"Why didn't you say anything before?" I asked. I remembered Fern's unease at my initiation, when I'd asked if she'd had a choice.

She shook her head. "I didn't know what I didn't know. We join so young. But I do know that forced, blind loyalty is wrong, period. I feel for you, Seph. But this is a chance for us to do things differently, to help lead the Aureum into a new era."

"I never took you for a revolutionary."

"You never know what you'll do until your back is against the wall." She jumped up. "Anyway, want to go again?"

This time, I fought with a measured fluidity that surprised me. When I pinned Fern, clapping filled the room.

"That was beautiful," Davina said. She and Alex stood in the doorway, a stack of books floating between them at shoulder-level.

I stepped back and Fern rose gracefully. "Presents?" she asked, nodding to the books.

"I thought we could all go through them together, in the kitchen. Sort of a study party?" Davina looked at me with tentative hope, and I realized the gesture for what it was—a peace offering.

"That sounds great," I replied. Alex gave me a lopsided grin that made my heart stutter. "I'll get cleaned up and meet you there."

He stayed behind when the others left, tucking a loose strand of hair behind my ear. "I have something I want to share, too. But first, you might want to check the room next door for something to wear if you want to clean up."

"Why?"

"Because all of your clothes are filthy and thrown into the corner like you're using them as kindling for a bonfire. Which you might as well, at this point."

"Shit." He wasn't wrong. Alex's military tidiness and my... haphazard way of arranging my belongings didn't exactly mesh. But he'd stopped casting long-suffering glances at my piles and let them be. "Can't you snap your fingers and make them clean? And wait, what do you want to tell me?"

He smirked and cupped the back of my neck, kissing me slowly before pulling away. "See you in the kitchen."

Shaking off the fog of desire, I started through the warren of hallways, crossing to the room next door that Simon had offered us on our first night in Canhaben. Another large portrait hung on the wall, a similar style to the one in my and Alex's room.

It was of a young woman, seated on the floor, holding an open book in one hand and propping herself up with the other. I recognized in her features a more grown up version of the little girl from Simon's family portrait. She looked to be in her late teens, and although her smile was sweeter than an angel's, the tilt of her head conveyed a playfulness that reminded me of Penn. This must have been their sister's room—Diana, he'd said.

Crossing to the closet, I found high-necked dresses in muted colors with matching shawls. All manner of shoes—boots, heels, and satin slippers—littered the floor. I skimmed my hand along the hanging clothes. They were made of fine, soft material, but were patched just like everything else in the house.

I went all the way to the back, but didn't find trousers or shirts. Resigning myself to living in dirt and sweat, a sturdy pair of boots laying on the floor caught my eye.

Could I be lucky enough that Diana and I wore the same size? I crouched down to examine them, running a finger over dusty leather.

It was then I noticed a frayed piece of black fabric laying discarded among the shoes. Praying I'd at last found pants, I reached for it. When I pulled, part of the wall crumbled, plaster flakes littering the floor.

"Damn it."

On hands and knees, I probed the edge of the small hole, assessing how bad the damage was. More plaster deteriorated beneath my fingers, exposing the outline of several dark shapes.

A secret compartment? Tearing more plaster away, I decided to ask Simon for forgiveness later. After a few moments of clearing, there was a rectangular hole in the wall just big enough to slip two hands inside.

I peered in. The tattered black fabric was actually a shawl that had been used to wrap something, the outlines visible beneath the thin fabric. There was also a jeweled hair comb, a large quantity of coins, and a surprising amount of weaponry. I stuck my head closer to the opening, eyes widening at the heap of daggers.

Wondering why Simon's sister had her own private arsenal, I gave in to curiosity and reached for the cloth-wrapped item. A book nestled in its folds.

It was tiny, both in width and length, not more than ten pages or so. The cover was nondescript apart from a few cracks running through the leather in which it was bound. It had no title, and no author's name.

I opened to the first page. The book was handwritten in lovely penmanship, but the words on the page weren't recognizable as any language I knew.

Damn.

It didn't seem like Diana's diary, and my curiosity wouldn't allow me to put the book down and walk away. Going inward, I touched the strands of my magic. They were ready and waiting for me—eager, in fact. Holding the book open, I bit my lip as I guided the threads toward the first page. I focused on my intent—my desire, to learn what was written in these pages.

The gold threads touched the words, and began to rearrange them. I held my breath, half in awe, half terrified I'd ruined the book forever.

The glistening strands stilled, then faded away.

What was left was perfectly legible. Kneeling in the closet, I began to read.

. . .

The stories of the lost worlds have not often been told, as their inhabitants perished along with them. Their secrets are carried by few, and those who do know them do not wish to speak of the great evil that was cast upon them. The survivors of one such world, once called Tiche but now only known as the ravaged place, told of a darkness that devoured the land so complete it stole everything in its path and left only emptiness in its wake.

The story of these survivors has been passed down through their generations, one that I will record in these pages so that they may find the next bearer of life and death, should they become.

Their land was one of many to succumb to the great darkness, spread by the gods-blessed. The closing of the doorways extinguishes the flame of life, plunging the world into a forever dark. In its death throes, the land will break off and fall into paradox. Once the land has been consumed, there is no resurrection possible.

The savage darkness can only be stopped by those who hold the power of paradox in their hands, to open again the threshold of the world so that it may become once more. The bearer of life and death has this power and more, for the lightbringer holds the threads of creation. They will call the air, fire, earth, spirit, and water, to make them one, and breathe life into the world.

I read the pages about five times, my eyes catching the words and holding them tight. This was what we were searching for. Diana had this information in her possession when she died, hidden away.

The last few pages contained several detailed diagrams with arrows, equations, and theories, so I didn't waste any time looking at that part. I had to get this to the others.

I practically skidded into the kitchen to find the Guardians and Simon already seated around the table. It smelled like fresh bread and woodsmoke, both courtesy of our host.

"I found it," I exclaimed, holding the little book aloft. "This is what we've been looking for. About the edge."

Sage let out a gasp of excitement. The rest of the Guardians stood, looking at me intently.

"Where did you find that?" Simon asked.

I faltered. "In Diana's room. There was a hidden compartment in her closet." Simon shook his head, his lips compressing into a tight line.

Flames from the hearth crackled in the silence as the book passed around the circle, hand to hand.

Sage rubbed their cheek. "If I'm interpreting this correctly, these are instructions to reopen the threshold. It's part elemental magic, part symbolic, part functional. Fire, water, earth, spirit—interesting," they mused. "And the void is called paradox."

"And once the threshold is open, life comes back to the world?" Sylvan said. Sage nodded, biting their lip as they continued reading.

Alex crossed his arms over his chest, firelight flickering across the planes of his face. "Having the threshold closed is protecting us."

"You can't seriously not want us to try to reopen it?" I attempted to meet Alex's eyes, but he stared into the fire, unreadable. The idea of returning to the edge stirred that magnetic feeling again, and it was getting stronger by the second.

"I'm just pointing out that we would be getting rid of an advantage."

"True," Hollis remarked.

"Of course you'd side with him," Casey scoffed, rolling her eyes. "And so what if something does come through? That's literally why we exist."

"I'm not siding with him," he snapped at Casey. "I'm just making an observation."

"There's no need to argue," Fern said, placing a calming hand on Hollis's arm. "We're just talking about our options."

"It's a good idea. I think we should give it a shot." Davina shut the book with a decisive snap, placing it on the table in front of her.

"Simon?" I asked. He stood slightly outside of the circle, leaning against the hearth. "What do you think?" The light illuminated the wear on his clothes, the threads hanging off the cuffs of his jacket.

"I think...I think you should try, if you can." He looked haunted, his face drawn. He cleared his throat and continued. "I think Diana tried to do what's written in the book, but wasn't able to. I don't think she could do it, because she wasn't you." He looked at me then, his stormy eyes rife with old pain.

Fern sent Simon an approving look. "Exactly. You're the light-bringer, Seph. It all makes sense now."

"I don't think that makes any sense," I protested.

"You've already done it," Simon answered. "When you were at the edge. No one has been able to bring it back like that, and believe me, they've tried. I think...we actually might have a shot at this."

I wouldn't have believed it if I didn't see it with my own eyes, but through his anguish I watched hope blossom on Simon's face. It might kill me if we crushed it.

"It's settled, then." I looked at everyone within our circle, finally landing on Alex. If this worked, we might be able to save thousands of lives.

"Shall we? Twilight is in four hours, and it looks like that's the best time to try," said Sage. They turned to Alex.

His eyes were on me, searching. He nodded, just barely. "Okay."

We set to work gathering the items noted in the book. Simon raided the dungeon workshop for dried herbs and hammered bowls. He consulted with Sage on the materials and quantities needed, while the others gathered the four elements.

When it was decided that gathering the spirit needed to open the threshold would require summoning a demon, the Guardians all tensed. Simon tried to reassure them, but if it wasn't for Sage's enthusiasm, the whole project might have slammed to a halt.

"Alex, it's fine," I said, scanning *The Book of Oberon*. "What do you think about Porax? It says here he's a gardening, earthy type. One of the nicer demons, I suppose."

Alex pinched the bridge of his nose. "A *nice* demon? Goddess alive."

"Yes, I think it ought to be him," I said, ignoring him.

He placed his hands around my upper arms, and I could tell Alex was being very careful not to shake some sense into me like he wanted to. "We have nine souls—spirits—between us. Our presence alone should be sufficient."

"Maybe. But I don't want to be wrong about this. If we don't need an actual spirit, then there's no harm done."

His fingers flexed, and his voice came out a bit strangled. "No harm done?"

"Are you going to let this get out of hand?" I asked him.

"Of course not." His hair was mussed, the rogue lock falling over his forehead. I felt the overwhelming urge to kiss him, so I did, tilting my face up and firmly pressing my mouth to his, opening to him.

He responded instantly, splaying his hand on the small of my back and drawing me in. His lips were like a firebrand, scorching every part of me they touched, and he tasted of tea and smoke. It was an altogether too pleasing combination, overwhelming my senses and blocking out thoughts of demons and danger and magic. My fingers curled around his shirt, and my stomach pulsed with heat. No, I would never get enough of this.

A loud cough made me flinch, but Alex didn't release me. He barely pulled away, touching his nose to mine, then planted a last soft kiss on my lips. Without taking his eyes off mine, he said, "What."

"We need the name of the demon we're summoning. Everything else is ready."

I slowly eased back. Simon looked less than happy about finding us wrapped around each other. Alex, on the other hand, seemed like this suited him just fine.

"We're using Porax. Here." Alex took the book from me and lobbed it at Simon, who caught it one-handed.

"You should come with me to fetch the materials," Simon said, addressing me but looking at Alex. "It's good practice for you."

"I'll be there in a minute."

With a last, dark look, Simon left.

"What is going on with you?" I asked, thumping Alex on the chest.

"Ouch." He rubbed the spot. "What do you mean?"

"That pissing match, with you and Simon. I feel like a damn fire hydrant."

Alex laughed. "Come on, Seph. You haven't noticed the way he looks at you? Whenever you're in the room, he can't stop staring."

"That's because I am his *friend*, and he trusts me." Saying it aloud made me realize for the first time that Simon and I were actually friends.

"It's more than that. He thinks you two belong together because of your parents, like he has some claim on you because of your Watcher blood."

I studied Alex's face, the hard line of his jaw, the hollow of his cheeks and the fine bridge of his nose. His eyes were tight at the corners, like chips of serpentinite. "Are you…jealous?"

He shook his head, giving me a tight-lipped grin. "Of course I am."

"There's no reason for that. You're the one I want." *The one I've been waiting for.*

"Can I show you something? It'll be quick, I promise."

"Is it going to be weird?"

Alex chuckled, then took my hands. "Close your eyes."

I did as he asked. I wasn't prepared for what happened next.

A succession of images flashed through my head. Me in the waiting room of Whitlock & Williams, my glacial stare melting as my lips curved into a small smile; sitting in Alex's car, tousled hair hiding my face like a hood, head bowed; holding his hand as we walked through a gateway together; in bed with him, drowsy and sated after loving him through the night.

There were countless more, things that I'd never noticed about myself but saw through Alex's eyes. The way my mouth went crooked when I concentrated, how my eyes appeared green and gold when the light hit them just the right way, the curves of my body that suddenly seemed not so boyish anymore.

But most of all, I felt what Alex had been feeling in each of those moments—curiosity about this strange and captivating woman, frustration that he couldn't lock away his feelings for me, desire that pulsed through him like a bass drum, his throat tight with need, laughter, joy, and love, so vibrant and startling that I had the impulse to close my eyes even though they were already shut.

The images trailed off, and I opened my eyes to find they were wet.

Alex brushed my tears away with his thumbs. "Can you finally accept how precious you are to me? If you were hurt, if something happened to you because of this…."

I wanted to tell him that I wouldn't be hurt, that nothing could happen to me if he was watching out for me. But I couldn't speak the words that would make me a liar.

"Nothing in life is guaranteed. You know that. Something could happen to me at any time. It could happen to you, for that matter." Ice collected in my chest at the thought, freezing my breath for a moment. "We can only try and protect each other as best we can."

"I guess that'll have to be good enough."

As we parted, me toward Simon and Alex to meet with the rest of the Guardians, I felt...seen. Cherished. And finally, accepted. Maybe that's all I really wanted in life. To know that in the midst of all of the beings in all of the worlds, someone would choose me.

32

The sky darkened toward dusk as we left Jupiter's to travel to the edge. Simon provided us all with ankle-length dusters and insisted we keep the hoods drawn low to hide our faces. Even so, we used power to mask our little band so that anyone who happened to see us would be met with a blurry impression of something that they couldn't quite make out, nor cared to.

It was chilly, the habitual haze of clouds and smog covering the sky like a dirty blanket. Steam pumped out of tall brick columns that still stood at the city's edges. Simon made pomanders for us to carry that helped cover the smell of the polluted air, which I thought was rather thoughtful until he said crossly that he didn't want anyone fainting, as it would be a hindrance.

On top of the dilapidated row houses crammed into the city were additional apartments, stacked upon each other crookedly. Spiral staircases reached from the street level to connect to structures that had all manner of roofs—conical, peaked, flat—and were constructed of sheet metal, wood, brick, iron, plaster, and stone. They looked like finely sculpted works of art that had then been broken apart and smooshed back together haphazardly.

We turned up the cobbled hill towards Lychgate Road. The broken trees and vines looked somehow wilder than before, like they'd rooted deeper since I'd seen them last.

"Gods," Fern breathed.

"Yep," Simon said.

We wound our way through the overgrown and fragmented paths as close to the boundary line as we dared. I wasn't sure if the edge was actually closer than the last time we'd been, or if it was only my imagination. The swirling energy of the place tickled the hairs on the back of my neck with awareness, and I felt that same pulsing potential as before. It called to me, and I had to remind myself to stay with the group, not to rush toward it.

The howling wind threatened to blow us all to pieces. Alex spread his hands and the wind died suddenly, like he'd placed a dome over us. After it was done, he flexed his fingers, looking at them. "It's harder to work arcana here," he noted. He already looked paler.

"It feels like the paradox is sucking it all away. It's…hungry." I could feel its teeth, their razor edges and driving need to consume.

"Let's hurry, then," Alex said.

Simon and I got to work arranging the ritual items at the points of a pentacle. There was earth, which I scooped into a hammered bowl; air, that Simon captured in a bottle with a cork stopper while we walked; water, which we brought from Jupiter's; and fire, from the slim ivory candle that I lit easier than drawing breath. My magic jumped in my veins, and despite Alex's observation, it seemed simpler for me. Like it wanted to be used.

Fern laid salt around the perimeter of our circle. The last thing to do was conjure spirit.

"Is everyone ready?" I received nods all around. The Guardians bristled with energy, on alert for the first time in weeks, their eyes bright, and some eager, with the possibility of danger.

Simon's face was tight, but he gave a slight nod. My pulse raced and sweat pooled in the small of my back despite the chill. I knotted my hair on top of my head and removed my coat, laying it on the ground behind me.

I placed a mirror in the center of the five-pointed star and shook more salt around it as an extra precaution. I added another bowl of soil containing herbs and seeds from Simon's basement laboratory next to the mirror. More stubby candles went around that, and I lit them with a wave of my hand.

Kneeling at the bottom of the pentacle, I read the summons that Simon had helped me craft. It was a plea, a call to the demon to appear by the offering of the fruits of the earth. I poured my whole heart into it, and felt the river of power under my skin gush to a roaring swell. The candles burned brighter, their flames shooting upward, and the water rippled in its bowl.

Then, a black smudge appeared in the mirror. The outline was blurry, but slowly became recognizable as the shape of a man with dark skin and large, feathery wings. Its wings flapped, and it spoke in a deep voice that resonated like a gong. "Who calls me?"

It fucking *worked*.

I cleared my throat. "The lightbringer calls you in our time of need."

Playing their parts perfectly, the others used their power to hold the demon in the mirror. My voice shook with adrenaline and effort.

"Air of the sky, water of the lake, fire of the hearth, soil of the earth, spirit of the otherworld, I bind and keep you."

I spun a tale of light and healing, of wholeness, of the tenderness and grief of the land that had been consumed by paradox, of its people who were scattered and dying, refugees of their own world. I continued on, long after I'd run out of words on the page and had to keep the story going on my own. My power beat like a drum, but instead of feeling drained, I was stronger and more energized than when we started.

The only problem was that nothing changed.

The wind continued roaring and the void of paradox was emptier than ever. In fact, another car-sized chunk of earth to our right cracked off and slipped into the chasm.

"It's not working!" Alex called. He was shaking now, and the wind around our little band had started to pick up again. The others were in a similar state, looking drawn and exhausted, their voices thready and weak.

I felt a tug on my arm, and turned to see Simon at my elbow. "We've got to stop!" he yelled. Sweat dewed his face. "We'll all die if we keep on." Fear was a living thing in his eyes, wild and wretched.

Why did I feel so strong, when they were all wasting away? "Go, then!" I yelled over the wind. Simon shook his head and tugged me back. I shoved him off, but then Alex was at my other elbow, and the two of them succeeded in dragging me back several feet. The demon we'd trapped in the mirror looked like a storm cloud and beat its wings like angry lightning. Then it was gone. The others' must have broken their chant, too weak to continue on. We were in full retreat.

I didn't want to give up yet. I could feel the power, could sense the world waiting to wake beneath the lifeless soil. I wasn't going to leave if there was still a chance. We'd gotten something wrong, clearly misinterpreted some part of the book's instructions. Part of me wondered if this was what happened to Diana and the rest of Simon's family, if they'd had their own life forces drained in trying to reopen the gateway. Fear wormed its way into my heart.

Hairline cracks spread under our feet, and the earth shook. We ran, full tilt, Alex gathering me into his arms and unfurling his wings. He launched into the air and the other Guardians followed, wings drooping as we lurched out of the cemetery. Casey held Simon, his face ghostly white.

They touched down at the top of the hill on Lychgate Road, Simon practically jumping out of Casey's arms. Sylvan stumbled to his knees, and Sage caught him. The sky over the edge was an angry bruise, clouds swirling fast as night descended.

"It didn't work," I whispered. "I can't believe it." Alex still had his arm wrapped around my waist, but I couldn't tell if he held me up, or if I held him. All of the Guardians looked utterly spent.

Simon threw his hands up. "This was a bloody mistake. I should never have—it was a mistake," he repeated.

"We can try again," I said. "We'll regroup—maybe we rushed it."

"No!" Simon thundered.

"Simon, I feel fine, I can go back—"

"No one's going back. Especially not you. As long as you're staying in my house, I forbid it." He turned on his heel and stalked away.

We were silent as a funeral march on the trek back to Jupiter's. I was relieved when we were back in the shadow of the house, wondering how this dilapidated mansion had started to feel like home. We trooped into the kitchen, which had become our default gathering place.

Once we were inside, everyone dispersed to their separate corners. Before Fern left, she laid a hand on my arm. "I'm sorry, Seph."

I swallowed hard, nodding. We'd tried, and failed. I hadn't been strong enough to save Canhaben. To save Simon. His world was going to die, and it was my fault.

"We don't have to give up," Alex told me. He'd remained behind, pouring us each a glass of water. He drank deeply, throat working.

"But Simon said—"

"Respectfully, Simon doesn't control us. Anyway," his voice lowered, "now's probably a good time to bring up what I wanted to talk about before you found that book."

"What is it?" The look in his eyes had anxiety clawing at my throat. "Alex, what?"

"I have a plan. But I don't think you're going to like it."

A relieved laugh spilled from me. "That's all? That's a good thing. Why won't I like it?"

"Because," he said, "we need to go back to New Orleans."

I blinked, unable to get any words past my surprise. "Well, you're right. I definitely don't love the idea of going back to the people who sponsored my abduction and subsequent torture."

Alex scrubbed a hand through his dark hair. "I have been thinking, and thinking, and thinking. There's no other option. We need proof the Aureum is killing off other worlds. That the Diurne tried to have you killed, and may have had someone else murdered." His brows furrowed, an anguished expression crossing his face. "I think we can make people see reason, if they only know what we know."

"Do you really think they'll listen?"

"I do. The Diurne has too much power," he continued. "I'm not the only one who thinks so. There will be others who agree."

I remembered my conversation with Fern, and wondered how many more dissenters were in the Aureum's ranks.

"If you're sure," I responded. "When are we going?"

He shook his head. "You can't go."

"And why the hell not?"

"Abduction and torture, remember? Why would we deliver you into the hands of the people who want you gone?"

Anger burned in my chest, chased by fear. "So I can stay here, safely tucked out of the way, but you can't? I don't think the Diurne is going to give you a cookie and a pat on the back if they catch you."

"They won't harm us. Guardian lives are too valuable. If we get caught, it's manageable. If you get caught?" His jaw tightened and he shook his head. "It doesn't bear thinking about. Not only that, but logistically it makes more sense. We know the space better and are used to working as a team of seven. As soon as we get what we need, we'll come right back. We can try again with the void, or even go to another world."

He tucked a stray curl behind my ear. "Seph. I love you too much to risk you. I can't force you to stay, but I can ask you not to go."

My heart thundered as giddy warmth spread through me. "You... you love me?" I was covered in sweat and grave dirt, my hair snarled and stress lines worn into my forehead. But Alex smiled, threading his fingers through mine.

"How could I not? I'm in love with you, Seph, and I will do my damndest to take care of you, to keep you safe, even if you don't want me to."

"Well, when you put it that way."

I wanted to say it back. Those three words were on the tip of my tongue, ready and waiting, but—when I tried to speak, only a choked noise came out.

He cupped my face, caressing my cheek with his rough thumb. "It's okay," he murmured.

You can let him take care of you, said my reasonable voice. *He doesn't think you're incompetent, or weak. He just loves you.*

"I'll stay here," I told him, covering his hand with mine.

Alex wrapped his arms around me, sighing into my hair. "Thank you. I'm sure Simon will be pleased."

I clung on, sinking into him. "If I ask nicely, I bet he'll teach me how to make some poisons." Alex stiffened, and I laughed. "Gotcha."

"Very funny," he said, trailing a hand along my ribs where I was ticklish.

I laughed, squirming away. "I still might, though."

———

The next morning, we began preparations for the Guardians to leave. Simon begrudgingly agreed to mix up a few handy herbal solutions, the type that could put someone to sleep or burn their eyes temporarily like pepper spray. I was supposed to help Fern catalog and sort all of the weapons we had between us, along with the pile I'd found hidden in Diana's secret cache. We were in the formal dining room that had patches of damp and mold on the walls.

"All right, I think we've got it all here," Fern said. We looked at the absolute arsenal spread on the long table that could seat thirty. There were knives, swords, maces, guns that shot salt and silver bullets, cross-bows, and even a double-headed ax that had belonged to Simon's grandfather.

"Jesus."

"Mhm. I guess we should start organizing these daggers by size, then move on to the swords."

We set to work, but Fern's efficient movements soon put my wandering mind to shame.

"I know you're not thrilled with having to stay behind," she said, throwing a hatchet into a pile one-handed. "And I'm sorry for it."

"It's fine," I muttered.

"I've known Alex a long time. He likes to have everything in its proper place, to be in control. He's a good man, Seph."

"I know—"

"But," she continued, "from a personal standpoint, it can be annoy-ing." She put a sword down and faced me. "He's the happiest and most relaxed I've ever seen him when he's with you."

"Really?" I couldn't stop the smile from pulling at my lips.

"Really. You'd have to be blind not to notice the way he looks at you."

We didn't hid our relationship from the other Guardians, but we weren't advertising it, either.

"Even Davina knows not to mess with a good thing when she sees it," Fern said, returning her attention to her pile.

I wrinkled my forehead in confusion. "Why would Davina care?"

"She had a serious thing for him for a while. It was an unrequited crush, but still."

My stomach cramped, like I'd taken a punch to the gut. Davina and Alex? She was beautiful, cunning, and deadly. Alex was a sexy, powerful, intelligent man. Both were practically Aureum royalty. They made sense on paper.

"Did they ever....?" I trailed off. Alex's past relationships weren't any of my business, but I couldn't prevent the flare of jealousy.

"Definitely not," she said, opening the cylinder of a revolver and checking for bullets. "Even if Guardians were allowed to date within their units, he's never been interested in her. She represents everything that's been forced on him—his duties, the family legacy. My sense is that Davina thought they would make a tidy couple, and take over both of their parents' places on the Diurne when the time came. But Sylvan's been half in love with her for years, too, and she's never given him the time of day."

I gripped a rusty-handled dagger too tightly. How must it have felt for Davina to constantly be around the person she had feelings for, and have to deny them? I'd tried to do that with Alex for a short time, and it had been hard enough. Sympathy lodged in my heart, although I knew Davina would've hated me for it.

"I think we're about finished here. Speaking of Davina," Fern said, rolling her eyes, "she asked me to cover kitchen duty for her. See you later, Seph." With one final smile over her shoulder, she departed.

I lingered over the weaponry, unable to get the idea of Alex and Davina being together out of my head. It was foolish and irrational, but I felt uncomfortable knowing it, as though I'd suddenly grown too large for my skin.

He was around Davina day in and day out, after all. Davina, with her perfect face and body, her skill, her—

Standing alone in that decrepit room, thoughts swirling around me, I had an urge to run from the dusty, moth-eaten house. Canhaben's signature gray sky was darkening, only weak rays of light piercing the streaked dining room window.

Everyone else would be busy finishing their preparations and readying dinner. If I really wanted to, I could leave, go get some air—even if the air outside wasn't clean, it would at least be a welcome change.

I could go back to the edge.

As soon as I had the thought, the threads of my magic came alive, pulsing. Pushing me forward. Alex and Fern and the rest were about to hare off, risking their necks. Why shouldn't I? Not that I was planning to do anything other than look. I'd be back before anyone knew the difference.

I walked swiftly through the halls until I came to the back entrance. Then I slipped into the alleyway like a thief in the night, taking a longer way around than usual to avoid being seen.

The crammed and sooty buildings slowly gave way to wider roads and a more residential area. Most of the houses seemed abandoned, and I imagined that their inhabitants had moved closer into the city as the world decayed. I passed one with its shutters hanging drunkenly off their hinges, and window boxes full with the skeletal remains of withered blooms.

Canhaben must have been a nice place to live, once. I tried to imagine it as Simon had described, a bustling center of trade and innovation. Then I imagined Simon as a little boy, running these already decaying streets, but with his family still intact, not yet destroyed at the hands of the Aureum.

As I started up Lychgate Road, I wondered if this was a terrible idea. But the others just didn't get it, didn't understand what I'd felt when we tried to heal the edge. They hadn't felt the void's hunger, hadn't known we were so close, if only we could find that last, missing piece. No, I couldn't turn back, not with the energy of the graveyard swirling over my skin, the wind tossing my hair like a teasing playmate.

But there was more to it. For some reason, this felt like the place I was supposed to be right now. It *wanted* me there.

I raced along the cracked and worn path, practically flying. Over the crumbling bridge, past the invisible barrier, and then—

It was just me and the edge of the world, the gale screaming in my ears and my heart thudding like it wanted to escape my chest, to fling itself into the void of paradox.

The vacuous darkness mocked me, like it contained all of my worst failures and fears. It was frightening, but compelling, too. I took a step toward it, not entirely of my own volition. Then another, and another, until I realized that I actually wasn't the one taking the steps—paradox was taking me.

I ground my heels into the cracked dirt, attempting to find purchase while electricity zipped over my skin. Mere feet separated me from the edge, and my senses were sharper than a blade knowing I could go over at any moment. I raised my voice, shouting to the sky in frustration and fear.

"What do you want from me?" Fruitlessness warred with the energy pulsing under my skin that needed an outlet, else I would surely combust.

We'd used everything the damn book said the ritual required; earth, air, water, fire, and spirit. What more could anyone possibly do? How many more people needed to die, to sacrifice themself to this pointless cause?

A sharp pain in my hand jolted me back to reality. My fingernails had dug into my palm right over the spot where I'd cut it that night in the cemetery when I met Penn. I looked down at the imprinted half-moons riding over the pale scar, and an idea struck me like a chord hitting just the right note.

Maybe people didn't have to die.

Maybe I just had to bleed.

33

The wind coming from the void shrieked, screaming at me, as my thoughts raced a thousand miles an hour.

Earth was already here, cracked and dry thought it was, along with air. My blood had water in it—fire, too. Even as I had the thought, sparks shot from my fingertips, bringing the scent of ozone. And spirit —what if it was *my* spirit that was needed? What if that was why it didn't work for Diana, or when we called the demon?

What was a little blood, if lives could be saved? If wrongs could be righted, if people could have hope instead of hardship, faith instead of fear?

I pulled out the knife Alex insisted I always carry with me, and held it poised over my open left hand. As if in protest of the idea, a jagged crack split the ground far too close for comfort—if there was any comfort to be had in this insanity. If I didn't act now then I would never find out, because I would be joining most of Canhaben in paradox.

Bringing the blade slashing down, I scored my palm deep enough that the blaze of pain made me gasp. Tightening my jaw against the sting, I squeezed my fist so the blood flowed in a steady stream onto the parched earth.

"Take it," I whispered. I was dimly aware that as the blood flowed, licks of blue flame raced over my skin, except where tears tracked down my face and made tiny raindrops as they fell.

The dark red pool of my blood spread across the ground like an inkblot, soaking into the dry earth and turning it almost black in the leaden light. I didn't think to stop it, just let it keep falling and falling and spreading and spreading until some part of me knew there was way too much blood on the ground for there to still be enough left in my body.

The red stain advanced along the edge like ocean waves that raced up to kiss the shoreline, except that it didn't retreat, just kept pushing until it traveled too far for my supernatural vision to see. Everywhere my blood touched, cracks in the desiccated ground sealed like two pieces of clay being thrown together on a potter's wheel.

The light changed. Clouds receded and a ray of sunlight escaped from them to beam down. The wind blew furiously, but the ray of sun grew larger and brighter. It shone directly into the void, but the blackness of paradox swallowed the light completely.

Everything else—the wind, the smell of dry grass, the dust blowing in my face—faded into the background, and I was alone with the world. I felt its heartbeat, slow and stuttering at first, then I trembled with it as the pulse became stronger and steadier. When it hammered in time with my own, I knew that it was done.

The wind died and the sunlight—actual sunlight, I could barely believe it—dimmed, though it didn't disappear completely. Though my legs shook, I felt solid as the world's beating heart lingered inside of me. I closed my eyes to take communion with it.

Dropping to my knees, I dug my fingers into the earth. I felt grass and damp soil. Opening my eyes, I saw a small yellow flower blooming under my hand. The earth was alive again, waking at long last after its eternal winter. My hand no longer bled, the wound sealed over with a pale pink line. Another scar to add to my collection.

The magnetic hold the edge had on me faded away to nothing. It didn't need me anymore. There was no point in lingering, so I walked back through the cemetery, past the point where the invisible barrier had been.

"Persephone?" someone called, a shouted question in the too still air.

I flinched, ready to explain myself to whoever discovered I'd left Jupiter's.

A tall figure picked its way through the gravestones, long strides eating up the ground. But it wasn't Alex, or Simon, or Hollis or Sylvan.

There were a few more creases and signs of age on the man's face now, but I recognized it all the same.

"No," I breathed, my voice raspy like I'd swallowed glass. That's what it felt like, at least. Tight, razor sharp pain slicing me from nose to navel.

"Hello, darling." His voice was lightly accented, rich and smooth like the untouched silt at the bottom of a lake. I recognized the man's half-moon smile as my own, and my heart bumped painfully.

"Dad? W-What are you doing here?" I asked, stumbling over the words. "How did you—I mean, when—" I pinched my arm, the pain sharp and real. My head spun, and I had to lean over and catch a cracked gravestone for balance.

"Hey, hey now," he said, knitting his brow. "It's all right, love. I know this is a shock, but wow. Let me look at you a second." His gaze ranged over me, hesitant but greedy at the same time. I watched his eyes widen as he stared into an almost exact copy of them in my face, the same color and shape.

"How are you here?" I choked.

"That's a bit hard to explain, darling."

"I don't believe this." I looked around for someone, anyone to explain what the hell was happening. "There's no fucking way. This is a trick. A hallucination."

"No, sweetheart." The pain in his voice was a living thing. "This is real. I'm real."

"Then prove it," I demanded, my voice holding all the warmth of a winter's morning.

"You were born as the sun set on the summer solstice, the most beautiful thing I'd ever seen, and ever will see. You had a head full of hair and the loudest cry. Your mom and I met in Gravesville when she waas waitressing. It was love at first sight, if you can believe that." A sad smile cracked his face. "I've loved you for your whole life, and I've missed you for so long."

"Anyone could know those things," I challenged, even as my heart gave a hard squeeze.

"You have three freckles on your left shoulder that look like a constellation, and a lily birthmark on your wrist."

True. But was that enough for me to trust the word of a stranger? Because even if this was really my dad, I didn't know the man standing before me.

"Where the hell did you come from? And what are you doing here?"

Regret was written all over his face. "Like I said, love, it's a bit complicated."

"I've got time." I folded my arms implacably.

"But I don't," he answered. "I only have a few moments before he'll realize I'm gone."

"Who is *he*? I've been waiting twenty-six years for you, and you can't even give me ten minutes?"

He frowned. "Why did you do it, Persephone? Why did you open the threshold?"

A muscle in my jaw jumped. "It was even a choice. There's no way I was going to let people here suffer if it could be helped."

"That's admirable, darling, and I am proud to see you've grown to be a caring young woman. But you need to close it again, as soon as you can. You don't know what forces you've opened yourself to."

"No. Why should I? Don't you care about your home being sucked into the void? Your friends dying?"

"What I care about is you. I know that you don't understand, and that you hate me for it, but I have only ever tried to keep you safe."

"I don't even know what I should hate you for!" I yelled. "Why don't you enlighten me?"

He remained silent, staring like he wanted to imprint the sight of me onto his memory forever.

"Why did you leave us?"

Our eyes held for a long moment before he looked away. "Fiery, like your mother," he said gently. I'd never known my mom to be fiery; meek and tired, was more like it. I felt a fresh flush of anger.

"You owe me." I had no problem playing the guilt card, not now when I needed to soothe the splitting ache in the center of my chest.

"You're right. I owe you this, and lots more besides," he agreed softly.

"Then tell me. Don't deny me this, after you've denied me for my entire life."

My father kept his eyes intent on me, as though if he looked away I would disappear. "Do you know why I named you Persephone?"

"I'm assuming not because you wanted to torture your child. Which you did, by the way."

He laughed, a short bark that rang into the early twilight. "No, darling. That's never what I would have wanted for you. If you're here, in Canhaben, then you've clearly found out my secret. Our secret," he amended.

"No thanks to you."

"No, I wasn't the one who helped you there. I'd hoped you'd never find out. That is my greatest failure," he said. "That I haven't been able to protect you."

"Most people would say that abandoning your child is the opposite of protecting them."

"Maybe for other children, but not for you, love. I left to save you. And before I did, I bound all of the parts of you that could put you in danger. That could lead them to you. If I thought I'd had any other choice, I wouldn't have done it. You and your mother are the most important things to me in all of the worlds. More important than my own life."

"So it was you," I said slowly. "That's why I was living a completely normal life until a few months ago."

"How did you break the binding?" He worried at his lip, just like I did when I was nervous.

I jerked my shoulder. "I bled in the graveyard on the night of the full moon. That's our best guess."

"That could have done it," he admitted. "Persephone, you are a daughter of the Nephilim. A Watcher. That means—"

"Yeah, I know what it means," I cut him off. "Simon told me."

A grin lit his face, and my breath caught again at our resemblance. "Ah, so you've met the Bishops. How is he?"

"Almost his entire family is dead. He lives like a hermit in a decaying mansion."

My father's face fell, instant sorrow clouding his features. "You don't know how sorry I am to hear that. Lucas was the closest family I had."

"Is he around here, too?" I asked, taking a step closer to him. "Are you the leader of a group of dead dads that have somehow come back to life to antagonize their kids?"

"Persephone, stop," he ordered, voice turning hard as flint. "You want to hear me out, you won't come any closer."

I halted instantly at the force of his words.

"A goddess appeared to me the day you were born, as I rocked you to sleep in the nursery. She warned me that they would come for you. That I should hide you away, and let you live a human life. I saw your mark, and I knew it was true."

"Hide me from who?"

"The Aureum, who have hunted Watchers for millennia for our blood and our power. And from other creatures, born of evil and madness."

"Well, they've already come for me. All of them."

Pride and sorrow filled my dad's voice when he spoke next. "I named you Persephone because she is the goddess who walks among the worlds of the living and the dead. She is tied to both, just like you. You're a gods-touched child of angels and demons, of heavens and hells, and every world in between. You have a power of which we know nothing but is likely to change everything. I bound you so that you would be hidden from forces which might try to seek you out, to use or destroy you. And I left so that I wouldn't draw attention to you, so that you could be fully shielded from them. But I failed." Tears fell down his face and dripped onto the collar of his shirt.

There they were, the answers I'd been so desperately seeking laid at my feet like an offering. If I had imagined this moment, I would have hoped to feel vindicated. Instead, all I felt was sorrow, my heart split wide open in his hands.

"Why couldn't you tell me all of this years ago?" I lunged forward and grabbed his sleeve, aided by a burst of magic born of desperation.

My father froze. Then he gathered me up, clutching me in a fierce hug and stroking my hair.

I burrowed my head into his chest. He smelled like smoke, and was warm. Too warm.

"You need to run, my love." With a final squeeze, he pushed me away.

"Dad, what—"

My father flung a hand out to stop me. Then he screamed in agony, his spine twisting into an unnatural curve. His body popped and stretched, and he dropped to his knees, his breath coming in guttural pants.

"Get out of here," he groaned. "Get away from me."

"What's happening? Let me help!" I cried, hands shaking.

"You can't!" A growl came now, past long, curved incisors, that shattered my concentration. "I just needed to see you, once," moaned the creature that had been my father a moment ago. "If you hadn't opened that damned threshold, you would have been safe."

The words cut off entirely, and he let out a deep snarl that made every hair on my body stand on end. The sound was low and menacing, beginning deep in his chest and then finally rippling out through slavering lips and jagged, yellowed teeth.

I backed away slowly, eyes locked on the beast before me. It was a massive wolf-like animal with pointed ears, its matted fur black as pitch. Its eyes glowed like two embers.

There was no trace left of the man my father had been.

<h1 style="text-align:center">34</h1>

Hunger and hatred replaced the love in my father's eyes. The creature he'd become stalked toward me, muscles bunching under its fur and saliva dripping from elongated canines.

But my dad *was* hidden away somewhere inside this hellish beast. I gave one more plea. "Dad, please come back."

It stared at me, eyes boring into mine. I thought I saw something like recognition flicker in their depths, but it was gone just as quickly. The monstrous black wolf reared its head, then raced toward me.

I ran.

My legs pumped like pistons and the breath whistled through my lungs as I darted through the graveyard, dodging tombs and twisted vines waiting to trip me up. My pulse thrummed loudly in my ears, and I tried to focus on something other than the slick fear coating my insides.

I hazarded a look backward, but immediately wished I hadn't. The beast was closing in, only feet away now. I put on an extra burst of speed to widen the distance between us. But my foot caught on a vine, and I staggered, barely picking myself up in time to avoid snapping jaws from closing around my ankle.

My muscles twitched as I began to feel the strain of my supernatural sprint. I couldn't run forever. *Keep it together, damn you,* said a voice in my head that sounded scarily like Simon.

What would Simon do? Well, he wouldn't have left his house in the first place. What would Alex do? Surely he would have known which word to utter at the creature that would either dissolve it into dust or send it back to wherever it had come from.

Except this wasn't just any old demon. It was my father. Or at least, it had been. I couldn't kill it—or him, if there was any chance at all that hurting the creature would hurt my dad as well.

I wanted to curse, to scream, to rage. If there was any moment for the goddess to hear my plea, to help me, it would have been then.

And for once, someone was listening. I heard a shout and looked up, barely daring to hope it was friend and not foe.

It was Simon. Or, not Simon. Penn had finally turned up. He stood atop a rise above the foul ditchwater.

"Oy!" he yelled, lifting his chin defiantly as I closed in on the edge of the bank. "Get over here!"

He didn't have to ask twice. I sprinted over the bridge, but the force of my footfalls must have been too much for it. The boards collapsed with splintering groans as I reached the other side and raced up the hill. Penn grabbed my hand to pull me up the last few feet and I lurched to the top of the rise, lungs searing with the effort.

The beast paced the lip of the bank on the other side. It bared its fangs and let out a spine-tingling growl.

"Why—did it—stop?" I mustered through panting breath, clutching a stitch in my side.

"Hellhounds don't like water," Penn replied, reaching under his shirt to pull a pouch from around his neck. Gone was the charming, dangerous stranger who I had encountered in Gravesville. His brows were drawn, his face etched in concentrated lines as he upended the pouch and sprinkled white crystals in a circle around us.

I seized Penn's arm, stopping him. "We need to get back to Jupiter's."

He shook me off, pulling more items out of a pack. "We can't outrun that thing. We can only try to fight it." Out came a mirror, a candle, a pearl-handled dagger, and a small cup that he filled to the brim with dark liquid from a vial. He traced an *X* with his finger into the ground and arranged each item so that they lay at its points. He spoke, so softly I could only see his lips moving.

My eyes met the hellhound's over the stream. It raised its hackles, then backed up several feet. "It's moving," I whispered over Penn's shoulder.

He glanced across the water, and his lips moved faster. He drew another small pouch from his bag. "When I tell you to, open this up and throw it in the beast's mouth. It's getting ready."

As if waiting for its cue, the hellhound took a running start, then sprang into the air. Time slowed down as its giant body seemed to hang immobilized over the wide ditch.

It landed hard enough to make the ground shudder. Penn covered his tableau to prevent it from scattering. The beast stalked us through the ruin of the graveyard, a predator who knew its prey was cornered.

"Get ready," Penn murmured. His gaze was trained on the creature, determined and calm. I wished I felt the same. My hands shook and my heart hammered. I pulled the drawstring pouch open, waiting for his command.

Without warning, Penn swallowed back the liquid from the cup and sprang from the circle, flinging the pearl-handled dagger at the hellhound. It spun end over end before lodging in the creature's shoulder.

"No!" I cried. "Don't hurt him!"

Penn turned toward my outcry for the briefest of seconds, but that was all it took for the hellhound to lunge. Penn threw his arm up to block the creature from tearing out his throat, and shoved it back with his bare hands. The hellhound flew through the air, slamming against a mausoleum. Penn's ritual had given him the strength of ten people.

"Now!" he yelled at me. I stayed within the circle, feeling slow and numb. "Do it!" he screamed again. The hellhound rose from a crumpled heap and shook itself. It let out another thundering snarl, lowering its head and pawing the ground like a bull chasing a red flag.

The urgency in Penn's voice snapped me out of my stupor, and I crossed the salt ring.

The beast kept both of us in its range of vision, pacing. It wasn't hard to believe that the creature stalking us belonged to hell. It smelled like burning rubber and sulfur, and this near I saw that the ends of its fur were singed.

I hefted the small bag, attaching black and gold threads to it. They wove around the bag in a protective net, holding it closed. Drawing my arm back, I aimed, then launched it at the roaring beast.

The bag went tumbling end over end, the threads of my magic keeping my aim true. It was ten feet away, then five, then one, then—

Some force grabbed the bag, wrenching it out of my grasp. The strings of power snapped, dangling in the air, and I felt as if I'd been punched in the gut. I cried out as I stumbled and dropped to my knees.

Penn reached for me, dragging us away from the hound, but the salt circle had been broken. "What happened?"

I shook my head, straining to draw breath. "It has magic."

The hellhound prowled, circling us. I got to my feet with Penn's help. We turned with it, not letting the creature out of our sight.

"You need to get the pouch back," Penn whispered out of the corner of his mouth, not taking his eyes off the beast.

"How?"

"Just do it. Use your bloody magic. I don't have much left," he said, rubbing his wrists. He did seem weaker, a bit more round-shouldered, and his feet were beginning to drag.

The bag was lying at the edge of the bank. One good shove would send it tumbling into the ditch.

"I need a distraction."

"Right," he said, and at that moment he sounded so much like Simon that I had to mentally shove the image away. "Ready?"

No. "Yes."

Penn clapped his hands together. "Oy! Ugly!"

The beast stopped its slow stalking and scented the air. I wondered if he—it—smelled my fear.

"Go!" he shouted, and launched at the beast. I ran to the edge of the ditch, reaching out with power, but it was as if the cut threads were still knitting back together. The bag wobbled, then stilled.

Penn gave a gargled cry, and I whipped toward him. He had fallen, but rolled, and managed to elude the hellhound's dripping jaws. I sprinted through the gravestones, then threw myself down, skidding on my knees toward the pouch. My fingertips skimmed the leather, but the momentum of my thrust pushed it over the bank, into the fast-flowing ditchwater.

"No!" I screamed. Without thinking, I plunged into the ditch.

The fetid water was freezing cold, and much deeper than I anticipated, coming to the center of my chest. The breath froze in my lungs for a second, but it didn't matter, because I was already diving to the bottom of the ditch. Encased in ice, my fingers scrabbled around the slick mud, stones, roots, and waste.

I breached the surface, coming up for air to hear a horrible scream. Panic flooding me, I dived again. Where the fuck was the pouch? My hands were rigid, my fingers barely able to move.

Shutting my eyes, I sprinted to my obsidian door. I wrenched it open and shot my hands out like I was pulling the whole world into me, the rivers and flowers and hills and that dark, dark sky.

Shining gold and black threads flooded through me, and I cast a net over the whole damn ditch, the banks and the rocks and the roots, until I dredged up the pouch from where it was trapped beneath a stone. Riding on the wave of my power, I lifted into the air, shooting up and onto solid ground.

"HEY!" I screamed, waving my arms. "Over here!"

The hellhound lifted its scarred muzzle into the air, nose twitching. To both my relief and horror, it galloped at me, eyes lighting up like burning rubies.

But I was ready. Holding the pouch in my hands, power lighting me up from the inside out, blue flame racing over my skin.

I was no longer prey. I was the predator.

I waited until it was a foot away, mouth open wide for the kill. Flicking my fingers, I sent Penn's pouch straight into its yawning maw.

There was a pop and a hiss, and a low keening from the hellhound. It collapsed and its eyes went dim, then its body started to fade, its outline softening until it became a jumble of blurred lines. Within seconds, it was gone.

Misery churned in my chest like the water below until I heard a low moan. *Penn.*

He was lying prone behind a tomb, only half of his face visible amongst the matted, dry grass.

I ran to him, placing a hand on his shoulder. "Are you all right?" I panted.

He moaned again when I touched him, and the part of his face that was visible screwed up in pain. I rolled him over gently, but he continued to utter low, distressed groans. The sleeve around his forearm hung in tatters, and there was more blood showing than skin.

"Oh, goddess," I mumbled, hovering my hands over him uselessly, swallowing back my gorge.

"She won't help now," Penn mumbled, eyes closed.

"You're going to be fine," I said, more to myself than him. "We just have to get you back to Simon. He'll be so happy to see you."

"Not bloody likely." His breath rattled in his chest.

"Let me help." I placed my hand above his wound, wishing I'd asked Alex how to heal someone.

"No," he ground out so vehemently that I stopped right away. "Take me to Jupiter's."

I didn't argue. Using threads of magic to assist me, I lifted Penn into a standing position, slinging his good arm around my neck.

"Quickly," he rasped. He'd gone pale, sweat edging his hairline and dotting the bridge of his nose.

I half walked, half dragged us back through the cemetery. Penn's mouth was tight with pain. But he limped on, only emitting a low hiss when we reached the bottom of the hill that led to Lychgate Road.

"I've got you," I said, reassuring both of us.

It wasn't pretty. By the time we reached the top, sweat coursed down my face, burning my eyes, from the effort of using my magic to pull Penn up the hill. The smell of rot and sewage clung to my skin, choking me. But we made it.

Then I heard a voice in my head, and relief washed over me. *What the fuck are you doing at the cemetery?* Alex's voice was tight, but I heard the worry beneath his frustration.

Come get me. I have Simon's brother.

Already on the way.

"Someone's coming for us," I told Penn, securing his arm around me. "Don't worry. We'll get you fixed up."

His head lolled on my shoulder. "Dint mean to."

"Sh, don't speak. It's okay." He was burning up, his skin like an open flame against mine.

"Nah," he murmured. "Gotta say. Didn't mean to...leave the card."

I stroked his hair, soothing. The effort of speaking was clearly costing him. "Don't worry about it."

"Was waiting." He took a wheezing breath. "Golden Ones...you did it. The edge."

I caught sight of Alex and Davina cresting a hill as they flew toward us. Her wings were raven black to his iridescent. "Oh, thank god. They're here, Penn."

They landed before us. Alex's face was almost as pale as Penn's as he looked us over, green eyes stark. "What happened?"

"Simon's brother, he was bit. There was a hellhound. I'll explain later, but he needs help. I'm fine."

"I'll take him," Alex said, shifting Penn into his arms. He took off, winging toward Jupiter's.

I wanted to collapse right there, but Davina put a hand on my elbow. She made an effort to arrange her face into more neutral lines, but her jaw was stone. "The edge?" she asked.

"I think I healed it."

With a tight nod, she scooped me into her arms and flew us over the city. Faces turned up to the sky, mouths open and eyes full of fear as they beheld Davina's wings.

We landed on the front step of Jupiter's, forgoing subtlety since we'd already been seen. Casey was waiting right outside the door.

"Where is he?" I asked without preamble.

For once, she was serious. "Kitchen."

Penn lay on the trestle table, pale and still as death. The other Guardians looked up when we entered, but Simon only had eyes for his twin. He did, however, spare me a fleeting glance when I explained what happened.

"He was bitten by a hellhound?" Hollis said, incredulous. "Jesus H., Seph, only you would sneak out and manage to run into one of those."

I left out the part about the hellhound having formerly been my father. "What's going to happen to him?"

"There's no cure for a bite from a hellhound," said Simon. His voice was lifeless and cold, like dead leaves swirling in a winter storm.

"There must be something," I said. I refused to believe that he couldn't be saved. We were talking about using magic, for Pete's sake. "I'm not going to let him die."

Penn's eyelids fluttered, then shut again. His forehead was hot and dry. The jagged bite on his arm—the flesh peeled back to expose muscle—had stopped bleeding. Black lines radiated out from the wound in a spiderweb pattern.

"He's not going to die," Simon said in the same, dead voice.

Relief surged through me. "Well, thank god." Then suddenly, Simon was in my face, and I couldn't see anything except his storm-tossed eyes. Lightning flashed in them. His lips turned up in a snarl.

"He's not going to die, because he's infected," Simon spat. "A bite from a hellhound will turn him into one, too. His body will die, his soul will wither away, and he will be trapped in the form of a hellbeast for eternity."

"Back off," Alex commanded, his voice hard, coming to flank me. He put a protective hand on my shoulder, but I couldn't even feel his touch.

What Simon said couldn't possibly be true. Before he'd transformed into the beast, I'd seen my dad whole and healthy, unless it *had* been some sort of intricate hallucination.

"No," I said. "No, no, no." I grabbed Penn's burning hand between mine, trying to send my golden threads into his wound. A twist of darkness lay under his skin, an evil that sizzled and spat.

Staring, disconsolate gazes surrounded me. Then I felt pressure on my hand. Penn mustered his strength, which was about as much as a newborn kitten's, pulling me toward him. He moved his lips, but no sound came out. I bent my ear toward his mouth.

"You need...to...*kill...me.*" He rasped.

I reared back, away from the ugly words. His eyes shone with desperation and fever, eyes that had a pinkish sheen to their whites.

We couldn't sentence Penn to eternity as a soulless, evil creature, both for his sake and ours. But did I have the strength to do what he asked? For I knew that it had to be me; I'd gotten him into this mess, and I owed it to him.

Simon cradled his brother's head, and tipped a cup of water to his lips. "Penn," he said, in a would-be normal voice. "Why didn't you come home?"

Penn's mouth flapped open and closed like a fish out of water. His skin was turning gray and waxy.. "Was...watching. Something...out there." His eyelids fluttered again, and he tried to raise his uninjured arm to point.

"You bloody fool," Simon whispered, bowing his head over his only surviving family member. "Why can't you just stay put, where it's safe? You can never just stay." His voice broke on those last words. I stared, unseeing, as Simon wept for his twin. We were interlopers on his grief that had only just begun.

"Simon," Fern said, her voice carrying a warning. "Look."

We followed her gaze to Penn's wounded arm. His fingernails had lengthened into points, turning the dark red of congealed blood. The black streaks radiating from the bite had enlarged so that they almost entirely covered his arm.

"It has to be done soon," Sage said. "He's turning. I can take his pain away, Simon. I can take his fear."

Simon gnawed on his lip, the places where his teeth touched turning white as old bones. "Get out," he snarled. "All of you." Feet shuffled somberly toward the door. "Except for you." He pointed an accusatory finger at me. "You stay."

I bent my head, ready to receive a penance that wouldn't even be close to what I deserved. I told Penn not to hurt the hellhound, to try and save any remnants of my father that were left in the creature. If he had been holding back because of me, then it was my fault.

"You've taken his life as surely as if you'd slid the blade in yourself," Simon said. "So you can go ahead and finish the job you started."

I deserved the guilt, shame, and wretchedness mingling in the spot just below my sternum. I couldn't keep anyone safe. I had to look Penn in the eyes, and watch the fate that I'd led him to.

"No," Alex interjected. "She won't."

"She did this." Simon stood, rage pouring out of him like a waterfall. "She's not turning me into a murderer."

"No one is turning you into a murderer," Alex replied. "The only one at fault here is the creature who attacked him. I'm so sorry, Simon." He was compassionate and sincere, but that only enraged Simon further.

"You're right. It's not just her. It's all of you. And if I hadn't let you darken my doorstep, then Penn would've come home straight away. He wouldn't be...this." Angry tears gathered in his eyes, turning them to glittering chips of ice.

"Then that makes his death equally my fault. I am responsible for my unit, for bringing them here. I'll do it in Seph's place."

"Fuck. You," Simon breathed. But he stepped back to allow Alex access to his twin. I felt his hateful glare on me, but I kept my eyes trained on a scar in the wooden table.

Alex was too good to let me suffer. And I? I was selfish enough that I let him.

35

Simon evicted us from Jupiter's the next morning. Even if he hadn't blamed me for Penn's death, we'd exposed ourselves to the citizens of Canhaben. It wasn't safe for us to stay. I was eager to go, to try and outrun the grief and guilt I'd be leaving in my wake.

I didn't consider myself a strong person, by any means. For most of my life, I had tried to avoid pain. The only risks I took were in my head, where I didn't have the chance to fail. I stayed stuck in the same boring job I detested for years, because it was familiar and predictable. I isolated myself with books and fantasies so there wasn't room for anyone else to hurt me in the very small world I'd built for myself.

So, I wasn't at all surprised that I'd let Alex do the things I didn't have the courage to do myself. It was selfish, and cruel, to let a person I loved look death in the eyes on my behalf, while I cowered in the corner. Simon, or anyone for that matter, couldn't hate me more than I hated myself.

Guilt lodged painfully in my throat as I packed up my few belongings. I left my father's letters on the bed for Simon, and put the silver ring on my finger and my dad's photo in my pocket.

"Are you ready?" Alex asked, slipping through the door of our room. He wore unrelieved black, the clothes clinging to his muscled frame. I could only tell where his weapons were hidden because I'd helped him put them on earlier.

We would leave from the cemetery in Canhaben, now that a gateway could be opened. From there, we'd travel to New Orleans and back to Aureum's headquarters. There was no option for me to stay behind anymore. Alex's plan was to use a distraction to draw the Guardians away from the archives, where he hoped to find records of the Diurne's plans. *Hope* was the key word. We were setting off on a wild goose chase that could end with us losing our freedom, or even our lives.

Simon didn't come to say goodbye, of course. He'd left shortly after daybreak, according to Fern, having prepared Penn's body for burial. He was laying his twin to rest in the cemetery, alongside his other family members. I wondered if he would plant parsley on his grave.

Simon was all alone now, and it was my fault. The thought pulsed in my head like a drumbeat as we traveled to the graveyard.

Already the world seemed to be healing. The thick vines that ensnared graves in a deathgrip had receded, and the sun shone weakly through the clouds. At least some good had come from this utter disaster. Anxiety had a chokehold on me as I wondered if I'd catch a glimpse of Simon's accusatory look, peering at me through the headstones.

Before we left, Alex gathered us around for one final review of the plan.

"Okay, everyone. This is it. Remember where we're going?"

"Greenwood. You've said it a thousand times, Alex," Sage said. "We know what we're doing."

"Doesn't hurt to go over it one more time," Davina replied. "Just to make sure there are no mistakes."

"And when we get there?" Alex continued, as if there had been no interruption.

"That'll depend on the time. We don't know if it works differently in Canhaben than it does at home," Hollis said. "Hopefully, it'll be the same, which means everyone'll be busy in the office suites. Casey, Seph, and I'll let off the explosion—er, minor distraction, I mean—above ground."

"While everyone's milling about," Casey continued, "Alex and Davina will slip downstairs in their disguises."

"After you two get through the tunnel, Sage, Fern, and I will seal the entrance. That should buy you two enough time to find what you need in the archives," Sylvan finished. "We'll be waiting back at the cemetery, and will slip off through a gateway once you've returned."

"Slick as a whistle," Hollis said. "Easier than pie. Simple as a—"

"Yep, I think we've got it," Casey said, rolling her eyes. "Now let's get a move on, before something comes through here and decides to have us for dinner."

"All right, then. Let's get going." Alex nodded to Davina.

She ran her hands through the air. "This feels strange," she said, then hooked her hands together and pulled hard, straining. "Like it's rusty or something." But the gateway, full of its usual midnight silk, stretched wide between her hands.

"Okay, everyone," Alex said, piercing us all with a final look. His gaze lingered on me. "See you on the other side." He stepped through without hesitation. Fern, Casey, Hollis, Sage, and Sylvan followed him, until it was just Davina and I left standing among the headstones.

"Wait, Seph." She took my elbow, stopping me. "I just want to say that I'm sorry."

I met her dark gaze. "For what?"

She shook her head, then looked away. "Just...for everything."

I paused. "Me, too." Then I stepped into the yawning black.

Hard rock, rusty sky, and dry desert air surrounded me as I dropped out of the gateway. It was cold, so cold that tiny pools of water pitting the bare, rocky ground were frozen. A gargantuan sun sat on the horizon, leaving the land bathed in a hazy red twilight. Stone mounds like termite hills speared out of the ground all around.

Frigid air burned my lungs, but all I felt were the frissons of panic coursing through my entire body, sounding an alarm far too late to be useful. A set of hands hauled me up.

"Seph? Where is she, where's Davina?" Alex asked urgently, his brows drawn.

Realization slammed into me like a punch to the gut.

"Alex, it's a trap," I said frantically, trying to draw him back toward the gateway. "We have to go back through before—"

But we were too late. Davina stepped out of the gateway, and it slammed shut behind her with a resounding *crack*. She whirled around, looking as confused as the rest of us. "Where are we?"

"Why don't you tell us?" I snapped.

Alex shoved me behind him. I tried to shove back, but he held me firmly. The rest of the Guardians flanked us, drawing their weapons and leveling them at Davina.

She held her hands up, fear showing in the whites of her eyes. "I don't know what's going on here. Seriously, guys."

"It's not her fault."

We all turned to look at Fern. Her usually kind features seemed harsher in the reddish light.

"I had to do it." Fern folded her arms, as if bracing herself for an onslaught. "There was no other choice. Not if things are going to change."

Shocked silence fell like the final curtain of a performance.

"Fern," Hollis said slowly, his seafoam eyes squinting like he was trying to pinpoint the exact moment of her betrayal. "Where are we, and what the hells have you done?"

"What I had to. The Diurne is on their way. And...and something else." She flicked her eyes toward a brownish smudge far off on the horizon. It could have been a cloud, but it was moving too fast. "We're on neutral territory, somewhere that levels the playing field. A prison world."

All I could think was that this wasn't the woman I'd come to know over the past few months. A pit opened inside my stomach, full of churning panic.

"Why?" Alex's voice was more rigid than the stone under our feet. But he had heartbreak in his eyes, and sorrow on his face. It was the first time I'd seen him slump.

"Alex, I'm sorry." The corner of Fern's mouth pulled down before she smoothed her face again. "This is the only way the Diurne would agree to listen. After we found out about the Aureum killing off worlds, I couldn't let that stand."

"But there are other ways," Davina said, her face crumpled like a tissue. "This is playing right into their hands."

Fern shook her head. "You don't get it, do you? There is no change possible without the Diurne's say so." She gave a mirthless laugh. "Even if our plan had worked, we'd be like a flea pestering a lion. The only way to change their minds is to work with them, not against them.

They've...." She cleared her throat. "They've agreed to give me a place on the council as an eighth member—if I give them Seph."

Casey drew a harsh breath, and Hollis's mouth dropped open.

Fern looked straight at me. "This is the start of the revolution. I'm going to change things for the Aureum. For the worlds, and for everyone who's suffering."

Sylvan shook his head, face ashen. "How could you?"

"We all have to bend the rules, now and then. For a good cause," she answered. Her words held a forced certainty.

"So help me, I will make you wish you'd never been born," Casey growled, marching up to Fern. She didn't even make it two steps before she slid slowly backward over the rock, as if dragged by an invisible rope around the middle.

"You can't hurt me," Fern said. "And you might as well stop trying to find a way out of here. Only those given permission can open gateways into or out of a prison world."

Sage and Sylvan had been clawing at the air, but stopped at her words. They talked over each other.

"You're lying," Sage barked.

"Who has permission?" Sylvan growled.

"Fern," Alex said, before she could answer either of them. "I'll do anything you want. You can hold me as a hostage, use me instead. Just let the others go." His eyes were pleading.

Fern's answering laugh was hollow. "They really only want Seph. She's the key to all of this." She turned to me. "I am sorry, more than you know. But I hope that in time, you can understand. One life for the life of thousands. Millions."

"What are they planning to do with her?" Alex said, finding my hand. I gripped him tightly.

"You won't be hurt, Seph. Part of the agreement I made with Edward and Mindara is that your life isn't forfeit. They made me a blood promise," Fern said.

After another beat of silence, I spoke. "Cora Roth."

Fern nodded. "She was like you. A Watcher and a Guardian."

My pulse pounded thickly in my ears. "So the Diurne made a deal with demons, because the devil they know is better than the devil they don't." I still couldn't believe that Fern—kind, nurturing Fern—had sold me out. "They've worked with demons to get rid of a Watcher before, so they can trust them to do it again?"

"That's right," she said, no longer meeting my eyes. "They want to hunt down all of the Watchers, those who carry demon blood, no matter how marginal. They think you're an abomination, that your ancestry makes you inherently evil and untrustworthy. But I am going to help change that."

Abomination, *evil*, and *untrustworthy* rang in my ears. Through it all, I couldn't ignore the icy licks of fear in my chest. But I was even more fearful for the people that stood with me. My friends. I looked at them, arrayed around me, faces set. I would protect them with my last breath.

"If I'm who you want, then let everyone else go." I stepped around Alex. He caught my arm, trying to pull me behind him, but I jerked away, power strengthening the movement. "This is between me and the Diurne. The unit doesn't need to be involved."

An invisible hand pressed on my back, then pressure forced me to my knees.

"Stop!" Alex commanded, his mouth a tight slash.

The pressure increased. He didn't realize that every attempt he made to protect me was going to cause more pain. The others flew at Fern, but she batted them away as easily as if they were gnats. Davina flung a dagger at her, but that, too, clattered uselessly to the ground.

"Your power won't work here," Fern said, letting up the pressure on my spine. "Please, stop. I don't want to hurt you."

I panted through gritted teeth. "Then don't. This isn't you, Fern."

Hollis lunged at her, teeth bared, then a howling gale blew over us. The Guardians went spinning to the granite ground, forced to their knees.

The Diurne—or maybe the demons—had done something to ensure the other Guardians' power wouldn't work in this prison world. But maybe a Watcher's would.

Shutting my eyes, I turned inward and groped for the threads of my magic. The gold was dull and lifeless, but the black—the black was strong, surging through my veins like liquid steel.

I stayed on the ground with the others, pretending pain had overtaken me. If Fern didn't see me as a threat, perhaps she would be lured into complacency. Sliding my gaze over my shoulder without turning my head, I searched for the brown smudge. It was closer now.

I had to act before whatever it was got to me, because I was almost certain it would bring my death.

Fern squeezed her eyes shut for a moment. "I tried to get the Diurne to leave the rest of the unit alone. But, they're going to deal with you all, too." She didn't have to explain what *deal with* meant for me to know that some horrible punishment awaited them.

"I thought you said they'd be here soon." Corded muscle stood out on Alex's neck. His eyes flicked to me, and his hands flexed toward the short knife I knew was strapped to the small of his back.

"They will be," Fern replied, though she sounded less confident than she had a few minutes ago. What if the Diurne's plan was actually to get rid of us all at once? To leave the defectors in a prison world where we would slowly starve to death or be destroyed by whatever forces kept the others' abilities harnessed?

"Then while we're waiting, maybe you could enlighten us as to how you planned this," Alex growled.

"Seph wasn't the only one who snuck out last night."

"You didn't have to stay," Casey shot. "You could've gone back to the Aureum. No one forced you to go along with this."

"It's the only opening I had. If I'd gone back empty-handed, there would be nothing for me to bargain with. But with Seph to offer them...." she trailed off.

Baring my teeth, I couldn't stop the low snarl that worked its way up my throat.

Ignoring me, she continued. "The Diurne has complete control over the Aureum. We could have tried to steal what we needed, tried to get to individual Guardians and change their minds, but I knew...even if we found evidence, we wouldn't have been able to convince the others to go along with us. Loyalty over all, remember?" Her lip curled.

"And you really think you're going to stop them from killing the worlds? One person, against seven senior Guardians who are stronger and have more influence?" Sage said.

"Roderick and Mallory will be on my side. I know I can get them to see reason," Fern replied coolly. "As long as I get a majority, the motion to stop the extermination program will pass. It might take years, but... change doesn't happen overnight."

"Gods," Hollis breathed. "You're just as crazy as those fuckers."

Fern's face twisted. "You should be thanking me."

"You're more brainwashed than all of us if you think allying with the Diurne is a good idea," he spat.

Fern raised her hands as if to strike Hollis. Alex, still on his knees, clenched his fists. I knew it was killing him not being able to protect us, but his face became the impassable captain's mask once again.

"The Diurne is using you and lying, just like they've done to all of us," he said, voice sharper than a black, killing frost.

As the Guardians talked, I had been slowly scooting toward Fern, stealing a couple inches at a time. But as I moved closer to her, the brown smudge in the distance advanced on all of us.

At this distance, I could see that it wasn't a smudge, but a sort of tornado. It emitted a low whine that made the hairs on the back of my neck stand up. Davina had been tracking it, too, and stole a brief glance at me. We didn't have much time left. I had to decide which was the bigger threat—the tornado, Fern, or the Diurne?

The atmosphere shifted and a billowing tear rent the air next to Sage. The midnight silk of the gateway undulated for just moments before a leg appeared, followed by the torso and head of Edward Eames.

It was now or never.

36

Everything came into sharper focus. The rusty sky became redder, the rock under my feet harder, and the air in my lungs agonizingly cold to the point of pain. In the millisecond everyone's attention shifted to Alex's father coming through the gateway, I launched at Fern. Her eyes cut to me when I was a whisper away. We connected and crumpled to the ground, rolling away from the others as we struggled. She disentangled herself and shoved me back, and we circled, each looking for an opening.

Davina, always ready, barked an order. "Close the gateway, before the rest come through!"

Sage and Casey flung themselves at the gateway, scraping and tearing to close it against arms and legs that emerged like an army of insects. Two more people managed to come through before they shut it. Mindara, and a young man with floppy hair—Yuto, that bastard.

They launched at my friends, jumping into the fray and striking out with power. Hollis came out of nowhere and tackled Yuto to the ground, while Casey met Mindara's charge with a roundhouse kick that sent her skidding along the ground.

Alex struggled with his father, doing his best to dodge Edward's attacks. Although he didn't have power, he was the younger and faster of the two. He managed to get behind his father and send an elbow drilling into his back. Edward looked like he had gone down, but tucked into a roll and sprang up, shooting a jet of light a hairsbreadth from Alex's right ear. Panic tangled with adrenaline in my chest.

A blast of heat rocked me, and I slammed into one of the stone mounds that resembled a termite hill. Fern held blue light in her hands, and I shoved power back at her, ducking behind the mound.

It shattered, shrapnel scoring my cheek. *Hiding is definitely out, then.*

Fern fought with her usual grace. Shooting arcana, she blocked kicks and punches with ease. Soon, it took all of my strength just to stay upright. I had a stray thought that maybe she'd let me win all those times we'd sparred, just to fool me into complacency.

"You can't beat me, Seph," she said, after landing a kick to my thigh that buckled my leg. "If you give up now, they won't hurt you."

We danced around each other, while I tried to keep my attention off of the sounds coming from behind me. I'd seen the others out of the corner of my eye, fighting two to a person with Edward, Mindara, and Yuto.

"You know that's not true," I panted, rolling away when Fern tried to plant her boot in my knee. Jumping up, I touched the river of black power that raged under my skin. I shot onyx fire, and it singed her hair. She retaliated by bowling me over with a harsh torrent of cold wind.

"You're handing me over to demons. Did you think they'd throw me a fucking tea party?" Blood dripped from the corner of my mouth, and I tasted salt and iron. I levered up, my knee screaming.

"It's the life of one against the life of many." Fern lunged, but my kick connected with her abdomen. She flew through the air, then hit the ground hard and skidded. But she was up almost as soon as she'd landed.

In a move that would have made Davina proud, I slipped the dagger strapped to my calf out of its sheath, aimed, then flicked it at Fern. It went tumbling end over end, finally landing buried to the hilt in her thigh. She screamed in pain, clutching at her leg, and fell.

Just after my momentary victory, I heard a cry that stopped my heart. Davina went down, clutching a knife protruding from her side. I took my attention off Fern, half turning in anticipation of running to Davina.

A blow sent me rocketing backward so that sky and earth pitched together in a tumult of iron and rust. I landed in a heap twenty feet away, with pain searing my left bicep. Pain, and something more. It felt like there was something lodged inside me, stabbing the muscle.

Fern stood, leaning heavily on her uninjured leg, holding a smoking gun. I looked down at my arm. Blood leaked from a perfectly round bullet hole torn through my shirt sleeve.

I tried to wiggle my fingers and almost passed out at the sickening dizziness clouding my head. Could I heal myself? I had never attempted it, and wasn't sure I had the strength to do so now.

Fern limped toward me, pain and fear marring her features. "You need to stay down," she urged. "I'm so sorry." With her good leg, she stepped on my arm, grinding her boot into my wound.

I retched, turning myself inside out as fire raced up and down my spine. Sweat sprang up all over my body, and I shook like I had the flu. Was this what it felt like to die? Hopeless, and broken, and as weak as the day I was born?

My eyes fluttered closed. I thought about Alex and Bri, my mom and Claire, Simon. I had let down the people who mattered the most to me in the world. But maybe if I died, they'd be safe. They'd be protected from the danger that had followed me ever since I'd bled in the graveyard.

And then there was a scream, and a rush of cold air. Pressure lifted from my arm and I opened my eyes to see a mighty terror cloaked in howling wind.

The tornado had finally arrived. It was made of blood and bone, a swirl of decomposing corpses that was so foul I just wanted to let my eyes drift shut again.

Fern turned and sprinted away from the cyclone of bodies, toward the Diurne and Yuto. Maybe there was no point, after all. Perhaps this was where the fates had decided to cut my life's string. I wasn't even me anymore, just a mass of fear and pain.

You can't give up, said the little voice inside my head. *Remember? You promised. Be smart and strong, and take care of yourself.*

The strength of everyone who ever loved me became the iron in my spine, the power in my limbs, and the courage in my heart. With my arm dangling uselessly at my side, I dragged myself to my feet and faced the raging tempest of blood and bone.

The storm towered above me, hundreds of feet of pure repulsion. Gruesome features of a face came together. There were the eyes, made of spheres of grimacing skulls. Organs and gristle formed the thick mouth, and the nose was a hollow slit.

The spectacle had stopped the Diurne's forces and the Guardians from trying to kill each other. Like me, they were all frozen in horror, helpless to stop the impending storm.

But they didn't have the black threads of my magic. I had the blood of the first demons, the Nephilim, running in my veins, dark as midnight and more powerful than the fire that licked along my skin. I would use the monster inside of me to call to the monster before me.

"I see you, demon! You don't frighten me," I called into the storm, channeling a confidence I'd never felt. My lips moved, but I couldn't hear the sound of my words over the howling wind.

It must have heard me, because the clusters of skulls with their horrible empty eyes shifted in my direction. The mouth smiled, and the wind slowed to a gentle flutter. The desecrated bodies disappeared.

In their place stood a handsome man, tall and dark-haired, bedecked in glittering jewels and rich silks. He was bearded and lean, and looked like an evil prince from a fairytale.

The man swaggered closer, until I could make out the thin red line circling his pupils. They dilated until his eyes appeared as bottomless obsidian pools, edged with blood.

"You are more beautiful than I imagined, daughter of Kore." The demon's voice was surprisingly genteel, and smooth as the silks he wore. "But you are too small to cause so much trouble." He cocked his head, examining me like I was a butterfly under a glass case with pins stuck in my wings.

I forced a breath through my teeth. "I haven't caused any trouble," I replied, flicking my eyes to his booted feet. If I looked for too long, those bottomless pools would swallow me whole.

His laugh was like a spill of golden coins. The sound was wrong, coming from behind those sharp teeth and rosy lips.

"You may address me as Prince Magoth, little witch. Surely even one who has lived in such ignorance as you has heard of me?" he asked, incisors flashing again.

Bile burned my throat. The demon they made a deal with was

Magoth? He was supposed to be a prince of hell. Whatever problems I thought we had grew by about a thousand times.

Think, Seph. I glanced up quickly, searching for anything that could somehow save our asses from this impossible situation.

His silk shirt and richly embroidered vest shone even in the dim light of this rust iron world, and the precious stones embedded in the rings adorning his fingers and collar sparkled dully. His pointed beard was manicured to perfection, not a hair out of place.

The prince was vain, rich, and sounded bored out of his mind. I needed to grovel for all I was worth, and entertain him to distraction. Hopefully the others would use the time to.... I wasn't sure, but they were the gods-touched. They could figure it out.

"It's an honor, Prince," I said, inclining my head in a short bow. "I never dreamed I would have the privilege of meeting you. You are correct in naming my ignorance. Someone kept my origins from me."

"Ah, yes. You speak of Ezekial." He pronounced my father's name in a strange way, the emphasis on a short *i*.

"You knew him?" I tried to keep my voice from wavering.

"Know him, little witch," Magoth corrected. "I am aware of your little...*rencontre* in the cemetery. A rather naughty mongrel he was, running off like that. Although it was delightful to punish him."

A picture flashed in my mind of my father lying in a broken, twisted heap on the ground.

I only have a few moments before he'll realize I'm gone, he'd said. He. *He.*

Lightning shot down my spine, and it was all I could do not to lunge at Magoth's throat and rip it out with my bare hands.

My gaze snapped up to meet the demon prince's. *Fuck. No.*

I let the lightning go, let it shimmer across my skin and engulf me in blue flame until my whole body was a firebrand, ready to burn. Holding my hands out, I shot a bolt at the demon. The air sizzled with the scent of ozone, and thunder boomed. But Magoth batted it away in a lazy gesture, grinning coyly and winking.

Then there was a small gasp of pain, nothing more than a quickly drawn breath. My gaze flicked to my side. Alex was there, caught in the corona of my flames. He held a knife in each hand, his mouth an implacable line, deadly focused on the demon.

My concentration broke and the flames died instantly. I grasped Alex's hand with my good one, sending black threads racing along his skin to soothe the burns. Pain echoed down my arms, then a wave of fatigue washed over me.

"Stay back," I warned him, keeping one eye on Magoth. The demon prince picked nonexistent dirt from under his fingernails, without a care in the worlds.

"No," Alex said simply. "I won't."

He still wanted to save me. There was no fight in his words, but his eyes blazed, and in that moment I felt all of his love and pain like two sides of the same blade, piercing and devastating, and I knew then that I'd never get enough of him even if we lived forever.

"Let me protect you, for once." I squeezed his hand, and he didn't say anything, just kept looking at me like I was the sun and he was a comet caught in my orbit. I desperately wanted to fall into his arms, but knew there couldn't be a more inappropriate time.

But it might be the very last time I ever felt his lips on mine. Tugging him to me, I kissed him, brief but fierce. I felt like I had flames racing across me all over again, but it was only the heat between us that set me on fire.

"Ah, young love," Magoth cooed, clapping slowly. "The devastation you will feel at your separation makes you all the more delicious. I can hardly wait, but then again, I like to play with my food before I eat it," he said, his lips pulling wide. "Call it my fatal flaw."

All I heard was, *we still have time*. I placed my rage behind a three foot thick wall of iron, letting it swirl from a distance, with Alex's calm, steady presence beside me. "What deal did you make with the Aureum, prince?" I asked. "What could they offer you that would make you join forces with your enemies?"

The tinkling of Magoth's laugh sounded again. "You don't know?"

From a distance, Edward let out a low groan. I hadn't even noticed they were still there. Mindara, Edward, and Fern were huddled together in a circle. Yuto was laid out on the ground, arms and legs akimbo. Hollis and Sage had their arms around Davina, whose eyes were fluttering open and shut. Sylvan and Casey flanked them on either side. They all looked as helpless as I had ever seen them, their stoic masks replaced with outright fear.

My hands shook, so I glued them to my sides. Agony flared through my wound. "I beg your enlightenment, prince."

The demon let out a long-suffering sigh, as though plotting my demise had been just a regular day at the office. Then again, for a prince of hell, it probably was.

"You are a freak of nature, my dear, and I say that with the utmost savagery. One who is handpicked by the gods to fight their war, who also has the blood of the Nephilim? You are indeed a dangerous creature."

"I'm not a danger to anyone," I asserted, my blood running to ice.

"Oh, but you are. Your very existence upsets the balance of the worlds. Where you walk, death becomes life. You have the powers of creation and destruction at the very tips of your fingers, and if you knew how to use them, then we would all be doomed, Proserpina," Magoth said, spitting the name like a curse. "Best we take you off the Golden One's hands."

I thought of the edge of Canhaben coming to life, and the flames I could call to my fingertips like a lit match. Just like the goddess who brought both life and death, who neither belonged fully in the light nor the dark. "Why would you help the people who want to destroy you and all your kind?"

"Because as long as the Golden Ones hand over the lightbringers, we go easy on their world. Well, not too easy, of course," he amended, winking. "And make no mistake—they will *never* get rid of our kind. We number as drops of water in the oceans, as stars in the skies." Then he shrugged. "It's just business, you know. Nothing personal."

"Right," I said, as I imagined slowly pulverizing him into jelly.

He yawned, showing his oversharp teeth again. "Well, it has been lovely having this chat. The fear coming off you all is just *delectable*. Especially your Diurne." He chuckled. "I cannot say I have seen such a miserable excuse for leadership since Commodus, and he set the bar when he got to the underworlds. You Aureum are the most dimwitted of all the so-called supernatural."

Edward blanched, then looked somewhere three feet to the right of Magoth. "Uphold your end of the bargain, and we will hold ours."

Magoth let out a loud, deep-throated squawk of amusement. "You know, I don't think I will." He tapped a long finger on his chin. "You have wasted my precious time, so I am changing the terms of our bargain." His voice boomed in a double timbre over the barren land-scape. "If you play with fire, expect to get burned."

Everyone cowered back as Magoth grew, first two feet, then ten, shooting upward at an alarming rate. Edward snapped one of the raised mounds sticking out of the earth at the base and used power to hurl it at Magoth. Some kind of giant bone fell from it, but I didn't stick around to see more.

"Run!" I shrieked, and pulled Alex back toward the others. His weight supported my injured side. I had forgotten how fast he was even without his powers, because we practically flew across the ground, the rest following, with Sylvan scooping Davina into his arms. I slapped my good hand onto her, and sent a healing shove around the knife wound that I hoped would staunch the bleeding.

"There's a crop of boulders, there, see? We'll take cover, then, Seph, you need to open a gateway," Alex panted. There was, in fact, an outcropping of boulders within sprinting distance, each at least twenty feet tall. The boulders were as bare and gray as the rest of the ground, only dotted with holes like swiss cheese where erosion had worked on them.

"I don't know how." I winced as our speed jostled my arm. My fingertips had gone numb, which probably wasn't good.

"I'll teach you right now," Alex said, practically throwing me behind a boulder. Sage ripped off the sleeve of their shirt and hurriedly made me a sling.

"You're okay," Sage said, fixing me with a determined look. "We're going to get through this. We won't let him have you." But their hands trembled as they tied the knot.

Deep in my bones, I felt that the trap had snapped shut. I wasn't going to escape. I needed to tell Alex that I loved him, a love so piercing and permanent it was a part of me, buried beneath my skin like the ink from our tattoos.

"Alex, I—" I started, but then I felt a curious shift in the atmosphere that made me pause, an almost imperceptible hollowing that could only mean one thing. *Unbelievable.* I followed Hollis's slack gaze to see a head of thick chestnut hair pop through a hole in the air.

37

"I'm hallucinating, right?" Davina wheezed, staring at Simon's face floating in midair.

"Simon!" I yelled. The rest of him came through, like toothpaste extruded from a tube. There were no gaps between him and the gateway, and we all realized at the same time when his last foot came out—

"No!" Alex shouted, lunging for the gateway, but he was too late. It snapped shut behind Simon like a rubberband.

"Fuck!" Casey yelled.

"Not exactly the reception I was expecting, thank you very much," Simon said haughtily. Then he saw me and Davina, dripping blood, and his eyes went wide. "What—"

"No time to explain," Alex snapped. Only moments—or was it hours?—had passed since we'd sheltered behind the boulders, and there were only precious seconds remaining until Magoth came for us. A boom reverberated through the air, along with a chorus of screams, and the wind raged like a vengeful god.

"How did you get through here? And can you get us out again?" Alex's voice was rough and his jaw clenched, the only sign that he felt as terrified and out of control as the rest of us.

"Well, I followed you through the cemetery, when I was—and, I saw you lot leave," Simon said, skirting around the fact that he'd been

346

burying his brother. "I overheard Seph talking to the short one, and it didn't seem right. I just—I had a feeling. And, well, I was obviously furious, so, I didn't come till now, but—"

"No, dumbass, *how* did you get here?" Casey spat.

Simon shrugged. "I spirit-called a demon to find you all."

"Do it again," Alex commanded.

"I—I don't think I can." Simon's face was ashen.

"Try!" he urged.

Head bent low, Simon crouched and pulled from under his shirt a leather thong with a small pouch. He reminded me painfully of his twin. *I'm not there,* I reminded myself. I couldn't afford to slip into the dark swirl of the past. I focused on the small differences that distinguished Simon from Penn. The way his hair was slightly shorter, waving just over the tops of his ears, where Penn's had brushed his shoulders; and the small scar that crested his upper lip, a thin white line slashing through stubble.

Simon spoke in a low voice, sprinkling herbs from the pouch into his hand. *Vervain.* A thundering voice boomed over us, obscuring his words.

"Come out, come out, wherever you are!" Magoth's cold laughter rang like a hammer hitting an anvil.

"I need to focus," Simon said, almost dropping the palmful of herbs with his shaking hands.

"I'll head him off," I said. "Or distract him, at least."

Alex's face was tight, like he wanted to argue. "Sylvan, Casey, stay with Simon and Davina. Sage and Hollis, come with us."

"Do not make me come get you!" Magoth boomed. "Or do. That could be fun." The ground shook under our feet, and we were caught in a shower of pebbles that spilled off the tops of the boulders in a miniature rockslide.

"Come here, quick. And hold hands." I had a wild thought and had no idea if it would work, but it was a last resort.

They did as I asked. I pushed dark power through our connected palms, sending the threads inside of Alex, Hollis, and Sage.

"Seph, no!" Alex shouted, wrenching his hand away. But it didn't matter, because it was done. I panted, feeling like a wrung sponge.

I'd sent every ounce of power I still possessed into the three

Guardians, who would make much better use of it. Now I just prayed they could hold onto it, and that whatever force prevented them from using their power here wouldn't have accounted for this loophole.

"You all know what to do with it," I said, doing my damndest to stay upright. "He doesn't know that you have power back. I'll distract him, and you go in for the kill." The others looked as shocked as Alex, but when I locked eyes with Sage, I knew I'd made the right choice.

"You can barely stand, for fuck's sake," Alex growled, wrapping his arm around my waist as I was indeed beginning to stagger. "You're pale as a ghost."

"It'll come back." Through the exhaustion, already I could feel the river of black threads replenishing. I laid my lips on his, and spoke into his warm breath. "I love you. Trust me. Now, go."

With my remaining strength, I ran from the cover of the boulders to face Magoth.

Gone was the handsome prince, and in his place was the face of a monster, towering above from a great height. Horns sprouted from a raw, red scalp, and his eyes were as round as shining silver dollars. The mouth gaped, a putrid scent emerging that almost finished me off. In the distance behind him, I caught a glimpse of Edward, Mindara, Yuto, and Fern, all sprawled limply on the ground.

"Hey, asshole!" I croaked as loudly as I could.

Magoth turned his great head in my direction, and unfurled a set of ragged, leathery black wings. He roared, a fearsome sound that made my ears ring. That surely wouldn't help Simon's concentration.

I threw my hand up in supplication. "Okay, okay, calm down. No need to freak out. Just quit with the monster act and I'll come quietly."

In response, Magoth swiped a wing in my direction. I didn't even have time for a quick repartee before it connected and I was thrown backward into the rocky outcropping. Pain bloomed along my side, indicating I'd probably cracked a rib. I couldn't stand anymore, but propped myself up against the boulder, listing like a drunk so that it felt like the boulder was shaking beneath me.

Then I realized I actually wasn't the one moving—it *was* the rock beneath me. Boulders weren't supposed to move and arrange themselves into suspiciously body-like jumbles, in which you could differentiate arms, legs, and torsos. And they most certainly shouldn't have roared in annoyance when Sylvan's musical shout of surprise floated through the air.

"Fucking hell," I coughed, clutching my side. "Giants?"

The not-boulders rose up, up into the air, shaking loose thousands of stones that pelted toward the ground. A particularly large rock was headed toward me and I braced for impact, but it never hit. Alex, Hollis, and Sage, who now ringed the stone giants, had thrown protection over the rest of us. The debris bounced away harmlessly, clattering to the ground and creating an almighty racket.

It was enough to distract the demon who was hellbent on our destruction. Magoth let out an earsplitting screech of displeasure, then charged the stone giants. Unfortunately, the Guardians were still in the middle of them, trying to avoid being squashed by sailboat-sized feet.

"Get them out!" I shouted, doubling over with the effort of speaking. Hollis was two steps ahead of me, sending ropes of black thread shooting into the breach. The ropes became netting, and they enveloped everyone, dragging them toward safety. Sylvan, Casey, and Simon were all splayed on the ground, gasping and shaking like they really were fish caught in a net. Davina looked unconscious, her side bleeding freely now.

Hollis joined Alex and Sage, sprinting around the stone giants to close in on Magoth. There were three of them, and they all charged the demon at once, striking with granite fists the size of Mini Coopers. One of the giants managed to pin a wing, but the demon ripped it free, although not without leaving a flapping tear. Magoth roared, then redoubled his attack, shooting fire at the giants. But fire was no match for stone, and the battle raged on.

"Did you get it?" I asked Simon breathlessly, because it actually was getting very difficult to breathe around the fire in my ribcage.

"Almost. But those mad things knocked everything about, and my mirror shattered. I can't call a demon without all the proper tools."

"You're descended from angels and demons! How can you not figure *something* out?"

"I'm not you, all right?"

"Simon, you can do this." I wanted to shake him, but instead spoke as calmly as I could manage. "Not to be dramatic, but if you can't get us out of here, we're all going to be either crushed to death or dragged to hell and barbecued." I searched his face, looking for anything that would motivate him. "Make your family's sacrifice mean something."

The will of a man who has been grieving for almost his entire life, yet has stayed alive himself, was not something to be trifled with. He wouldn't let us all be killed. He lifted his eyes to meet mine, and I saw angry purpose reflected back at me.

Simon backed away from our injured and bedraggled group. Planting his feet, he turned his face to the rust-red sky. He raised his arms, then a warm wind began to swirl, cutting through the chill in the air. His eyes fluttered shut, and he seemed to turn inward, blocking out the world.

I looked over my shoulder at the battling supernaturals. The three Guardians were holding their own, dodging and shooting their borrowed power at both the giants and Magoth, and wielding their weapons like they were sent from death itself. Every time they landed a hit, there was another attack to answer. My heart was in my throat watching them—watching Alex fight with his incredible speed and strength that still wasn't enough to turn the tide.

The wind picked up, and soon it howled in my ears and whipped my hair into a frenzy. Simon stood as firm as a mountain in the gale, not wavering an inch. Then his eyes snapped open, and the storm-tossed gray had turned the light green of the sky before a wicked storm, shining like two new pennies. A frisson of shock, and something darker, tangled underneath my battered ribs.

"It's done," Simon said, his voice no longer his own but a more ancient sound reminiscent of crumbling temples and sacrifices given at the foot of an altar.

The wind itself took on a dark hue, and concentrated into a circle with Simon at the swirling black heart of it. He looked like a dark god, a sorcerer, able to bend the very atoms of the worlds to his will. The darkness solidified into smooth, midnight silk. Simon was somehow anchoring a gateway.

"Alex!" Casey called over the howling wind. "Let's go!"

Without missing a beat, the three Guardians left the battle and sprinted toward us, Alex bringing up the rear, continuing to shoot power over his shoulder at Magoth.

I allowed a small bubble of hope to rise. *Come on, come on, almost there—*

Light exploded. I flew through the air, landing hard on my back and knocking the wind out of me. Searing heat raked across the back of my eyelids. Deafness settled over my ears, then high-pitched ringing, but I was still able to hear a single, muffled scream.

The ground had cracked wide open in a jagged slash, stone sheared away to create towering cliffs. Bubbling, steaming water rushed in to fill the void like a flash flood. Massive chunks of granite, the remnants of the bodies of the stone giants, bobbed to the surface of the water for a moment, then sank, replaced by scattered ash that floated on the surface of the pseudo lake. Lightning cracked overhead, thunder boomed, and the air became as hot and dry as the inside of an oven. The smell of sulfur curled up to burn my nostrils.

And, to my abject, fear-curdling horror—Alex was on the other side of the pit, laying at the feet of the demon.

The others were strewn around the cracked ground like abandoned toys, but were stirring. Only Simon had maintained his footing, stormed-tossed eyes fierce and standing strong with the gateway around him, beckoning us to come through.

We couldn't, not with Alex alone on the other side of the pit, a hairsbreadth from the demon who wanted to kidnap me and take me into hell like my namesake.

Unlike the daughter of Demeter, there would be no spring return for me.

But I had no magic, could barely stand. Unless—

If I could give power away, maybe I could also take it.

I plunged through the concentric darkness around Simon and latched onto him, leeching that power into me. I *felt* like a leech, blood-sucking and parasitic, but I had no choice. And, oh, it felt good, felt *right*, this magic flooding through my veins, intoxicating me. I hadn't realized how bereft I'd been without power until I filled myself back up. I forced myself to stop before I drained him dry.

A strange feeling came over me when the flood of magic slowed to a trickle, like something was missing. It only took me a split second to identify that it was the absence of pain. My arm no longer bled, and my ribs had ceased throbbing.

The magic wasn't like my own black and gold threads—it felt like I'd borrowed someone else's clothes that didn't fit me quite right, but were still soft and luxurious against my skin. It whispered in my ears, telling me I could have anything my heart desired. Anything at all, and if I just wished it, it would come true.

Simon didn't give any indication he'd felt me take power from him. But the swirling darkness of the gateway faded, and it took on more of a grayish hue. His face had a chalky white pallor, although his eyes continued to burn brightly.

If I didn't get Alex back now, we were going to lose our window, and be stuck in the same room as all of the people who wanted to kill us.

The others staggered to their feet like survivors on a battlefield, which, I supposed, they were. "Go, now," I said to Hollis, pointing at Simon. "Take the others. We're coming."

My borrowed power whispered in my ear that the air would catch me if I jumped. I ran, launching myself over the lake. The air cradled me like an embrace, sending me through clouds of vapor and smoke that smelled like hellfire.

I dropped in front of Alex, who had managed to gain his footing but struggled against invisible bonds. Part of me almost collapsed with relief as I touched him, my hands streaking over him feverishly to find a way to free him.

"Now, now, that's no fair," Magoth boomed.

Staring into the hideous face of the demon, I was prepared to bargain.

"Let him leave," I demanded. "It's me you want. I won't fight you anymore, if you just let him go."

Magoth's wings retracted, then disappeared. His body shrank, fangs shortened, and animal hide melted back into human flesh. He looked again like the handsome prince, almost human, except for his eyes. They remained bright yellow with slits for pupils, like a snake's.

As his serpentine gaze met mine, there was an uncomfortable pressure on my ankles and wrists, then a weightiness. I tried to take a step and uncouple my hands, but was stuck.

"I am displeased," the demon stated matter-of-factly, as if he was telling a waiter his steak had been cooked well-done instead of medium-rare. "And when I am displeased, there will be pain, and suffering. Well, more pain and suffering than there might have been," he amended.

"Please," I begged. "I'll do anything you want. Torture, enslavement, anything. Just let him leave."

"If you had come along quietly in the first place, your little coven could have gone home and been reading their bedtime story by now," Magoth said. "For the inconvenience I've suffered, I will take two souls instead of one. These are the new terms."

I sensed Alex trying to catch my eye, but I refused to look at him. If I did, then...I wouldn't allow myself to imagine all of the ways he would be tortured, or—*no, don't go there.* I strained against my bonds, but nothing moved even a millimeter.

Sweat dripped down my face, plastering my hair to my forehead. I didn't know how to fight a demon and win. But I did know how to negotiate.

"What if you took someone else in his place? I mean, does the second soul have to be his?"

Magoth's eyes gleamed, then his mouth curved into a cruel smile. "Ah! A Sophie's Choice, as you call it! Although I cannot take credit for inspiring that one, it was a proud day for my kind. My my, you are doing my work for me, little witch. All right, then. Who would you like to choose?" He snapped his fingers, and Simon, Yuto, Fern, Mindara, and Edward appeared lined up in a neat row, frozen but for their blinking eyes. I sagged in relief. Alex's unit had gotten out.

The four Guardians looked bewildered. Simon was the same as he had been moments ago, pale and staring with a pool of darkness lapping around him, as though he wasn't conscious of his surroundings. Almost as if he was in another world.

I'd hoped those four hadn't been able to escape. In fact, it's what I was counting on. "Can you uncuff me? I want to look into their eyes when I tell them I'm dragging them to hell."

The demon chuckled, then shook his finger at me, yellow eyes shining merrily. "You have a bloodthirsty streak. I like it. But you have already tricked me once, and although I admire you for it, I will not let it happen again. You will remain chained, but I shall allow you to approach them. Any funny business and you go straight into the pit. Understood?"

I nodded my assent. Magoth was mercurial, flashing from enraged, to polite disinterest, to indulgent, like he was my favorite demon uncle. I needed to capitalize on his giving mood before he shifted again.

Shuffling over to the prisoners, I stared into each of their faces and pretended to weigh my decision. Although their lips were clamped together, their eyes said everything they couldn't. Fern's were overlaid with icy fear. Mindara's gaze was rigid, her jaw set. Yuto's were unfocused, like he couldn't quite believe it all. Edward's held pure terror.

I smiled grimly, leaning in close to him. "I've been wanting to do this for a while," I whispered.

Drawing back, I punched him square in the nose as best I could with my manacled hands. He keeled over, stiff as a board, unable to make a sound, but a steady stream of blood trickled from his nostrils.

Not only had a wash of satisfaction rolled over me, but when my fist made contact with his face I'd sucked power out of him, just like I'd done to Simon. The influx of energy zinged through my bloodstream, like I'd chugged a bottle of champagne.

"Ah, excellent choice," Magoth said, clapping his hands together.

"No, it's not him. I'm just paying him back for selling me to you. But, I have made a choice," I said, slowly pacing down the row. "All of them have wronged me in some way. Obviously, Edward is the whole reason we're here. Mindara gave him permission to execute his plan. Yuto is their lackey. Fern is the one who laid the trap." I briefly considered hitting her, too, as payback for my arm, but decided against it. It was time to act.

I pointed to Simon. "I'm choosing him." Fern's eyes fluttered shut in relief. "He stands for everything in my life that's brought me pain. If my father hadn't left his world, hadn't come into mine and found my mother, none of this would have happened." I curled my hands into fists, tapping into my rage toward the Diurne and Magoth.

"Fine. Let's get this show on the road, as the humans say. They do have some excellent idioms, despite being idiotic enough to cook their own world like a rack of spit-roasted werewolf ribs. But, I digress."

The chains on my wrists and ankles vanished, but they'd been replaced by Magoth's iron grip. He had me in one hand and Simon in the other. I tried to suppress my recoil of disgust at his flaming touch. I hoped he couldn't tell that my heart beat like it wanted to escape my chest.

"Wait," I said, digging in my heels. "Can I say goodbye? Please?" Magoth hesitated, but I remembered what he'd said about separating lovers. It would be too delicious a meal for him to resist.

He sighed heavily. "Make it snappy." He pushed me toward Alex, and I felt tension around my chest like I was being spooled out on a ball of twine.

Alex was covered in grime and blood, and his eyes were ringed red from smoke. There was a gash across his left cheek that was still bleeding, and a bruise blooming across the hard line of his jaw.

And yet, he was still the most beautiful person I'd ever seen. He took my breath away, again and again.

He took my hands, looking at me with a fierceness that made me burn. My pulse scrambled, but for a different reason now. I was terrified, but still so grateful that the universe had put Alex Eames in my path.

He bit his lip, then started to speak. "I'm—"

"If you say sorry, I'm going to kick your ass," I said, instead of, *I'm the one that should be sorry. I'm the one that risked your life. I'm the one who was too selfish to let you go.*

"I love you, Persephone Hart," he breathed, using a bound hand to draw me close. "And I always will." Then his lips were on mine, soft and strong and burning and sweet, as if he was trying to tell me all the things he thought he'd never get to say. I hated that I tasted his goodbye in the kiss. I cursed myself, and men who were bigoted and power hungry, and most of all the goddamn forces of evil that were trying to ruin my happy ending.

"I love you, too," I whispered into his neck. I molded to him until there was no space left between us, then said, so quietly that even I couldn't hear myself, "Get ready."

I cupped his cheek in my hand and pressed a finger to the gash, healing it instantly. His eyes widened in surprise, but I hid it by laying my lips on his, breathing in the smell that was purely Alex underneath the hellsmoke.

"Okay." I turned to Magoth. "Let's do this."

The demon yanked my invisible chain and I stumbled, catching myself on Simon. I sent a little zip of power into the exposed skin of his forearm.

Then Magoth's demon hands were on me again, dragging us toward the lake. The water frothed and roiled, like the world's most purgatorial hot tub. He smiled triumphantly, then tossed us over the edge.

38

I may not have had wings, but I felt like I was flying.

Instead of dropping like a pair of stones, Simon and I hovered just below the cliff face, as if resting on a low bank of clouds. In the second it took Magoth to realize that we were not in fact plunging toward hellfire and brimstone, I had already shoved Simon back toward land.

With stolen magic burning in my veins, I simply had to think something to make it true. I threw a barrier of impenetrable fog between Simon and the demon. Then I lashed out at Magoth with the business end of the flaming whip I'd conjured in the same breath. He spun away across the surface of the lake like a rock skidding across an icy pond. Pivoting to Alex, I slashed his chains with the whip.

"Get them through the gateway!" I yelled, while I spun around to face Magoth, prepared to go head-to-head with a nightmare.

I'd decided to rescue the other Guardians, even though they didn't deserve it. But I didn't do it for them; I did it for Alex, because that's what he would've done. We were playing to our strengths. He was built for saving. I was built for destruction. And boy, was I ready to destroy something.

Magoth took the form of the great winged creature, which, while terrifying, gave me the advantage of speed. Unfortunately, it gave him the advantage, of, well—everything else.

He roared in fury, belching flames. I smiled grimly, the magic whispering that I could fight fire with fire. All I needed to do was ask for it.

As flames arced across the sky, I pulled them into me, reveling in the heat. I absorbed their energy, letting it churn and coalesce into a mass of power that spread through my limbs and almost stole my breath.

Alex, silhouetted by his glorious, sweeping wings of ivory, joined me at the edge of the lake. We dodged a volley of flaming arrows. He scattered them into the water with a mighty beat of his wings, where they hissed and sizzled out.

"Nice one." I shot all of that harnessed fire toward Magoth, effectively creating a living wall of flame between us.

Alex looked at me with awe and something else, hair flopping over his sooty, sweat-stained brow. "Let's finish this so we can go home."

"And where exactly would that be?" Gravesville was likely overrun with our enemies, and Canhaben had been exposed, too.

He gazed at me, the gold in his eyes flashing like the sun, then smiled his heartstopping smile. "With you," he said, like it was the most obvious answer in the world.

An idiotic grin spread over my face, despite the fact that I had nothing to be smiling about. "I have a plan. I need you to get him about...there." I gestured to the midpoint of the lake. "And no matter what happens, don't stop flying."

Alex's eyebrows dipped.

"Trust me," I said, and let my skin flicker faintly blue under a current of electricity.

"Always," he answered, squeezing my hand. He spread his wings and soared toward Magoth, like some kind of avenging angel. Then again, that's exactly what he was.

Alex taunted Magoth, flying just out of reach like a bothersome insect, pestering him. Magoth roared, swiping a long-fingered claw, but Alex was too fast, too agile for the demon's larger size. The demon gave chase, and the two winged figures, one large and dark, one small and light, headed for where I stood on the opposite shore.

The lake churned, waves lashing at sheer cliff walls. Grimacing, I steeled myself. Then I took a deep breath and dove into the steaming lake, taking care to aim for a spot that wasn't on fire. I braced for impact, but the water was gluey and gelatinous, sucking me in with a stomach-churning squelch.

The upside was that the flesh hadn't instantly melted from my bones. The downside was that it was like swimming through cement, almost impossible to make any headway against the dense substance.

I struck out determinedly, letting magic flow through my muscles to propel me forward. I looked up, tracking Magoth, calculating how far he had to go until he was directly above me. I sent up a flare of red-orange flame, making sure that he knew exactly where I was, as Alex soared past overhead. I said a little prayer, filled my lungs to bursting with fetid air, and dove beneath the murky surface.

Just as I had sent the flare above, I sent it below, casting a ring of light into the subaquatic landscape. The entirety of my plan hinged on a complete guess formulated in about ten seconds of thought. If I was wrong...well, I couldn't be.

Stroking and kicking, I swam toward the bottom of the lake. I counted the seconds in my head, going deeper and deeper, as far as I could safely go and get back to the surface alive. I just hoped it was far enough.

Suffocated as I was by the oppressive water, I thought of fires, of volcanoes, of nebulas, of their heat and light and power, of new beginnings, and openings, and the feeling of being embraced by people who loved me. Power ebbed and flowed through me like the changing of the tides. It concentrated in the space between my ribs, and I clamped down on the swirling energy, but it was like trying to hold back the Titanic with a single frayed rope.

The surface of the water finally broke, like a demon-sized cannonball had been launched into it. Magoth plunged into the depths, his leathery wings sending forceful waves that buffeted me like a buoy in a storm.

He'd taken the bait.

I braced to keep from losing my grip on the power that threatened to burst its dam. Magoth was closing in now, just five strokes away. My lungs burned. Four strokes away, and the brightest fear I'd ever known wrapped its fingers around my throat. Three strokes away, and everything became clear as a bell. Two strokes away—

Now. Aided by magic, I shot upward so that I was positioned above Magoth.

I let go of that frayed rope.

Power detonated with a supersonic boom, and I spiraled upward toward the surface like a rogue rocket. If it had the effect I'd hoped, the demon would be going in the opposite direction, forced downward. But I couldn't see anything, because there were bubbles and air pockets clouding the water, coming out of the gateway I'd opened at the bottom of the lake. Was that a black-tipped wing, being sucked down into what had become a whirlpool, all of the water draining through the bottom like pulling the plug in a bathtub?

The lake coughed me up onto the cliff's edge, straight into Alex's waiting arms. I fell against him, choking on water. He held me up while simultaneously running trembling hands over me, checking every square inch for injuries.

"Thank the goddess," he breathed on a sigh, crushing me to his chest. He encircled me with his wings so that we were cocooned together, blocking out the rusty sky and steaming lake.

"I'm okay," I spluttered, although I felt like a boneless, battered piece of meat.

"What did you do?" he asked, cupping my face. "When I saw you go into that water...you took years off my life, Seph."

"I opened a gateway in the lake," I coughed. My throat was on fire and my lungs burned. "And sent Magoth back through it."

"You did...what?" Alex's mouth hung open. "Where did you learn gateway magic?"

"Turns out it's not as complicated as I thought. I just went with my gut."

"Incredible," he said, shaking his head in disbelief. "Only you would be brave, and when I say brave I mean *stupid* enough to do that." But he said it with such incredulity that I decided to take it as a compliment.

"Yeah, well." I cleared my throat. "Can we continue the praise in a safer location? I don't think Simon is going to last much longer."

He brushed a kiss over my lips. "Let's get out of here. You brilliant, brave woman."

"Damn straight."

Alex folded back his wings, then I took his hand, and we walked toward Simon together. Toward the rest of our lives.

My thoughts had been caught up in a tight net, only focused on defeating the demon, but now they spilled out, flooding me with relief that made me wobbly and lightheaded. It was over. At least, for now. We still had to sort out the Diurne, but that could wait. We'd rest, regroup, then come back stronger than ever.

"So, how do we do this?" I gestured to Simon. "Just walk into the dark stuff?"

"It seems that way. He should take us to the same place that the rest of the unit is waiting, wherever that might be. I think if we hold onto him, he'll come through with us."

"Okay, then. Let's give it a shot."

I touched a finger to the shadows circling Simon. It was burning hot, and, like quicksand, my arm slid right through right up to the elbow.

"So far, so good. Let's do it together." Reaching for Alex, I felt his strong, steady hand on mine. I looked back and he gave me a reassuring nod.

"Here goes nothing."

I tipped forward into the ring of midnight silk, and it hit me. This was real. We had survived. Joy budded in my chest, stretching out hopeful tendrils.

Until I felt Alex's pressure on my hand disappear and was left bereft, grasping at nothing.

"What?" I gasped, then turned, half in and half out of the gateway, and saw the end of the world.

Magoth, in his monstrous form, had crawled out of the pit like some hideous spider. His barbed tail was wrapped around Alex from chest to ankles clinging like a deadly vine.

Numbness spread through my chest, and a dull knocking feeling pulsed under my ribs. Everything was wrong. Just a second ago—hadn't it been only a second?—we were hand in hand, victorious after having just missed death by inches. There was a glitch in the fabric of time and space. We'd been dropped into an alternate reality.

Alex's eyes stared vacantly as he looked down at the scaly black tail, and I hoped we were sharing the same hallucination. Time slowed to a crawl, so that I could see every emotion that crossed his face in quick succession: surprise, horror, fear, anger, sadness. Acceptance.

He looked at me then, a look of such love that tears pricked the backs of my eyes, a look that I hated because I saw the goodbye that I never wanted reflected there. He gave me one last dizzying, heartbreaking smile. A fissure formed in my chest, splitting the length of me, bringing me to my knees.

Magoth yanked his tail, and dragged Alex into the pit. One breath he was there, and the next he was gone.

"No!" I screamed, leaping after him, but found I was trapped in a vise. Simon's arms had snaked around me, holding me tightly to him so I couldn't move a muscle. I stood there, frozen in my worst nightmare, looking at the horribly empty space where Alex had been.

"You owe me," Simon said in that ancient and terrible voice.

Then he pulled me in, and I was falling, falling through blackness that lasted for an eternity, seeing only the look in Alex's eyes as he vanished.

39

Through the haze of my despair, some part of me that was still functioning noticed everything was green. We'd landed in a mossy forest, and I had the impression of light filtering through a high canopy of trees, dusting the forest floor with mottled sunshine. Water fell somewhere in the distance, splashing on rocks.

It would have been beautiful, if I had given a fuck about anything other than trying to get back to Alex.

"NO!" I screamed, again and again, running around the little clearing. "Simon, GET UP! We have to go back!" I yanked at his prone form, pulling him upright. He was back to his normal self now, no longer green-eyed and other-worldly. "Hurry! If we go now, we can follow them, I know we can. SIMON!"

"No, Seph."

"Do the gateway thing again, or, actually, I'll open one. Okay, yeah, just hold on." I waved my shaking hands through the air, trying to find the catch that would bring us back to the world where we'd just been, but felt nothing. The air was dead and still under my fingers. "Come on, help me!" I cried.

"I said, no. It's too late. We can't go back, I've lost the power." Simon grimaced and shook his head. Then, even worse, he looked at me with a pitying expression.

"What the fuck do you mean?" I whirled on him. "Yes, we can. We can go right now, I don't know why you're wasting time!"

He took my arm, turning me around to face him. I refused to meet his eyes, but my heart was beating a mile-a-minute and the dull thud that had been under my ribs started to take on a dense, sinking quality. My stomach clutched, as if trying to reject the feeling.

"Seph—"

"HELP ME!" I screamed, pounding on his chest. I was wild, with white-hot panic lancing through me. This wasn't happening. This couldn't be happening. In fact, maybe I'd fallen asleep, or gotten knocked out, and this was all a dream. I stopped my assault on Simon and slapped myself across the face, the crack of it ringing out across the clearing.

Simon grabbed my wrists, pinning them down by my sides. I shot an electric current across my skin, but he held on, his mouth twisted in pain. It wasn't until I smelled burning flesh that I stopped. Instead of letting go, Simon pulled me in, wrapping his arms around me as I struggled against him.

Alex couldn't be gone. I'd feel it, wouldn't I? I seized a fiber of hope, and found the thread of connection that tied me to him. Excitement pooled as I gave a slight tug, then pulled harder, until I came to the end of the thread and nothing was there but a loose end.

All the fight went out of me. Simon stopped me from falling, and slowly lowered us to the ground as I let go and sobbed into his chest. It was real. Alex was gone, and I was trapped here, and there was nothing I could do.

I didn't know how long we stayed like that, me keening and him holding the shattered pieces of me. When I eventually quieted, I noticed the light had faded almost completely. In this world, wherever we were, twilight fell in a haze of soft pink and lavender. Stars began to peek out, twinkling merrily. I couldn't stand the sight of them. Of anything.

"I'll find some wood, shall I? We can have a fire, get warm." Simon cast a worried glance at me, as if fearful of what I might do if he was out of eyesight. He needn't have been. I was numb, my limbs hard and immovable as the statues in Angel's Rest back in Gravesville. I didn't feel warmth, or cold. I felt nothing. I *was* nothing.

At some point Simon returned and started the fire. Sparks jumped out of a bed of twigs, and he added sticks to the meager flame as the kindling caught, wincing slightly as he worked with blistered hands. I wondered if I should feel guilty for burning him, but searched and couldn't find anything. We didn't speak as we sat there, staring into the fire. Eventually he stood.

"You can get some sleep," he said. "I'll keep an eye out here." It hadn't occurred to me that we might be in danger. But I couldn't have felt fear, because the worst had already happened. I ignored Simon and stayed put, seeing nothing and hearing nothing but the crackle of licking flames.

———

I woke to a dazzling sunset, so stunning that had my heart been working, it would've ached. It seemed unfair that something so beautiful should still exist, when the most beautiful thing in my world was gone.

The sun, smaller and paler than the one back home, was beset by shocking ruby and violet clouds. The sky had begun to fade into layers from palest ice to deepest ocean, signaling it was that time again. The strange hour between day and night. It looked just like the night I'd met Penn in the cemetery. The night my story really began.

I knew I'd slept because of the nightmare. It was the same one, over and over. Alex falling into the pit, with me trying myriad ways to save him. But I always ended up watching the horrible acceptance in his eyes as he fell into unrelieved darkness, while I stood there, helpless. I sat up, Simon's jacket slipping from my shoulders.

Simon was awake, his eyes bloodshot and gritty. He at least had the decency not to ask if I had slept well. I'd woken myself with my own screams a few times.

"Ah, you're awake. You've been out almost the whole day. I was able to find some nibbles for breakfast—or, maybe it's dinner, now. It's not much, just some burdock and a few rosehips, but thankfully this place appears to have some of the same plant life as Canhaben, so I'm fairly certain we won't be poisoned," he said in a rush.

I glanced at the impoverished offering that was still covered with a light dusting of soil. It looked wholly unappetizing, but my stomach growled so I brushed off one of the scraggly roots and took a bite. I forced myself to chew and swallow, but the taste actually wasn't bad. I picked up another. Simon gave an encouraging smile, and we ate in silence.

"Where do you think the others are?" I asked. My voice sounded rusty and my throat ached.

Simon answered slowly, as though to keep from spooking me. "I have no idea. I felt them, er...go through. But I couldn't tell you why we landed here instead of with them."

I nodded. That was the answer I needed. My nightmarish brain must have come to a resolution as I slept, because I felt surprisingly steady, even more so now that I had something in my stomach. I'd thought about what Alex would've done if our positions were reversed, if I'd been the one taken by a demon and he'd been left standing on the edge of a cliff watching me fall.

He'd have gone after me. I knew without a doubt in my mind, in my soul, that he'd have been relentless in trying to save me, even if there was nothing left to save. So that's what I was going to do. I would do everything in my power and beyond to find him, and if he was still alive, to bring him home. And if he wasn't, I would exact a revenge so devastating the only thing left in my wake would be the flames that had become as familiar to me as my own face.

"Are you ready to go?" I asked.

"Go where, Seph?" Simon sounded weary, like he didn't relish the idea of restraining me again.

"I'm not asking to go back to that world," I said calmly. "But I am going to try and find Alex. Then when I've got him, I'm going to pulverize the Aureum into dust."

"Sorry, *what*?" He gaped at me.

"I'm going to go get Alex. You can come with me if you want, but I don't mind going alone. Actually, it might be better if you go back to Canhaben. You'll be safer there." I stood and pulled off Simon's jacket, holding it out to him.

"Hold on just a minute," he said. "You're in no state to go gallivanting off on a suicide mission. Seph, I might have been...not myself, back there, but I heard and saw everything. Alex is—"

"You don't know that." I held up a hand to silence him. "We don't know anything. All I saw was him go into that pit, alive. There's a good chance Magoth wants to keep him that way. He is a son of one of the Diurne Council members, which makes him a powerful bargaining chip." They also wanted a soul, and now they had one; it just wasn't the one they'd intended.

Simon blew air out of his lips. "Oh, well, if that's all. If, and only *if*, he is still alive, they could also be using him as bait, for you. But you knew that already."

"Yes."

"And you would willingly walk into a trap in which you will be at best tortured, and at worst killed?"

I stared coolly at him.

He sighed. "In the name of Asael, Seph, is he worth dying for?"

Was love worth dying for? I thought of my mom, and Bri, who I missed like a lost limb, and the rest of Alex's friends that had become my family, who I would've loved for their own sakes even if he hadn't already. I thought of Simon's family, who had all died for a chance at a better future for their loved ones. And Alex, of course. Always Alex.

"I love him. And that's the only thing worth living for, Simon."

He closed his eyes and covered his face for several long moments. "Okay, then. *Fine*. I'll go with you, even though it's fucking mad, and we will likely both be killed."

"That's the spirit." I felt a little whisper of warmth then, knowing I wouldn't be alone on this journey, and that even though I couldn't feel Alex didn't mean he wasn't out there, hoping for me like I was hoping for him.

I would be brave, like him; have faith, like him. I would be strong and smart, and stay alive.

I held out my hand to Simon. "Come on, then. We better get going."

ACKNOWLEDGMENTS

Well, hell. I can't believe we're here.

I started writing *The Strange Hour* in February 2021 in the midst of a job crisis. I'd been miserable at work for months, and figured I'd come to the end of my mental rope. And at the end of the rope was writing.

Maybe every author (it still feels weird to think of myself as one) or every reader (yes, that's more like it) has a drawer full of childhood story scribblings. I know I did, but I likely trashed them out of shame in my teenage years. At the time, evidence of my deepest and most ardent desire to be a writer was sooo embarrassing. And it continued to feel that way until I reached the point where I figured, fuck it, I literally have nothing left to lose!

Writing the initial draft of *The Strange Hour* began as part thera-peutic exercise (looking at you, rage quitting scene), part personal fantasy, and part lifelong obsession with graveyards. What if I, as a person in my mid-twenties, discovered some secret ability and was able to start anew? What if I discovered my courage and found my passion, and those led me to a whole other world full of adventure and romance and heart-rending emotion?

Well, dear reader, I found it! I found it in the pages of my book (*my* book, utterly wild, I will never get over how weird this is). I found I could create worlds, tell stories I would want to read, and exercise my creative brain that has been a little good at a lot of things, but not a lot good at anything.

So, what I'm trying to say is—this book started out as being for me. But now, because of all the support I've received through this long-ass journey to even get here, it's also for all of you—the readers. So, thanks for that, y'all.

First and foremost, I'd like to acknowledge my husband. Thanks for believing in me every step of the way, and for not rolling your eyes or laughing in my face when I said in a very shrill voice that I started writing a book. Thanks for dealing with my hyper-focus and the nights I spent with this baby instead of you. Without you, I'd never have a hope of writing Seph and Alex's love story. Love you, babe.

Thanks to my sister, for being my lifelong reading buddy and fellow fantasy lover. And to my friends, particularly my tiny blond angel—you all inspired the friendships in this story.

Thanks to my community of writers and critique partners, along with everyone else who spent their valuable time reading and giving me feedback. You all have made me more of an okay writer, and pointed out my truly heinous use of the word 'that'. (I've taken it out about 500 times just in this acknowledgement section!) I appreciate you all more than you could ever know. And, thanks to all of the folks who beta read for me—you've been an invaluable part of the process of writing my first book.

I'd like to acknowledge a resource I used for inspiration while writing this book, *The Dictionary of Demons* by M. Belanger. It was immensely helpful in teaching me about demons and angels, as well as the lore surrounding them. Some demons and information in *The Strange Hour* are pulled from texts and mythology in real life, while some were fabricated by me. I hope I didn't muck anything up too much.

And finally, special thanks to my developmental editor, Laura Bossicart, and the artists at Ebook Launch for my brilliant cover design. You all really helped this book shine.

ALSO BY R.G. WESLEY

The Graveborn Series

The Strange Hour

The Book of Shadows, coming 2025

www.ingramcontent.com/pod-product-compliance
Lightning Source LLC
Chambersburg PA
CBHW030108310726

48970CB00004B/1202